THE
Black Hawk

JOANNA BOURNE

BERKLEY SENSATION, NEW YORK

THE BERKLEY PUBLISHING GROUP
Published by the Penguin Group
Penguin Group (USA) Inc.
375 Hudson Street, New York, New York 10014, USA
Penguin Group (Canada), 90 Eglinton Avenue East, Suite 700, Toronto, Ontario M4P 2Y3, Canada
(a division of Pearson Penguin Canada Inc.)
Penguin Books Ltd., 80 Strand, London WC2R 0RL, England
Penguin Group Ireland, 25 St. Stephen's Green, Dublin 2, Ireland (a division of Penguin Books Ltd.)
Penguin Group (Australia), 250 Camberwell Road, Camberwell, Victoria 3124, Australia
(a division of Pearson Australia Group Pty. Ltd.)
Penguin Books India Pvt. Ltd., 11 Community Centre, Panchsheel Park, New Delhi—110 017, India
Penguin Group (NZ), 67 Apollo Drive, Rosedale, Auckland 0632, New Zealand
(a division of Pearson New Zealand Ltd.)
Penguin Books (South Africa) (Pty.) Ltd., 24 Sturdee Avenue, Rosebank, Johannesburg 2196,
South Africa

Penguin Books Ltd., Registered Offices: 80 Strand, London WC2R 0RL, England

THE BLACK HAWK

A Berkley Sensation Book / published by arrangement with the author

PRINTING HISTORY
Berkley Sensation mass-market edition / November 2011

ISBN: 978-0-425-24453-1

BERKLEY SENSATION®
Berkley Sensation Books are published by The Berkley Publishing Group,
a division of Penguin Group (USA) Inc.,
375 Hudson Street, New York, New York 10014.
BERKLEY SENSATION® is a registered trademark of Penguin Group (USA) Inc.
The "B" design is a trademark of Penguin Group (USA) Inc.

PRINTED IN THE UNITED STATES OF AMERICA

10   9   8   7   6   5   4   3   2   1

To Karen

Acknowledgments

To my wonderful editor at Berkley, Wendy McCurdy, and my agent, Pam Hopkins, of Hopkins Literary Associates. You have always believed in me. Thank you.

I am grateful to my patient beta readers: Leo Bourne, Mary Ann Clark, Laura Watkins, Madeline Iva, and Wendy Rome. I owe much to the support and friendship of the excellent folks at the Compuserve Books and Writers Community: Diana Gabaldon, Deniz Bevan, Jen Hendren, Jenny Meyers, Donna Rubino, Beth Shope, and others too numerous to mention. The Beau Monde, a special-interest chapter of RWA, has provided endless expertise on all things 1800-ish. Anything I got right is because of these wonderful people. All mistakes are my own.

One

1818
London

THE PAST CAUGHT UP TO HER IN THE RAIN, IN BRADDY
Square, six hundred yards from Meeks Street.

She'd been wary as a wild bird all the way across London.
No footstep echoed her own. Nobody showed a flicker of interest. But she knew someone was following. She had been a spy a
long time.

Her gun was no use in this wet. She kept her knife in hand,
ready, under her cloak.

In the end, it did no good. The square was a confusion of
housemaids scurrying home and clerks bent under their umbrel-
las, resentful. They emerged out of the rain, brushed by, and
disappeared into a landscape of gray. A young messenger boy
ran toward her, his jacket pulled up over his head, a slouching
cap hiding his face. Ordinary. He was wrapped in ordinary.

At the final instant, she sensed intention. She twisted. Slashed
out with her knife. Hit him through the cover of his coat he
twirled in her face. Heard him gasp. She felt the jolt and shock
as his body slammed into her. She had a glimpse of his face.
His knife scraped her chest, missing the blow to her heart, cutting her clothing. Cold pain speared up her arm.

He pushed her away and ran past, his boots splayed side to

side, scattering gravel. It was the mark of the assassin to strike and run.

She dropped the knife and took her arm where she'd been cut. *Sapriste*. Her hand came away red. The blood went pale with rain and washed from her palm even as she looked at it.

I'm bleeding. She pressed her arm tight to her ribs. Her dress was cut through. The slice down her arm ended in one single, deep jab. It had hit something important and the blood spilled out.

So small a thing to let the life out of her body. It barely hurt at all. Just death. Only death.

So she hurried. She let her cloak slip off. She held her blood in, trying to buy another few minutes. But all her time was seeping away.

Meeks Street was north of the square. The Service chose a quiet street. No one entered unless he had business there. Number Seven was halfway down. She staggered onward, not trying to keep dry or be inconspicuous or watch for enemies. Trying to make the last hundred yards.

She had expected death to be more spectacular, somehow. She had thought it would come at the end of a long Game, with the last roll of the dice still spinning and everyone watching and holding their breath for her. She'd be caught and shot by one army or another. It had seemed the most fitting end.

She'd expected the simplicity of the firing squad. Its neatness and order. Its finality. Instead, she was bleeding to death on an ugly English street, and she had no idea why.

Now she'd never find out. Even the question faded as she concentrated on putting one foot in front of the other.

Gray curtains of water wove in the wind. Two men barreled by, almost knocking her down. They were English gentlemen, seeing no one and nothing beyond themselves. They'd find blood on their coats when they got home and mourn their spoiled clothing and never know what had happened an inch under their noses.

She'd made them bloody aristos. Funny. It struck her as funny.

Nobody noticed her dying. Every door was closed. Every curtain drawn.

She passed low walls, punctuated by stone posts. Then she was at Number Seven. She knew the way even when she couldn't see very well. The door was painted green. The knocker was a bronze rose. She covered it with her bloody hand and banged down hard and went back to holding her blood in.

She leaned on the door, her forehead against the green paint. *It is strange that it does not hurt. I have been in pain so many times. This final time it does not hurt at all.*

Really, she was not ready to die. She had a long list of things to do.

The door opened and she had nothing to lean upon. The ground crested upward to meet her. The rug was scratchy on her cheek, surprisingly hard. She felt herself rolled over. She was looking up at a woman, not much more than a girl. She didn't know this one, did she?

Hands pushed her own hands away and came down strong around her arm, at the wound. Someone shouted. She could tell it was shouts from the urgency of it. It sounded distant in her ear.

When she opened her eyes again, he was there. Black hair and a thin face, dark as a Gypsy. Serious eyes.

She said, "Hello, 'Awker."

"Hello, Justine," Hawker said.

Two

SHE DID NOT DIE ON THE DOORSTEP. SHE HAD NOT died more times than she could count. Perhaps this would be another.

She opened her eyes. After a while she knew where she was. She was lying on the dining room table at Meeks Street, looking up at silver loops and flowered sconces holding half-burned candles. The ceiling was white, molded plasterwork with garlands of leaves.

She heard Hawker say, "Will she live?" and the long, rude, impatient man who was a surgeon replied, "How the hell would I know? Now get out of my light." She could not tell if this reassured Hawker, but it gave her considerable comfort. Surgeons were honest butchers. She did not trust polite doctors with their slimy patter of Latin and their soft hands.

The table was flat and hard under her. She hadn't noticed them cutting her clothes away, but she was naked. Several people held her down. It was Hawker who took her left shoulder and looked into her face.

Dark closed down upon her. She was in the heart of the pain. Had to get away. Had to. She fought.

The surgeon said, "Keep her still, damn it."

Hawker said, "*Chère. Ne me quitte pas.* Look. Look at me. *Ici.*"

Light came back. He was above her, his clever, handsome face grave. Hair fell in his eyes. Hard eyes. They had been old and cynical when he was a boy. "Look at me. That's right." His fingers dug into her shoulder. "Be still. You're here with me."

"I didn't want to come here," she said.

"I know. Quiet, now. Chouette, look at me."

"I don't hate you." Did she even say that? It was too much effort.

"She's fainted," someone said. "Good."

She had not fainted. She saw shadow and darkness, heard their voices, felt—oh yes, she felt—the pain. But it was as if it happened to someone else, several feet away.

A man said something. Hawker answered, ". . . before the blood washes away. Find out where this happened. Pax, I want you to . . ."

The surgeon did not pause in hurting her. "See if there's anybody left out in the rain who needs me. Every time you people—" and he said, "Hold that," to someone.

She said, "I was not fast enough. I must tell you. The papers . . ."

"Later," Hawker said. "Talk later."

She was not going to die, then. Not possibly. Hawker, of all people upon the earth, would awaken her and force her to speak if her life were ending and she had only minutes left. He would be brutally efficient, wringing the last morsel of words out of her, if she were dying. One could depend on him.

Another voice. "The house is secure." A man's face, grim and scarred, looked down at her and went away. William Doyle.

Then Hawker was telling someone to knock on the doors on Meeks Street. Did anybody see anything?

Under it all, the mutter of the surgeon. "Don't you slip away on me, you bastard . . . And here's the bugger causing all the problems. Little bleeder going at it like hell for no reason. I need to—Will you people hold the damn woman still!"

There was a pattern of greater pain and lesser pain. The surgeon set stitches, talking to himself as he worked on her arm. It was predictable in its dreadful bite and pull. She counted. Put a number on each second. Stepped from one second to the next. She could get through ten seconds. Start again. Ten more.

"Nice musculature. Healthy and no fat on her. I suppose she's one of yours." It was the surgeon's voice.

"Yes. Keep her alive," Hawker said.

Someone said, "Doyle is . . ." and a murmur after that. Someone said, "It's coming down in buckets," and then, ". . . found it under . . ."

"I'll look at it later." Hawker's voice.

More voices. She did not listen. Soft darkness, most perfectly solid, crowded in from all sides like so many insistent black pillows. She had slept in a bed with black velvet pillows in Vienna.

A clangor of pain struck and she was being lifted. Corners of the room spun by, confusing and dizzying.

The surgeon said, "You know what to do. Watch her. Make sure it doesn't start bleeding again. Put her to bed and keep her there."

"I shall devote myself to that goal," from Hawker.

"You are barbarians." She did not say they were *crétins* and clumsy idiots because she was a marvel of tact and endurance. "I am naked. Deal with this."

She was being carried upstairs past the large mirror in the hall. Past the line of maps in frames. After so many years, Hawker's arms were still as comforting as bread and milk. Familiar as the rumble of thunder.

I have never forgotten.

He was not tall or massive. Not a walking mountain of threat like William Doyle. Hawker was the menace of a thin, sharp blade. He was strong in the deep fibers of his body. Tough as steel in the sinew and bone and straps of lean muscle.

Behind them, at the bottom of the stairs, she heard William Doyle say to someone, "She's too old for you, lad. She was too old for the likes of you when she was twelve."

One of the young men of this household had looked upon her nakedness and become interested. Her last, thin thread of consciousness found this amusing.

Three

ADRIAN HAWKHURST, KNIGHT COMPANION OF THE Order of the Bath, former thief, master pickpocket from the rookeries of St. Giles, Head of the British Intelligence Service, stood beside Justine's bed, watching her breathe. He could trap air in a bubble. Whistle it out a wooden reed. Wave it around with a fan. He couldn't push air in and out of her lungs. He couldn't do a thing to keep her alive.

Doyle said, "Did you ever go into that shop of hers and talk to her?"

"No."

"I wondered," Doyle said.

"She wasn't a threat with Napoleon gone. She was nobody the Service had to watch."

"You kept an eye on her," Doyle said. "Her and her shop."

"Yes."

Justine was naked under the covers, pale and vulnerable. Bricks, hot from the oven, wrapped in flannel, were tucked up and down the bed, keeping the chill out. He'd laid her down inside that barricade. When he pulled the blanket up over her, she didn't move.

She'd have a new scar when she healed. That made five. He knew the story of every one. He'd kissed them all.

She'd always been pale as the moon. Skin you could almost see through. He used to lie beside her in the candlelight and trace the line of a vein up her arm to the pulse in her throat, then down to the mound of her breast. Or he'd follow one thin track up her leg to the silky, soft nest he never got tired of playing in. She was opaque now, as if the light in her had retreated to the core of her. It was gathered up there, keeping the chill out, keeping her life's heat in.

Fate carries a sting in her tail. He'd wanted Justine back in his bed. Now she was. But look at the price of it.

Doyle came up beside him. "Luke says she has a good chance."

"It's his job to say that."

"He's too busy to lie."

"Friends will always find time to lie to you. A heartwarming thought in a cynical world." He set his knuckles against her cheek. Skin fluent as running water, sleek as air. He felt the vibration inside from her blood pulsing.

Even after all these years, he'd still wake up in the middle of the night, hard as a rock from dreaming about her. He'd never stopped being hungry for this woman. "I wanted her back, and here she is. Fate's a perverse bitch."

"Always." Doyle slipped his hand inside the blanket, to Justine's shoulder, testing the temperature. "She'll make it. She's hard to kill."

"Many have tried."

Her hair spread everywhere on the pillow. Light-brown hair, honey hair, so golden and rich it looked edible. He knew how it felt, wrapped around his fingers. Knew how her breasts fitted into his hands. He knew the weight and shape and strength of her legs when they drew him into her.

A long time ago, she'd shot him. They'd been friends, and then lovers, and then enemies. Spies, serving different sides of the war.

The war was over, this last year or two. Sometimes, he walked outside the shop she kept and looked in. Sometimes, he found a spot outside and watched for a while, just to see what she looked like these days.

The last time they'd exchanged words, she'd promised to kill him. He hadn't expected her on his doorstep, half-dead, running from an enemy of her own.

I have the most dangerous woman in London in my bed.

Downstairs and distant, the front door to Meeks Street opened and closed again. He couldn't hear what his men were saying in the study, just the front door and the sound of rain coming down, urgent and hectic, like it meant business.

"Pax traced the blood trail to Braddy Square. That's where it happened." Doyle reached inside his jacket and drew a knife from an inner pocket and passed it over. "He found this, lying in a pool of blood."

"Justine's." A black knife with a flat hilt. Deep hatch marks on the grip for fighting. Balanced perfectly for throwing. "I gave her this." Razor sharp, of course. Justine knew how to respect a blade. "It's been a clever and useful piece of cutlery today. It's drawn blood." He looked past the knife, down into Justine's face. "You cut him, Owl. Good work."

He remembered putting this knife in her hand. Saying, "You shouldn't walk around without one." Gods. They'd both been kids.

"She's carried it awhile," Doyle said.

"A long time." He could feel that in the steel—the years she'd kept it close to her skin. Why had she held on to it? "Now all we need to do is find a Londoner walking around with a slice cut in him."

"Which don't narrow the field as much as I'd like. And he might not be English. Could be the Prussians or Austrians are still irritated with her." Doyle scratched the stubble on his cheek. "Or the French."

"Given the length and ingenuity of her career, there are Swedes and South Sea cannibals annoyed at her."

She'd kept his knife all these years.

He slid Justine's blade, still with the dried blood on it, under her pillow, putting the hilt to the left. That was the way she'd kept it at night, back when he knew her well. Maybe she'd thrash in her sleep and feel it under there and be reassured. Maybe she'd reach for it in her dreams and use it to hold death off.

Her breath caught in her chest with a rattle. Then silence. Cold sluiced over him. Time stopped . . . till she grabbed air again and settled to a slow in-and-out.

Not dying. She wasn't dying. "I don't like the sound of that."

"She hurts," Doyle said. "They do that when they hurt. It doesn't mean anything."

A friend always lies to you.

She muttered something—he couldn't make out the words—and turned her head on the pillow. She was shaking in all her muscles, as if the pain were trapped inside her body, trying to get out. He said, "This isn't sleep."

"No."

"I used to watch her sleep sometimes, back when I knew her that well." He'd get out of bed after they made love and go stoke up the fire. He used to stand in the cold, naked, looking down at her, thinking how perfect she was. Not quite believing it was real. "She falls in deep, every muscle loose. It's the only time she's not a little watchful. Then she wakes up all at once, all over, smooth as a cat. Probably there's cat in her ancestry someplace. Those old noble French families . . ."

"No telling, with the French. Inventive people. And she is still strolling about armed to the teeth, even in these piping days of peace. We took a gun out of the pouch in her cloak. Loaded. Not fired recently."

"I keep telling her—" He steadied his voice. "I used to tell her, you can always trust your powder in the rain. It's reliably wet."

"Might be why she had that knife in her hand instead of a gun and she ain't dead. She was also carrying this." Doyle took out a handkerchief and unwrapped it carefully to show a soggy, square mass, layer on layer of thin paper, pale pink with dilute blood. "Newspaper clippings. Unreadable at the moment."

Wet paper. That would be fragile. He didn't touch. "That would be the papers she's talking about. Somebody thinks the popular press is worth killing over."

"Might be the *Times*. Might be the *Observer*. This had the bad luck to fall in an inch of water. We'll dry it out and separate the sheets and see what we got." Doyle refolded the handkerchief. "It'll take a few hours."

"She'll tell us when she wakes up. Shouldn't be long."

Doyle nodded. He gave a last long look at Owl before he walked over to the window. He was dressed like a laborer today . . . a big, ugly, thuggish, barely respectable giant in sturdy clothes. His hair was wet and the gray streaks didn't show. The scar that ran down his cheek was fake. The imperturbable strength wasn't. "Still coming down like all the saints' frogs. Hope the basement doesn't flood."

Good weather for killing. Nobody would have seen Justine

or the shadow that stalked her. Back when he hunted men, he'd chosen this sort of day.

"I sent word to Sévie. She'll want to be with her sister." Doyle started to close the curtains.

"Leave the curtain. It's still light out. She likes light." Then he said, "She's shivering."

"The room's warm enough. The chill's coming from inside her." But Doyle went to nudge at the fire basket with the toe of his boot. Sparks shot up the chimney and out onto the hearthrug.

Soft thuds on the stairs turned into clicks headed down the hall. Muffin had attached himself to one of the agents, keeping him company, making him conspicuous.

A minute later Pax came in, carrying a tray. Muffin, a dog the size of a small pony, his rough, gray, untidy coat glazed with drops of water, followed. "Broth. Luke says to spoon this into her, if she can swallow."

"Set it down." Doyle stripped down to shirt and waistcoat and slung his wet jacket over a straight-backed chair. He rolled up his sleeves, looking ready to hold off a few bruisers, barefisted.

Pax said, "Fletcher and his crew are working their way out from Braddy, asking questions, trying to pick up her trail. We think she may have come directly from her shop. Stillwater and a half dozen are searching the square. Everybody else is in the study, dripping on the rug, drinking tea."

The men and women who belonged to him were gathering. They'd want to see how he was taking this. Want to lay down the words people said at times like this. They'd need orders. "I'll be down in a minute."

Muffin came over, looking worried, and nosed in under an elbow to stick his big square head up to the pillow to sniff over Justine's hair, memorizing her. He approved of the Justine smell. Didn't like the blood and antiseptic of the bandage. A few more whuffles up and down the bedcovers and he was satisfied. He clicked across the room to assist Doyle.

Doyle was hunkered down to lay coal on the fire, piece by piece, acting like his hands didn't feel flame. When he was through and stood up, Muffin took his place and thumped down in front of the fire, taking one end of the hearth to the other. The coal scuttle rattled. He stretched his chin on his paws and curled the great plumed tail to his side.

"I brought the knife." Pax set bowl and spoon from the tray

on the table beside the bed. "Luke says it fits the wound." He looked at Justine soberly.

"Show him." Doyle motioned.

Pax had brought it up on the tray. He passed it over, hilt first. "Fletcher found this under a ledge, thirty feet from the blood. Tossed in on purpose, looks like. Don't touch the edge."

The knife was a flat, matte-black, deadly curve, elegant as a crow's wing.

He knew it, of course. "Another of my children has found its way home. What well-trained knives I have." The weight of it, the balance of it, were completely familiar. He turned it over in his hand. "And look. Somebody's engraved it for me. The letters *A* and *H* . . . for Adrian Hawkhurst. That does make a truly personal gift."

"From someone who does not wish you well," Pax said dryly.

"They're not friendly to Justine, either."

"It's yours? You're sure?" Doyle said.

"Mine. Without doubt. See this?" He ran his thumb on the shaping of the swage. "That was supposed to steady the turn in flight. It didn't, so I only made an even dozen. I gave one to Justine." A glance at Pax. "You got one. Fletcher got one. I gave Annique one and she immediately misplaced it, careless woman that she is. I lost two in France, sticking them into people. And I left three behind with my baggage when I fled in undignified haste from . . ." he had to think, "Socchieve, in Italy."

"So they're spread broadcast over Europe," Doyle said.

"That's nine." Pax was never happy till the numbers added up. A shop clerk at heart.

"There's three tossed in a drawer in the workshop downstairs."

Doyle hooked a finger in his waistcoat pocket and curled out with a pocket lens. Typical of Doyle that he walked around with a magnifier. Wordlessly, he handed it over.

Under the glass . . . "No wear on the edge, for all it's sixteen years old. A few nicks, probably where it fell today. We have lots of dried blood, just turning brown. That's an hour old, at a guess. And . . ." There was a white film, as if somebody had drawn the blade through milk and let it dry. Nobody ever put friendly things on a knife. "The blade's dirty. Poison."

Pax said, "Luke thinks so. He doesn't know which one."

Damn and bloody codswallowing hell. Poison. He dropped

the knife down. Took the three steps to the bed. Pulled the blanket off Owl. He'd reopen the wound. It wasn't too late to—

"Hawk—" Pax caught his wrist. "Hawk. Leave it. It's clean. You didn't see. She left a trail of blood all the way back to Braddy Square. Anything that was in there washed out." Slowly, Pax let go. "There can't be much poison left in her."

It doesn't take much.

"The Borgia touches don't work." Doyle wasn't looking at him. He was pulling the covers back over Owl, studying her face. "It's been over an hour. Pupils are normal. No sweating. No swelling on that arm. Her mouth isn't dried out. Her pulse is fast, but that's from the pain."

You could buy five hundred poisons in London if you knew where to go. Fast ones. Slow ones. *Name of God, Owl, which one? What did they put inside you?* "I never used poison. It encourages sloppiness."

Pax said, "Even in the middle of the war, there weren't many men who poisoned. That narrows the field."

The war was three years over. Doves of peace were flapping every bloody where. But something from the bad old days had slithered out of the past to reach up and claw Justine.

"They used my damn knife." He stooped and retrieved it. Holding the knife, he could remember the feel of making it. The first time he shaped the edge on a grindstone. It took hours to get it exactly right.

Some knives wake up. They get to be a little alive. Nobody'd ever been able to convince him otherwise. This was an angry knife, full of purpose. A killer.

But you didn't kill her, did you? There was that much loyalty in you.

He flipped it in his hand, threw it into the doorframe. It thunked in solid, an inch deep. Muffin jerked up out of a doze and trotted over to hide behind a chair.

He worked it out of the wood and set it on the mantelpiece, cutting edge to the wall, where it wouldn't hurt somebody accidental-like.

Doyle said, "They're piled up like cordwood downstairs, without orders, losing daylight." When there was no response, he said, "I won't let her die while you're gone." And then, "Don't waste what it cost her, coming here."

Justine would be the first to kick his arse out the door. She'd send him out to do his job. He could almost hear her telling him to get to work.

He leaned down to her ear and whispered, "Stay alive for me, Owl. Remember. You promised to slit my throat while I slept. I'm going to hold you to that. We have unfinished business."

She lay, unquiet, her forehead pinched in tight lines, her lips shaping words that didn't get spoken. Still breathing. Still alive. The knife had missed her heart because she fought back like the she-devil she was.

He straightened up. "I'm going to kill the man who did this."

Doyle said, "I know."

PAX wasn't fast enough, following Adrian out the door.

"Stay," Doyle said.

"I have to—"

"It'll wait five minutes." Doyle crooked two fingers. "Get on the bed and lift her up. We'll put some of this broth into her." He took the bowl.

"I'll send Felicity up."

"Justine doesn't know Felicity. She knows you. Even half out of your head, your body knows when it's strangers touching you."

"She doesn't know me well enough to want me handling her, naked." But he went around and lifted her carefully, trying not to joggle the arm with the bandage. He kept the sheet between them so he wasn't touching her skin. "She's Hawker's."

"She won't mind. Hell, she won't know unless you go bragging about it. And we won't enlighten Hawker." Doyle took broth in the spoon. His voice hardened as he spoke to Justine. "Drink this."

She swallowed. She didn't open her eyes, but she swallowed.

"You're a man of many skills." Pax shifted uncomfortably, holding a woman who belonged to Hawker with discretion and disinterest.

"Four kids, and Maggie taking in every stray in England." Simple pride filled Doyle's voice when he talked about his wife.

Another mouthful. Justine came a little awake and drank thirstily when the bowl was set to her lips. Then she lay her head back against Pax, falling into sleep. After a minute, Pax shifted away and gingerly settled her down to the bed.

"That's good then." Doyle picked up a straight-backed chair, one-handed, and brought it over to the bedside. He sat and propped his boots on the frame of the bed. "I'll take it from here. Tell Felicity to send in some tea."

"Should I put that knife away? Hawk's knife."

"Might as well leave it be. I think he has plans for it."

"You see what it means, don't you? Using one of his knives?" Doyle nodded. "I see, all right."

"I don't think Hawk does. Not yet. He's distracted." Pax let his eyes touch Justine.

"It'll come to him when he's thinking clearly."

"Men all over Europe know Adrian Hawkhurst's knives. The Black Hawk's knives. Somebody wants to make it look like he killed her."

"That's the general idea. Yes."

Four

THERE WERE NOT MANY PLACES FOUR TRAITORS could meet. Their long association and their shared past were secrets held close as the fingers of their hands. At first, that caution was the order of the man who brought them to England so many years ago. After he died—after he was killed—it became their own wise and suspicious practice. Now it was habit.

The man dressed as an executioner said, "He's almost six, isn't he? And he's big for his age."

"He's old enough to have his own pony, of course." One of the women spoke. She wore the extravagant dress and blank, uncanny mask of the Carnevale of Venice. "I was hoping for a more . . . ponylike pony."

Two men and two women stood in a curtained alcove outside the ballroom. They were a little patch of French bindweed planted in the garden of England. They committed treason by breathing. But it was old treason. They were a conspiracy with the juice long since dried up.

Till the blackmail. Till the murders.

Violins, flutes, and a cello played. Fairies and pirates, shepherdesses and English kings skipped and bobbed a Scotch reel up and down the ballroom.

The woman in the Carnevale mask said, "I spoil him. We

always spoil the youngest." She folded and unfolded her fan. "He looks so small up on that brute of a pony."

The woman dressed as Cleopatra looked away, bored. She had no children.

"He's named it Palisade. What kind of a name is Palisade for a pony? That's a wall isn't it?"

"The defensive wall of a fort. Good name. Strong." The compact, heavily muscled man wore the tabard and armor of a medieval Knight Templar. Underneath, he looked like the soldier he had been.

The Humphreys' masquerade ball was always held the first week of May. It was one of the traditions of the Season. But Sir George was only a baronet and Lady Humphrey's father was in shipping. The Humphreys cast a wider net than they might have liked. The company was less exclusive, the dancing more boisterous, the manners a shade less refined. Young squires from Yorkshire, who'd somehow missed making a splash in the ton all Season, paraded the fringes of the ballroom and thought themselves devilish fine fellows. Mamas brought awkward daughters, who would not be officially out till next year, to commit their first, inevitable gaucheries in anonymity.

French spies met behind the potted plants.

Carnevale Mask said, "I don't want a strong pony. I want a docile one. It's eating its head off, trying to grow. I catch a very sneaky look in its eye sometimes."

The four talked and waited, half hidden by a heavy expanse of blue curtain. They spoke of the weather, scandal, politics, of a pony eating its head off in a stable near Hampstead village. They sipped punch. When it was clear no one lingered to overhear, they fell silent.

The one dressed as Cleopatra spoke first. "The surgeon left at five. They sent a boy to the apothecary. She must still be alive."

"That was damnable work." A fierce whisper from Carnevale Mask.

"Damnably stupid too. We're all lucky he wasn't caught." Cleopatra's face was hidden by a mask of feathers and beaten gold. She wore a black wig. Her arms were heavy with wide gold bands. "Or she wasn't caught."

The Knight Templar said, "Stabbed in the middle of Braddy Square, for God's sake. It can't be one of us. None of us would take that chance."

"And yet, he succeeded," Cleopatra said. "It was genius, in its way. The rain hid everything. He struck on the doorstep of Meeks Street and escaped. I'd call that bold, not stupid."

The executioner said, "He condemned all of us to disaster. The British Service won't forgive this. They won't forget."

"Maybe it's a damn coincidence," the knight said gruffly. "The town's full of sneak thieves. It could be—"

Cleopatra cut in, "I received my letter. I was told to be in the bookstore in Hart Street, waiting for the magistrate's men. Ready to give evidence." She let that sink in. "We all gave the same description. We implicated the same man. We all followed orders."

The executioner said, "One of us held the knife. When she dies, it's our murder."

"Only one of us is guilty. Only one." The woman of the Carnevale mask gripped her fan like a weapon.

"One murderer." Cleopatra's jewelry, the gold and the gilt, chimed as she lifted her glass and drank. "But three of us willing to lie and send a man to the gallows. Is there a hotter hell reserved for the murderer?" A sly look. "Will you save me a seat by the fire, Amy?"

"I didn't kill anyone."

"You'd say that if you had the knife stuffed in your corset. Shall we take it in turns, protesting our innocence?"

"I swear, I didn't—"

"We are all so very good at lying," Cleopatra said. "Swear, if it makes you feel better."

The Templar held his hand up, silencing. He wore a chain mail hood and mask the color of steel. His armor was rings of silvered tin, bright and mobile as fish scale. When he moved, metal clicked against metal like the gears of a clock. "What do we know?"

"Military Intelligence saw nothing." Cleopatra rolled the wineglass back and forth between her hands, gazing down into it. She was the most discreet of expensive courtesans. One of her men held a position high in Military Intelligence. "Their man who watches Meeks Street didn't like the rain and had taken himself off to a tavern. They have heard only rumor. No one's made the connection between Meeks Street and the killings. Do you know the name of the man we've been accusing?"

"Don't." The Templar spoke sharply. "We know. All of us know."

"It is the Head of the British Service. The Black Hawk."

"And that is why we will fall." The executioner leaned on his ax, head bowed, gripping the two-sided head. "Justine DuMotier and the Black Hawk were lovers once. When she dies, he'll hunt us down like dogs." He raised his eyes, going from one to the other. "Perhaps he should. Gravois and Patelin deserved what they got. DuMotier didn't."

"She was Police Secrète. Like them." Cleopatra shrugged.

"Like us." Under the mask, under the helm, the Templar's mouth drew a grim line. "She was a soldier fighting for what she believed in. She shouldn't die like this."

"We tell ourselves we have no choice." Carnevale Mask followed one bright figure through the pattern of the dance. Her oldest daughter. "They've won, you know. We've become the monsters they tried to make us. We—"

A man dressed as Henry VIII paused at the curtains to the alcove and peered in. Cleopatra wore thin folds of pleated linen. Her pale body with its gilded nipples was clearly displayed beneath. She had become wealthy selling that beauty. Henry VIII gave a long, appreciative, lip-licking smile.

The executioner lifted his ax and tested the edge. Henry VIII decided to stroll onward.

When he was gone, Cleopatra said, "It's too late. It's always been too late. What can we do?"

The executioner said softly, "We can stop."

They held a long conversation with their eyes. Four French spies, pretending to be the grandson of an earl, the widow of a baron, the bluff military gentleman, the notorious courtesan.

"I will stop this. Here and now," the executioner said. "For me, this is the end. When the next letter comes, I'll ignore it."

"The end." Carnevale Mask still watched her daughter. "No more. Whatever it costs."

The Knight Templar bowed his head.

"Justine DuMotier will be the last to die." Cleopatra went back to watching the dancers.

"If she dies," Amy said.

Cleopatra said, "We were well taught. That knife will have been poisoned. She won't live through the night."

"I can't believe one of us did this."

"I believe it very easily," Cleopatra said. "We've all killed. Even you, sweet Amy. And you always used a knife."

Five

JUSTINE HAD TOLD THE BOY TO MEET HER AT THE
guillotine. It was not because she was bloodthirsty—indeed,
she was not—but because they would be inconspicuous here.

She was dressed as a housemaid today, in honest blue serge,
white apron, and a plain fichu. In this, she became indistinguishable as the tenth ant in a line of ants. She held her basket
to her chest and leaned on the wall that marked the boundary
between La Place de la Révolution and the Tuileries Gardens.

She was too young to pretend to the august status of lady's
maid. A thirteen-year-old must be a housemaid, no more than
that. But a housemaid was exactly what a respectable woman
would take with her when she went to an assignation in the
Tuileries Gardens. A housemaid could be left to stand in a corner of La Place de la Révolution, bored and resigned, while her
mistress played fast and loose with her marriage vows.

So the housemaid assumed her appropriate expression of
boredom and resignation and waited. Hawker would find her
easily. She was still when everyone else was in motion. Nothing
is more apparent to the eye.

This was a good spot for enemy spies to meet. From a hundred yards away Hawker could look across La Place de la Révolution and assure himself she was quite alone. The chattering

stream of humanity that flowed through the square would allow him concealment as he approached. Beyond, to her right, the tight, milling anarchy of the arcade and shops of the Rue de Rivoli offered a dozen paths of escape. Her good intentions would be clear, even to an English spy of limited experience.

Or perhaps not. She would not trust herself if she were an English spy.

She frowned, working that out, and kept watch for him.

In the center of La Place de la Révolution stood the guillotine. The boards of the platform were dull brown. The stones to the right-hand side were nastily, thickly black where corpses had been rolled into waiting carts. But each morning at dawn men washed the instrument and whetted the blade suspended above the chopping block. The edge of the national razor gleamed silver.

There would be no work for the machinery of death today. For the first time in months, no heads rolled. Robespierre was three days dead, and everything had changed. Perhaps, just perhaps, it was the end of the Terror.

The citizens of Paris, who were toughened to the most horrendous sights, treated the empty guillotine as one more festival. They came in their dozens and crossed the vast, impressive spaces of the Place to gawk and circle about the platform, poking one another and pointing. Men carried their young children on their shoulders. When they passed nearby she could hear them saying, "Look, son. That is where the tyrant Robespierre died. I saw it myself, with these eyes. He wore a bloody bandage over his cheek and he screamed when they tore it off."

She did not care that this was a great moment of history. Her sister was not yet four—the age of those children being shown this "history"—and she would not have taken Séverine anywhere near this abattoir for any reason under the sun.

Hawker settled to the wall beside her, his arms folded, his eyes on the guillotine. "So that's where they did him. Robespierre."

Hawker was not there . . . and then he was. Close enough to touch. She had not been aware of his approach. How annoying. If he had been a fellow member of the Secret Police, she would have asked him to teach her this trick of becoming part of the crowd, invisible. But he was not Secret Police. Not yet.

She would try to recruit him. He was young—her own age, no older—and he would be impressionable.

They shared the wall companionably. She said, "You did not come to see the great man die? That was incurious of you, Citoyen 'Awker."

"Doyle kept me busy. I don't know why he bothered. It's not like I've never seen a man die."

Madame had done the same—set tasks to keep her away from La Place de la Révolution. "I am sorry you missed the spectacle."

"There'll be others." He leaned with his shoulders against the stone and his arms folded. When he shrugged, it was a ripple of his whole body. "No shortage of deaths here lately."

"Comme tu dis."

His hair fell across his forehead, black and straight as poured ink. He was always pushing it away as an annoyance, casually, without thought, the way an animal might toss back its mane. He was a good-looking boy in a dark, exotic fashion.

He said, "I suppose you're keeping busy lately."

It was an oblique reference to her many activities. "I am."

"How's the sprat?"

Because she had involved herself with British spies, they now knew more of her than she wished. Hawker knew the most. He had met Séverine. "She does very well. You should not wear that waistcoat."

He frowned at her. "I like it."

"I had supposed so, since you are wearing it, but it does not go with what you are pretending to be, which is a tradesman's son. Unless you wish to portray that you have no taste at all."

"I might be." A minute later, "No stripes, huh?"

"Not stripes of that color. It is vulgar."

"Thanks for pointing that out. Sometimes, when I'm talking to you, I get a revelation as to why certain folks meet a grisly end."

They had met one week ago. She had learned much about him and surmised more. He was the most novice of British spies, an ingenious boy who learned with frightening speed. He was of the lowest class of English. He had very little patience. She had not seen him show fear. He possessed a dozen rare skills, some of which she needed very badly. This was what she knew of him.

In the same time, she had allowed him to learn almost nothing about her. He knew she was one of the great, secret smuggling chain that slipped refugees out of France, saving them from that very guillotine. He might not know she was also of the French Secret Police.

Pigeons strutted up and down the platform of the guillotine, self-important as sentries. Bold boys climbed and dodged up and over and around the steps where Robespierre, Danton, Desmoulins, Lavoisier, and Herbert had walked to death, and before them, the king and queen. Every few minutes, a bored soldier would come over and chase the boys away. The pigeons scattered. In a while new examples of both returned.

"I got your note," Hawker said. "I must be stupid. I'm here."

She had left messages at a café Hawker knew and at a stand on the Rue Denis where she had seen him buy a newspaper. Citoyen Doyle, who was Hawker's master and an English agent of the most exemplary type, would not have returned to those places. He would not have been lured by her beckoning. Hawker was less wise.

"You are kind to come. Especially when I did not tell you why." Of course she had not told him why. Even in the short time she had known him, she had learned his great weakness. He could not resist a mystery. What Frenchwoman worthy of her salt could not make of herself a mystery?

She was thirteen, but she was a Frenchwoman. Really, he stood no chance against her.

"I know why. You want something from me." His eyes slid to her . . . and away. "You'll get around to asking for it in a while."

She did not contradict him. Side by side, they looked across the Place, watching for anyone who might take undue interest in them. There was a certain camaraderie.

"You ever see anybody chopped?" He jerked his head toward the platform. "Up there?"

"Once. When I was eleven." She had come to La Place de la Révolution alone, in a cold rain, and she had been colder inside than any rain that fell from heaven.

Hawker glanced over, prying at her face. "Somebody you knew?"

"An enemy." They had dragged Monsieur Grenet from the tumbrel, the third in line of fifteen who would die. The demon who had defiled her shamefully for so long had become a shaking, white-faced old man, held upright between soldiers. She had been savagely glad to see him so diminished.

She had been too small to push her way close to the block. The crowd seethed and shifted between her and the execution. She did not get to see everything. She had heard the shrill whine of the blade dropping. Heard the knife thunk on the block. She caught one glimpse of the aftermath when his body was rolled aside like so much garbage, and it was over. "I am the one who sent him to the guillotine."

Across the square, a flurry of pigeons flew up, kicked into motion by a small child chasing them. Hawker's eyes flicked to that, then back to her. "And you were eleven. Deadly brat, weren't you? Did it help any, killing him?"

"No."

It had not stopped the rage. It had not warmed the chill inside her.

Grenet had been her father's friend. The day her parents died he came and took her and Séverine away from their *appartement*. He had a wife and children at home, so he could not take her there to do shameful things to her. He had taken her to a brothel where men of his corrupt tastes debauched children. For months, he visited again and again. He was one of those who demanded that she smile and tell him she liked what he did.

She said, "He was one of several dozen I would like to kill. And his death was too fast."

"Sometimes fast is all you get. Can we stroll away from here? I don't like being out in the open. Makes me wonder who you might have invited to meet me."

"You are cynical for one so young. If I wished to betray you, which I would not bother to do because you are entirely negligible, I would perform that betrayal in an alley with several large accomplices. But, certainly, let us remove ourselves from this unpleasantness. I have been advised to avoid public places, in case there is disorder."

"Half the town's walking around, hoping somebody will start a riot." He narrowed his eyes at a band of laborers, swaggering in a group, pushing through the crowd. "Those fellows, for instance. You can see them thinking about it."

He was right. Under everyone's voice, under the laughter, under the holiday atmosphere, they were all waiting. "No one is quite sure what to do next. It was simpler when we feared Robespierre. Now there are fifty devils to take his place, and we have not the least idea what to expect."

"Let's go expect it somewhere else. I don't like the smell of blood unless it's a throat I cut myself."

It was chilling that he said that and meant it. Hawker was in many ways like a fine gun. At rest, well made, efficient, and even beautiful. Pull back the cocking piece and the gun became deadly. This boy, elegant in motion, perfect in feature, cold as carved crystal, was the cocked gun. He was, in fact, rather frightening.

"One does not slit throats in a public square."

She had never, in point of fact, slit a throat, but she would not admit this to Hawker. He was the entirely genuine murderous spy, and she was not. With a small pang, she envied him.

He strolled beside her, his pace relaxed, his posture all ease and enjoyment. His eyes were amused and sleepy. Lies, all of it. The energy contained within his skin hummed in the air between them like a sound. He was more alive than anyone she had met. It was as if he carried an invisible top in the center of his chest, spinning strongly, that made her own nerves buzz in sympathy. He was not a restful person.

Ah, well. She would put his deadliness to use. She let her basket swing free. "Come with me. I have something to show you."

Six

MOST GIRLS, WHEN YOU FOLLOW THEM INTO AN ALLEY, are selling you a quick poke, with the possibility of getting knocked over the head by their pimp. Owl, on the other hand, could be engaged in a broad range of sinister plots.

She brought him to a stone church, small and so old it was sooted up black. There was straw and paper blown up against the bottom of the iron railings of the fence. He'd had a map of Paris pounded into his head, so he knew where they were, but he didn't know the name of this church. Either he'd forgot or it wasn't marked on the map in London.

Whatever saint used to own the building, now it was a shrine to Saint Horse. There were three big geldings out in the church-yard, standing together, lipping at the straw spread around, fill-ing the place with horse droppings and attracting a swarm of flies.

The French did that when they kicked the priests out and closed down the churches. They used them as stables and hay barns. They'd built a wood ramp up the front to the big double doors with the carved statues around it so the horses could get in and out.

The door at the side was locked up snug and suspicious-like. Owl produced a set of lockpicks she had about her person and set about dealing with that. He stood in the doorway, scratching his privates, which was going to make most people look away, shielding her from the curious.

There were various touchstones that said you had fallen among disreputable folk. Carrying lockpicks was one bad sign. On the other hand, Owl was taking long enough getting the lock open she almost counted as honest.

"I'm not going to offer to do that," he said. "It'd just annoy you."

"If you do not wish to annoy me, be silent. I am trying to be quiet about this."

Which was what he would have said if he was housebreaking and one of his confederates kept flapping his lips. Or churchbreaking. He hadn't spent much time in churches, once he got past his first youth and graduated from the trade of snatching poor boxes.

She had pretty hair—shiny and light brown like good ale. When he wasn't keeping an eye on the street he watched it make an escape out of the side of her cap. Every time she pushed a dozen strands up over her ear, a few more snuck out and started hanging down in the breeze. All this passed the time till she got the lock sprung and picked up her basket and went in.

It was cooler inside and dim and it smelled of horse. Two windows—one in the front, one at the other end—were still full of glass, colored like it was made of sapphire and ruby. The rest were boarded up, that being what you had to do if you go smashing all the glass out. A lesson to mobs everywhere.

This was all comfy enough, if you were a horse. They'd covered the stone floor with straw and put up wood slats to make some stalls across the front, under the windows. There were twenty good-sized horse bastards in here. A couple of them swung their heads around, looking right at him.

He didn't know a damn thing about horses, except they bit you when they had a chance or kicked you if that end happened to be closer. If you avoided them in the stable, they ran you down in the streets.

Two grooms were working up at the far end, one of them carting a bucket, the other with his back to them, stroking his way down the side of the horse with a brush.

Owl hissed. It sounded like a little wind coming in at a keyhole. "Do not stand there like a turnip. Come."

He followed her, sneaking past a horse left on his own in a big stall. Owl had decided that one wasn't going to bite. She was probably wrong. Horses spend their time just waiting to break your bones and stomp on you. It's all they think about.

The door she headed for opened up easy. Just as well, considering how long it took her to pick locks. They slipped into a room with cabinets on all the walls and a stairwell off in the back. He had only a second to take this in because Owl closed the door and it got black as under a hat.

He didn't mind dark—it was what you might call his area of expertise—but if he'd known they were going to bump around in it for any length of time, he'd have brought a candle.

"This way." Her voice came from a ways ahead, where he hadn't expected her to be. You'd think she did that on purpose.

Fine. He put one hand out to skim along cabinets. Put a knife in the other. One of the prime characteristics of dark is that it's full of people who want to do you harm. At least, that had been his experience.

They said the churches were rich before the Revolution. No telling what kind of stuff the priests left behind. Gold cups. Jewels. Bags of coin. If he'd been alone, he'd have stopped to take a look through those cupboards, just in case something trifling had been overlooked.

Ten paces and the cabinets ran out. Now he had stone wall under his fingers. His foot hit a stair—sturdy, solid-build, wood, curved in a circle, headed up. Air flowed down from above, carrying the wind in from outside and a small, sharp lemon smell with flowers at the edges. That was Owl. No aspect of that girl that didn't have a bite to it. He didn't hear footsteps, but she rustled the way women do, faint and subtle.

So. Upstairs. He counted the steps as he went in case he had to retreat with some deliberate speed.

The good news was, she probably hadn't brought him here to gut him. If she wanted him dead, she'd be sensible about it and stab him in the street. She was complex, not perverse.

He took the steps two at a time, which was why he ran into her, full-tilt, in the dark. Because she'd stopped to wait for him. He didn't run into her hard, but she jerked like he'd poked her with a stick.

He felt shock in her muscles. Her whole body went stiff,

ready to fight or run. He stepped back, quick-like, but tension kept right on drumming in the air around her. "Sorry."

"It is nothing." A stiff little answer, in a tight voice that barely escaped her throat.

She didn't much like men. He'd seen that the first time he laid eyes on her. Seen all the signs that said some man, some-time, had done a right professional job of hurting her. Where he came from, he'd known a lot of women like that.

She said, "Ahead, there is better light. Perhaps you will refrain from stumbling over me until we get there."

He could have said he wasn't the one standing stock-still in somebody's path, but he didn't.

When the stairs circled again, light started filtering down from the top. A hundred and six steps more and they got to the trapdoor, already opened. Owl crawled up onto the platform of the bell tower. His eyes stung, coming out into the sunlight. Sparrows came out of nests tucked up in the edges of the roof and flew back and forth, objecting.

He'd never been in a bell tower before, largely because there was nothing to steal in them. But this . . . This was prime. You could see all the way from the Seine out to the hill at Montmar-tre with the windmills on top. Notre Dame really was on an island. It looked like a bloody map.

All four sides were open. Up top, over his head, the roof had a beam across it from corner to corner, thick as a tree trunk. That's where the bell had been. You could see the grooves where it used to fit. The wood floor was scraped up where they'd dragged the bell across. They'd have taken it off to melt down for cannons. There was a square in the floor where the bell ropes must have come up. Big enough to fall through. Somebody'd set three boards across the space.

Owl put her basket on the stone sill and leaned over, show-ing off a pretty, rounded arse. He didn't take any notice of that, since she was a French agent and didn't like being touched any-way. But when she was grown up a little, she was going to drive some man mad.

She pointed southeast. "They are outside. You will see them." She'd brought field glasses in her basket. "Take this."

What she handed over was a nice sturdy set of optics, stan-dard issue for the English military. It was just a wonder and a mystery how the French got their hands on so much British equipment, wasn't it?

He wasted forty seconds thinking how much money a man earned smuggling and being wistful about it. But he was a spy now, not a member of the criminal classes, and he was reforming himself, so there was no point in thinking about profits from smuggling.

He shook hair out of his eyes. "What am I looking at?"

"That street. The long wall. You see it? The gate is green."

He was good with maps. "Rue de la Planche."

"It is. Do not boast to me. Look at it."

He adjusted the optics, set his elbows on the ledge to keep the view steady, and followed where she was pointing. Swung past. Came back again and found it. Adjusted the glasses. And he had it.

That was another exercise Doyle kept setting him—using glasses just like these and finding his target fast as blazes. "A house. Green shutters on the windows. Iron bars. It is just a pleasure to see somebody take provident care of their possessions."

"Go back toward that gate."

The double doors in the long wall had gouged pale half-circles into the stone of the street, opening and closing a thousand times. The gates were closed at the moment.

"In the courtyard behind that." She brought out another pair of glasses and stood at his shoulder, mirroring his concentration. Since he was a noticing kind of fellow, he observed she had a little white-handled gun left in the basket.

She shaded the lenses with the flat of her hand. "Good. They are all there."

Shade the glasses from the sun and they won't glint and give away your position. Doyle taught him that. And wasn't it disconcerting that Owl, who probably worked for the French Secret Police, knew the same trick.

"What do you see?" she said.

The courtyard was mottled brown and gray. Cobblestone with dirt. Dark boxes and crates were stacked up everywhere. One small wagon. Two handcarts. There was a big, light-yellow pile of hay. No horses. There were fourteen . . . fifteen people.

Two men attacked a boy about half their size, whacking at him with sticks, while everybody else stood around and watched.

The boy dodged and twisted like an alley dog, keeping out of reach. Just barely.

Hawker feathered at the optics, fixing on the boy, trying to bring his face in. It was tempting to lean forward, trying to see better. Doyle had cured him of that particular bad habit by clouting him on the head every time he did it.

And that was not a boy running every which way between the crates. That was a girl. She wore trousers and a loose shirt and she didn't have any tits on her, but when she flipped around, dodging a kick, long braids fell from their mooring and swung on her back, pale as wheat. She was twelve maybe. Younger than he was.

One of the men managed to hit her a good one across the back. Then the other man moved in. She got away, scrambling up over a pile of boxes. They chased her. Once, she tripped longwise and didn't roll away fast enough and got herself kicked in the belly.

Around the edge of the yard, a dozen boys did nothing . . . Hawker squinted into the eyepiece. No. That was probably girls and boys. Hard to tell from here.

Five minutes. Ten. Eventually it stopped. The men backed away. The girl struggled back to her feet and leaned over, arms braced on her thighs, braids falling straight down to brush the backs of her hands.

The two men motioned another kid over and began the creative process of beating the hell out of him in a purely instructive way. The girl limped to join the group lined up along the wall. It made him hurt, just looking at her.

He glanced across at Owl. "Some men take their pleasure in strange ways. Is that what you brought me here to see?"

"Yes." She held her hand out for the field glasses, wrapped them up carefully in a checked cloth, and gave some attention to settling both pairs, and the gun, neatly in the basket. "What do you think?"

I think there's men better dead. "She's a nimble little thing."

"She has been in training for a few years, I would think. She is good at fighting. Today, they are being taught that one may be hurt and hurt and hurt again and still continue. It is a valuable lesson. Those men, the *Tuteurs* who rule that house, repeat it frequently. Let us go. Someone might possibly look up and see us in this tower where we have no business being."

"Who are they?" He stepped in front of Owl, blocking her way. Not touching. A man risked whatever part of his body he laid on Owl, careless-like.

She looked away from him, down into the spiral of descending dark in the opening of the trapdoor. "They are called the *Cachés*. The hidden ones. They are being groomed to be sent to England."

With the last words, she went off down the stairs, as if she'd said everything that needed saying.

Since he knew a fair amount about women, he didn't hurry. He came along slowly after her, counting steps so he didn't trip at the bottom, hearing her footsteps in front of him. At the bottom of the steps he could see the outline of the door. Owl was blocking off some of the light at the lower edge.

If he'd been waiting there, he'd have stood off to the side so he didn't give away where he was. Lots of tricks Owl didn't know yet.

He took the last few steps and reached past her to spread his hand flat on the door before she opened it. "What do you want from me?"

She whispered, "We will talk outside. I—"

"We will talk here. Explain, or I walk out and leave you."

She made some gesture he felt in the air. "You bluff. You will not walk away after what you have seen. You have no choice but to listen."

"You'd be amazed what kind of choices I have." He opened the door an inch.

Her fingers touched his arm. "Wait." It was enough to stop him.

He was looking at a smooth, pretty face that didn't belong to a child. Determined eyes. Eyes that suggested it was probably not a good idea to cross her. He didn't know what she saw when she looked at him.

She stood and breathed on his shoulder long enough to make a warm, damp spot. Then she spoke, low and fast. "That place is called the Coach House. They made carriages there, years ago, in the work building behind the courtyard. There is a school now in the house where the master once lived."

"A damn strange school if you ask me."

"When one considers its purpose, it is not so strange."

"Are we going to stand here and play guessing games? Spit it out or swallow it."

"I am deciding what you should know." A moment passed. "I take a great risk. In all of Paris, there are no more than a dozen people left who know the Coach House exists and what happens there."

"Well, I'm not one of them yet, am I?"

"That is because you are an *imbécile* and keep interrupting me." Another minute passed. "They are orphans, those children. A man of the Police Secrète searches for young orphans of a particular quality." The long slit of light from the door fell on her face. Her mouth pulled in at the corner. "There have been many orphans in France, since the Revolution."

"They're a glut on the market lots of places." The streets of every city ran full of strays in various stages of starvation. He knew. He'd been one. "Common as lice."

"These children are not so common. They are the clever ones. Some are so beautiful they make the eye ache. They are brought there at eight or nine or ten years and it begins. In that house, every spoken word is English. They eat English food and learn the lessons and games of little English schoolchildren. You would not know they were born French. They are trained to fanatic loyalty to France and to the Revolution. Then they are sent to England, to be spies."

Interesting. "Not much use sending kids that age, if you ask me."

"You say that, you, who are younger than many of them. I would be amused if I had leisure to be amused with you." She shook her head. "Think, 'Awker! Someday, they will not be children. They will be grown men and women who have worked their way into the circles of power."

"That's planning a long time ahead."

"We speak of the Secret Police. Twenty years is a nothing. Governments rise and fall, but the Police Secrète remain."

"And that is a thought to take home and have bad dreams about."

"Do not smile at me in a superior manner. We speak of dangerous matters here, not foolery."

"I'm listening."

"Probably not, but I will speak anyway." She bent her head closer and lowered her voice to a whisper. "The children are reborn in the Coach House. The Tuteurs strip away from them all they have, even their names. When a place is found for them, they are sent to England and pass as orphans, or as children lost from English families. They are so young, no one questions whether they are what they appear to be."

That was a satchel of news to bring home to Doyle. Kids planted in England, waiting to be let loose someday. Spies still in the pod. "You know a lot about it."

"It is part of my charm to be knowledgeable in many fields." She batted his arm. "Move aside. I want to go out into the light to speak of this."

He didn't budge. "Why did you bring me here?"

"We will put an end to this. You and I. Tonight."

He said a couple of French words he'd learned recently. He wasn't sure what they meant, but it was something obscene. "Don't tell me your people couldn't have stopped that, Chouette. Any day. Any week. If you gave a damn about—"

Her hand twisted into the cloth of his coat. She held him, furious, snarling into his face. "We did not know."

"You knew."

"*Écoute-moi, Citoyen 'Awker.* You are the newly minted spy. You strut about with your insouciance and your black knife and you understand no more than a flea. This is the battle of shadows we fight here in Paris. There are a hundred factions. There are secrets the Secret Police themselves do not know. Men too powerful to be challenged." She let go of him. Pushed him away. "The Tuteurs who rule the Coach House were such men. They were untouchable."

She stood, breathing heavily, her teeth gritted. If he kept quiet, she'd get to the rest of it.

She did. "Three days ago, the Head of the Coach House followed Robespierre to the guillotine. Now, secrets creep into the daylight. Men say openly that the Tuteurs of the Coach House have committed the most evil acts."

"What exactly does that mean when you put it in plain words? Being as I'm an expert in evil, I take a certain interest in the variety of depravity in this—"

"Do not play the dunce. You are not the only connoisseur of evil here. We have all waded deep in blood since the Revolution." Her voice was brittle as glass. "You may accept my judgment. The men who placed those children in England were monsters. They have committed enormities. The Secret Police themselves are appalled."

"What enormities?" When she didn't answer, he said, "Go ahead. Name them. Impress me."

She set her fist to the wall. Just set it there and looked at it. "Many of the Cachés—most—became children built of smoke. False names and false histories. English children who never existed. But some were more solid than that. Sometimes, the Tuteurs traded a child for a child." She hit the wall, suddenly, with the side of her fist. It must have hurt. "Stand aside. I will go out from here. I am sick of darkness."

He let her shove him away. When he followed her outside, she was waiting for him at the iron railing that separated the churchyard from the road, holding onto one of the bars with her free hand, looking at the ground.

He said, "Now you tell me what that means. A child for a child? What's that?"

She breathed deeply. Twice. "Sometimes, the Cachés became real English children. They became orphans without close family, sent to live with distant relatives." She let go of the railing. "How do you think so many very convenient orphans are created? Walk beside me. I must tell you what we will do tonight."

"Hell. Are you saying . . . ?"

"I am not saying anything. Now, attend." She strode down the street, every bit of her the firm, busy, basket-on-her-arm house servant. A kitchen maid in a hurry. Not one speck of spy showed. "These Tuteurs must close that house if they wish to avoid an accounting for what they have done. They must place the last children in England, and do it quickly and brutally. I will not allow this."

"Because you're so concerned about England." He lengthened his stride to keep up with her.

"Because they will choose the easy placement. There will be no false persona prepared for the Cachés who are left. They will take them to brothels in London and sell them to important men."

He shouldn't have felt it like a punch in the stomach. Kids in St. Giles sold themselves every day for food and a roof overhead. Lots of the girls he'd grown up with ended up in brothels. Some of the boys too. He didn't like to think how close he'd come to it.

Deliberately, he slowed down, making her slow down too. "You think this is my business, somehow."

"I have made it your business. You cannot forget what you have seen."

She'd taken him up to that tower to see that skinny girl with her braids flapping out, dodging and hiding. He was supposed to think about that girl, locked up in a brothel.

Owl was a fool if she thought any of that made a difference to him. He said, "I can't do a damned thing about it, anyway, so—"

"But you can. We can. Tonight, I will go into that house and take the children out. I have laid my plans. All is prepared. You will aid me in this, or you will not, but do not tell yourself there is nothing you can do."

"I'm not going to help you."

She stopped and turned to confront him. She looked so bloody innocent. She had a face like a flower, pale and open. Fine threads of her hair fell down alongside her face, picking up sunlight, shining. "I will be at the bookstore on the Rue de Lombard at sunset. If you are there, we will together perform this little theft of the property from an arm of the Secret Police." She smiled, all winsome, not fooling him and not trying to. "It would be a brave and wily act to take so many potential agents from the French, would it not?"

"It would be a good way to get myself killed."

"Then stay at home tonight and pull the covers over your head. Perhaps you will be safe." She considered him keenly, and she changed her basket from right to left arm. "I shall expect you at sunset. Wear something . . ." she twiddled her fingers toward him, "unobtrusive. *Au revoir.*"

She walked away from him with a spring in her step, looking like her basket held five rolls and an apple instead of a gun, field glasses, picklocks, and God knew what else.

Seven

JUSTINE DID NOT GO TO THE FRONT DOOR OF THE brothel. She walked around to the back entrance, to the kitchen.

Men come to a brothel for the women, but they stay for the food. Babette, who ran the kitchen with a spoon of iron, was worth several times her weight in whores. Senior members of the Police Secrète schemed to lure Babette to their kitchen.

The grooms who kept the horses and swept the yard—Joseph, Jean le Gros, Petitjean, and Hugo—were sprawled at the big table by the kitchen window. René, who was an agent, very clever though he was young, was at the end of the table beside his cousin Yves, another agent, newly come from the country.

They called to her as she walked by.

"Justine. Ça va, petite?"

"What's the news, girl?"

"Over here, love. I've kept a warm spot on the bench for you."

Their clogs scuffed the floor as they bunched together to make room for her. The plate of cheese was pushed forward enticingly. The bread indicated. Jean le Gros patted the space beside him and grinned. He was a man of many words and few teeth.

She had topped up her basket with news sheets. One must look very innocent when carrying a gun. She tugged a *Journal de Paris* loose and tossed it in René's lap as she passed by, to read aloud for everyone. The grooms loved to hear about the men who came to this house. Nowhere in Paris were politics more hotly and intelligently debated than in Babette's kitchen.

Many times Jean le Gros and the others passed to Babette interesting words one fine visitor had said to another in the stable yard when there was no one to hear but the horses and a stupid old groom. Political revolutionaries spoke a great deal of the equality of man, while continuing to act as if servants had no ears.

It was hot in here, with the coals of the hearth raked to orange under the copper pots and chickens simmering down to stock. Babette stood at the long board, up to her elbows in flour, dough plump and obedient under her hands. Séverine was beside her, standing on a chair, wrapped in an apron many times too big for her, her front and her arms powdered with the flour, a very small round of dough before her, somewhat lumpy.

It was good to be home. She would enjoy a day of the mundane and familiar before she must embark upon her dangerous enterprise. One does not take the small joys of life for granted when they may not be granted tomorrow.

Séverine glowed. Too wise to bounce about on a kitchen chair, she contained all that joy inside herself, spilling it out in words. "Justine. Justine. I made rolls and we ate them for breakfast. Madame had a roll and Babette and Belle-Marie and I had a roll. Four rolls." She held up a white hand, showing five fingers, then pointed to the shelf with the salt box and the smaller mortars. "I saved one for you."

She had indeed. Oddly lopsided, it sat on a little blue-patterned plate. It was impossible to guess what path her sister's life would follow, but Séverine would not become a cook.

"That was a lovely thought and it is a beautiful roll. I shall take it upstairs with me." With any luck, she would feed it to the sparrows who inhabited the roof outside her bedroom window. If Séverine came with her, she'd eat and praise every rock-hard bite. The others, including the doll, Belle-Marie, had done so.

"Babette is letting me make tarte aux pommes with her. See. Next, we peel apples. I can almost peel an apple. Will you be here for dinner, Justine? They will eat vol-au-vent of chicken upstairs, and we are having oxtail stew in the kitchen, even though it is very hot today. Madame said that everyone will need sustaining food in times of momenterous changes. Babette let me chop carrots. And we bought parsley and I helped wash it."

For three days . . . four days, maybe longer, she had spent no time with Séverine. The overthrow of Robespierre, in which she had played a small part, seemed a poor excuse for neglecting her sister. Now there were Cachés to rescue. She would be busy all night.

There was always more to do. Spying would eat you alive if you let it.

She leaned across the kneading board to kiss Séverine on her forehead, keeping her basket stretched to the side so it would not get floury. It is hard to clean flour out of guns. "That is a very pretty ribbon." Séverine had red ribbon tied in a loose bow around her braid, the long ends trailing. "Did Babette give it to you?"

"It was the man on the stairs who wanted to take me for a walk with him. He knew you. He said he hoped I would grow up to be as pretty as you are." She lowered her voice. Séverine had already learned that some words must be kept quiet. "I did not like him, but Babette said it would be polite to wear the ribbon until the man leaves the house."

Babette said, "Leblanc," and then, quickly, "I was there at once." It was spoken softly so the men at the table would not overhear. "He had some business to conduct and wanted to take a woman and the little one with him as disguise. I did not allow it."

Leblanc dared to approach Séverine. Rage was cold as ice, empty as night. She had never understood why people spoke of the heat of anger. "Thank you," to Babette, who would know the complexity and depth of her thanks.

She set her basket on the floor and went to Séverine. She picked at the knot in the ribbon with her fingernails, keeping the cold deep inside, so Séverine would not sense it. "I will put this away, safe." *I will give it to the old woman who sweeps the street.*

If Leblanc had laid a finger upon Séverine, she would shoot him. "He was with her only a moment?"

"Less than that." Babette cut the ball of pastry with a knife. "I brought her away and kept her by my side. I pay no attention to the orders of that canaille. Then Madame returned sooner than he expected, and his plans came to nothing. He is with Madame now."

Maybe she would shoot Leblanc anyway. He was an annoyance to Madame. It was a good time to dispose of enemies, this, when there was much disturbance in the city.

Séverine had acquired a smear of flour upon her cheek. Justine brushed that away with the tail of her apron and took the moment to hold her sister and kiss her face and become very floury herself in the process. They both admired the small, nubbly roll that was for her and she tucked it carefully into the pocket of her apron.

"I will eat it tonight with my dinner, before I go out." She sent a glance to Babette, saying she would be gone late into the night. Babette nodded. Séverine would be cared for, protected by that great bulwark of peasant strength.

Tomorrow, she would spend the whole day with her sister. Perhaps they would go to the Tuileries Gardens, if there were no riots, and Séverine could chase the pigeons.

MADAME'S sitting room was on the second floor. The halls were quiet. The women of the house were napping in their rooms or chatting in the salon. A few would be out, even in this heat, strolling the parks to loll prettily on a bench in the shade and smile at gentlemen.

Justine had changed from her housemaid clothes to a pretty dress in the new soft style, the waist high, the bodice crossed with a drape of fabric. It made her look older than she was and it was immensely fashionable.

She scratched upon Madame's door and entered, her footsteps making no sound on the deep pile of the rug. Madame, who was aware of everything that happened around her, glanced up and smiled. Leblanc pretended he did not notice her.

He had taken Madame's most spacious chair and sat with his boots up and splayed crudely on the embroidered footstool. His clothes were expensive but vulgar. He was of a family of provincial pig farmers. He carried about with him a hint of the sweet stench of pigs and, in his eyes, something of their bustling intelligence and arrogant self-interest.

Leblanc was one of the new men of the Revolution, violent and shrewd. He had risen quickly in the Secret Police. He was a powerful man. Even Madame was cautious around him.

"Madame." She curtsied deeply. These days it was a political statement to curtsy. It aligned one with the Girondists and the moderates, against the Jacobin fanatics of Robespierre. This was a comfortable political place to be when Robespierre's blood was scarcely dry upon the guillotine.

She held her chin high and made the dip of the knee that was exactly appropriate to greet a jumped-up pig farmer. Leblanc was a Jacobin. It would do no harm to remind him of the current weakness of his position.

If Leblanc were compounded of farmyard dirt and rancor, Madame was spun of steel. She wore a pale lavender dress, cut so low across the bodice that her breasts were clearly visible. Her dignity was such that it did not seem indecent. It was as if she came from a pagan time when the human form was sacred and nudity was without shame. Her hair, black and smooth as ebony, was swept up with silver combs and allowed to fall free in the back. She wore no jewelry whatsoever. Not the least ring or trinket.

Madame stood at the rosewood secretaire holding a letter. She noted every nuance of both curtsies and, in the deeps of her eyes, approved. "My dear. Your work went well?"

"Oh, yes. All is prepared."

"Good. We will discuss that in a moment, when Jacques has left." Thus she set Leblanc in his place. "He brings a letter I have been awaiting. You will read it in a moment."

"Is that necessary?" Leblanc frowned.

"It is always interesting to hear your opinions on the management of agents, Jacques." Madame folded the letter. "I will think about this before I reply. I must consult Soulier." She dropped it to the blotter on the writing desk.

Leblanc followed her gesture with cold eyes. "Tonight, then."

"Not tonight. You need not concern yourself with this. If you wish, you may return to the amusements of the parlor. My women will see to you."

"I am not amusing myself." He stood up, brushing his sleeves, as if to dislodge the contempt Madame's glance had left there. "I do not play with whores when the Republic is in turmoil. I am gauging the temper of the city. Important men come to your salon."

"To play with my whores. Sordid, is it not? One trembles for the future of rational government. For Justine, I will repeat what I said before. No one in my household is available to you for your work. Not the scrub maid. Not the cat in the stables. No one."

"You make a great fuss over a trifling matter." Leblanc shrugged. "I would have returned the infant in an hour or two. Now I must detach experienced agents from other work to accomplish my business. You inconvenience everyone with your insistence on—"

"Do not approach members of my household, Jacques. If you sneak behind my back in my own house, you will find the door closed to you."

"A thousand apologies," he spread his hands theatrically and inclined his head, not hiding the smirk of triumph, "if I have trespassed." All the time he peered beneath his lids at Madame, avid for some response. But he had not scratched the surface of Madame's great composure.

"You disrupt my house with your intrigues. I will not have my people upset." She spoke as one does to a tradesman who has made a delivery of inferior goods.

"I live to please you, Lucille." He was not as skilled in sarcasm as he believed.

"Let us hope you continue to do so."

This was how mortal enemies spoke to one another in the Secret Police. Threat and counter-threat. She watched Madame and hoped she would be half as subtle, someday.

Leblanc made a great business of taking his leave. He bent over Madame's hand, then he took hers, giving himself the excuse to touch her. "My compliments to your small sister. She is delightful."

There could be no reply to that.

She stood at the door of the parlor after he left to make certain he went down the stairs and did not loiter. Then she left the door open. A closed door invites eavesdroppers.

Madame had taken up a magnifying glass to examine the seal of the letter. "You have allowed him to discompose you."

"He makes my skin crawl. I do not want him near Séverine."

"It will not happen again. Babette was there in moments." She set the magnifying glass aside. "For all his many faults, he does not molest children. His preference is for girls just come to womanhood. Like you."

"I know. He would smirch her a little, because he cannot have me. In revenge."

Memory struck like a spear. For an instant she felt men rutting on her body. Felt them smother her in their smell, poke their slimy tongues into her mouth. She was so sick with hate she could not breathe.

Madame stood and shook out her skirts, drawing the eye, breaking the hold of the past, bringing her back to the present, to the sunlight, to the pleasant parlor. To safety. "He will borrow a beggar child for his scheme and use one of the whores of the Palais Royale. It is what he intended from the first. He only sought out Séverine to torment you."

"And to challenge you. I am surprised he dares. Many people have disappeared in the last few days."

"To the general rejoicing of all. But you will not assist him to disappear, petite."

With Robespierre dead, a great power struggle was under way for the control of the Police Secrète. For three nights Madame had gone into the streets alone and returned to the house late, in quiet triumph. Once, covered with blood. Several of the men who had vanished were Madame's great enemies.

"I would be thoroughly careful, disposing of him, Madame. I will not be busy tomorrow, and I am very good with my gun."

"You are admirably skilled, but I will not indulge you in that way." It was gently said, but firmly. "Now, look here." She took the letter from the desk and studied it a moment. "See how this has been opened? There is the smallest sign of misplacement in the resealing. Leblanc is purposefully insolent. I assume he has found a new patron."

"Why should I not eliminate him for you? I have watched events long enough. I am ready to work."

"Then understand the work I need you to do. My child, you are clever. You see the mind and heart of others. That is a weapon beyond compare. Leave poison and the knife to amateurs." Startlingly, Madame chuckled. A warm, earthy sound. "You will find that making fools of men and plucking forth their secrets is more gratifying than killing them. One cannot, alas, rid the world of all of its Leblancs."

"I would like to try. He looks at me and licks his lips. It makes me sick."

"It gives him great satisfaction to know that."

No one was more wise than Madame. "You are telling me to dissemble more skillfully."

"You let him decide what you will feel. You delight him by showing your anger. Is that what you wish?"

"No." How often had Madame told her to deal dispassionately with men?

"Leblanc is an open enemy. But he is vain, greedy, and predictable. As things stand, there will be one of the Jacobin party in that position. He is less dangerous than whoever might replace him."

"I hate him."

Madame went to look out the window, down into the courtyard. "If you allow it, hate will eat you hollow. It is not good to be hollow. Ah. He leaves. Come. Observe him as the bug he is."

The front courtyard of the Pomme d'Or was bounded from the street by a high wall of square, biscuit-colored stone. The cobble was gray, crossed with lines of mud from coach wheels. A dozen orange trees in huge white planters stood at intervals against the wall, their green, shiny leaves glinting of silver where the afternoon sun hit. Leblanc strode away, stuffing his fingers into his gloves as he walked. It was a pleasure to see him this way, small and retreating.

"He develops a bald spot. How amusing." Madame let the curtain fall back. "Let us speculate, you and I. What is Leblanc's purpose in coming here to play annoying little games with my people? It was not to deliver that letter."

This is what she teaches me. To be dispassionate. To consider this man as a problem of logic. "He tests you. He wants to know if I can be used to hurt you. He came for Séverine . . ." She thought of Leblanc near Séverine, and she could not be detached and calculating. Quite simply, she wanted to kill him. "He sought her out to see if she could be used to control you. Or me."

"Now he knows."

It was a hard lesson Madame set her. She swallowed. "I have allowed him to see that I am vulnerable. Because of that, I have put Séverine at risk."

"I believe you have," Madame said gravely. She understood. She kept her own daughter well hidden in the countryside, where she could not be used as blackmail or threat. "She would be safer out of Paris, where Leblanc and others like him cannot reach her. You know my friends who keep the school in Dresden would welcome you both. You would be with young girls your own age."

The porter closed the gate behind Leblanc. What could one say? Only the truth. Madame would send her to play the innocent in some respectable school in Dresden. To live among giggling schoolgirls. To pretend to be heedless and wholesome. "I have not been a young girl for a long time."

"Child . . ."

"There are roles even I cannot play."

Perhaps Madame sighed. "We will speak of this again. Are you ready for tonight?"

It was a relief to turn to practical matters. "All is arranged. Every detail." Her gun was cleaned and loaded and her clothing set out, upstairs. She had tied together the last strings of her plan this afternoon. "I will free the children. La Flèche has promised to take them onward. We will use the freight barge at the Jardin des Plantes and slide downriver at dawn. The Cachés will be to the coast within a week."

"That is well done."

"It will be the last great operation of La Flèche, I think, now that Marguerite will depart from France tomorrow. She was not only their mastermind. She was their heart. I do not think they will carry on without her."

La Flèche was the best of the several secret rescue organizations—clever, well organized and reliable. Hundreds of miserable souls, fleeing the guillotine, owed their lives to La Flèche. She knew them well, having spied upon them and reported all their stratagems to Madame. The Police Secrète found many uses for an organization that smuggled men into England. "I will miss spying on them. Marguerite de Fleurignac throws herself away on the Englishman Doyle. This business of falling in love is a great stupidity."

"And yet, I believe she will be a happy woman in England, with her large English spy. And still useful to France. She will doubtless give refuge to the Cachés you free, once they are across the Channel."

"Nothing is more certain. She would care for every child in the world if she could reach her arms around them. She leaves Paris soon. Perhaps tomorrow. Citoyen Doyle will see to that."

"These new husbands . . ." Madame smiled.

"He is very protective." The English spy Doyle was like a great mastiff. He was a formidable enemy, but what he took under his protection was safe for all time. "He calls her Maggie, you know. I suppose she will become used to it."

"And the boy Hawker?"

She had to smile. "He is mine."

Madame bowed her head with a touch of mockery. "I congratulate you. Even the English are not sure he is theirs."

"For the space of one night, he is mine." In the midst of many troubles, amusement filled her. "Oh, I have been Machiavellian. You would have been so proud of me. I did not argue passionately. I showed him the barbarity of that place and told him what was planned. He will not permit it."

"You trust your judgment of him? He has killed men, my child. He has a reputation for cold-bloodedness."

"It is deserved. But he has weaknesses, as all men do. I watched him carefully. He is driven by his curiosity. And, most especially, he does not like to see women hurt. I took care he should see one of the girls being mistreated upon the fighting field. Now he is tied to my cause."

"That was astute."

The praise filled her with warmth. "One may hang many hopes upon the hook of a single small decency."

"Do not forget he is an enemy, Justine."

"He is a most useful enemy." In all of France, she could have found no more perfect associate. There was a core of honor in him, though he would have denied it vehemently. Once he was committed, he would not turn back. "I will use that ruthlessness of his."

She ran plans through her mind, as a woman might run a strand of pearls through her fingers, every pearl familiar in shape and texture. "If we are caught, I will see the blame falls upon him and the English. Everything works out perfectly."

Eight

BY THE TIME JUSTINE RETURNED TO THE KITCHEN,
Séverine had left.

"It is too hot. She has gone to play in the loft." Babette waved
to the kitchen window, toward the stable and the shed behind it.
She was brushing a dozen wide, fluted circles of pastry with egg
yolk, using a little brush made of feathers, making progress with
the tartes now that she had less assistance.

Justine had not eaten, so she stole an apple from the big bowl
and dodged away from Babette's scolding, out to the stable yard
behind the brothel.

The yard was kept in the most perfect order and cleanliness.
Madame said—she was very practical—that men would expect
to find clean girls in a clean house. Jean le Gros worked in front
of the stable door, currying one of the coach horses, keeping an
eye on everything. When she walked by eating her apple, he
called, "La petite is off that way," pointing to the shed, and,
"That pig-faced piece of dung is gone." No harm would come to
Séverine while Jean watched.

The storage shed hugged the back of the stable and held all
things that were outworn but not yet useless enough to throw
away. The loft above the shed was a considerably more interesting
place. It was a very secret place, that loft. Hard-eyed men—and

some women—came to shelter for a night or two and left under the cover of dark, carrying messages. Some were agents of the Police Secrète. Some were Madame's own couriers, loyal only to her. Many were sent here by La Flèche.

That had been her own particular work for La Flèche—hiding those who must flee France, taking them onward to the next link in the chain that would lead them to safety. Under Madame's orders, she had become a trusted member of the great smuggling organization. That was a noble work in itself, of course. It was also useful to the Secret Police to have an agent within those counsels.

When the loft was not occupied by desperate people, this was Séverine's playhouse.

The door to the storage shed was left open, always, as if nothing of importance happened here. The main room was dull and innocent. She picked her way between feed bags and wooden boxes. A ladder slanted up to the open square in the ceiling. She bit strongly into the apple, held it with her teeth, and climbed the ladder to emerge through the opening of the trapdoor.

A path was cleared the whole length of the loft, from the small window at one end to the large window at the other. Lumber, broken furniture, shelves of old dishes, crates, barrels, and piles of moth-eaten blankets jostled together on both sides.

In the relatively empty space below the window, where fugitives made rough beds of straw and blankets, Séverine had invited her favorite doll and a subsidiary doll to take luncheon upon a square handkerchief spread upon the floor. They were eating pieces of bread, small stones, and leaves from the chestnut tree, served on cracked plates.

"You have come, Justine. I am so happy. We are having dinner, Belle-Marie and her friend and I. Here." She patted the boards imperiously. "I will share my bread with you."

"I am just in time, then." She pulled herself the last steps into the loft. "I am famished, you know. My morning was busy." She came and sat and composed her skirts around her. It was not necessary to eat the somewhat dusty bread, only to raise it to her mouth and pretend to eat. "That is very good. You may finish this apple. I stole it from Babette."

"We will pretend Babette is a giant and you have stolen the apple from her castle."

"That is exactly what I did. I am too clever for any giant. I always escape with their treasure."

"You are immensely brave." Séverine took a bite of apple and held it to Belle-Marie, who presumably ate some.

"Belle-Marie is looking fashionable today." The doll wore a little cap with real lace. One of the women of the house was skilled with a needle and had made that cap, and also the apron and the blue dress. Justine accepted the apple from Séverine and took a bite and offered it back.

"It is Théodore's turn now," Séverine said.

Théodore had been carved from a bit of thick board and wrapped in red cloth. His arms and legs were nailed on and could move. "Perhaps he does not like apples."

Séverine giggled. "Of course he does. Jean le Gros made him for me."

That was enough of an explanation, she supposed. There was a crude face carved on Théodore and a fine big mustache drawn on in ink. "He is a soldier," Séverine said. "He is Belle-Marie's particular friend."

So Théodore got his bite of apple. Séverine was content to finish the rest of it. The dolls, after all, had their lovely plates of round white stones.

Séverine had opened the windows at both ends of the loft. It could not be said to be cool, but a little breeze found its way here, often enough. The loft was shaded by the height of the stable. It was as comfortable a place as any to pass the heat of the afternoon.

Under the disorder and the deliberately cultivated dust, this was a place of refuge. One could rest here . . . and she was very tired. This last week, her days had been filled with schemes and excitements and work that must be done. Robespierre had fallen. The government had changed. There had been a small amount of riot and fighting. She had been soaked in the rain, not once but twice, and had run the length of Paris a dozen times arranging small matters with huge consequences. She could not remember when she had last slept.

She said, "I must work tonight. I'm sorry."

"It is all right. Babette lets me sleep in her room, you know. She is teaching me to knit. I am making a shawl for Madame, but that is a secret you must not tell anyone."

"I will be as silent as soup."

"You are very silly. Soup is not silent. Soup goes . . ." and Séverine made a slurping sound.

"I will be silent as a potato then. Potatoes are the quietest of vegetables."

The festivities upon the napkin continued. Séverine discussed the weather politely with Belle-Marie and Théodore.

Justine took advantage of the decrepit chair that was overturned behind her. Blankets were stacked here, ready to make up rough pallets for the next occupant of this refuge. She pushed them about to make a pleasant softness and leaned back against the chair and closed her eyes. In a while, she must go to her room and sleep. For now, she would enjoy being with Séverine, who had abandoned the plates on the floor and was walking both dolls over the tops of some barrels.

Justine said, "What are they doing now?"

"We are through with luncheon. We are going to the office of the *avocat*."

"That's good."

"Théodore will give Belle-Marie a nice settlement. He is very kind."

She opened her eyes. "What?"

"He will take her to live in the Faubourg Germain in a grand *appartement* and buy her pretty clothing. He has promised it."

"Oh. Well." She sat up. She did not feel like dealing with this. She did not know how.

"She will give him her youth. It is like Virginie, who is giving her youth to Monsieur le Citoyen Barbier. She has a beautiful bracelet from him. She showed me. It has red stones in it."

Belle-Marie and her Théodore decided they would go to the park instead. So they jumped from crate to crate, going to the park. Then Séverine pulled a box over to the window and stood on it and looked out to wave at Jean le Gros.

"Look." Séverine leaned very far out the window. "Jeanne has brought a new man home. I hope he does not have diseases. Virginie says we will all catch diseases because Jeanne has the brains of a peahen and brings home any man she meets in the park. Will we catch diseases?"

"No."

She cannot stay here. What am I going to do?

Nine

"WERE YOU FOLLOWED?" THE OLD BITCH SAT DRINK-
ing coffee, glaring at Hawker.

She wasn't just any old bitch. She was Carruthers, Head of
the British Service for France. She could order him killed just
as easy as stirring sugar in her cup. Easier, because she liked
sugar and she didn't like him.

A fellow might as well talk to a pillar of iron spikes when it
came to reasonable discussion. He said, "People don't follow me."

"Really?" Just a well of skepticism, Carruthers. You had to
wonder if she trusted her own earwax.

"I switched back on my trail a dozen times. Crossed the
Seine twice. Went all the way down to the Sorbonne. It took me
an hour. I didn't lead anybody here."

"He has the skill." Doyle had all the parts of his gun laid out
on the table where he'd pushed his plate away. "It's his neck,
too, if the French stumble in here."

"If he's left a trail here, the French won't get a chance to kill
him." The Old Bitch picked up her cup and looked over the top.
"Tell me what the girl said."

He could do that. He started at the beginning—meeting Owl
in La Place de la Révolution. "First off, she asked me if I'd seen

Robespierre die. Called him the 'great man.' But sarcastic-like.
I said . . ."

He knew how to report. He used to do this when he worked
for Lazarus, back when the King of Thieves owned his soul,
such as it was. When Lazarus wanted information, a fellow gave
it to him fast, not wasting words and not making mistakes.

Working for Carruthers wasn't all that different from working for the cold-blooded bastard who ran the London under-
world, except now he lied and stole for England, and he was
likely to get killed by the French instead of dancing in the air
on the nubbing cheat.

He went back over his encounter with Owl, word for word,
as near as he could remember. Doyle cleaned his gun. Two
more agents came in, took chairs, and listened. Althea—she
was the other old lady spy, but fifty times more reasonable than
the lead-plated bitch—brought out eggs and toasted bread and
laid it down in front of him.

Maggie sat on a stool to the side of the kitchen under the
window. She was five days married. Married to Doyle over
there. They were generally within sight of each other when they
could manage it. She was spending her honeymoon busy as a
cat with two tails, but not the way you'd think. Or not only that.
She had maybe two hundred gold louis piled up on a barrel top
in front of her. She was counting them into bags and writing out
notes, giving orders for La Flèche business she wouldn't be
here to see to, personal. She'd be leaving France tomorrow.

Maggie was another one who wouldn't let Bitch Carruthers
get peevish and slit his throat.

He finished up his report with, ". . . said she'd expect me at
sunset and I should wear something unobtrusive."

They all sat, considering him.

Doyle fingered the crop of bristle that was establishing itself
on his cheek. He hadn't shaved, since he might need to go out
and look scruffy on the streets. "So she says they're about to
close this Coach House operation. You have to go in tonight.
That's not much warning."

"I doubt the timing is accidental." Carruthers had a way of
looking at you so you almost doubted yourself. "You saw a
dozen children, learning to fight."

"Thirteen. They're doing a good job of it. If Owl is right—"

"Justine DuMotier," the Old Bitch corrected.

"Her. If they learn English as well as they're learning to fight, they'll pass for English kids. No problem."

A long stare from Carruthers. She turned to Doyle. "Do you believe this?"

"It's an elaborate lie, if it's a lie. Why bother?"

Carruthers came back with, "The boy's not worth the trouble of arresting. You are. Are they after you?"

When Althea went around pouring coffee, she poured some for him too. The cup was thin as paper and the color of blue jewels, with curly gold leaves painted on it. The only time he touched something like this was to steal it. It didn't feel right, drinking out of it.

They started talking back and forth, all of them arguing, and left him to eat in peace.

"If the girl belongs to the Pomme d'Or, then Soulier's behind this."

". . . and the very wily Madame Lucille. They're both old enemies of the Jacobin faction, particularly Patelin. This could be aimed at discrediting him."

". . . internal politics of the Police Secrète. The DuMotier girl's being used by them, at the very least. Probably she's an agent herself."

"If the boy gets caught, it looks like a British operation. That undermines Patelin without pointing the finger at . . ."

"Which is what they have in mind. Blaming us."

". . . a chance to find out which side Soulier's supporting in the next . . ."

The air's so thick with intrigue nobody's going to be able to breathe. He put jam on bread and piled the eggs on and rolled it up tight to eat. He had most of that inside him before he noticed he wasn't doing it right. The Old Bitch had that kind of look on her face.

No eating with your hands. Just no end to the things you weren't supposed to do. He started to lick his fingers. And stopped. You weren't supposed to do that either, apparently. He was damned if he'd wipe jam on his togs.

"The napkin," Doyle said.

He'd laid it on his lap, like you was supposed to, and forgot about it. So now he used it and stashed it away again.

He said, "I know what we have to do."

That stopped the talking.

"We stop trying to guess what everybody's up to. I meet Owl tonight, and then we know. I go find out."

Althea sat down comfortably in the cushioned chair at the end of the table. "The problem with that, Hawker, is that this smells remarkably like a trap."

"And I have no intention of losing my rat to a French trap," the Old Bitch said. "I'll send a man to watch the DuMotier girl and see what she does. You," she looked directly at him, "will stay home."

"You're wrong." It was out of his mouth before he knew he was going to say it. Stupid.

Nobody said anything just immediately. Doyle put the cork back in a little bottle of gun oil, tamping it down hard with his thumb. He didn't seem concerned one way or the other. Noncommittal, if you went searching for the exact word.

"Explain yourself." Lots of spiked and rusty edges in Carruthers's voice.

"You're going to have to root out a whole platoon of these Cachés they've planted in England. It'll take you months and you'll probably miss some. In one night, I can give you thirteen you won't have to track down." He glanced around. No expression on any face. "I won't do anything stupid. If it's not going to work, I'll back away."

They lounged around, waiting for him to say some damn thing or other. He didn't know what.

He said, "You're not risking much. Just me."

Nothing.

So he said, "They're kids."

Doyle stopped scraping cinder out of the frizzen and set it down. "He should go. I would."

"Fine then. We'll send him into the middle of a Police Secrète power struggle," Carruthers sounded irritated, "where he'll be just about useless to me. He won't see what's going on under his nose, and there's no time to teach him."

That simple, that easy—he'd won his point. With the British Service he was out of his depth most of the time.

"Send someone with him," Althea said.

"Who'd frighten her off. And I take the chance of losing two agents."

Two agents. Carruthers said two agents. Meaning one of them

was him. He missed some of what they said next while he was trying to decide how he felt about being an agent.

". . . and more experienced," one of the men said.

"We'll send Paxton." That was Althea. "He's young enough to look unthreatening."

Paxton. Everybody's pet. The perfect agent. Paxton wouldn't forget to use his damned napkin. Paxton probably didn't slurp his tea. Probably he was no use at all on a job.

But the Old Bitch thought it was a glorious idea. "Pax will keep him out of trouble. You," she turned to Hawker, "are walking a fine line. An agent gets to contradict me three times in his career. You've used one of them. You will now write a report of everything you saw and heard this morning."

"I can't—"

"The ink and paper are in the cupboard. Work at this table. Make two copies."

Great. Just bloody great.

Ten

JUSTINE, WEARING TROUSERS AND SHIRT, WAS INTI-
mately entangled in this small space with the boy Hawker.
His knee thrust into her ribs. Her elbow poked his belly. He
remained unconcerned to the point of insult. She might have
been a large dog or a sack of grain placed in his way.

"You're squashing me." He shoved at her buttocks as if they
were melons at market. "Move."

"Two people cannot fit here. Frankly, I do not need—"

"And keep your voice down."

She hissed, "I am silent as the grave compared to you."

"Like hell."

One thin brick wall separated them from the house of the
Cachés. The Tuteurs would be downstairs, playing cards or
reading, but they would be alert these days, suspicious and vigi-
lant as crows. "This is my project and I—"

"Are we going to spend all night talking, or are you going to
shift your arse out of my lap?"

She was not the possessor of the body that did not fit here.
Hawker created the problem. He was composed of flat and hard
muscles that did not budge an inch when she pushed them. He
was heavy and uncooperative as wood.

He was correct in this much—they had no time to waste.

She said, "I will scrape the last bricks free. Do not remove them yet. Do not, in fact, do anything."

"We both work," he said.

She picked up the chisel and pushed herself away from Hawker till her backbone rubbed the splintery wood of the crossbeam. "Then do not be clumsy."

"I've done this before."

The candle of the dark lantern spread a circle of light barely six feet wide. Within that space were boards laid down to make a floor and the ribs of the rafters. Beyond was an ocean of darkness. They could not afford more light. Some crack in the eaves might gleam down to the coach yard below. Too much light would leave them blinking and blind when they entered the hallways of the Coach House.

At the far end of the attic, Hawker's friend knelt in the dark and kept an eye on the street. He was called Pax. She had met him briefly once before, though he gave no sign he remembered that. Tonight he pushed his way into this operation to protect Hawker's back. The spies of England did not trust her to the width of a thread.

Citoyen Pax was the first of many unforeseen difficulties. Possibly she would find some use for him.

She wiped sweaty hands on these pants she wore. She had scrambled through many attics and basements in them. They were less indecent than skirts, but skirts would be cooler.

She took up the chisel, holding the shaft slack in her fist, tapping the butt with the flat of her other hand. Softly. Carefully.

The attic ran above the workshop where men had once constructed coaches. This end—this wall under her hand—was shared between the workshop and the old house where the master coachbuilder and his apprentices had once lived.

She had plotted to free the Cachés since the first moment Madame discovered what was being done here. This was her second night of sweating and choking in the close air, chipping away at the mortar between the bricks.

Now everything was held in place only by a little plaster. The mortar was of some substandard sort. It crumbled from its brick in pea-sized morsels that she teased out with her fingers and laid into piles behind her. Each time she cleared a brick she chinked in a wedge of wood to hold everything in place.

All was precarious. All was poised to give way. A single

incautious pressure, and the bricks and plaster would crash into the upstairs hall of the house.

Hawker was, indeed, deft in his work. He bent to the wall and set his forehead on it. His hair was tied back with a black ribbon. His face was grimy from crawling about in this attic and smeared with white powder from the mortar. His lips held a tight, intent grimace. He began scraping between bricks with the point of his knife.

She said, "You will ruin that blade."

"I got lots of knives."

She watched him work for a moment, disquieted by the edged beauty of his face. Lines of his hair fell in thin slashes of black. His lips were strongly marked. He was like one of the old Celtic spirits who still lived deep in the woods in the province she came from. They appeared in twilight of high summer and tempted girls to lie with them. Her nurse had told her the old stories. Someday soon, Hawker would be admirably suited to tempting silly young girls.

She said to him, "You will bring the Cachés this way. Not down the stairs. Through this opening. You understand?"

"Right."

They had discussed this already, but it did no harm to repeat instructions. "And out to the street. Get across the street and around the corner. You will be met. That's the end of your work. My friends take them onward."

"Where?"

"They will be safe. I would not spend this much time and trouble to be careless at the end."

"I'll find out. You might as well just tell me." He chipped away.

"You do not need to know." All was prepared. The Cachés would leave Paris in hidden compartments of the barge now tied to the quay at the Jardin des Plantes. They were not the first human cargo smuggled out of Paris in that barge.

They worked in silence for a few minutes. The loft was stifling. Sawdust from old carriage-making clogged her nose and lay on her tongue like cloth. The single flame in the lantern added to the suffocating closeness.

Sweat from Hawker's face dripped on her arm. His knee pressed into her side. He did not fidget, though he must be as uncomfortable as she was. He was a steady comrade for this work. Curled up, cramped, and hot, his concentration was absolute. Most obviously, he had dismantled many walls and broken into many houses. It was not an admirable history, but it reassured her at this moment. She had chosen him well.

"Last row," Hawker whispered. "We pull them out starting from the top."

Of course, he would try to take charge. "And you will be altogether silent, if you please. Starting now."

"Wait." He stopped her hand. Released it. He reached out to open and close the door of the lantern, covering and uncovering the light.

His friend materialized, crawling without sound from the dark, dressed in black, his hair darkened in an unconvincing way and his face smeared with dirt. Perhaps they thought she would not recognize him again. They were overly optimistic.

"Go over it one more time," Hawker said. "This breaks through into the upper hall."

"If I have calculated correctly. You will find the door to the attic. The Cachés sleep there, up under the roof. I have seen them looking out the window at dusk."

"And the door's to the right."

"So I believe. When I was working here, doing this," she touched the ranges of exposed brick of the wall, "I heard them pass. That way." She gestured. "The door will probably be locked upon them. I have lockpicks."

"I brought my own."

"That does not amaze me. You and your friend—"

"He's not my friend," Hawker said shortly.

She let her eyes run over the British spy who had been foisted upon her. "You and your associate will convince the Cachés to leave. That is the whole of your work, to get them out of the house. Mine is to see that you are not disturbed while you do this. I will be downstairs."

"Those two men that I saw—the Tuteurs—they're downstairs."

"Those two men at least. Maybe more."

"You're going to stop them."

"If it becomes necessary. I have a gun. And I have brought a knife." She swallowed the chalky air. In this small space, a great, hot silence closed around them and they breathed each other's hot breaths, like animals.

Hawker regarded her without favor. "Did you ever actually fight anybody?"

"That is not your concern."

"It is when you're guarding my back."

"I have killed." She did not say that it was not with her own hands. "I know how to fight. I have trained with a man from the army."

"Lessons. Now I'm impressed."

"Matters are as they are. I suggest you accommodate yourself."

Hawker said a single word, very rude.

"We will follow the plan as I have laid it out." She waited.

The single candle was hidden within the dark lantern. Hawker was compounded of various sorts of shadow—inky black, shadow like smoke, ash-gray shadow. The knife he held did not reflect the smallest particle of light. It was as if he held darkness itself.

At last he turned away and touched the center of the upper row of brick. He did not answer directly. He flicked a last bit of mortar away. "Let's break through."

He used a lockpick to make the first small hole and put his eye to it. "Good. They're not dancing minuets on the other side. It's dark and quiet."

They removed the bricks. Hawker's skinny, untalkative comrade made himself useful. He accepted bricks from her and from Hawker in turn and stretched to the eaves to stack them out of the way.

Eleven

THERE'S A WAY INTO ANY HOUSE. YOU CAN KNOCK on the door and talk your way in, pleasant-like. You can kick the door down and tromp in with clubs and a gang at your back. Or you can crawl on your sly, silent, dusty belly for sixty feet, scrape some bricks loose, and chew your way in like a rat. Hawker preferred the sneaking route to open and brutal force, which was why he'd become a thief instead of joining the army.

The hole they'd gnawed through the wall came out in an empty hall—Owl was right about that—about six feet up from the floor. You couldn't take a hold onto the bricks themselves, getting down. That was asking for the whole place to fall apart. You had to jump. Six feet wasn't what you'd call a long way down, but it was a long way to drop and land soft as cotton, which was what they had to do.

He went first, ignoring some gesticulating from Owl. He didn't trust either of his cohorts when it came to the fine points of being quiet. He trusted himself. He hit the floorboards loose and springy and turned it into a roll and came down at the end, flat and limp as a doll. He didn't make any noise.

He was alone in a long corridor with closed doors. No sound of breathing behind any of them doors, which was what you might call an indication they were empty, but not a promise you could take to the bank. Light leaked out of the hole they'd made in the wall. He braced himself on the plaster wall, making a ladder for Owl. Letting her put her feet on his shoulders and climb down, hand and foot, over him. Then Pax did the same thing, only heavier. Nothing like breaking into a house together for getting to know somebody.

Owl dressed right—head to foot in black, boy's trousers, hair pulled back and braided, covered with a dark scarf, soft boots. She'd left her woman's clothes in a bundle outside when they first came in. She wouldn't pass as a boy, not close up, not to a blind man, but she could move fast and easy and nobody cared how she looked anyway.

Pax brought a lit candle with him and left the lantern behind in the attic where it'd be useful in the escape. That was showing a modicum of common sense. Hawker's old master, who'd taught him to thieve, used to say, "Always take pains over your escape route. It's never wasted."

The minute she was down, Owl slipped off to the left, going from door to door, looking in, and leaving everything open behind her. Bedrooms. Men's clothing. Lots of books and papers. They'd have those rooms to hide in and leap from ambush if they were hunted along this corridor. Pax ghosted off to do the same down the right side, setting his boots to the floor silent as philosophy. All of this with no need for a word between any of them. That was a good sign.

This was a barracks-looking sort of house. No carpet in the hall. No furniture. No place for a cat to sit. Ten or twenty framed samplers on the wall. Not like anybody lived here at all. Not like it was somebody's home.

The door to the attic turned out to be next-to-last on the right-hand side. He went straight to it, which was half figuring out where it must be from long experience in the way houses were laid out and half luck. He hoped he impressed everybody.

Owl had worked her way to the head of the stairs leading down. She stood, breathing slow, getting herself steeled up for what came next. When she'd done that a minute, she took a little gun out of the pouch under her shirt.

He trotted down the hall—quiet about it—to intercept her. She looked mulish, but she stopped.

He held out his hand and she gave him the gun so he could

take a look at it. It was small, but not a toy. A serious gun, well maintained. A working weapon.

When he gave it back, she held it right—low against her side, on the half cock, thumb on the hammer. She'd been well taught. She might last all of a minute and a half in a real fight.

He mouthed, "Good luck," and hoped like hell she wouldn't need it.

Then he headed for the attic to play his part. He passed Pax, still searching rooms. Taking the stairs upward was like climbing into a dark throat. What they had here was—what would Doyle have called it?—Stygian darkness, whatever the hell that meant. Funny how his old profession—stealing—and his new one—spying—both involved a lot of fumbling his way around in the dark.

The fourth tread squeaked, like he'd stepped on something that objected. He'd been hugging along next to the wall just so that wouldn't happen. It was a shame and pity the way some householders didn't fix these little defects in their house.

At the top of the stairs, he ran his hands up and down the doorframe. The door was not just locked, but barred, like they were keeping jaguars and highwaymen behind it. A board thick as his hand was laid across the door in iron holders. Serious impediments to exit on this door. They were keeping somebody in, not out.

He put his ear to the wood and there was not a sound inside, which would ordinarily mean he was about to break into some furniture storage. In this case, it probably indicated somebody was going to stab him the minute he nudged the door open.

He'd had the chance, once, to apprentice to a fence, him being handy with numbers and knowing a fair amount about stolen goods. He should probably have pursued that line of work.

He lifted the bar up. Set it to the side, out of the way. Next on his list was this padlock. Nice and solid. Cold. Heavy. Expensive work, by the feel of it. His picks slipped into his hand with velvet silence since he kept them wrapped up nice and quiet. There was no feeling in the world sweeter than a fine pair of lockpicks between the fingers.

Except maybe a girl's breasts. Maybe the flower between her legs. That was the sweetest toy in the world. But lockpicks were a close second.

He shouldn't be thinking about girls when he was on a job.

Doyle would have said something sarcastic and made him feel like a fool.

He saw Pax before he heard him, since Pax was bringing the candle and he made about as much noise as the ghost of a mouse. Pax didn't creak on that fourth step. Then he stood, not flapping his mouth, holding the light at a useful angle.

Hawker'd admit it—Pax knew what he was doing. Didn't make him one wad of spit more likable.

The tumblers scraped. The lock clicked free. Pax cupped his palm around the candle flame so it wouldn't blow out if they encountered any breeze in the course of their next activities.

The door swung out smoothly, showing a tight, narrow room with no lights inside.

A pack of kids stood together at the far side of the room. They were dressed in short, white nightshirts—the same for girls and boys. Counting quick, he summed it up as thirteen of them. The girl with blond braids, the one he'd seen fighting yesterday, was in front. On her right, a boy the same size. Pink and blond for the girl. Really beautiful. Brown and wholesome-looking for the boy.

Still as doorsteps, every one of them.

So far, so good. "We're friends," he whispered. "Give me a minute to talk . . ." *before you start yelling.*

This wasn't much of a room for a baker's dozen of kids to sleep in. Slanted ceiling. The only place you could stand up was in the middle. The little window at the end had no reflection in it. No glass. Just a hole in the wall with iron bars across it. Too small to crawl out of even if you were a skinny kid.

No beds. No furniture. No dressers. Blankets were parceled out in two rows, one on each side of the attic, on the floor. That was how they slept. One blanket under them. One over. No pillow. No padding. No sheet. Clothes stacked in a neat pile next each blanket, a pair of shoes set square beside it.

It was hotter in here than outside. He knew all about attic rooms like this. Roast in summer. Freeze in winter.

The bedrooms he'd seen downstairs were comfortable enough.

The kids' faces and bodies were honed down into hungry angles. Not a plump one in the lot. And they were locked in. He felt Pax behind him, being silent.

The blond girl said, "Who are you? What do you want?"

She was the leader then. It showed in the way the others kept an eye on her and ranged themselves out from a center, where she was. Street thieves in the St. Giles rookeries traveled in mean, dangerous little packs that acted like this. They were run by girls, often as not.

He said, "I want to get you out of here."

"Why?" One blunt word from the boy at the front.

"Does it matter?"

None of them blinked. Absorbed attention was the order of the day.

He said, "Have they told you Robespierre is dead?"

"We were told."

"Then you know everything's changed. This Coach House of yours . . ." He didn't spit on the floor. Doyle said gentlemen didn't spit. That left him not knowing how to express his feelings with the eloquence they deserved. "This place. It's done. Finished. Over. You're the last." He took a step into the room. He saw the girl think about attacking him and decide to put that off for the moment.

He said, "This is what they didn't tell you. There's no place for you in England. Nothing's prepared. There's no one left to set you up. You won't be put in families or schools. You'll go to brothels."

The girl remained cold-eyed. "Why do you concern yourself?"

Damned if he knew. But Doyle would do this. Maybe this was what a gentleman would do. "Stay, or get yourselves out of this kennel. You have three minutes to decide."

"They're testing us," a boy said. Another nodded.

"It is the British."

"They will cut our throats," a girl said in a sweet voice.

The blond girl said, "We serve France. We will do whatever we are called upon to do."

"We are loyal to the Revolution," the boy beside her said. The others murmured about loyalty and revolutionary ideals and steadfastness.

He didn't have an endless supply of time.

Light slid in and out of corners of the attic room. The faces of the Cachés shadowed and unshadowed. Pax came up beside him. He said, "Is somebody downstairs?"

There was no noise at all. No light coming up the staircase. That was just Pax being nervous.

He turned in time to see Pax change the candle from left hand to right. "It is the least of my worries," Pax stretched and closed his fingers, uncramping them, and looked from one Caché to the other, "whether you believe me or not." He could have been talking about the cost of radishes for all the emotion in his voice. "Take what we offer, or stay and accept what will be done with you." Pax looked from one face to the other. "This is no test. No trickery."

A dozen seconds ticked off. The girl in long braids said, "We are not cowards. It is the moment to stop pretending that we are." She swept around, full of authority, wearing a nightshirt with dignity. "Choose. Remain here or come. If you're coming, dress. Carry your shoes."

Not everyone decided to leave. He and Pax argued with them for a while, but three stayed behind.

Twelve

SHE WAS NO INFANT IN THIS BUSINESS OF SPYING. She was on the rolls of the Secret Police, working for Madame and the great spy Soulier. For them, Justine became the servant girl, passing without notice, lingering and listening, gathering up whispers and rumors. For them, she had crept into the confidence of the tariff smugglers of Paris and kept their lookout and walked their secret ways. She had become a trusted member of La Flèche and plucked men and women from the very shadow of the guillotine. For two years, she had been a spy.

This was the first mission she had planned by herself. This time, there was no one to turn to for advice and direction. When she stepped her way silently downward, she was on her own, and her stomach was filled with spears of ice.

The stairway wall held samplers worked by the Cachés. There was sufficient light coming from the hall below to read the stitching. *I live to serve France.* The next one said, *I will die to do my duty to France.* The house was filled with such cheerful mottoes.

She felt Hawker's silent comments follow behind her as she descended. She ignored him. She carried her gun exactly as if she had killed battalions of men. It was comforting to play the role of an experienced spy, even if she fooled no one but herself.

Hawker broke into the Coach House with a panache that spoke of many houses invaded, many schemes brought to illegal fruition. She had no such confidence. But everyone must begin somewhere. He had no special monopoly on death.

The stage was set, the curtain rising. The Tuteurs of this Coach House, Hawker and his comrade Pax, the Cachés . . . they were all committed to the drama she had plotted. She was committed as well. There was no going back.

Hawker's job was to prod the Cachés on their way. He would be impatient and sarcastic and uncaring, what the English would call "damn your eyes." The Cachés would believe him because rudeness is always convincing. Those who wish one ill are all amiability.

She was their last defense. If they were discovered, she would delay pursuers and give the others a chance to get away.

She had come to the bottom of the stairs where the banister ended in a soft curve, worn by many hands. She took the last steps carefully, her muscles thick and slow with fear. Her heart thudded inside the tightness of her chest, as if her whole body were a fist squeezed around that beat. Her mind was sharp as broken glass.

She was sourly afraid. Sick with it. Some dispassionate part of her spirit looked at herself, being afraid. *I will not let fear control me. If I do, I will become nothing. I will not do that. Never again.* She wrapped up the fear to be a small, whining bundle tucked away inside herself. She had learned to do this in moments of great danger. This was why Madame had taken her as protégée.

To the right, down the long corridor, forty feet away, a dim lamp cupped a yellow glow that sketched out the doors on both sides of the hall in oblong shadows. To her left, in a mirror beside the front door, the lamp reflected like a tiny star, hung deep and distant. The mirror was not here to set a hair ribbon straight or comb the hair. It held a view of the upper and lower halls. One would see every movement in the house. The mirrors in the halls of the Pomme d'Or were given the same work.

The gun she carried felt natural in her hand. Endless hours of practice made it so. *Perhaps I will kill tonight. I have told Madame she may use me for such work. I am ready.*

She was young. Thirteen. But someday, she would become the kind of woman who walked in the dark and carried a gun and performed great acts. Someday, she would not even be afraid.

She rounded the newel post. The reflection of the candle in the mirror disappeared and reappeared as she crossed the hall.

There were no obstructions to avoid on her way to the front door. No cabinets or cases or chairs to rest in. No small tables carrying a graceful statue or a Chinese vase. The masters of the Coach House were men of grim ideology and small, meager vision.

At the front door of the house, she slid the bolt, disengaging metal from metal in utmost silence, and lifted the latch. The door swung in well-oiled discipline, making no noise, playing its part in her schemes. The night slid past her into the hall.

The open door was a deception and a distraction for the Tuteurs. It would send them searching the courtyard before they went upstairs and found the gaping hole in the plaster. She gained three minutes of delay and confusion to cover their retreat, just by opening the door. If the worst happened, she would run this way.

She slipped down the hall to stand beside the parlor door, her back to the plaster, the gun fully cocked now, upheld in both hands, cradled between her breasts, muzzle upward. Her clothes were soaked in dirty sweat. Inside her, she was an endless ocean of cold.

Hawker went about his work with due care. There was no sound from the upstairs hall and no light fell upon the stairs. There was only the distant night candle, twitching in the great dark, and the infinitesimal answering light in the mirror.

She set her ear against the plaster. She could make out a buzz in the parlor, a slow rhythm of exchange, back and forth. She heard the masculine voices, not the words. She did not know—and Madame had not been able to ascertain—how many of the Tuteurs still survived and were in Paris. But Gravois and Patelin, the Tuteurs who oversaw the daily running of the Coach House, would be here. Tonight, they would be on edge. They were familiar with every creak of every board of this house. No one could be more dangerous.

From their tone, the men in the parlor spoke of some serious subject. Perhaps they made plans. There was a sense of purpose and organization in the shape of speech and response.

She listened for any pause in the give and take of men's voices. That would mean they had heard something.

Her finger was a light caress on the trigger guard. She would kill the first man through the door, easily. Then she would be left with only her knife. She was no dreamer. She could not win in a knife fight against the trained killers who ruled the Coach House. They were twice her size, three times her age, with a thousand times her experience.

A vision filled her mind. Her own death, vivid and red. Falling under knives and gunshot and the blows of boots, messily splattering her blood in this spartan hallway, across these well-scrubbed boards, onto the whitewashed walls and the trite political cross-stitch.

She shut the thought away. She would picture only what she must do. If they came out of the parlor, she would shoot, drop her gun, and run. She'd planned her path across the courtyard. The best route up and over the wall. She would escape into the streets and leave them shouting and bewildered behind her.

She did not fidget. She knew how to stand long hours without moving. She relaxed each muscle except those she needed to hold the gun. She did not burn up her strength.

When she was eleven and her parents had died and she was betrayed into the child brothel by her parents' friend, she had learned to stand perfectly still. It had been a fancy of that house that the children played nymphs and fauns. They stood naked beside the dinner tables, draped with woven garlands of flowers, holding a lamp or a tray. Sometimes they were covered with fine white powder so they would resemble statues. They stood still as statues, hour after hour.

She was not beaten when she trembled from weariness and failed in this game. They whipped Séverine instead.

This was another house where children were beaten when they did not please their masters. She would enjoy killing Citoyens Patelin or Gravois or whoever was unwise enough to walk through this door first. The blood spattering these walls would be theirs.

They did not deal with the innocent daughter of the noble house of DeCabrillac. That child was gone forever. They faced Justine DuMotier, agent of the Police Secrète. She had not been destroyed. She did not give her enemies that victory.

Outside, the wind shifted and nosed into the hall with a

sound like breathing. She narrowed her mind to this moment only and then to the next moment that came after it and did not think any more about dying or the failure of this mission. Madame said, "There is a mighty army of what could be. Do not exhaust yourself fighting it."

Time passed. And passed.

Her eyes had become so accustomed to the darkness that she saw when the empty, dark space at the top of the stairs grew faintly light. She heard, not voices, but the softest shuffle of feet. A scrape against a wall. The Cachés were climbing into the hole in the wall. Escaping. Good. Good.

Minutes passed, heavy as if they were cast in lead.

Inside the parlor, a chair grated on the floor. The voices fell silent.

They'd heard something. She swallowed. Gathered herself to fight. Tensed her legs, her arms, her shoulders. Prepared to spring and shoot the instant the door opened.

Evil chances poured through her mind. Her death, Hawker's death, and terrible revenge upon the Cachés. Madame disgraced. Séverine alone in a country at war.

My fault. Everything. My fault. Suddenly and completely, she understood what it meant to be the one in charge.

Don't think of that. It's almost time. Be steady. She laid her finger beside the trigger with immense care. The pistol was perfectly still in her hands. She listened for the scrape of the door. Soon, she would turn and fire. *I am not afraid.*

When she ran, they would follow her out into the street. Hawker and his friend could kill at least one man. She was sure of it. Maybe two. Hawker's reputation said he could kill a man.

Blood pounded in her ears. She held her breath, listening.

In the parlor, the rhythm of speech began again.

So it was not discovery. Not disaster. Not yet. She removed her touch to the trigger. This was worse than fear, this reprieve. She was filled with nausea and cold, trembling. It was hard to keep her breath even and quiet. Words of a psalm repeated in her mind, stately, full of weight. *I will fear no evil. I will fear no evil.* She held on to those words. She, who had given up belief in God long ago.

Then Hawker was at the top of the stairs, casting a gray, stepped shadow, coming downward on its path, making no sound. He was beside her, unexpected because he moved so quickly, as if there were no distance across this hall.

He set his fingers on the barrel of her gun to say, "Put that down." Made a motion to say, "We've finished here. Come," and, "Good job. Let's get the hell out of here."

She lowered the gun, uncocked it, and tucked it away in the pouch under her shirt. The Cachés were on their way. It was done.

There was light outside.

Hawker turned the same instant she did. The window and the open space of the door lit up. Someone was in the courtyard, carrying a lantern, walking quickly toward the house, making little noises.

There was time, barely time, to throw herself across the hall to the far wall. To take one side of the front door as Hawker took the other.

The hall filled with light. A man stepped into the doorway.

Thirteen

SHE SAW THE MAN'S FACE AND KNEW HIM AND FELT a fierce exultation. She did not know when she drew her knife, but it was in her hand when she attacked.

The moment hung clear and motionless in the air. Time did not move.

Drieu had slung his jacket over his left arm across the valise he carried. In his right hand he held the lantern. His waistcoat was unbuttoned in the heat, his shirt blatant and white down the length of his chest.

She used both hands to hold the knife. She drove it into that white, into his belly, up under the breastbone and almost cried out with the triumph of it.

She had been taught to use the knife at the great marketplace at Les Halles, stabbing again and again into a great slab of hanging beef. She thought, *His belly is softer than a side of beef.*

A sickening intimacy joined her with Antoine Drieu. He shocked and shuddered against her body. It was as bad as copulation—hot and bestial. His damp clothes and his horrible hot breath smothered her face.

Hawker was beside her, at her shoulder, doing exactly what needed to be done. His hand closed over the man's mouth, keeping the cry and gurgle inside. His thigh, his foot, cushioned the valise as it fell. Knocked the lantern onto the crumpled jacket, keeping it quiet.

She held the hilt of the knife. Blood seeped warm and sticky onto her hands.

They supported the body upright while it struggled and died. Till it became only an ugly, huge weight.

Antoine Drieu was dead. She had dreamed of this a hundred times. She had schemed this. Planned to go to Lyon, undetected, and somehow murder him.

She had killed a French agent. *If they find out, I am dead.*

Her skin tightened to goose bumps. Her stomach heaved. She was filled with terror and relief and lightness and a kind of horrible joy.

One less. One less, of the men who had me in the brothel.

It was a shock when Hawker elbowed her impatiently. He said, "Leave the knife in," using no breath at all. No sound. "Bring everything."

He took Drieu's body against his shoulder. Bent halfway over, balancing the weight. Lifted it across his back. He was very strong, Hawker. She had not exactly realized that.

The lantern had fallen to its side, but the candle had not gone out. She found drops of blood splattered on the doorstep and smeared dirt across them. All would be brown and unrecognizable by daylight. There was surprisingly little blood anyway. It seemed one must leave the knife in the wound. Now she knew.

The lantern, coat, bag. She closed the door with exquisite silence. Followed Hawker and the ghastly load he carried. They both perfectly understood that the body must not be found in the courtyard. The Cachés must not be connected to this murder. She must not be. Even the British must not be connected.

Hawker stopped and turned with the body so she could plunder the corpse for a key. It was in the vest pocket. Her hands were weak and shaking. She could scarcely draw it forth and fit it in the lock. The huge gate swung out to let them through, making no noise about it. She slitted the door of the lantern to show only a small, secret, unobserved light upon the ground, picked up the valise, and stepped out into Rue de la Planche. She pushed the gate closed behind her with her shoulder.

The houses along the street were dark and silent. To the left, fifty feet away, candlelight slanted through a gap in the shutters of a second-floor window. Citoyen Pax stood in the street, square in that patch of light, showing himself in a manner that must be deliberate.

He beckoned. A small figure emerged from the alley that ran beside the Coach House wall, raced past him, across the road, and hid in the long range of shadow on the other side. One could barely see others already there, two or three of them in a line, still as rocks.

Hawker headed in the other direction. He was a dozen paces ahead, so she followed quickly. Where the road curved, just where they could still see the Coach House, he stopped to lean his burden against the wall. He scowled out from under a lolling head and arm.

Her heart beat, fast as a shrill little drum. She would not show Hawker her fear. She would not. "We will stay here a minute. I must wait till the Cachés are free."

"Right. We'll stand here gaping in the street for a bit." He was annoyed. "Where are your friends?"

"My colleagues are not seen until they wish to be seen." Hawker was glaring at her with many accusations, so she said, "I had to kill him. There was no choice whatsoever."

"Probably not." He did not sound appeased.

"It would be best to put that down." She gestured with the lantern. "It looks heavy."

"It is." He grunted and lowered the corpse of Drieu from his back and propped it, as if sitting, against the wall. Improbably, the posture seemed quite natural.

They spoke low, though they would not be overheard by anyone inside the Coach House or behind any of these dark windows up and down the street. It was not respect for the dead. She did not know what it was.

Far down the Rue de la Planche another shadow flitted from the alley, crossed the road, and joined the others in the wide slab of shadow. One more Caché, free.

Hawker wiped his hands on the clothing of the corpse. "You would kill somebody sizable."

"It is unfortunate, I agree."

Hawker went down to one knee beside the body and started going through Drieu's pockets, despoiling the dead.

She said, "The corpse cannot be left here."

"I knew you were going to say that. When Pax finishes, we'll take the body along between us like a drunken friend, being helped home. Give me his coat. It'll hide the blood."

"It is too far to take him to the Seine, but there is a graveyard a few streets north. I see a logic to putting bodies there."

"The Cimetière des Errancis."

He must show off his knowledge of Paris. "*Comme tu dis.* There are many unhallowed political dead in that place. Possibly no one will notice one more corpse among so many. There may even be an open grave."

"And that is a pleasant prospect. Or I can leave him in an alley. That's the preferred method where I come from."

"He deserves no better." Someday, she would be that cold-blooded. Someday, she would shrug, just as Hawker did at this moment, and turn her attention to the next pocket. "When they find him, no one will be surprised if he is left like refuse in the streets."

She set the lantern onto the stones of the street and released more light to help Hawker's investigations. Herself, she turned away and did not watch. How stupid that she did not want to look upon the body of Drieu, or touch it, though she had been glad enough to kill him.

"You know him," Hawker said.

"Antoine Drieu. He is a corrupt and wicked man."

"Was. He was corrupt and wicked. Now he's just inconvenient." Hawker methodically laid the bits and pieces of everyday life beside the corpse—a tinderbox, a watch, a penknife, a silver toothpick case. Deft and unconcerned. He made no wasted motion. "Was he one of those Tuteurs at the Coach House?"

"He works in . . . He worked in Lyon. But he was of the Jacobin faction. The Coach House is wholly their operation. He may have come there from time to time. He . . ." she made herself say it, ". . . he liked to mistreat children."

"Ah." Hawker did not ask one question. He saw too much with those cynical dark eyes. He guessed too much about her.

"I have not seen him in more than a year." Drieu was dressed for travel in dark pantaloons and coat. The strip of light crossed his plain gray waistcoat, horrible with blood. The shiny red was a blow to the eyes.

"If you're going to throw up, go do it somewhere else." Hawker did not look up at her, which was delicate of him. He continued to turn out pockets. "The first one's the hardest."

She wanted to tell him this was not her first killing, that she waded to her ankles in gore every day of the week, but there is nothing more pointless than telling lies that will not be believed.

"It helps if it's somebody you hate," he said. "Next time you might give some thought to how you're going to dispose of the body."

"I know how I am going to dispose of the body. I will give him to you. You will leave all the papers you find upon the ground there and not attempt to steal them."

"Me? Nothing here for me." He turned his attention to Drieu's valise. "Just a pile of travel documents. Looks like he was leaving France. Not fast enough as it turns out. And they are useless to me unless I grow six inches and get thirty years older all of a sudden. I'm keeping the money."

"I do not give a damn what you do with the money."

"Owl. Listen to me. You always strip the corpse. Otherwise you might as well tuck a note on him saying, 'This was business, not stealing.' Always take the money."

She knew many spies—good and bad, skilled and clumsy, some nearly as young as she was. She had never met one like him.

If she had been with anyone else tonight, she would be dead.

He had been keeping an eye on the street. He lifted his head from his pillaging of valises. "Looks like your friends have finally showed up. We may brush through this more or less intact."

A sliver of moon, white as bone, hung in the sky, giving no light. An old woman hobbled out of the darkness toward Pax, bent over, leaning on a cane, approaching slowly so he would have time to study her. It was Blackbird.

"She doesn't look like much." Hawker buckled the bag and stood up.

"That is her genius. We are in luck. They have sent us one of the best of the smugglers, with a hundred lives saved at her hands. She will take the Cachés to safety."

"Good. Because I am sick and tired of dealing with them."

Tiny and barely lit, the figures of a shrunken woman and the tall Englishman leaned together, talking. A shadow ran across the road. All was going well. "It won't be long now."

Hawker said, "That's ten. We're done."

"There are more."

"Three of them aren't coming."

She did not understand at once. Then she did. "Damn you. Oh, damn you to hell. You left them behind."

"It's their choice."

Her hand went to the gun that hid under her shirt, heavy and hard and cold upon her belly. She must go back. "You've made it more dangerous. I've wasted—"

Hawker grabbed her, jerked her around, and slammed her back to the wall. "Stop it."

"I will not leave three children in that house. I will not. Never."

He gave a hard push to keep her there. "They won't budge. You're not going to throw the others away trying to save three of them."

"You do not tell me what I do and what I will not do." Rage boiled from her heart till she choked with it. Till she could not speak for the thickness in her throat. "No one says what I must do. I decide. I—"

"They decide. Not you."

She twisted, viciously, against the cage of his hands. He was incredibly strong. She threw herself, all her strength, against him, and it was nothing.

Then she was free. Suddenly and completely free. He released her. He stepped away. "Go ahead. Go in and convince them, Citoyenne Golden Tongue. Get yourself killed like a bloody fool."

"And you are an idiot."

"I'm not idiot enough to blunder in there, thinking I can change their minds."

"You did not try hard enough." But she stood where she was, shaking. With anger. With fear. With great and terrible grief. "You did not try."

"We were lucky to get any of them out. They think it's a trap."

She knew. Oh, she knew. She had lived her months in captivity when she was a child whore. Trusted no one. When men came to free them, she had hidden in her room, trembling, hugging Séverine. She had feared them all, even Madame. "They do not know what will happen to them. They cannot know. They do not understand."

"You aren't going to convince them."

"No." She made a fist. Slammed the stones of the wall, hurting herself, making no noise. "I will not let this happen. I will not lose three children."

"Then you're going to lose them all. These kids . . ." he jerked his thumb to the far end of the street, "the ones we got out . . . those ten kids are a mouse hair away from panicking and running back into the cage. They'll do it if we don't move them along."

"I will wait then. Wait until they leave." Her body shook and she could not stop it. "When they are safe, I will go into the Coach House and drag the others out."

"Not short of knocking them over the head and tying them up, you won't. You think anything else, and you're just stupid. I don't think you're stupid."

He listed the reasons this could not be done. He would not be silent, though she interrupted him and sneered at him. Everything he said, she already knew and did not want to admit to herself. He battered her mind with his certainty. His relentless common sense.

He ended up, ". . . at which point those Tuteurs are going to come pounding up the stairs and gut you like a fish."

"I have been taught to fight."

"I don't care if you've been taught to fly like a bird. They'll kill you. They won't even raise a sweat doing it."

The night was silent and heavy with heat. Tiny and far away, Blackbird gestured to the children. Each in turn slipped around the corner, out of sight, moving as small, slight darknesses rippling the greater darkness. Ten of them.

I have saved only ten.

Those last three would not be persuaded. She knew that in the pit of her belly. In her heart, in the cold reason of her mind, she knew that. She shivered under her skin, sick with the bloody murder she had done and this corpse that waited at her feet. Sick with failure. "If I do not go back, I condemn them to hell."

"Close enough." There was light to see his lips twist. To guess at the expression in his eyes. She did not want pity from him. "You can't save them."

"I must try."

"That's not running an operation. That's a complicated way to commit suicide." He let her think about that. "Either way, you're dragging me along with you."

"This is nothing to do with—"

"If you go in, I go in. You decide if you lead me in there to get killed." He did not look like a boy when he said that. She did not doubt for one instant that he would follow her back into the Coach House.

On the stage of her mind, she could see many ways to die. Nowhere did she see a way to save the last three Cachés. "They are children."

"They're not any younger than you."

She stood with her hands empty. It was defeat. "You are a bastard."

"My mother always swore she was married. I kind of doubt it. Owl, I've had longer to think about this than you. If I could come up with any way—any plan at all—we'd do it."

"I will not forgive myself for leaving them behind."

"Most of us have something to keep us awake at night."

"You make light of—"

"The hell I do. You think I don't have nightmares?" They stood awhile, looking at each other. He said, "If they weren't trained fighters, I'd try it." He nudged the valise with his foot. "You get rid of this."

She would scatter the belongings of a dead man across Paris. Leave a shirt rolled behind a drain spout. Stuff a boot into some gutter.

She realized, suddenly, that her hands were covered with drying blood, sticky and somehow slimy. The lantern disclosed the slumped dead body. Overhead, the stars burned steadily, pitiless in the night sky, watching her, knowing her for what she was. Not brave. Not passionate. She was so much the realist, so cowardly, that she would leave three children to fall into hell.

If she had still possessed a soul, it would have died tonight.

Down the street, the drama of the Cachés' escape was coming to a close. The children were gone. Blackbird followed, limping around the corner, playing the feeble old woman. Citoyen Pax stepped back and disappeared into shadow.

She said, "Your friend Paxton is headed this way."

"We'll start carrying corpses out of the vicinity. Hold a minute." Hawker shifted his body, not blocking her path, just getting her attention. "Take this."

He had pulled a knife from somewhere, like magic. He held it by the blade, offering her the hilt.

"Your knife?"

"You shouldn't walk around without one." Neither of them glanced to where her knife reposed in the chest of Citoyen Drieu. "Go ahead. I have a couple more on me."

"You are very provident." His knife was warm from being next to his skin. She felt this when she tucked it away beneath her shirt. "I will return it to you."

"Keep it. We aren't going to see each other again." He had become entirely sober. Greatly serious. "I got something to say."

He was wrong in that much. They would meet again. In the small world of spying, it was inevitable. And the next time they met, they would no longer be allies. "Tell me."

"Go with the Cachés."

"It is my intention. I will follow till they are safe. You need not worry."

"I don't mean that. I mean, go back to that brothel you call home, you collect your sister, and get out of France. The Cachés are going. You go with them."

How strange this hard young English spy was in agreement with Madame. He said almost what Madame had said. "I have no intention of leaving France."

"Then you're a fool. You're living in a goddamned whorehouse. You've got your sister there." He chopped his hand down. "You're trying to be a bloody damn spy. Of all the stupid—"

"You are a spy. True, you are only the very junior, new spy. The damp chick of a spy, fresh from the shell. But—"

"Will you be quiet and listen?" He ran his fingers up into his hair. His eyes swept left and right as if the words were floating in the air. "We're not talking about me."

"We are not talking about me either. At least, I have no wish to discuss this."

"When I go spying, it's better than what I was. Better than what I used to do. I'm making something of myself. But you're not like that. You're . . . you're books and eating neat and using a handkerchief. You have all that inside your skin."

"I have not the least idea what you are talking about."

"You're quality. Stop playing with the notion of spying. Go to England. Be quality." He shook his head, impatient.

It was so simple. Why did he not see? "'Awker, I am a whore. I have been a whore for two years."

"Then leave that damned brothel and stop being one."

"I do not mean yesterday and the day before. They do not touch me at the Pomme d'Or. No one, not in the least instance. Not one finger."

"Then you're not a whore."

"It does not change anything. It is too late. I cannot become clean again. I cannot be—"

He snorted. "You can be any damn thing you want to be. Go to England. Change your name. Lie through your teeth."

"For some things, there is no lie big enough." Did he imagine she had not thought of this? The knowledge of what she was lay down at night to sleep beside her. Stared at her from the mirror every morning. "I was a child whore in the most fashionable and degenerate house in Europe. Many men came to me while I was in that dreadful place. There will always be men who know me."

That silenced him. It was the truth, and they both knew it.

She said, "I can escape France, but I cannot escape what I am."

Hawker raised his hand as if he would touch her, but stopped, deliberately short. He let his hand drop. "What about Séverine?"

"I will take care of her. I have always taken care of her." She knew what she must do, of course. She had made her decision. The sorrow of it expanded in her chest so she could barely breathe, it was so huge. Before she turned and left she said, "I will protect Séverine. I will do whatever is necessary."

Fourteen

WHEN THE FIRST LIGHT OF DAWN CRAWLS OUT OF
bed and staggers over the horizon, evildoers head off home and
solid citizens take to the streets. In his disreputable past,
Hawker would have been yawning his way back to his own den
of thieves as the sun came up, having finished a long night of
assault with intent or maybe breaking and entering.

He'd reformed, even if he still headed home at daybreak.
Last night, he'd disposed of a corpse, picked himself a heavy
pouch of coin off the dead man, and palmed a packet of documents, some of which might turn out to be interesting. It wasn't
much different than his old life, when you came right down
to it.

He walked harmlessly alongside Doyle and Maggie and
their bits and pieces of baggage and the donkeys. The sky was
turning milk white, with most of the light coming from the
east, behind them. The air was stuffy and flat. It was going to
be scorching hot later on. The city was just going on the
griddle.

Doyle had decided to leave Paris, since there were a number
of men thirsting for his blood right now. He was also getting
Maggie away safe, the political situation having become unsettled. Every time the good citizens of Paris got unsettled they

started pulling aristocrats out of the houses and hanging them from the lampposts. Maggie was an aristo. Time for a cautious man to take his wife home to dull old England.

Doyle strolled at donkey pace, his thumbs hooked in his waist-coat pockets, portraying stolid and stupid to anyone who might take an interest. He kept an eye behind them and to the right, motioning Hawker to scout ahead and watch the left-hand side.

When they turned the corner and left the Rue Palmier, Owl was ahead, waiting for them.

She sat on the steps of a big respectable house, getting away with it because they were still in the damp and poorly lit dawn and the householders hadn't come out to chase her away. She dressed like a housemaid—neat, with a big white mobcap on her head and a thick, plain fichu knotted on her chest. Owl had shoved a brown leather bag to the side of the steps, which might be important. She held Séverine on her lap.

Owl said, "Good day to you, citoyens. It is a pleasant day to be walking free under the sun, is it not?"

"Very." Doyle came up beside him. "You're waiting for us?"

"For Marguerite, though this is a matter of interest to you as well."

Owl was . . . wound tight. She cradled her sister, gentle-like, but look close and you'd see her hands clamped like iron on the kid's dress, as if any minute Séverine was going to fall off her lap and get eaten by rats.

The streets were empty as a beggar's pouch. Nothing out of place and no tick of movement. The donkeys weren't twitching their ears. But Owl was scared of something, or angry about it, or both.

Maggie went over to Owl, and they settled in to chat like market women passing the time of day. Looked like everybody was going to pretend like the donkeys and the bags were just decorative and nobody had anywhere in particular to go, least of all to the gates of Paris, and there was no hurry to get out of this town before something untoward happened.

Doyle's hands kept being unconcerned and innocent, down near his knives. He gazed idly across the windows everywhere and kept close to Maggie.

They should be safe. Owl would never, under any circumstance on earth, put her sister in danger. But what the hell was going on?

Owl passed Séverine over to Maggie and they discussed the sprat for a while. Nobody in any of the houses coughed. Nobody came walking by. It was so bloody quiet they could have been standing in a painting. He distrusted quiet, just on general principles.

Funny how Owl looked different, sitting there without the kid in her arms. She looked alone, folded in and closed up with her arms around herself. She said to Maggie, "You were right. A whorehouse is no home for a child," which was what everybody had been telling her. She said, "A war is coming."

There was another giant revelation for you. War, riot, mayhem . . . It was all coming. Owl and him would be on opposite sides.

He eased his way back to keep an eye up and down the street since everybody else was talking single-mindedly and not paying attention to the surroundings.

Owl looked back and forth from Doyle to Maggie, making quick, brittle little comments. Maggie held the kid. It looked natural, like they fit together.

Then, word by careful word, staring into Maggie's face, Owl said, "You will take Séverine as your own. You will take her away from France and keep her in safety. You will watch over her. You, yourself."

Take Séverine? What was this?

"She will be no trouble on the road." Owl was talking fast now, not giving Maggie a chance to answer. Owl's hands pushed at the air as if she was shoving objections aside. "She has learned to be quiet. She will go with you willingly when I tell her she must. She knows to say nothing at all and to answer to any name she is given."

Doyle got grave and quiet, deep voiced and dead serious. "You're giving your sister to us?"

"I give her to Marguerite." Owl fumbled around for the valise she'd stowed away. That would be clothes for the kid in there. She pulled the bag out and held it, looking at Séverine.

There was no way to say what he saw in Owl's face. Once he'd watched a man get knifed in the belly and know he was going to die. It took him a while to get it done. That was how he'd looked the whole time.

Maggie and Doyle talked low, back and forth. Doyle nodded. Then he put his hand on the sprat's head. "Séverine is mine. I'll treat her no differently than a child of my blood, born in wedlock. I'll set her welfare before my own life. I will love her as a father. You have my word."

Back in London, back in the gang he'd lived with, they called that a blood oath.

Owl knew what she'd done. That flat, black, blank behind her eyes was her knowing exactly what she'd done. No telling how much Séverine understood of all this. Might be a lot. She was a smart little kid.

Maggie put her hand out toward Owl. "How can I take your sister and leave you behind? Do you think I wouldn't welcome you? Come with us."

Hell. Hell and damn. That wasn't going to happen. If Owl wasn't on the rolls of the Police Secrète, she reported to somebody who was.

He didn't stay to listen while Doyle told Maggie why Owl couldn't come to England. Lots of things to do that didn't involve watching that. The load on the donkeys had to be shifted and balanced and tacked down to take account of a new bag. He had to make a place for Séverine to ride.

They talked. He tried not to listen too much. After a while, Owl came over, walking like a marionette, stiff and awkward. She lifted the bag to where he'd made a place for it. "I have packed clothing for her. Things she will need. Her . . . doll."

"Some people wouldn't leave this to the last minute. The kid's going to make them conspicuous." He wasn't gentle. Owl didn't want to break down in front of Séverine. She was close to doing that.

"What is more inconspicuous than a child? Would anyone suspect a family traveling across the countryside with a small child? No and no. Everyone should take an infant or two with them upon their missions."

He shrugged and made a clicking with his lips, which was one of those French noises he was practicing.

"She is a better companion than you, in fact, because she has been trained to keep her mouth closed and follow orders, which you have not."

He'd made her angry. Good. She didn't look as dead inside.

"I follow orders." He hauled out the blankets, rolled them, and tied them on the donkey, making a sort of half-moon shape where Séverine could ride. "It's that hair of hers. Might as well attach a red flag. That has to . . . Here." He took a string of leather and went to braid up the sprat's hair and tie it. "That's better. But she's dressed too well. You should dirty her up. Put some mud on her."

"I am pleased to know she will not be in your hands, Citoyen 'Awker."

That was enough prodding to get her spine stiff. To let her blink back tears. She walked with Maggie, saying good-bye to Séverine without saying it. Touching her sister's back once.

Last thing, before she left, she handed over their real name. DeCabrillac. Their father was a count, which it was just as well he hadn't known when he was shoving her arse out of his way back in the Coach House.

When Owl left, she walked away fast and didn't look back.

Doyle motioned him over. "I wish I could take that girl with me. It's a shame and a sin sending her back into that shambles."

Nothing much to say to that.

Doyle said, "She's going to be dangerous in a few years. On their side."

"She's dangerous already."

"You go follow her. Make sure she gets back to that damned brothel safely."

No hardship. He would have done it anyway.

He found her two streets away, sitting on a doorstep, her head in her hands. She didn't look up to see who it was that stopped in front of her. Probably she recognized his boots.

He said, "We can go get her back if that's what you want."

That was a lie. He wasn't going to take the sprat away from Maggie. Owl had done the right thing, and she knew it.

"You know very well there is no going back." She took her hands away from her face and put them together on her knees, a pair of fists, facing each other.

"Just so you understand."

"I have kept her safe for more than two years. Clean and cared for and well fed. That is not a small thing to do. I was eleven when I started."

"You took care of her fine."

"I taught her the letters. And to speak some German and English." Her fists tightened in her lap. "Babette is teaching her . . . Babette was teaching her to cook."

"Useful stuff."

"It has never been right, never, that the child of my father should grow up in a brothel."

"I can see that."

"She is not safe in Paris. There could be fighting again. Any disaster at all. If I am killed, there might be no one left to protect her. I have to send her away."

He sat down beside her, one step up, so it'd be like he was taller. She needed somebody taller, and he wasn't yet. There was plenty of room on the step, but he sat close and put his arm across her shoulder. "I know."

"There is no one better on this earth than Marguerite to care for her. Séverine will be safe in England. They will have a house for her where everything is pleasant and . . . English. With a dog."

"Doyle likes dogs. Big ones." Not the right thing to say. "And little ones. He'll get her a . . ." He didn't know a damn thing about gentlemen's dogs. He knew about alley dogs and fighting dogs. ". . . hound."

She wasn't paying attention. "It is not possible for me to be with her. You understand that. I will never, never, never permit it that someone points to her and calls her 'sister of the whore.' I will not let that happen."

"Well, now it won't. You've done what you had to."

She gave up on trying not to cry. She put her face against him and shook. She kept it muffled on his shirt. There wasn't a damn thing he could say.

Fifteen

1818
Meeks Street, London

THEY WAITED BY HER BED, DRINKING TEA, THEN coffee as it got later. For a few hours, Hawker thought she'd escaped the poison. After sunset, he knew she hadn't.

It came over her like cold mist lying down on a hill. The restless, nervous, pained movements stopped. She lay on the bed in a limp, unnatural stillness. Her breathing changed. Caught. Ratcheted. Became shallow gasps. She was dying, and there was nothing he could do.

A shudder. Then another shudder ran through her. A strangled sound in her throat.

He put his hand on her chest. *This isn't happening. I won't let this happen.*

He heard Luke's footsteps in the hall. At last.

Luke dropped his medical bag by the door. Strode to the foot of the bed. He stripped the blankets off her in a single motion.

"She can't breathe," Doyle said. "It's getting worse."

"Tremor? Jerking in her muscles? Stiffness in her neck? Her back?"

"Not that." Doyle pulled the cover the rest of the way off.

Luke felt the muscles of her calf. Hooked her ankle up and flexed her foot back and forth. Ran his finger along the bottom of her foot. "Not responsive. Paralysis."

Her lips had gone blue. Panicked, half-conscious, she convulsed, trying to suck air in. She gurgled ugly, shallow pants.

Slowly, painfully, horribly, she was suffocating before his eyes. And she couldn't move.

"Help her, damn it."

"There's nothing I can do," Luke snapped. "Her muscles aren't working. Not even any reflexes. The diaphragm can't—"

She needed air. He'd give her air. He opened her mouth with his fingers and blew air inside her, hard.

It puffed back out. He blew in again.

Luke said, "Do that." He leaned over to look in her face. "Do that again."

The air was getting inside her. She was less desperate.

"There's a Frenchman." Luke ran his hands over Justine's ribs, feeling them expand with the air. "Frenchman. Can't remember his name. Wrote a monograph. Lay her down." He put the heels of his hands below her breasts and pressed down all his weight. Air whistled out of her. "Blow in again."

She was trying to breathe. Hawker did it for her.

"This Frenchman talked about doing this for drowning men." Luke pushed down. Her breath whooshed out. The bed sagged. "I didn't think it would work."

The air had to get out of her, before he could put more in. They needed a hard surface. "The bed's too soft. Get her down on the floor."

She flopped on the rug like a rag doll. He knelt at her head.

"She's bleeding under the bandage," Doyle said. "Bleeding bad."

"Then stop it," he snapped. He gave her air.

"More. More," Luke said. "Enough." He waited a beat. Shoved downward on her chest. "Good. Again. Let me know when you start to feel light-headed."

Another breath into her. "Damned if I'll let you die." He knelt beside her and breathed for her.

They took turns keeping her alive. Past midnight, she started taking in air on her own. When she got reliable at it, they lifted her back to the bed and set chairs around it. They just sat there, staring at each other, exhausted and relieved.

At three in the morning, the fever began.

* * *

SHE felt so hot. Her arm ached, sharply. Pain radiated through her body, into her chest. Pain had been in the dreams with her.

She was on her back, naked and damp. Her skin crawled with heat. Itchy with the heat. The light coming in the window said it was dawn. Still raining.

Someone had followed her in the rain and stabbed her. She had never been careless. Her attacker must be very, very good.

"It was one man. I didn't see his face. Just a glimpse." Her throat was dry. She made almost no sound. "Water."

"Don't move. I'll help you drink."

". . . Papers."

"Safe. Downstairs. We're drying them out. Drink this."

She ached hollowly, as if a bell of pain clanged in her chest. He put an arm behind her and let her drink. Then she was flat again, looking up at the ceiling. He looped her hair around his hand and laid it to the side on the pillow, out of the way.

There was no square foot in the hallways of her body that did not hurt. The covers were hot. Stifling. It was too much trouble to move. Easier to just be too hot. She closed her eyes.

She was safe. Hawker would not let anything happen to her.

Sixteen

DOYLE FOUND PAX IN THE STUDY, SITTING CROSS-
legged on the hearthrug, toasting wet newsprint on an ash
shovel. Three clippings, dry, crinkled and curling at the edges,
lay on the bricks.

Doyle came over to watch. "Hawk sent me down to see how
you're getting on."

"It's slow. How's the breathing?"

"Good. She's breathing easy. That part looks over with."
Doyle brought a pair of glasses out of his jacket pocket and
hunkered down. He pushed the clippings into line and looked at
them. "The fever's worse."

"How bad?"

"Bad. She's out of her head with it." He rearranged the
papers, smallest to largest. "I hope Sévie gets here in time."

"She'll hurry."

"I wish Maggie was upstairs, keeping Hawk's woman alive."
Doyle put on his glasses and picked up the first clipping.

"I was wishing for Camille. Hell of a time for wives to be
working in France. You sent messages?"

"It'll be finished, one way or the other, before they get the
letters." Doyle turned a clipping over and then back again.
"Looks like this is cut out of the *Times*. It is the obituary for one

Antoine Morreau, bookseller in Paternoster Lane. 'Dead, suddenly, at his place of business.' No desolate family is mentioned, so we will assume he is unmarried. A respectable address, so we will assume he is prosperous. Why did our Justine find this particular death of interest?"

"He got himself murdered, if that's interesting." Pax took up the ash shovel and went back to dealing with damp newsprint.

"Not in and of itself, 'specially." Doyle took up the next page. "'Monstrous Crime in Paternoster Lane.' 'Shopkeeper murdered in a wanton daylight robbery.' Our bookseller had his throat slashed and his money box broken. We continue . . .'" He picked the last sheet. "It looks like a dark-haired man did the deed and ran off. 'Neighborhood shocked.'"

"I read that. More than a week ago. Ten days, I think. You were still in Scotland. I didn't think it was worth filing, even with the French link."

Doyle ran a considering finger along stubble on his chin. "Paternoster Lane. They do not normally stab citizens over their shop counters in that part of town." He picked up another piece of paper. "This is the *Observer*, reporting the same thing, the bottom half of which is no doubt interesting but we can't read it. Felicity can hie herself off to the Strand to their office to make a copy. And I will drop by Bow Street to see what they know about our dead bookseller."

"Cummings will be annoyed." Pax tested wet newsprint with the point of his knife. The top sheet wasn't ready to separate off. "London murders fall into his territory."

"Annoying Military Intelligence and Cummings is jam on the bun."

Pax offered a view of the paper he was lifting loose. "Another somebody, bloodily dead."

"'An incident in Finns Alley.' That's off Dean Street in Soho. I'd stab somebody in Finns Alley if I was setting about the business. 'The public is asked to come forward with any information.' They don't mention outrage and shock, that being in short supply in Soho. 'The body is identified as . . .' Looks like Monsieur something."

"A Monsieur Richelet. This is yesterday's *Times*."

"Justine's collecting dead Frenchmen. Everybody should have a hobby. This one died late Sunday night. Day before yesterday." Doyle glanced up to where light was coming through a break in the curtains. "No. Two days ago, now. We'll still have the paper upstairs."

"I'll catch George before he burns it. It looked like just another random death. Only showed up in the *Times* because one of the witnesses was an army man of some distinction."

"A sad commentary upon the human condition."

Pax set the shovel flat on the hearth. The upper sheet was mostly dry. He freed the last corner and eased it away. The page below was still wet. The general gray tinge made it hard to pick out words. He said, "The *Courier*, I think."

"With a more complete account of the same murder. 'A Stabbing in Soho.'" Doyle took the handle of the shovel and slanted the writing toward the fire to get better light. "And what else do they have to say? 'Violence in the foreign community. When will it end?' That is something I ask myself daily. According to eyewitnesses, a slight, dark man of foreign appearance fled the scene."

"This," Pax rested the point of his knife on a line near the bottom of the clipping. "This is what Justine came to tell us."

"'Do sinister Eastern assassins threaten our streets? The curious black knife left in the body—'" Doyle stopped. "God's avenging chickens."

"Exactly."

Seventeen

TWENTY-ONE YEARS BEFORE
1797
Oxfordshire, England

FRIQUET WAS SMALL AND BROWN WITH DELICATE hooves and a way of nosing gently among the tangle of grass and weeds that grew along the bank of the stream, taking this plant and leaving another. When Séverine rode out with Pascal the groom, she could not allow Friquet to indulge himself in weeds. Pascal had strong opinions about what ponies should eat and worried about Friquet's digestion ceaselessly.

Pascal was French, though he had no accent. He had a sad history and had been sent here to be healed by Maman, although he did not know it. Eventually he would stop being nervous and angry and go away to school. There had been several such grooms.

She was not supposed to know that part of his job was to protect her. Papa worked for the government and was very important. He was a spy. Her friend Hawker was also, though he was less important because he was younger. There were always several men working in the garden or the stable who protected everyone.

Pascal had gone onward to the stable. She was allowed to be by herself once she had crossed the stream and was within sight of the house. Friquet waded into the water and ate his watercress and chickweed in peace. She could pick her own watercress to eat and think about things. Pascal could not say she was not allowed to eat plants from the stream, but he looked disapproving.

It was raining a small amount, but that did not bother her. She sat under the tree where it was all moss and she would not get her dress muddy. The tree kept most of the rain off. It was an oak and had probably been here when Cromwell burned the manor in Thinch. One night, when she was out with Papa and they were hiking quietly through the woods, finding their way around using the stars, Papa had showed her where Cromwell's troops marched over Thinch Hill and explained why they had come that way instead of another.

She ate watercress, putting it leaf by leaf on her tongue. Papa was in France, being clever against Napoleon, although she was supposed to tell anyone who asked that he was in Bristol on business. They didn't know about Papa in the village.

Down the stream where the bushes were thick a hand emerged from the greenery, and then a face under a black shawl, and then . . .

"Justine!" She did not run headlong through the slippery wood to her sister. She looked around first to see no one was watching, then tangled Friquet's reins in a bush and walked, fast but oh so carefully, along the bank. She dipped her head and ducked into the bushes and crawled between the leaves and scratches. They were together inside the arched, dark space. "Justine."

Justine had beaten down the ground between the bushes to sit and wait for her. There was room for both of them. When they had embraced and Justine sat down, she climbed into her lap. She was far too big for this now that she was seven, almost. It was comfortable for neither of them. But still she did it. When she took Justine's face between her hands and studied her, their heads were on a level. Justine's skin was cold, so cold. "You are well? You have not been hurt?"

"But those are my words, petite. Are you well? Are you happy? Tell me everything."

There was so much to say and they had very little time. Justine was an important spy for France, though she was only sixteen. When she came here and concealed herself in these bushes, it was no game. She must not be found on English soil. It was especially dangerous for her here, near Papa's house. Papa and her sister must never, never meet.

So much to say. There had been a trip to Oxford to the dentist with Molly, who was the upstairs maid and had a toothache. There were puppies at Mr. Richard's farm, and she had been allowed to pick which one she wanted. It was a bitch puppy and she had named it Harmony. It would come home with her in two weeks, when it was old enough. She was reading La Fontaine with Monsieur Rochambeau who sniffed and sniffed when he went into the rose garden.

She snuggled close to her sister, trying to warm her.

"La Fontaine." Justine stroked her hair. "I carried a book of his fables for a while, until I lost it. I have them memorized."

More news. The kitchen cat had kittens in the barn. A girl had come to be the nurserymaid. She was like Pascal the groom, one of those called the Cachés, which meant "hidden," because they were French but pretended to be English. She cried a great deal in all the corners of the nursery, but then the old ladies who were not really her aunts missed her and decided that it did not matter that she was an imposter. "Hawker came to take her back home. He said she was a right little misery and we were well shut of her."

Friquet pulled his reins free and wandered off to sample the banquet upstream.

"Move a bit. Let me . . ." Justine took a bag from the pocket under her skirt. "I have brought this to you, through perils uncounted."

The bag was filled with twists of paper, a little discolored by water. Inside each paper, sugar drops. The first one she opened was blue and white and red, colored like glass from Venice.

"They are from Paris," Justine said. "They may taste of salt. I had the merest whiff of difficulty coming ashore."

If Justine brought them, they would be the most perfect of their kind. The seawater was not important. Not at all.

She sat on the ground and leaned against Justine's knees and sucked upon a peppermint drop. Justine said, "I've been in Italy. That's why it has been so long since I came to you."

"There is a war there." When Papa was home, he read to her from the newspaper, after dinner, when he and Maman sat close together with her on the sofa in the salon.

"The fighting is over for a while. There will be a treaty." Justine put one arm around her. They watched barn swallows swooping over the lawn that ran from the parterre down to the river. It was not really raining if the swallows were out. "This is a pretty place. I like to think of you being here, in that house."

"I will think of you in Paris, if that is where you will be."

"Perhaps." Justine's voice said she would not be in Paris. She would be somewhere more dangerous.

She could feel Justine getting ready to leave. Quickly, she said, "Wait. Just a minute more. Did you get my letters? All of them? I sent you pictures."

"I have all of them. They were in Rome, at the embassy, when I came through."

"I have three letters from you. The one with the canary, the one with the black-and-white cat, and the one with the bowl of broth."

"There will be six more, if they all come. Alas, they never do." Justine made a gesture. She was very French in her gestures, like Maman. "I must go, petite."

She held Justine tight, loving her and always, always frightened for her. "You will be careful."

"There is no need. My life has been boring as a piece of bread these last few months. I sit and drink coffee in the café. I write reports and walk in the countryside all day. It is a healthy life, I assure you." The last thing, as always, Justine kissed the top of her head. "You will tell Marguerite I was here."

"After nightfall." That was as always. Justine would not let her keep secrets from Maman.

When she had watched until Justine was gone and the bushes were quiet again, she went to catch Friquet. He did not much mind being caught because he knew they were going to the stable where they would fuss over him and give him bran mashes and carrots. He was muddy up to his hocks from wading in the stream.

Because she wanted to make the meeting with Justine last as long as she could, she walked through the meadow and up the lawn, leading Friquet home, sucking a peppermint drop, remembering every word.

She would tell Maman about Justine's visit after dinner. They would not find Justine.

Eighteen

JUSTINE DID NOT LINGER NEAR THE HOUSE OF WILliam Doyle. He knew she came here from time to time to see her sister. So far, he had not tried to stop it. She did not fool herself into thinking she would come so close to his stronghold unless he allowed.

Just lately she had not endeared herself to the British. There had been an incident in Italy. The English really should not involve themselves in the wars of Italy.

The route of her retreat involved much crawling through mud. She followed the small stream and the cover of bushes. In the day and a half she had waited for Séverine, she had spotted several men patrolling. There were two now, one in the garden and one on a hillock in the woods, who made only the smallest pretense of working. And . . . Yes. She pulled back a stand of gray-green weed. The grim young groom who accompanied her sister everywhere leaned at the wall of the stable, polishing the metal of a bit, his attention on the patch of bushes where he had left Séverine.

Her sister was well cared for. She was held within that mansion as in careful cupped hands. She was given the pretty riding habit and the sleek, playful pony. Given the tutor—he had been a great scholar in France before he was broken and tossed aside by the Revolution. That was another soul Marguerite gave refuge to. Alert, dangerous veterans of the war, some missing an eye or an arm, patrolled the perimeter. Three monster dogs coursed the grounds after dark. If there were any peace and safety in the world, William Doyle folded it around his wife and the children in his house.

She came to the green swath of lawn where the river widened. When Séverine arrived at the house there would be less scrutiny in this direction.

Rain fell around her, soft and intricate, the tap of it becoming indistinguishable from the splash of the stream. It was not possible to tell where gray sky ended and gray rain began. After so many months in Italy, England seemed very wet.

She stood with her back to a tree, letting emotions run over her and around her as if she were a rock in a river with the water going past. There was a hardness at the core of her life, like a rock. A spy of her sort is very alone. She never felt so alone as when she had been with her sister for a short time and they must part again.

It was weak of her to keep coming back this way, just to talk to her sister. It would be kinder to make a clean break while Séverine still loved her. Before she understood what her sister had been. Before Séverine asked questions and Marguerite must tell her about the brothel in Paris.

The drizzle thickened. Mist rose and all was hidden. Another minute or two and she could—

Cold metal bit at her throat.

A knife point. Fingers gripped her hair, pulling her head back to expose her neck. The instant closed around her in terror.

A man stood behind her, with death in his hand. She did not flinch. It is not wise to flinch when someone holds a knife to your throat. A sensible woman does not move at all. Hold still. Breathe. She wavered in place the smallest amount with the pounding of her heart.

A voice said, "Owl?"

No one else called her that anymore. "'Awker."

It was his body, immovable behind her. His breath on the back of her neck. She should have recognized it somehow.

The moment throbbed with danger. Hawker would not kill her. She was sure of that. Almost sure. But he might well drag her off to prison. One does not lightly invade England. One does not capriciously approach the household of important British agents, however much it is the home of one's sister.

The knife no longer pricked at her throat. Roughly he turned her around to face him. "What are you doing sneaking around?"

"What do you think I am doing? Bird-watching? I come to Séverine." Calmly. She spoke calmly. No mean feat. It was a hard, dark, unforgiving face that confronted her, devoid of humor. And there was the knife.

She had seen him six months ago, in Verona. Their eyes met across the Piazza dei Signoria. They were both pretending to be Italian. France held the city, but matters were complicated by the Austrian army marching about the countryside trying to take it back, and the Veronese hated all foreigners equally, which was not unreasonable of them. She and Hawker had both deemed it prudent to turn in the opposite direction and walk away.

He had grown since she last stood this close to him. He was not tall. He would never be tall. But he was now taller than her.

She said, "I must see her, you know. I do not come here often."

Hawker put his knife away in an inner jacket pocket, a single ingenious disappearance. He gazed upon her, looking dangerous. Looking familiar and being very much a stranger. "You shouldn't be here at all. Now what do I do?"

"You will let me go, of course. I am not spying upon all these fields of cows. I have no work in England at this time. Do you think agents do not take holidays?"

It had begun to rain harder, which was the favored choice of English weather. Hawker was bareheaded and water dripped down his forehead, pulling his hair into thin black lines, sharp as the knives he was so menacing with. He was becoming very wet. This would not sweeten his temper.

He said, "The trouble dealing with you, Owl, is that there's no way to tell whether you're lying."

"What use would I be to my country if any passing British Service agent could tell I was lying? I will admit it puts me at a disadvantage when I happen to be telling the truth."

"Fortunately, that doesn't happen often." He looked around as if the dripping woods and the little running stream would give him advice. "This is awkward. I should probably take your weapons off you."

"A cautious man would do that, certainly."

"But I don't think you'll stab me a couple hundred feet away from Sévie. It's surprisingly difficult to get rid of a body in Oxfordshire."

"As you will know by experience, no doubt."

He would not harm her. The possibility of that had passed. He also would not drag her into William Doyle's house in disgrace and indignity. "Neither of us will do anything to hurt Séverine. It is the most perfect of truces, is it not?"

He only growled at her, less pleased with this stalemate than she was.

She said, "Why are you here, anyway? It is very strange of you to be wandering in the damp shrubberies of Oxfordshire. Me, I would be inside in front of one of your English fires on a day like this."

He wiped his face with the sleeve of his jacket. "Right you are. I don't know why I'm standing in the rain anyhow." He turned his back on her and stalked off into the drizzle.

She had forgotten, in three years, how much he was master of such simple, brute subtlety. A shrug, a turning away, and he discovered whether she meant to attack him. Or he invited her to escape so he need not be bothered with deciding what to do with her. She would not, however, shoot him or try to run away. She possessed her own subtlety. She followed him and caught up and walked alongside. "Where are we going?"

He gestured ahead, along the path. "I have a place up that way."

Of such unpromising material, great plans are born.

She had thought of him, often and often, in the three years since they parted in Paris. He was a person one remembered vividly. Sometimes, confronting some particularly egregious stupidity of this long war, she imagined telling him about it. She could almost hear a caustic, cynical reply spoken over her shoulder.

She had collected every small scrap of rumor about him, all across Europe. She still carried his excellent knife. And here he was. They met upon a neutral ground. Fate served him up to her on a lordly platter.

Perhaps . . . A great *perhaps* grew in her mind.

He was no longer the grubby boy she had known in those desperate times in Paris. He was expensively and well dressed. Not as a young country gentleman or a town beau, which were modes altogether different. He wore the loose soft collar and casual neckcloth of the liberal artistic set. He might have been a student or painter walking about on holiday, strolling through the countryside with friends, going from inn to inn, carrying luncheon and a sketchbook in that leather bag over his shoulder.

He glanced at her from time to time as they walked. He said abruptly, "You grew breasts."

"Thank you. Do you know, there are many things one may notice without commenting upon."

"When did you get to be a woman, Owl?"

"I was a woman when you first met me."

He shook his head, perfectly serious, as if he'd given the matter consideration. "You were a kid. A scrawny one."

"*Tu es galant*. I am immeasurably flattered."

They spoke French, having fallen into it naturally, without thinking. He sounded utterly Parisian now, with the bare soupçon of the Gascon tongue underneath. If she did not know better, she would have thought he came from the south of France when he was a child. This suited him, with his Gascon looks and the arrogant assurance of the Gascon male. His voice was deeper than it had been.

"We might speak English," she said. "I have never heard you do that."

But she had. She remembered suddenly. Three years ago, in Paris, when she was following him secretly, she had overheard him hiss a dozen harsh words in an English she barely understood, it was so much the language of the London poor.

"They don't want me speaking English." Humor sliced across his face. "I don't do it right."

She would like to hear him speak English, "not right." It would make him seem even more himself. "I will cajole you. I have lured many men into disobedience."

"I'll be one more of your dupes." He said it in English. "I fall into lots of bad habits."

Ah . . . but he no longer spoke the Cockney of London. His English had become overprecise, slow, careful of every syllable, as if it were not his native language. It was a pleasure to see him a little ill at ease. He had entirely too much self-assurance.

She, on the other hand, was very proud of her English. She had almost no accent. "You have not explained why you make the squashings about in the wood of the house of Doyle. Why are you haunting the bushes?"

"Somebody's got to keep an eye out for French spies in the underbrush. And what do you know, I found one."

"I am the delightful happenstance, am I not?"

"Too bloody right."

Nineteen

THE DIRT LANE WAS MUDDY, OF COURSE. EVERY LANE in England was muddy. She followed him and they kept to the grass in the middle, between the wagon wheel ruts. A fine drizzle fell lightly upon them.

"Not far," Hawker said over his shoulder. He walked like a cat, both assured and infinitely circumspect, with not one wasted motion. And also like a cat, there was no inch of him that was not elegantly constructed. Bone to bone and nerve to nerve fit together as deftly as the parts of a clock. It was as she remembered.

It would be Hawker. Hawker and no other.

When had she decided? Was it the moment he lowered his knife from her throat and they knew each other, there in the brush by the stream? Was it when he spoke his careful, uncomfortable, upper-class English to her? Or had she known this for months? From the beginning?

For a year she had planned, putting one face and then another into her thoughts, and saying, "No. Not that one. He is not right." Had she discarded every other possibility because they were not Hawker?

I thought it would be a matter of cold calculation, but it is not. He is the man I want. If not here and now, with him, I think it will be never.

How stupid of me.

The stone cottage at the end of the lane was tiny, smaller even than the smallest of the farmhouses she had passed in Oxfordshire. The twists of the lane had brought them again to the stream. It could be seen through the woods behind the cottage. Beech trees rose on every side, a very soft green. The door of the cottage faced open country.

"Doyle owns it," Hawker said abruptly. "He bought the land a while back. There's ruins of a big house out that way." He waved to the right. "Burned down fifty years ago. This was the gamekeeper's cottage." Hawker had become studiously casual. "I ride up from town and stay here when I want. They keep it ready for me."

The grass was scythed on either side of the path in the front, and someone had planted flowers that splashed color into the gray mist. Hawker would perhaps think these things happened of themselves.

He ducked under the lintel going in—the threshold was that low—and paused on the braided rug that lay across the doorway to shake his head like a dog, scattering water. A small thing, but it told her he was at home here. He would be less wary, perhaps, in a place he felt safe.

He turned to look at her through the open door. He'd collected silver points of rain upon him everywhere. On his coat, in his hair, in his eyebrows, on his eyelashes.

"You do not lock your door," she said.

"They don't in the country." Hard, dark eyes ran up and down her. He stood aside to let her in. "Pointless anyway. Just encourages somebody to break a window. Do you know how much it costs to buy a window?"

The cottage was a single room with plaster walls and a stone fireplace at one end. A table, black with age, was pushed against the wall under the window. There were books everywhere—on the wide windowsill, on the bureau, on a table between the two big, comfortable chairs that faced the hearth. French books, so far as she could see. Clouet's *Géographie Moderne* on the table. Lalumière's thin volume, *Sur l'Égalité*, dropped in the chair cushions. Hawker was making a Frenchman of himself in every way but his loyalties.

Propped on the mantel over the fireplace was one of Séverine's watercolors, framed. This was someone in blue—perhaps Séverine—beside a large brown dog. Or possibly a pony. The brown rectangle with door and windows was recognizably the house of Doyle.

"They leave the place empty for months when I'm not here." The bag Hawker carried thumped onto the table. "A waste. I'm about never in England."

"You are in Italy, causing trouble for me. I will make tea."

She left her cloak on the straight-backed chair next to the table and knelt to the hearthrug. How does one make such a decision? When had it happened? She could not place a finger upon the moment everything changed, but she had decided.

The coals were orange under the ashes. It took only an instant to blow fire into life and lay down a few lengths of beechwood shavings and build a blaze with the kindling.

Hawker closed the shutters at the window over the table, giving them privacy from the day, then crossed to the other windows. Two in front. One in back. "Tea's about all I have to offer. I eat at the house or in the tavern in the village."

Or he stayed here alone, she thought. There were signs of his solitary meals. A half loaf of bread was cut-side-down on the table. The shape under the checked cloth was a cheese. A bowl held two apples. And he had tossed remnants of orange peel onto the fire. They curled like old leaves in the ash. She could smell the acrid, not unpleasant bite of burned citrus.

She pictured him sprawled, loose limbed, in one of the deep, chintz-covered chairs, his legs stretched to the firedogs, peeling an orange, absorbed in the book in his lap, with the lantern lit beside him. It would be a domestic scene, if one imagined a domestic scene with panther, couchant, at the fire.

The black kettle was half full and still warm from lying on this hearth. He had been gone from the cottage for two or three hours, then. The kettle and the heat of the hearthstones spoke of a fire built, tea brewed, boots and coat warmed, before Hawker had gone out into the cold mist this morning.

He put himself into a rush-bottomed chair to take off his boots, using the toe of one upon the heel of the other to loosen them. He wore thick knitted stockings like a good countryman. These he removed also and tossed to keep company with the boots.

She rearranged herself from kneeling to sitting on the hearthrug. The gun she carried in the pocket under her skirt thumped against her thigh. She pulled her knees close to take off her own boots.

"If you plan to run, leave those on," Hawker said. "This would be a good time for it. I can't chase you in the woods without my boots."

"If I wanted to run, I would shoot you first and you would also not chase me in the woods. You would lie here bleeding."

"That is what they call a cogent point."

She pulled off her boots and arranged her skirt around her legs. The cloth clung and sucked and made her damp and uncomfortable. Nothing is more gloomy than sitting about in wet clothing. She poked at the fire, hoping to remedy that dampness somewhat.

She liked his hideaway, both the superficial clutter and the underlying austere neatness. A stack of shirts had been left lying upon the coverlet of the bed. The red painted chest on the floor was open, showing more clothing inside. Hawker went, barefooted to tame this disorder.

Agents are well organized in this way. They live, ready to pack their belongings in a handful of minutes and decamp hastily. The life of a spy is uncertain.

He came to stand beside her, to frown down and think deep spy thoughts. When she leaned back to look up at him, his hair dripped three distinct drops onto her face. "Sorry." He pushed wet hair back from his forehead with the back of his fingers. "You don't have to do that. I don't need somebody to make a fire for me."

"*Comme tu dis.* But it is not altruism. I am warming my hands over these coals and your kettle. I have skulked in the bushes for hours. Skulking is cold work." In truth, she had spent much of yesterday and all the last night wrapped in her cloak, half buried in old leaves, waiting for her chance to see Séverine. "You may hand me that teapot, and the cups too. I will put them on the hearth to take the chill off. All the crockery in England must shiver continually."

"Chilblains in the china. Well-known English problem."

The teapot he took down from the mantelpiece was plain brown, such as could be found in any cottage up and down these hills, or in France, for that matter. The handleless cups were slightly more refined, but they were still crockery that might be slapped onto the table of any country inn.

She felt a moment of annoyance at those dishes. Maggie could have found something finer for him. The country manor of Doyle was like the great houses of France, filled with treasures.

Hawker picked up the teapot, one-handed, his hand wrapped familiarly through the handle, his thumb holding down the lid. He collected a pair of cups with the other hand, hooking them both with one finger, letting them clank together. He was as casual with the tea caddy, unstoppering it, peering in to scoop out tea leaves.

The teapot and cups were valueless. The blue-and-white tea caddy was Chinese porcelain of the Ming dynasty. Her father had kept one very like it in a glass case in the red salon at the chateau, before the Revolution.

Hawker tamped the scoop of tea leaves against the lip of the jar, carelessly, with a fine melodic ring. He did not know.

Marguerite was wise. She took what Hawker carried from his past and gave him the rush chairs, the heavy, cheap teapot, the well-scrubbed old table. She offered him his future in those fine books and the soft chintz chairs by the fire. Then, casually, upon the mantelpiece, Marguerite set a piece of porcelain fired when Joan of Arc was young.

Hawker would find everything in this small cottage easy and familiar, because Marguerite made it so. Someday, when he moved easily among the rich and powerful, he would not even realize it began here.

She lifted the teapot so he could turn scoops of tea leaves in. He had artist's hands. Sculptor's hands. Such hands are not delicate and white with long fingers. They are strong, precise, exact, and purposeful.

His chin was shadowed with a need to shave. She had known a boy three years ago. She did not really know this young man.

I do not know how to ask. Everything I can say is ugly. I do not want this to be ugly.

She gave her attention to pouring hot water onto the tea leaves. Rain drummed on the roof. Since they were not talking, since they were not looking at each other, it seemed very loud.

He said, "As soon as you drink that, you should leave. It's getting worse out there."

I must do this now, before I lose my courage. "I am hoping to spend the night."

Twenty

SHE CHOSE WORDS CAREFULLY, TO CLARIFY MATTERS beyond any possibility of misunderstanding. "It is my wish to spend the night with you, in your bed."

There. She had said it. It was now too late to take it back. Her mind, which had many cowardly corners, immediately went looking for plausible ways to pretend she did not mean what she had said.

Hawker was silent. He would be this self-possessed if tribesmen of the Afghan plains burst through the door and attacked him with scimitars. The refusal to be ruffled was one of his least endearing traits.

Time stretched, very empty of comment, while she swirled the teapot gently and he was inscrutable.

Finally, he took the oil lamp from the end of the mantel and busied himself adjusting the wick, lighting it with a paper spill from the fire. "The hell you say."

"But, yes. That is what the hell I say. You need not treat this as an inconvenient importunity. Even you do not have hordes of women proposing to share your bed." *I expected him to be stupidly pleased. Instead, he is suspicious of me.* "I will pour you tea. Yes?"

"Thank you."

"You need not thank me. It is your own tea, after all." Once, she could have offered him an explicit choice of sexual acts. In six languages. Now she had no words. She could not even call to mind the French ones. She lifted the lid of the pot. "I will add water. The tea is a little strong."

A nod from him, and she did the pouring of hot water into the pot. Then she poured two cups of tea.

This time, I will be in control. I will be the one with all the power. This is how I will free myself. Memory wriggled like dark worms at the edges of her mind. She pushed it away.

He took the sugar bowl from the mantel and stood, holding it. "Do you want sugar?"

"It is kind of you to offer. Yes."

"I have sugar tongs and spoons around here. Maggie keeps putting silver tableware in here, which is an incitement to theft if I've ever seen one. I shove 'em out of sight and that blasted woman they send to clean goes and hides them someplace else, just to make a point."

"It is the subtle warfare of the servant classes. I am frequently a servant, so I sympathize." She held up both cups, resting in their saucers. "Do not go seeking sugar tongs, which are probably well concealed. Two lumps for me. You may use your fingers."

He slid two fingers into the bowl and brought out sugar lumps scissored between first and second finger. Dropped one into his cup, clever and deft. Two into hers. He never took his eyes off her face. "You and me go to bed."

It was impossible to say anything. She, who had mouthed so many unclean words, so many bawdy songs, poems, ditties . . . could not get that small "yes" off her tongue.

"You want to . . ." He made a gesture. A rude one.

She nodded.

"It's a dull day that doesn't bring some surprise."

He walked away, taking off his coat, hooking it over a peg on the wall. Underneath, he wore a waistcoat of such vivid burgundy one blinked. His knife sheath rested between his shoulder blades, the knife hilt upward. The harness had its own peg. He rolled up his right sleeve to unbuckle another knife sheath. His shirt was full sleeved in an old-fashioned way, the better to hide weapons.

He was unarming himself. A hopeful sign.

In her teacup, the layer of dissolved sugar swirled like silk at the bottom. She drank and watched him over the rim of the cup.

When he turned, she saw that he was aroused. Very aroused. His coat had kept that hidden. A little shock ran through her, as if she had taken a step that was not there, and her pulse raced.

He did not hurry, coming toward her, but practiced the nonchalance of a bird of prey circling something in which it has developed an interest. When he was close, he leaned on the stones that surrounded the hearth. He paid no attention to the insistence in his breeches. He would not be ruled by his cock, would he? He was not apologetic, either, but seemed wholly unconcerned.

She was the one who did not know how to deal with this. She had sought this confrontation. Sought him. Now, the reality confounded her.

I should not be nervous. I have unbuttoned the breeches of many men.

She imagined herself closing her fingers gently around that bulge and his cock growing even larger and harder under her touch. She knew how to drive a man to unreason with her hands and her mouth. She had been so well trained.

That was what haunted her. Not hunger. Not humiliation. Not waiting in cold corridors, dressed in schoolgirl white, till a man called her into the parlor to hurt her. Not even pain.

She woke in the night, trembling and sweating, because of what she had done. Smiles, practiced in front of a mirror. The sly admiring lies of a whore. The clever tricks of pleasing men. She had not pretended to become a whore. She had become one.

I will never be clean of it.

"Hey." Hawker laid the flat of his hand on her cheek. It was warm from holding the teacup. "Hey. Owl. It's just me."

She looked into his eyes. The moment held a perfect stillness. The rain drummed the slates of the roof, empty of judgment. The fire was harsh and hot all on one side of her body with an indifferent, inhuman intensity.

Nothing could be more masculine than that hard palm of his hand. She had become the center of a determined and focused hunger. Hawker's hunger. It was hard in his body and his spirit. Clean-edged as one of his own knives. She read all that in the single touch on her face.

Soon, he would thrust into her and she would receive him.

A man. Inside her. She waited for the slick chill of nausea to uncoil in her belly. It did not come.

HAWKER ran the side of his thumb along her cheekbone, feeling the soft of it. Strange to know a woman like Justine DuMotier was soft to the touch. In her eyes, the pupils were contracted to tiny hard points. If she wanted a man's hands on her, he was a caterpillar.

"Why me?" he said.

"There is not one man in a thousand who would ask such stupid questions when a woman offers herself to him." Now she looked annoyed. That was better.

"I'm an unusual man."

Touching her distracted him, so he stopped doing it and folded his arms. Her skin still called to his fingertips. Sort of an itch, making him want to touch her some more. "Why me? Why here? Why now?"

"Oh, then. Reasons." She huddled into herself, hunching a shoulder, looking sulky. "I have heard rumors of you and I am curious. Is it so strange I would wish to pass a pleasant afternoon with . . . an old friend? We have been something like friends, have we not, though it is inconvenient for both of us. There is no reason we should not come together *pour le plaisir.*"

"For pleasure." But she wasn't hungry for him. Not a sign of it in her anywhere. "Do you do this much—go to bed with men?"

"You know what I am. There is nothing I do not know of the many acts of love."

That didn't answer his question, did it?

She raised her cup from the stones of the hearth and hid her face behind it. Hid her eyes by looking down into the tea. "It is not so surprising I wish to lie with you. You have acquired a reputation, did you know? You are said to be a young steed in bed. I stayed in an inn in Milan run by two widows. They had many interesting tales to tell about you."

Milan. The merry widows. Oh, yes. He remembered them kindly, and not just for being warm and welcoming and what you might call educative in bed. They cooked like angels. "I offered to marry them both, but they didn't take me up on it."

"They admired your skill, however. You would blush to hear

them speak of it. There was also the foolish young kitchen maid you sent away from your room in the night, telling her to come back when she was older. They have not forgotten that."

"I'm a prince of a fellow." He squatted down next to her so their eyes were level. "What are you up to, Owl?"

"Nothing evil, I promise you. A few hours of your expertise in bed. With you, I might . . ." She drank the last of the tea. "I did not come here with this intent. Now it seems inevitable, as if it were destined. I have been thinking about this for more than a year."

"Thinking about going to bed with me?"

"Sometimes. I have imagined others, but it did not . . ." There was a little tremor in her hands where they were wrapped around the empty cup. "It did not turn out to be possible, after all, when I faced them."

He'd made it a policy never to take on a woman with a herd of private nightmares. He broke that rule more often than he kept it, but that didn't stop it being a good one. If he had any sense, he'd stomp off into the rain and find a bed in Doyle's house.

But Owl was shaking. A woman like her, afraid.

And, by God, he wanted her. He kept pushing that out of his mind, but it kept coming back. She'd turned into a woman. She had breasts, for God's sake. Nice ones, from what he could see. He could almost taste them. But he wasn't going to play the fool for a lovely body. Not even Owl's lovely body.

Then she said in a small, flat voice, "I am weary of being a coward," and he was lost.

She's leading around three thousand demons, give or take. I guess I could kill a few. "I keep hearing that. 'Justine DuMotier, the coward.' Battle of Arcola and you underfoot through the worst of it. They sent you into Verona, alone, and you went. Coward right to the heart."

"Do not be stupid. That is our profession. If it terrified me, I would take up knitting." She breathed out. The air brushed his face like she was touching him. "I wake from sleep, shaking. When I think of being with men, I am afraid and ashamed and my stomach is unwell. This will stop, when I have done this with you."

"It might. Owl, it might not."

"You are skilled. You have that reputation. You are known

to be discreet. We will part, and our paths do not cross often."
She looked up with an absorbed and grave expression. "We will
do this once. It should not take long. I know what to do to—"

"You don't know a damn thing. You're worse than bedding
a virgin, which I will mention is something I do not do. You
know too much that's wrong."

"I am very skilled. I am not ignorant. I—"

"You are ignorant as a clod of dirt. If I had any sense I'd just
walk right out of this and go sleep in the rain." Looked like he
didn't have any sense. "I'm not flattered, in case you're wondering. There's a name for men who pleasure women for a living."

She'd gone motionless, the way you do in an alley when
there's men hunting you. Or maybe like she was afraid she'd
shatter apart if she wasn't careful. "Are you saying no?"

Not on your life. "Just pointing out some of the complexities.
You're an enemy agent, for one thing, which is a complicating
factor of some magnitude."

He settled back on his heels, digging into the knot of his
neckcloth, thinking. She'd been hurt so bad.

He never understood the way some men treated women.
Himself, he never got tired of the marvel of them. The sounds
they made when they felt good. When you made them feel
good. There was nothing in the world like it.

Maybe they could outrun her ghosts. "I should have sense
enough to let you be . . . but you're so damn beautiful."

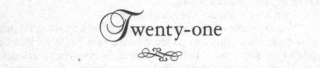

Twenty-one

HIS KISS—THE FIRST ONE—WAS COOL ON HER FORE-
head. It felt like he said hello to her body in this way. It reassured her.

He leaned back. She saw that his eyes had gone vehement
and dark, as if he deliberately laid aside a layer of civilization
along with his neckcloth. He tossed it, without looking, up onto
the chintz-covered chair.

Three buttons held his shirt closed at the neck. He was fast,
getting them undone. One button. Two. Three. She appreciated
the speed. It would be best to get this over with as quickly as
possible.

He said, "You're going to drive me mad. You know that?"

"It is not my intention to—"

"Well, it's too late, innit? Set the damn cup down before you
drop it."

She had been holding it protectively between him . . . and
her. She put the cup down into its saucer on the hearth.

He reached to cradle her chin in long, clever fingers. "Let's
try this." He kissed her mouth.

I do not like the kissing part. It's not the worst, but I . . .

She lost the thread of that thought as he nibbled upon her
lips. Nip, nip, nip, traveling from one side of her lower lip to the

other. He licked her upper lip as if he reveled in the shape of it against his tongue. Her mouth opened to him and he plucked at her lip with his teeth and sucked. He was not tentative.

It tickled. No, not tickled. It was little shocks that made her want to turn away. Or move closer, somehow.

She put her hand up to her face. Not to stop him. To touch . . . her mouth. His. The joining of the two.

He had already drawn away.

"Right." He did not sound entirely calm. "All the parts in working order. We get our clothes off next. Give me a minute."

Some men liked to take off her clothing. Some wanted her to do it herself, while they watched. The fichu kerchief she wore, crossed in front, was tucked into her bodice. She eased one end free, touching the curve of her breast as she did so. Teasing. She had done this many times—

"Stop it," he snapped. "Just undress. And stop goddamned thinking about everything."

"You are very bad tempered. I do not stop thinking because you order it."

"Then think about me." He unbuttoned his cuff and shook his arm so the sleeve loosened. He was scowling. "I'm going to risk getting kicked out of the Service, taking you to bed. You bloody well be here, body and soul, when I do it."

Body and soul. He wanted to touch both her body and her soul. No. That would not happen. That was not what she had planned.

He pulled his shirt over his head in ripples of white linen, and came out, still frowning. He crumpled the shirt in his fist and tossed it behind him and stood up, making it one continual motion. He reached both hands down, wordlessly, to take her hands and pull her up to stand beside him.

He skimmed his breeches down and kicked them away and he was naked. His cock was upright and large, which he continued to ignore. She had made many compliments to men in this regard. Now, when she might have spoken sincerely, she said nothing and resolutely looked elsewhere.

He was the same brown everywhere. That was from being in Italy. She had seen the boys and young men, naked as fishes, swimming in the heat of the day, in the harbor between the boats or beside the bridge of a river, and envied them that freedom.

He was so thin. The British gave him no peace and no rest. They used him as a courier when he was not set to more serious work. His ribs showed, each one separate and defined. The muscles of his belly, his shoulders, his arms, were stark as rocks jutting from a hill, smooth as peeled wood. He was a fierce and violent simplicity, like a force of nature. There was not the least softness upon him anywhere.

She would be able to put her hands upon him. She could do this. She could do it now.

She watched her own fingers draw the line of his collarbone. Warm skin overlaid the unyielding hardness of bone. The line of muscle in his throat was just as hard. His pulse beat very fast. She could see that in the valley at the base of his throat. She could feel that under her palm.

His cock . . . She should stroke his cock. She thought of touching him and no horror descended.

She felt empty inside. The fear was not there. She did not know what to feel instead.

"I'm proud of that. We'll admire it together, later on." He nudged her in closer to him. Set his mouth against her hair and breathed in. "You smell of the fire. You smell . . . domestic-like."

"I made you tea. I am very domestic."

He talked more, rambling on about the cottage. He had stayed here for a month last winter, healing up from a fall. The year before that he'd learned to ride the damn horses in the stable at the great house. Doyle was teaching him to sneak through the woods like a bloody great rabbit.

His voice poured warmth over the cold inside her. He knew what she was. Knew what she had done. There was no condemnation in him. He had done terrible things, himself.

He kissed her eyelids, closing her into the darkness with him. He was there with her. In the heat and solidity of his body. In his breath on her face. In kisses on the corners of her eyes, that did not hurry. He went deep into her mouth. When men kissed her in that way, she must—

"Stay with me, Owl." His fingers closed tight around her face. "Me. Not the damned ghosts."

He tangled his fingers into her hair and held her while his mouth took hers. This time, he was not careful and gentle. He came to her, dark and overwhelming. He was the Mohawk of the alleyways when he kissed her. The street rat, not the gentleman. All the brutality of his nature, all that he controlled and denied and tried to tame, revealed itself.

He said, "What do I taste like? Tell me."

"You are very stupid."

"Oh, I am. This is the stupidest thing I've done in a long time. Tell me what I taste like."

"You taste like darkness." Cautiously, she stretched upward and explored that flavor in his mouth. That possibility. "And tea. And . . . oranges."

"You taste like ghosts." Even while he kissed her, he was suddenly taking her clothes off, clever and fast as a man playing music on strings. "Stop negotiating with them. Leave 'em be. There's just me. I want everybody else out of your head."

There was no more time for calculation or uncertainty. She had not felt the buttons fall undone, but he was pulling her sleeves down her arms, so it must have happened. She heard the slither of her stays unlaced. Felt them open and fall free. When he kissed her shoulder, he pushed the sleeve of her shift away with his lips. The undercurve of her neck, the top of her breast, the hollow behind her collarbone . . . everywhere he kissed was bare and sensitive.

She had thought he would seduce her slowly. She had imagined a long, slow journey, dogged by nightmares. Instead she was whirled from one moment to the next. She stood, barefoot, with one of her breasts quite exposed and all of her filled with perplexity.

"Right." He pinched up a fold of the linen of her shift. "Next, I get you out of this."

She was shaking. Not fear. Not distaste. The trembling of a racehorse at the start of the course. "You are not so great a lover as your reputation." She had not meant to say that. One did not say such things to men. "You hurry."

"No point giving you time to think. Do you please yourself? With your own hands?"

"What do you mean?" But she knew what he meant.

"In bed, alone at night, do you give yourself pleasure with your hands? Do you stroke yourself here?" He touched, lightly, to her shift where it covered her lower belly.

He was without shame. She had not thought it was possible to make her blush.

He said, "Good, then. We couldn't do this if that nubbin between your legs didn't make you happy."

One does not speak of such things. "You lack subtlety."

"I'll get to it, one of these days. Subtlety. I got a whole list of things I plan to learn."

He was pulling her shift down her body, and his eyes were deep wells, mysterious and contained. He did no more than brush her skin when he took her last clothes away. So fast. So matter-of-fact. She might have been alone, removing her own clothing, except that she felt his fingers through the cloth.

She was naked. He was naked and aroused. *I am not ready for this. I need time to think. I need—*

Hawker lifted her from her feet, into his arms. She held on. There was only his skin beneath her hands and pressed to her side and holding her. The world swept by in a rush of confusion. He was the most real of all realities. Alive, solid, unyielding, sure of himself. He was perfectly, absolutely made of strength.

Fear struck through her. Memory of—

He did not carry her to the bed. He kicked the door of the cottage open. They were outside in the light, in the rain, in the sound of wind.

Rain fell into her face, across her breasts and belly, shockingly cold. His body shielded her from the worst of it. Ten paces and they were under the loose cover of tree branches. Under the beech tree that stood in front of his cottage.

"Don't you dare change your damn mind. Understand me?" He set her to stand and pushed her bare back to the tree. The bark poked long rough lines and ridges against her. Her feet slipped on the cold, soft cushion of moss. She was warm only where their bodies met. Where Hawker was hot and dense against her belly and thighs.

"Close your eyes," he said. "Do it!"

She closed her eyes.

"Listen." His voice fell like a stone through the buzz of rain. "What do you hear?"

She heard sharp taps, thousands of them, becoming one muffled note that rose and fell with the wind. The rain rode that wind in sideways to where they sheltered, sneaking under the leaves, pelting Hawker's bare back that protected her. Little drops worked their way through the leaves above and fell onto her shoulders.

He said again, "What do you hear?"

"I hear a madman who has brought me out to freeze in the rain."

"You hear rain. It's making a wall around us. Nobody can get close. We're alone." His mouth closed over her mouth. He was heat and flavor and demand. His body was the only warmth in the world. "What do you smell? Tell me."

He crushed mint, carrying me here. I smell that. And rain. Cool, gray rain that is clean and washes everything away. "I am cold and you are entirely mad."

"But you're with me, aren't you?" Knuckles persuaded her chin upward till her mouth was an inch from his. "Every freezing inch of you is here with me. Kiss me back. It's your turn."

Rain slanted in past him and hit her face with little cold darts. Drops slid down her forehead and cheeks, into her mouth.

He said, "Don't think about it. Just do it."

When she kissed him, he tasted like rain. She sucked it off his tongue and his teeth. She drank him in. A column of energy built in her body, beginning where their mouths joined, that spun and twisted inside her.

Still kissing, he muttered, "Oh, yes. My God, yes," and bit down on her lips. Response jerked inside her, pulled her loose of all control. She could feel herself shaking.

"What do I taste like?" he demanded into her mouth. His hands took her breasts, shaping them, gentle, gentle across the nipples. He brushed them with the side of his thumbs and her blood jangled in her veins.

"Rain." It came out a whisper. It was hard to get her breath. She put her arms around and him and pulled close.

His voice. "Taste me. Be here, with me."

She tasted soap on his lips and the stubble of his chin. Harsh soap. No perfume. Not like the others. He was compounded of simple flavors—tea, rain, soap, smoke, flame.

Under everything, she smelled Adrian himself. She had not once imagined the smell of his skin. It dragged her to him, like fingers pulling at her skin. She stretched upward and filled her mouth with his hair. Set her teeth into the texture of it and tasted. Sucked the rain from it.

He nuzzled her aside to get to her ear, biting, licking, filling her mind with his breath. "Feel this," he said. "And this." Somehow his lips, his teeth, found her breast with its goose bumps and the pucker of cold. So sensitive. He warmed her nipples with his tongue. A hum, deep in his chest, appreciative, vibrated on her there. The words, "So good," were in there somewhere.

The hint of his teeth sent frantic, nervous energy to pluck between her legs.

She squirmed with it. Not away from him. Toward him. His hands spread wide on her ribs, to hold her. His arms hardened to steel. He lifted her off her feet and slowly let her slide against him as he brought her down to earth.

They were slick with the rain, chilled, almost shivering. But there was no cold where they were together. His cock was the center of all that heat, hard and insistent on her belly.

A man. The edges of her nerves flicked and twisted like leaves in a high wind. He was very much a man. He would—

"None of that." He lifted her upward again. Let her glide with agonizing slowness down the architecture of his body. A thousand shocks pricked where every part of her was against every part of him. Surface to surface. One to the other. Complexities interwoven.

He said, "Look at me. Who am I, Owl? Who's here with you?"

"'Awker." His name was a talisman. Hawker did these things to her. Rain fell in her face, washing everything away. All the past. All other hands, other men, all the smudges on her soul. The dark cloud of them dissolved, and the rain carried them away. Ghosts, washed away. Gone. Leaving her clean.

Hawker was real. Nothing else. She gripped her hands on his shoulders and leaned to him. Yes. She opened her legs around him, to hold him to her, to make her warm.

Cold roughness at her back. More kisses to her breasts. She was gasping now. His hands soothed downward over breast and belly till he stroked between her thighs, then upward to the joining of her legs. Skillful and sure, he found the fold there and touched inside. She cried out.

"Just my hand, giving you pleasure. That's all. You and me. *Pour le plaisir.*"

Him, touching her. Only pleasure. Dark, secret pleasure, like the night. Dark fire. She rocked against his hand.

"I want to be inside you," he said. "I can't hold out much longer. You ready for this?"

Anything. It did not matter, if only he would keep touching her. She nodded once, jerkily.

He slipped his hands around her. Brought her to him. At the end of the long caress of his skin against her skin, he was inside her.

They hurt me there—

He bit down hard on her earlobe, and she lost the thought. Rough bites to her lips tore every dark memory away before it took hold. He was a storm contained in a body. He swept over her. He kissed deep and she whimpered into his mouth, overwhelmed.

He thrust. The pang of it shot through the tension inside her. She was the center of a thousand sensations. Shock upon shock as he eased outward. Entered again slowly. Fully.

He was still talking to her. She didn't try to understand the words, only heard the tone of his voice. Determined. Unrelenting. His hand found her. Was between them. Caressed, so softly, so skillfully, rhythmic, following her as she twisted and gasped.

Faster now, he thrust deep, driving against her. She tried to climb him, while her legs slipped and slid on his thigh. She throbbed and could not escape, she was so unbearably open. Did not want to escape. Offered herself and gloried in it. Heat swept through her, down every pathway of her body, sweeping decision and fear ahead of it.

She dug her fingers into his back. Opened her mouth and bit his neck. Braced her feet on the ground, arched backward, and drove herself toward what he gave her.

He was everything she needed. Unceasing. Steady. Sure of himself. He knew exactly what to do. She released the last restraints in her mind and trusted him.

She was seized and tossed by the climax. Grabbed and shaken as by a great fist. Inside, she closed around him again and again, and every time was a new beat of pleasure. She heard herself cry out in a sound like pain.

He was pleasing himself now, with rough, quick thrusts inside her. Absorbed. Drinking his own pleasure. Lost in her.

He has done so much for me.

She gave back to him, as she knew how to do. Rose to reach for him. Took his hair strongly with her fingers and pulled his mouth to hers. Licked, teased, played with his mouth. Used all her knowledge upon him. Gloried that she knew so much.

Below, she clenched herself around him, where he was within her. Squeezed him tightly. She knew the muscles to use. Had practiced and practiced. She contracted against the hardness inside her.

This, she could give him. This, she knew how to do.

But this time it was no indifferent service. This was beyond words different from anything before. She had not known, could not have imagined, how the tension twisted and exploded. Joy came from everywhere and gathered there, where she held him. She tightened and tightened and felt him move and was struck with ecstasy. Breathless with it. Dizzy.

He was no careful and controlled expert. Not any longer. He had become wild, pounding into her. He was beyond thought. Mad. Consumed. A cry rasped in and out of his throat. His body shocked and stiffened.

His last thrust withdrew. She felt him shudder in her arms and spill himself against her thigh.

They held each other. While he shook. While she trembled and her bones melted and she let her head fall to his chest. While he gasped into her hair.

His grip opened and closed on her shoulders. It was long minutes before he spoke. "Well. That was . . . That was very good." His voice was gritty. Hoarse.

She did not want to open her eyes. She was crying. She could not imagine why she was crying. "I will not tell you . . . You are conceited enough." Then she said, "It was good. I didn't know it would be that good."

"Me neither. Joke's on us, innit?" He breathed heavily. "Let's get inside before you catch an ague."

"Yes. That is wise."

"We'll see how we do in bed." He did not make her walk back to the cottage in her bare feet. He carried her in his arms while it rained down on them, hard, every step of the front path back to the door. She became cold, as well as filled with amazement.

He dried them both in front of the fire. They made love in bed, very slowly, and it worked there too. He had the most skillful and amazing mouth.

Twenty-two

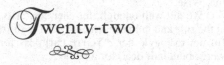

1818
Meeks Street, London

SHE WAS IN HAWKER'S ARMS. SHE KNEW THAT before she knew where she was. It was rare and important, being with him.

Even now, after so many years, she dreamed of him. Sometimes, when she first woke up, she'd think he was with her. She'd feel his arm under her head, his body naked beside her. Then the day would come and wash dreams away. Then it was not his arm under her. It was a pillow. It was not his body. It was the rolled and tumbled blanket. Time after time, she slid out of a dream and she was alone, but for an instant, the bed smelled of him.

This time, it wasn't a dream.

She lay awake for a time before she opened her eyes, hurting and vaguely angry about it.

She was in bed, in a quiet room, under a soft blanket, held by Hawker. She glided back to consciousness, riding the currents of that certainty. She was with Hawker, so she was safe. In all the world, there was no flesh, no bone, no sound of breathing she would mistake for Hawker's.

"I can tell when you're awake," he said.

Her mouth was dry. "You always could."

"A matter of being cautious." He unwound from her and

tucked the blanket into the space he'd emptied. The bed moved. He sat up to lean over and look down at her. "I never quite trusted you, you know, not even when we were closest. I just thought it was worth the risk. You were always worth the risk."

I was stabbed because I came to warn you. "You do not trust me. Wise."

"We did well enough, for enemies." His smile pulled down at the side and didn't reach his eyes. He shifted his weight, careful not to joggle her. "You're harmless for the moment. You were about half dead for a while."

"How long?"

"It's been three days. A little more."

So long? She thought of days frittered away, like small coins out of a pocket. Pouring from her mind, like grains of silver. "I don't remember."

"Just as well."

Someone had put her in a night shift. Her left arm was an ache from shoulder to fingers. Under the bandage, she itched. She held her hands up. So heavy. Her joints felt like old iron wheels and gears that had lain abandoned for a long time and were now set moving again, creakily.

Bruises circled her wrists and ran in regimented lines, forearm to elbow. Blue finger marks showed where someone had held her.

"I am bruised." Events took shape in her mind like shadows in fog. She had been in Braddy Square, trying to get to Hawker, to warn him. She remembered being stabbed. Staggering toward Meeks Street. "Who did I fight?"

"I held you down when you were being sewed up. You objected to that for some reason. And later, when you were out of your head with fever." He rolled smoothly off the bed and stood over her. "I hurt you doing it. No choice."

His voice said how little he had liked hurting her.

Oh, Hawker. We have hurt each other so much.

He was unshaven, which always made a ruffian of him. He wore trousers and a loose shirt, open halfway down his chest. She had felt it next to her as she slept, cradling the edge of her dreams—the warmth of him, the creases of the linen of his shirt, the old, familiar comfort of his skin.

He poured from a pitcher to a small cup. "Everybody wants you to drink this. I have seldom encountered such unanimity of opinion. I'm going to slip in next to you and hold it up. You sip out of the side here."

It was not water, but lemonade. Exactly right. She was very thirsty.

They looked at each other while she drank. He was deeply tired. His face was pared to the bone, to sarcasm and deadliness. He had watched her come very close to death, she thought.

"That's better." He eased her down to the pillow again. "You almost slipped away from me. There was one time there, you stopped fighting. I thought it was over."

"It was not. Not this time." When she lay still, the pain was not great. There was much to be said for holding still. "Lie beside me, if you would. For comfort. I am in pain and I'm cold."

"My pleasure, anyway."

She started to laugh and took the warning her body gave and did not. "The papers? You have them. Important."

"I have them." He lifted the blanket and crawled in beside her. So many times, he had done that.

"I will tell you what I saw . . . when I wake up." One more thing to say. "Do not send for Séverine." She would come all this long distance and worry about her. "It is unnecessary."

"Go to sleep, Owl."

"Do you know? You are the only one in the world . . . who still calls me Owl."

The darkness was huge and friendly. She would rest in it awhile.

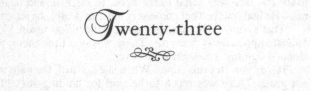

Twenty-three

HAWKER PICKED UP HIS RAZOR. IN THE MIRROR over the dresser, he looked back at himself with hard, steady eyes. A killer's eyes.

"She's alive for the next little while." Alive. Exhausted. Sleeping. Just sleeping. Felicity was watching her.

He'd never got into the habit of using a brush to put soap on his face. Just lathered up between his palms.

"Let's say there's two groups. One of them goes poking knives into various Frenchmen. The other is trying to gut Justine. Both of them are mad at me and both have some of my knives handy." He shook his head. "Not likely."

No argument from the mirror.

He tried the razor along the hair on his arm. Nicely sharp. He did like a good edge on his steel. Swish his hands in the basin. Pull his skin taut with his thumb and shave the right side. No hurry.

Wipe soap off the razor on a towel. Rinse it in the basin. "Not two groups, then. One. They go after the Frenchmen to frame me. They go after Justine because it'll hurt me."

Finish the right side. Wipe the razor down again. "They know me fairly well."

Now for the left side. "But it's easier to shoot me one balmy evening. Who's going to take the time and trouble to be that convoluted and that patient? Who hates me that much?"

One name came to mind.

Shaving's a meditative business. He did the short, careful strokes under the chin. Always a tricky part.

Wipe the final soap off the razor. Wash the blade.

"Try this. Say Justine's been collecting my knives for a while. She kills a pair of Frenchmen, planning to lay it on me." Dry the blade with the clean corner of the towel. "Before she dispatches another hapless French cove, one of her confederates gets peevish and pokes the knife into her."

Fold the razor. Lay it down beside the bowl. Take a new towel and wash his face. "That gives us one group, with infighting. And Justine behind everything."

Toss the towel away with the other one.

A long time ago, he'd thought it was special between him and Owl. They were friends, right to the heart. Being enemies didn't change that. Even when he was staggering around, half dead, with her bullet in his shoulder, he kept thinking they were friends.

His eyes looked back at him, particularly bleak this morning. "Owl won't stop, you know. She never gives up. If she's behind this, I'll wake up one morning with my throat slit." He fingered his throat. "Because I'm still a damn fool when it comes to that woman."

No answer to that either.

He strapped on the arm sheath, settled his shoulder harness, checked the knives, and wished he was out in the field where he might get to use them. He was in the mood to confront somebody a good deal more dangerous than Lord Cummings, Head of Military Intelligence.

WHEN Hawker walked into his office, he saw that Cummings had taken a place behind the desk. He was sitting in Hawker's chair.

He'd never decided whether Lord Cummings played the fool on purpose, or if it just came naturally to him. He looked the part of an aristocrat. He was straight-backed and silver-haired, sporting a long, thin, supercilious nose. He sat behind the desk, looking distinguished, pretending to be absorbed in the newspaper he'd picked up. He'd brought along his cur dog, Colonel Reams, who did not look distinguished.

Felicity leaned against the wall just inside the door of his office, keeping a gimlet eye on the visitors. She muttered, "About time," as he passed.

He barely moved his lips. "You felt it quite necessary to put them in here?"

"You said to be polite."

"Not that polite."

She'd let Military Intelligence invade his office just to see what they wanted to get into. And to annoy him. He gave her a "we'll talk about this later" look and motioned her out.

Back when Adrian Hawkhurst was still Hawker the Hand, stealing for a living and associating with questionable companions—in the flower of his youth, as it were—he'd walked into many an alley to find an enemy sitting in ambush. This felt the same. It was enough to make a man nostalgic.

Cummings had settled his arse into the carved oak chair that belonged to the Head of Service. It was black with age, worn smooth by the behinds of twenty-nine men who'd been Head of the British Intelligence Service. It dated back to the time of Good Queen Bess. To Walsingham, who'd founded the Service.

It's mine now.

Cummings didn't do anything by accident. He wanted anger. Now, why did Cummings want him angry? Dealing with Military Intelligence just drove the humdrum out of the morning.

Reams stood to the side of the office, a thick-bodied, red-faced bulldog of a man. His hands were gripped together behind his back and he sneered at the map on the wall. He wore scarlet regimentals, as usual, though he didn't have any particular right to a Guards uniform. One of Military Intelligence's little fictions. No battlefields for the colonel.

Reams looked particularly self-satisfied this morning. Possibly he felt he'd done something clever. He was probably wrong.

The map held a hundred numbered and colored pins, set from Dublin to Dubrovnik and points east, as far as India. His agents. Austrian, Russian, and French agents. Trouble spots. Nothing Military Intelligence would make head nor tail of.

"The lumpy yellow shape off to the right is Austria," he said helpfully. "The square blue one is France." He jostled the colonel off balance as he strolled past.

"Watch it, you—" A glance from Cummings, and Reams swallowed the rest of his comment.

Cummings took his time folding the newspaper. He tossed it on the desk, toppling a pile of unopened letters into a stack of reports, making a point, doling out his second nicely graded insult of the morning. He'd got them in before they exchanged a word. "Good. You're here."

"A pleasure to see you, Cummings. As always."

"You haven't answered my messages."

"How careless of me." There'd be notes from Military Intelligence somewhere in that pile on his desk. How wise of everyone to ignore them. "The press of work . . ."

"I don't have time to wait on your convenience." Cummings tapped his fingers impatiently on the arm of the chair. The hand rests were carved wolf heads, snarling.

British Service wolves. Not Military Intelligence. He knew just how they felt. He wouldn't mind snarling himself.

"Always so awkward to settle upon another man's convenience. And you've come all the way across town to do it." He skirted around the desk and sat on the edge of it, chummily next to Cummings, his boot heel hooked on to a drawer pull. He showed his teeth, copying the wolf heads.

Cummings slid back in the chair, harrumphing. "I mean to say . . ."

Let us loom over the man. I get so few opportunities to loom. "Why don't you tell me what we can do for Military Intelligence today."

In Cummings's world, men in authority sat at desks and gave orders. Inferiors stood at attention. Sitting down meant you had power.

In the rookeries of East London, men in authority kicked you in the guts to drive home the salient points of their discourse. Sitting down just put you closer to somebody's boot.

In his office, the rules of Whitechapel applied.

Cummings had propped his cane against the wall. He reached out and put it between them, the ivory head clutched in his hand. "I say . . ."

"Yes?" For two days he'd lived on coffee and anger and

watched Owl fight for her life. When he looked down at Cummings, he let some of that show in his eyes.

Cummings cleared his throat. "Mean to say . . . you should speak to that girl of yours, Hawkhurst. Damned if you shouldn't. She left me standing on the steps ten minutes before she opened. She was blasted impertinent. Wouldn't leave the room when I ordered her to."

You do like to order my people around, don't you?

"She talked back to me." Cummings sucked his lip in and out, deploring the situation.

"We all have that problem."

"I suppose you keep her around because she's a toothsome little thing. You have a reputation for liking the ladies, Hawkhurst. You have that reputation."

"Do I?"

The cane jiggled nervously in Cummings's hold. There was a blade hidden inside. Anyone would know that from the way Cummings carried it, even without the wide gold rim that circled the head. Hardware like that meant a cane dagger.

A rich man's trinket. A short dagger, with no hilt but that little hexagonal rim. Good for one sneaky, unexpected strike. Useless in a fight.

Cummings fingered it as if it were a favored piece of his anatomy. "I envy you Service Johnnies sometimes. Pretty petticoats stashed away at headquarters. Drinking coffee on the Via Whatever-o in Rome. Jaunting off to the opera in Vienna. No real work for you, now that the war is over. Nothing to do but write up reports and shoot them off to the Prime Minister."

"We keep busy in our own modest way."

It wasn't the British Service out of work. It was Military Intelligence. When the last of the occupation army pulled out of France, Military Intelligence went with them. Cummings was reduced to spying on Englishmen, playing informer and agent provocateur to discontented Yorkshire weavers. Intercepting the mail of liberal politicians, hoping to find something treasonous. Harassing purveyors of naughty etchings in Soho.

Military Intelligence was being whipped through the newspapers as the "secret police" of England. It wasn't just the radical press that said it was time to close them down.

His lordship liked to see himself as the spider in the center of a vast web of international intrigue. Now the only agents in the field in Europe were British Service. Cummings spied on the British Service, fishing for minnows to carry back to the Prime Minister, Liverpool. Always gratifying to be the object of interest.

"But you haven't told me what brings you to Meeks Street." He hitched himself more at ease on the desk and let his boot swing right next to his lordship's immaculate, buff-colored trousers. Cummings couldn't get to his feet without scrambling like a crab, losing dignity. "Not that we aren't delighted to—"

Doyle came in, with no sound to announce him. Silent as the grave, Doyle, when he wanted to be. He said, "Cummings," being blunt to the point of rudeness. Then he gave a respectful, "Sir," in Hawker's direction.

That was Doyle propping up the fiction that Adrian ran the place. Listen to Doyle, and anybody'd think Adrian Hawkhurst was somebody important. Somebody an earl's son deferred to as a matter of course.

"Join us. Cummings is about to reveal why he's graced me with his presence today. I'm . . . what's the word I want?"

"Intrigued."

"Exactly. I knew you would have the *mot juste* in your pocket. I am intrigued."

The wide chair pulled up on the other side of the desk was Doyle's. It was big enough to hold him. In the years Doyle had been reporting to Heads of Section—five of them now—the chair had taken on his shape and something of his character. It was not unknown for new Heads of Section to sit at the desk and hold conferences with the empty chair, asking themselves what Doyle would advise in a particularly sticky situation.

Doyle sat down, playing Lord Markham to the hilt, showing off the Eton and Cambridge and the estate in Oxfordshire. He'd changed into a suit of gentleman's clothes. Nothing fancy, because you didn't decorate a man like Doyle. Understated. It wasn't what he wore that made him look like Lord Markham. It was the hundred subtle little gestures and flickers of expression that did it. Right now he was applying a nicely graded aristocratic disdain when his eyes landed on Reams.

Doyle had unassailable credentials. Adrian Hawkhurt's were more . . . imaginative. One popular theory was that Tsar Paul got him on an English noblewoman. Then there was the rumor he was a Hapsburg, exiled for doing something too disgraceful for even the Austrian nobility.

A soft grinding noise. That was the cane twisting into the rug. Cummings said, "I'll get to the point then. You brought a woman here, injured. Do you know she's a notorious spy? She's a French émigré we've been keeping an eye on for years. A shopkeeper in Exeter Street."

Justine would smile, being called a shopkeeper. Hadn't Napoleon called the English a nation of shopkeepers? He glanced at Doyle. "Notorious spy? That does sound familiar. We have one of those tucked away upstairs, don't we?"

Reams snarled, "For God's sake, man. You have blood on your front door."

"How biblical of us."

"She was attacked in the square," Doyle said. "It's been reported to the magistrate."

"Sneak thieves. They're everywhere. I didn't know street crime in the capital fell under your jurisdiction." He watched Cummings.

Who seemed angrier than he should be. Why was that? "She's alive? She'll recover?"

"Yes."

"Did she see who attacked her? Can she identify him?"

"No." He didn't expand.

"Well, then. Well." Cummings gathered in his cane, gripped the head of it in both hands. Awkward because he was crowded in, he scrambled to his feet. "These things get exaggerated. Rumor said she was at death's door. Heh. Death's door is the door to Meeks Street. Amusing, that."

"Diverting."

On his feet, Cummings began a fussy pacing back and forth, flourishing his cane. Reams glowered from the sideline. Cummings huffed and hemmed. At last he came out with, "There's something you should know."

"Tell me." Maybe he was about to find out why Cummings was in his office.

"Private, really. You want Markham to leave. Don't want to say anything about this in front of him."

"There's nothing he can't hear."

Cummings shrugged. "You may wish you'd chosen privacy."

Another trip across the office. "There have been a pair of murders in London. Frenchmen. Antoine Morreau, bookseller. Pierre Richelet, publican in Soho. Both stabbed. They passed themselves off as Royalist émigrés. In fact, they were French secret agents."

Cummings was pleased with himself. He knew something more. He was enjoying himself too much to just say it right out loud.

"Police Secrète." Reams pronounced it like an Englishman. "Both of them."

Doyle rearranged himself. The chair creaked. "How long have you known about them?"

"Does it matter?" Reams demanded.

"If they were killed because Military Intelligence let something slip, it matters."

"We don't leak information." Reams shifted on his feet, a bantam bull, pawing the ground. "You can damn well—"

"Reams got a letter." He didn't have to tell Doyle this. It was obvious. "An anonymous letter. Probably yesterday. They didn't know before that, or they would have pulled them in to harass."

Reams's face turned red.

"Their real names," Cummings said, mellifluous and superior, "were Gravois and Patelin. They were senior officers of the Secret Police under Robespierre. I'm sure you'll find them somewhere in your records."

He didn't have to search the records. Those two, he remembered. The Tuteurs of the Coach House. He'd very nearly met them one night when he was young enough to be an idiot.

Reams subsided against the wall, muttering, "Don't know why there's Frenchies everywhere. They have their own country."

"We took the matter to Bow Street." Cummings nodded to Reams. "Tell them."

"When we got the let—" Colonel Reams rubbed across the buttons on his coat, shining them up. "When we connected those two murders, I went to Bow Street. Tied the cases together for them, you might say." He let the pause drag out, enjoying himself. "They'd spotted some similarities. What they don't understand at Bow Street, though, is intelligence."

So many things one could say. So tempting. But he let the colonel wind to his conclusion.

"They were both stabbed," Reams said. "They were goddamned French émigrés. Dead ones now. The knives were left sticking in their gut where they fell."

Almost poetic, the colonel.

"I asked to see the evidence boxes." Cummings tucked his cane under his elbow, getting ready to leave. He'd done what he came for. "The murder weapons were flat, black throwing knives of a most distinctive design. I recognized them at once, of course. A British agent used knives like that in France during the war. A rather infamous agent."

"The Black Hawk." Reams laughed. "They had your initials on them, Hawkhurst. I told Bow Street they're yours."

Twenty-four

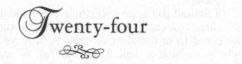

JUSTINE'S SHOP, VOYAGES, HAD A SOLID, PROSPEROUS look to it. The windows gleamed. The name was spelled out on the front in green letters edged with gilt. There was a proper mercantile bell on the door.

From across the street, Hawker heard the faint jingle as a muscular clerical gentleman emerged, hunched in the rain opening his umbrella, and strode off carrying a large, oblong package under his arm.

It was short of noon, but lamps were lit inside the shop, paying blackmail to the mucky gloom of the day. He and Pax had pulled back to the line of shop fronts, just to give the carriages a challenge if they wanted to soak somebody. They stood in the doorway of an antique dealer across the street from Voyages. Nothing much else happened, except everybody got wet.

Inside Justine's shop, two customers stood at the counter and examined every possible aspect of some small metal instrument, passing it back and forth between them. The shop clerk, a Negro, tall and thin as an ebony cane, advised and discussed and sometimes pointed. This went on.

The clerk was calling himself Mr. Thompson now. He'd used a half dozen other names when he worked for the French.

Pax said, "Somehow I never expected Justine DuMotier to end up a shopkeeper on Exeter Street."

"A surprise for all of us."

"Everybody buys here. Good business. Doyle watched her for months when she first set up to see if it was legitimate."

"I know."

"I figured you knew everything you wanted to know."

Three years ago, when Napoleon fell, Justine DuMotier disappeared from the sight of man. He'd looked for her everywhere, worried as hell. Paris was full of occupying armies. Petty, rancorous men tracked down Napoleon's followers to pay back old scores. The new French government was thinning the ranks of the Police Secrète, not being frugal with the bullets.

It had been months before the Service spotted her in London. More months, before he got back to England himself.

He remembered. He'd landed in Dover, ridden up from the coast in a night and a day, dropped his kit at Meeks Street, and walked straight here. To her.

It had been late afternoon of the day, and foggy. The shop was lit up inside, the way it was now. He'd stood . . . He'd stood almost exactly at this spot and watched her at the counter of her shop, fifty feet away. She'd unrolled a big map and was showing a gentleman customer some river on it, or a sea route. Something that involved leaning over close and tracing a line with her finger.

He'd stayed in the shadow, watching. Didn't go into the shop. The war was over, but it didn't make any difference. The last words she'd said to him dug a chasm he hadn't dared to cross.

"What do you think that is?" Pax said, meaning the instrument everybody was so fascinated with, inside.

"Sextant maybe. A small one. And that's the case for it."

"We don't buy from her," Pax said. "The Military Intelligence boys do. The navy officers. The Ethnological Club. The Service goes to Barnes instead."

"That's tactful of us."

"We like to think so."

Voyages designed and sold gear for travel to the far corners of the globe. Now that the war was over, Englishmen were pouring out of dull old England, headed to Egypt, South America, India, and every port in the Orient. Voyages was the first stop. They knew what you needed. They'd buy it for you or make it, and pack it up neat. The expeditions Justine supplied never ended up hiking through the monsoon in wool underdrawers. Her guns didn't misfire during some sticky dispute with Afghani bandits. That clerical gentleman with the umbrella wouldn't run out of soap and ipecac while he was bringing enlightenment to the Maori.

Voyages also did a roaring trade in luncheon hampers with nested teacups and a little brazier for under the teapot, suitable for picnics when exploring the far reaches of Hampstead Heath with an elderly aunt.

"She makes a good living," Pax said. "Half of England's traipsing around the remote and uncomfortable."

"Getting bit by snakes and skewered by the outraged local inhabitants."

"It's the English way." Pax refolded his arms. "Those two don't look like they're leaving anytime soon, do they?"

The black man placed another enigmatic metal instrument on the counter. A theodolite. Everybody took a look at it.

"Not soon," he said.

Pax shifted an inch, edging out of the path of a persistent drip coming down from the roof. "Speaking professionally, if I wanted to kill Justine—just a simple death—I'd shoot her in the shop."

"Speaking professionally, that would be a wise choice." He kept his voice level. Rage had been simmering away inside him for a good long while. He'd keep it there, boiling away in his gut, till he needed it. "They waited till she came to me. They must have known she'd come."

"Then they know her. They can predict what she'll do."

"A small, elite group. The man who did the stabbing was watching her and waiting. Probably from . . ." He looked up and behind him, got rain in his eyes. "One of these windows."

"I'll bring the boys. We'll start asking questions, up and down the street."

"The pub over there has a front table with a view of the shop." In the last two years, he'd sat there sometimes, pursuing a lengthy acquaintance with a glass of gin, knowing Justine would walk by and he'd get to see her. There could not be anything in the world more pitiable than a man afraid to face a woman. Unless the woman was Justine DuMotier. "Ask in the shops if anyone's been looking in that direction. But it'll turn out to be a room upstairs."

"One of those." Pax glanced across houses, assessing likelihoods. They'd avoided ambushes in the war years, knowing where shots were likely to come from. Sometimes, they'd been the men doing the shooting.

That was the dark secret of the assassin's trade. It's not that hard. A stab in the alley. The pull of a trigger. People were so damn fragile—ten breaths or two minutes bleeding separated life and death.

Justine had turned out to be hard to kill. A nasty surprise for somebody.

Pax said, "Looks like they're winding up."

The pair in Justine's shop finally agreed that the first mechanical device, whatever it was, suited their purpose. The black man set it carefully in a box, left the room to go into the back of the shop, and came out with brown paper. There was more talking, all round, while he wrapped the box. Everybody nodded and shook hands. Then the two men left and walked down Exeter Street in close conversation.

He said, "And we have the place to ourselves."

They crossed the street. Pax, beside him, watched the right hand. He watched the left. He didn't feel eyes on him right at the moment. But then, he'd been wrong about that on some notable occasions in the past.

At the door he pulled his hat off and shook the rain off. He set it back on his head so he'd have both hands free.

The bell jangled as they walked in. The black man, Mr. Thompson, looked up from a book, open flat on the counter. His eyes slid across Pax. He saw Hawker and knew him.

Twenty-five

THOMPSON WAS WELL OVER SIX FEET TALL AND WORE the intensely black skin and long, sharp features of East Africa. He dressed plain as a Quaker, in black, his shirt and cravat startlingly white. His face stayed impassive, but his eyes snapped to alert. He called, without turning, "Mr. Chetri."

Someone moved in the room in back. A chair scraped. Footsteps padded softly. The other clerk came in from the back, polite and attentive. His eyes fixed on Adrian and narrowed.

This was Chetri, no other name known for him. Like Thompson, Chetri had worked for the French in the East and around the Mediterranean. He was north Indian, gray-haired, fine-featured, square in body, quick of movement.

For a long moment both men found Adrian Hawkhurst absorbing. Two critical examinations plucked over him, head to foot. Assessing.

He'd seen these two any number of times from a distance. Studied them through the window glass. Quite the little nest of retired French agents here on Exeter Street.

"Something has happened to Mademoiselle Justine." Thompson spoke fluent English, with the cadence of the African language of his birth underneath and a French accent overlying it all. "Tell us."

Behind him, Pax threw the bolt on the front door and turned the sign to Closed. He could be heard, walking down the shop, pulling the shades down over the windows.

Chetri came to the counter and held the edge, tight fingered. "You have news of Mademoiselle?"

Thompson said, "There has been no message. I opened the shop myself, yesterday and today. This has never occurred."

"Always, she sends word if she will be away."

Time to say it. "She was hurt, but she's alive. She was in an accident." He watched the faces, eyes, hands, the muscles around the mouth, knowing Pax was doing the same, making the same assessments he was.

Shock. Worry. Their eyes turned to consult back and forth. Natural to do that. It rang true. He read relief in the way shoulder muscles relaxed and breath leaked out. In fingers loosening. They'd expected to hear Justine was dead.

An emphatic foreign phrase from Chetri. That was a string of syllables to save in mind and ask an expert about when he had a chance.

Thompson stepped closer. "How is she hurt? Where have they taken her?"

"She's safe."

"But she did not send for us." Thompson said, "She is badly hurt, then."

"Safe." He could give that reassurance. "She's out of danger. She's asleep now, but she was awake and talking a little. We had the best surgeon in London working on her."

Chetri pressed fingertips hard to the wood of the counter, making tense brown pyramids of his hands. Holding still. "She is at Meeks Street? It must be, or we would have news. I will close the shop at once and return with you. I will see her."

Nobody was getting close to Justine. "Maybe in a few days."

"I am not merely an employee of Mademoiselle. We are friends. My wife and daughter will be honored to care for her. They have some skill in nursing. I must—"

Thompson interrupted. "You won't be allowed in. Look at him. He won't let any of us near her. Not even Nalina."

"Who knows a hundred herbs of healing. These British will kill Mademoiselle with their ignorance. I will go to her."

"And be turned away. Why should they trust you? Or me? Or Nalina?"

"Pah." Chetri shook his head impatiently. "We are hers. Does he think she is a fool to keep enemies this close?"

"He thinks no one can be trusted. Would you wish him to be gullible?" When Chetri said nothing, Thompson said, "If she cannot defend herself, he must." He turned. "Ask your questions."

Pax had been walking around the shop, poking into things, opening up the wooden medical boxes and peering in at the bottles and muslin bags inside. He looked over. "When did you last see her?"

Tuesday, it turned out. Mr. Chetri came from behind the counter to stand at the head of the long table and put his hand on the back of one of the wide wooden chairs. "Here," he said. Mademoiselle had taken breakfast here that morning. A roll and coffee, as always, while they prepared the shop for opening.

Thompson said, "The bakery boy brings the newspaper as well as bread. I make coffee for her myself, in the manner of my homeland."

"The coffee is not important." Chetri made a chopping motion. "It was not yet seven. This is what happened. Mademoiselle tosses the newspaper down and leaves the shop, hurrying as if devils pursued her." What devils, he could not say. One did not demand of Mademoiselle Justine where she is going or why.

She had returned three hours later. Perhaps four hours—before noon—and still hurrying.

It was raining heavily by that time and Mademoiselle was soaking wet. There was one client in the shop. The foolish young man from Oxford who wished to collect little bugs in the Hindu Kush. He would be shot by tribesmen almost at once, unfortunately. One preferred repeat customers. But Mademoiselle said nothing to him. She went upstairs—

"She took newspapers with her," Thompson interrupted. "She took last week's newspapers from the back room and carried them upstairs with her."

"Why?" From Pax.

"She did not tell us." Thompson was patient. "And we did not ask. Let me finish saying what I have to say."

The right-hand wall of Justine's shop was hung with lethal instrumentation, a collection of fifty or so. Spears for poking holes at some distance. Sabers for cutting from horseback. Knives for doing it close up. Bloodthirsty woman, Justine.

Pax picked down a kris knife to examine. Pretty, but impractical. "Go on."

Chetri said, "In twenty minutes she descended to the shop. She was worried."

"Not worried," Thompson contradicted. "Angry. Very angry."

A nod. "She cleaned and loaded her gun. The little Gribeauval she carries. She sat here," Chetri patted the chair back, "and did so. She put her knife into the sheath inside her cloak, as if she would need to use it. She gave us no instruction, except to say we should close the shop."

"I am ashamed," Thompson said. "She loaded her gun, took a knife, and left in the rain. I did not offer her my escort. I knew she was going into danger, and I did not go with her."

"She would have refused," Chetri said. "You would only have annoyed her."

"Yes. But I did not offer. I did not ask."

Whatever ambush Justine walked into, she wouldn't have dragged them in with her. "Did you know where she was going?"

The black man said nothing.

"We must show him," Chetri said. Then, "This is the time. This is what she spoke of."

Thompson did not hesitate or show uncertainty. He simply thought for a while before he spoke. "You are right."

Abruptly he left. He strode toward the counter and around the end of it, to the door that led to the back. In his plain black suit, he walked as if he wore robes that spread out around him.

Chetri lowered his voice. "She was enraged when she walked into the shop yesterday. Furious. As soon as we were alone in the shop, she went to the shelves in the back room . . ."

Noiselessly, Thompson returned. He carried a plain wood case and laid it upon the table. "He is wondering why you babble secrets to him, Mr. Chetri." He gave the other man no chance to reply. "We are not fools. We would not speak like this to anyone else."

"We follow Mademoiselle's orders."

"Three years ago she told me—told Chetri as well—that if anything happened to her, we were to go to Number Seven in Meeks Street and seek out the dark-haired, dark-skinned son of a bitch who ran the place."

"You forgive us," Chetri said. "We only repeat what she said."

"When she said, 'dark-skinned,' she looked at me and laughed and said, 'Perhaps not so dark.' She said, 'He is called Black Hawk, but he moves like a cat.'"

Chetri spoke up. "I went—we both went—to spy upon the house in Meeks Street. To look at you. We had heard of you, of course, Sir Adrian."

With a small click, Thompson turned the box. It was yew wood, without carving or inlay, thinner than a gun case, but with the same utilitarian design. "I was to give you this, if anything happened. She said I was to trust you."

Thompson's face had become grave, closed, and immovable as obsidian. He released the simple hook that clasped the lid. "That day, she opened this box. This is why she armed herself and went into the rain, to whatever fate awaited her there."

The box was empty. The gray velvet lining showed three identical imprints where three knives had rested, parallel, point left. He didn't have to pull his own knife to know it would fit right into place.

That was one mystery solved. Knives were sticking into Frenchmen across London. This is where they came from.

Somewhere, somehow, Justine had got hold of three of his knives.

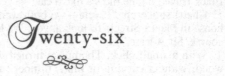wenty-six

SIXTEEN YEARS EARLIER
1802
La Pomme d'Or, Paris

HAWKER HUNG IN THE NIGHT, BALANCING AGAINST the side of the building, just touching the windowsill. He heard Owl inside her room, being busy, making the little rustles a woman makes, getting ready for bed. When he was sure there was nobody with her, he scratched at the shutters.

She came to let him in, wearing a peignoir the color of peaches over her night shift.

For five years they'd been lovers, and he never got tired of the sight of her. Her hair was loose down her shoulders in honey-dark rivers. Her feet were pink and bare on the floorboards. She looked cross.

He crouched on the window ledge. "I keep expecting to find you in some pretty apartment on the Rue St. Denis." He knew every fingerhold on the shutter and the open casement. A good thing. He was clumsy tonight. "But it's the same pokey old attic."

"It is a very safe attic, *mon vieux*. There is nowhere in Paris so well-guarded as an expensive brothel."

"Yet here I am, getting in without let or hindrance."

"You, of course, are the exception to many rules. It is a pity you will break your neck one of these days, showing off. It will be mourned by all the women of Europe. A more sensible man would simply—"

"Walk in the front door. I know. That takes all the fun out of it." Even if he wanted to tell the world he was in Paris, he wasn't dressed to stroll into a place like the Pomme d'Or. They'd looked at him twice even in the livery stable where he'd left his horse.

He stumbled when his feet found the floor. His legs were giving way now that they knew he was at the end of the road. "Am I welcome?"

"If you were not welcome, I would not have opened the window. Or perhaps I would have opened the window and then pushed you to a sudden death on the stones of the courtyard. In either case, you would receive the hint." He could smell the clean bright smell of her. Lavender. "You may give that extremely dusty coat to me, if you please. You have been rolling in the dust. Fighting?"

"Falling off a damned horse."

"I will be tactful and not point out how maladroit you are." She took the cuff of his left sleeve and began to ease it downward. He didn't wear a tight fashionable coat. It came right off. She made one of those disapproving French shrugs. "You are hurt. Why did you fall off a damned horse? And where?"

"Careful. That's sore. I fell off . . . somewhere." He honestly didn't remember. He'd been moving for ten days straight, eating in the saddle, sleeping rolled in a blanket in the bushes. "I think it was yesterday. I was going downhill."

"You have no affinity for horses. That is strange in an Englishman."

Two floors downstairs, somebody tinkled away at a piano. Skillful about it, for all he knew. They had one of the best pianists in France working in La Pomme d'Or. It went along with the best food and the best paintings on the wall. The best women.

Justine wasn't one of the women. The French Police Secrète hadn't made her a whore, though they might have tried it. She was Owl, who confounded them all and went her own way. So far as he knew, the only man she slept with was him.

He never told her he didn't go to other women. For five years it had been only her. Nobody else. Nobody, not even when it was months that went by without seeing her. He wouldn't have admitted that under torture.

She slipped his coat down over his shoulders and down his arms. Unbuttoned his waistcoat. His senses filled up with swirls of the apricot color she wore and the sweep of her hair. Everything about her flowed like water.

He'd have let her hurt his ribs, just for the pleasure of feeling her hands on him. But she didn't hurt when she undressed him. She was neat and quick, getting his shirt untucked, pulling it off over his head.

His shirt joined his coat and waistcoat on the floor. She ran her fingers lightly over his chest, up and down his ribs. "You look as if you have been laid upon the road to be trampled by an advancing army. You have many bruises, for one thing. They are very ugly."

"You, on the other hand, are luminous as daybreak. Exquisite as . . ."

"Sit," she said. "On the bed. And be silent. I do not wish you to collapse facedown on the floor and become even more inconvenient to me. You have burned yourself away to nothing at all."

Pain jabbed in his side when he sank down. Linen sheets on the bed and one light blanket. Everything was orderly, simple, well arranged. Everything said "Owl."

He sighed out a deep breath. "It was a long ride."

"So you fall from the horse because you are exhausted. I am all out of patience with you." Her hands were light on his shoulders. "If you are determined to kill yourself, ask me to do it. I would earn great praise in certain quarters if I brought you down. Have you broken any bones? There is a surgeon downstairs in the parlor tonight, only half drunk. I can bring him to you."

"There are two hundred and six bones in the human body and not one of them is broken. Remarkable, isn't it?" Who'd told him how many bones a man had? Doyle maybe. Or Pax. They carried that kind of useless information in their heads.

Her breasts, small, perfect, and kissable, rose and fell, about six inches from his mouth. He wanted to start, right there, and taste his way across her body. He wanted to put his head down onto her breasts and fall asleep. "Feels like I've been beaten with rods. Very Turkish."

"One may expect you to explore such novelties. You are very stupid to fall off horses, but I do not suppose you will change."

"For you, my sweet—"

"Oh, be silent. Your boots demonstrate all the reasons women should not entertain men in their rooms. I will remove them so you do not suffer doing it. I am a marvel of sensitivity every time I am with you. I astound myself sometimes."

He must have closed his eyes. When he opened them, she was at his feet, taking his boot in her hands. The sight of her, kneeling between his legs with her hair spread out over the edible, edible silk on her shoulders . . . He couldn't have found words anywhere on earth, in any language.

Inevitable, wasn't it? He could barely move, but he managed to get roused up like a rabbit. He was almost too tired to talk, but he wasn't too tired to spring up hard, pointing to Owl like a compass seeking north. What they had between them was natural as breathing. Always. Every time.

He didn't try to touch her, just looked. That was the joy of being a man. Looking was its own reward. Hunger welled up, and it felt warm and fine.

"You are not entirely exhausted." Dry words from Owl. She took on the second boot, being gentle. "Do you plan to use this particular yard of gallantry, perhaps?"

He laughed. She could make him laugh. "I'm filthy. I don't belong in any woman's bed, least of all yours. But, damn, I want you."

"So I see. I am vastly flattered." When she stood, silk like apricots, like peaches, flowed across his thighs. Cool yellow fire, infinitely tempting. "You are in several sorts of pain tonight, are you not? I will get you a brandy."

She kept brandy on the shelf with her books. Wasted on him, of course. He'd never told her he liked gin better. He could admit he'd killed an Austrian captain, who needed it, but he wouldn't tell her he drank gin by choice. She'd think worse of him.

"This particular brandy, they make near my old home from the lees of the grape harvest. It is very potent." She gave one of her fugitive grins and went looking for a glass.

Women move different from men. Their joints don't fit as tight. They glide from place to place without any obvious assistance in the way of bones and muscle involved.

Narrow and clever feet slipped in and out of the slit in the peignoir, not making a sound on the floorboards. Her toes were naked and pink as raspberries. One day soon, when he didn't ache so much, he was going to kiss her toes. Take them into his mouth and suck on them, one by one. She'd twitch when he did that. He liked it when she twitched. "I kiss your hands and feet, *gnädige Fräulein*."

"That is very pretty. Your German accent has improved. Here. You will see this is the cut crystal you gave me in Vienna. I took a fancy to it and brought it back home with me." She held the glass till he had it firmly in both hands. "Tell me why you have tormented yourself and several horses, racing to Paris. It is not merely to see me."

"Oh. The usual. Civilization is coming to an end. War is imminent. The sky is falling and we have to go tack it up again."

He'd gone to Service headquarters first, to the new house over on the Left Bank. He'd dropped a copy of the letter in Pax's lap two hours ago. Carruthers was already calling in agents. Setting them to work.

His job was to tell the French. That was his assignment from London.

The Service knew he had a line into the French Secret Police. They didn't know it was Owl. Nobody knew about him and Owl.

Owl said, "And what is the usual?"

"It's not good. Give me a minute." He sipped eau-de-vie, which was strong enough to lift his brain case. "But I'm carrying one piece of good news. Hand me my coat, could you?"

The package was wrapped in his handkerchief and wedged into an inner pocket, beside his left-hand knife. He'd tried to protect it when he fell, but it looked a little flat. He slit the twine and handed it over.

Owl let brown paper wrapping drop to the floor. Pulled the end of a thin blue ribbon and let it fall. Slipped the lid off. She stood, holding the little painted box with the tips of her fingers. The ride from London was worth it, just to see her face go unguarded like that.

His small, unofficial commission. It wasn't the first time he'd played courier. "Rock cakes, they're called. In Sévie's case, one of those appropriate names. She sends her love and that letter. I'll tell her you enjoyed them, when she asks."

"You may do so, because I will." She ran a finger over the little brown cakes, then picked the folded letter from the side. "Drink the brandy. You're shaking."

She slid the lid back into place and set the box on the table, on top of the letter, so it was hidden. She wouldn't read it at once. She'd save it for later, savoring the moment as long as possible. He knew her so well.

"Just tired." He drank again. "Last time you gave me brandy was outside Zurich."

"When you came to warn me, in a benevolent manner. You were exhausted that time as well."

"And on the run."

"We both were. It is remarkable how often we manage to annoy the same people."

"The Austrians are easily annoyed."

"*C'est vrai.* Now, tell me why you have come from England. What matter is so serious you barely trust yourself to speak of it?"

"In my coat. I'll show you."

Owl did not hand him his jacket. She ransacked the pockets herself. If she hadn't been French, and blue-blooded and a spy, she would have been an ornament to any gang in London.

He sat on the bed and let the brandy sear his mouth where he'd bit his lip, falling. It didn't stop the shivering in his muscles. Didn't clear his head.

"One passport," she muttered, "in the name of Pierre Thibault, harmless citizen of Rouen. That is you. A handkerchief. One of your knives."

"I know what I'm carrying. Nothing interesting." He brought nothing into this house she couldn't see. Nothing the whole French Secret Police couldn't print in the newspaper.

"Do you know, you are almost stupid with not sleeping." She turned the coat over. "Now I find another of your knives. I do not know any man who has such a fascination with knives. A candle stub and a tinderbox. We are prepared for all eventualities, are we not? Playing cards. A set of picklocks. And one book . . . which seems to be a very dull survey of mining sites in France, published in Lyon. I do not suppose this is a clever work of codes."

"It's just a book about mines. What you want is in the front of that."

"Ah." She came to stand beside him while she opened the letter. "This is in English."

"It was written by an Englishman. The British embassy is full of them."

"Do not be facile." She read the letter quickly, from beginning to end, then looked over the second page more carefully. "There is much about buying a horse and complaints about his mistress. He finishes . . . he has overheard a plot and is it not curious? This Englishman, this John—"

"Millian. The Honorable John Millian, attached to the embassy in Paris."

"He claims to have overheard a conversation while he is at dinner somewhere—"

"The Palais Royale."

"He does not say which restaurant or café in the precincts of the Palais Royale, so it is useless. He does not say who spoke, so it becomes more useless. He records only part of what he has heard. He also spells it wrong. Why have you brought me this?"

"Because three days after writing that letter and sending it off to London, Millian fell out a window and splattered his brains across the Rue de l'Aiguillerie."

"Ah. That is unfortunate."

"Particularly for John Millian. He took a dozen strands of hair down to the street with him, torn out by the roots, clenched in his fist."

"He was not alone when he fell."

"So we assume. The letter got sent to London, and it struck his friend in the Foreign Office as so interesting, he sat on his thumbs for a month before he brought the letter to us. To the Service."

"Who send you posthaste to deal with it, at last. We are always called in when it is almost too late."

Three candles lit the room. She went to the closest and studied the effect of light shining through the paper. "There is no writing hidden. You will tell me there is no British code involved."

"None."

"I see no French code words. We are left with the dozen words your Monsieur Millian overheard." She frowned as she read, "*'La Dame est prête.'* That does not tell us so much. Only that the woman is ready."

"If that's even what he heard."

"We must trust it is, or we have nothing at all. Next, one says, '*À Tours.*' That is the city of Tours, I think. And then, '*L'Anglais arrange tout.*'"

"There's an Englishman who'll arrange everything."

"How nice for them," she said. "Then we learn, '*Le fou va aller à Paris.*' The fool is going to Paris. This means nothing."

"Except we're about to get another fool in Paris, a commodity with which the city is plentifully supplied."

"None of this says anything useful. The conspirators in the Palais Royale might as well have remained silent. They end with, '*Patiente. Napoléon va mourir en août. C'est certain.*'"

"He predicts Napoleon will die in August."

"But he will not. We will make sure of that. Your Monsieur Millian spells French vilely."

"The least of his faults. He also didn't speak French very well. There's no telling what he actually heard."

"'The woman is ready.' So a woman is involved. That is one solid bit of information. Tours is another, as is the Englishman who arranges everything. But the meat of this nut is that Napoleon will be attacked in August."

"Now you know what we know."

"It is already August."

"Yes." He closed his eyes. He'd memorized every pen stroke of the letter.

"So slight a messenger, this letter, to tell us of so great a disaster. You know what will happen if Napoleon is attacked by an Englishman."

"We'll be at war again." The treaty patched up between England and France had lasted for a year. It wouldn't hold forever, but any day men weren't shooting at each other was a good day for somebody.

"War. Within a week," Owl agreed.

Armies in the field. Thousands of men dead.

"*Casus belli.* Doyle called it that." Always had a way to wrap things up in some dead language, Doyle did. The cause of war. *Casus belli.*

That was why he was ordered to bring this letter to the French Secret Police. After ten years of fighting, rational men on both sides were sick of it.

"I will copy this." She folded the letter. "Several times. There are people I must inform. Give me your glass. You are finished with it."

"What? Oh. Yes." He put it in her hands. He should stand up and walk around to keep himself awake. Ask what the French knew about the plot, if anything. Put his shirt on. Leave. Find a bed at headquarters. Carruthers would want to talk to him. When he yawned and started to get up, Owl shoved him back to the bed.

"You will wait and not go wandering off into the night. You will probably fall into the Seine and drown."

He yawned again. Bone-cracking yawn. "I'm not fit to stay here. I should—"

"You should sit and be quiet. I must read this again." She studied him impatiently. "No. Lie down. You need not go anywhere, and I may have questions for you again. This is all you have? This one letter?"

"One letter. A couple mouthfuls of words spilled out in a Palais Royale restaurant or gaming den in front of a damned idiot who barely spoke French."

"It is not much to work with."

"It's so close to nothing it amounts to the same thing. The gods must love war. They're making it hard to stop this one."

He let her bully him into lying down. Let himself fall across the blanket. Let her swing his legs up on the bed. His muscles had turned to jelly and it didn't seem worthwhile trying to get up. He closed his eyes.

Not a soft bed. Justine didn't sleep in a soft bed. But the linen was worn silky by the turning of her body, night after night. The pillow smelled of her.

Paper crackled. Owl sat at the table, reading. Checking the words again and again.

She said, "I do not think it possible your Monsieur Millian made a mistake in the word *Anglais*. He will have heard it often."

"He probably got that part right."

"It may be code. 'The Englishman arranges everything' may speak of the arrival of some émigré or the storage of spikes and guns in a warehouse in Dijon. There are hordes of disgruntled royalists. This may be yet another band, with no living, breathing Englishman involved at all."

"Hope so."

He heard her uncork a bottle. Then the scratch of pen on paper. "August."

"Today's the tenth." He didn't have to tell her that.

"If it is to be in August, we have no more than twenty-one days." Her pen continued. "I will be canny in choosing where to place this information. There are men in my service who would like the war to resume, just as there are Englishmen who wish that."

"Yes."

She came to him, rising from her chair, crossing the room. Silk slithered like water spilled along his bare arm when she pulled the blanket across him. Like being licked. He was so tired. Too tired to say anything.

SHE copied Monsieur Millian's letter six times, in a fair approximation of his handwriting, in the exact lines and spacing he used, in case this turned out to be a cypher that depended on the placement of words. These would go to the three men most senior in her service, immediately. She must also take a copy to Leblanc, who would be useless but must be included. She would send one copy to Soulier, the Police Secrète's chief in London. She would keep one copy herself.

Napoleon must not die.

This filled her mind as she wrote the first copy and the second—the utmost seriousness of this task. Napoleon was all that held France together. He was the great man of this age. He renounced the worst excesses of the Republic but kept the great gains. Because Napoleon held France, all men could vote. The Jew, the Black, the poorest peasant in the field—every one of them was French and free. He even invited the émigrés back to France, without penalty, if they would only renounce the special privileges of noble blood.

The Republic had been purchased with rivers of blood. Only Napoleon could preserve it.

She would protect him and the Republic.

She tried not to think of Hawker while she wrote. It is a discipline to set aside pain and do one's work. It makes one strong.

After an hour, she finished and set the last pages aside to dry.

She held the quill, watching a drop of ink gather at the tip. *My lover is an Englishman. This cannot continue.*

Her bed was so full of Hawker. His body disconcerted her, always, with its fierce energies concentrated inside his skin. He lay on his back, half naked, his head turned toward her, his arm across his chest upon the sheet. She did not think he had broken any ribs, but he was holding pain inside him as he slept.

He lay, sunk fathoms deep in exhaustion. All the deadly knowledge of his blood and bone was quiescent. He was like a well-honed sword someone had carefully set down. Sometimes she forgot how beautiful he was when they had been apart for a long time.

The gathering of ink at the end of her pen would drop in an instant and make a mess of this clean sheet of paper. It would be stupid to let that happen, would it not? She touched quill to the lip of the ink bottle.

His country and mine will fight again. It is inevitable.

France, every day, showed the world that men could be free. The kings of Europe could not permit this. They were resolved to destroy the Republic. If an Englishman schemed to kill Napoleon, it was part of a larger plot to topple everyone into war.

We will be enemies when war comes.

Hawker made not the least noise or movement when he slept. It was as if he had trained himself to concealment, always and everywhere. He was the least trusting man she knew, but he trusted her. He should not. It pierced her like a knife that he would sleep so deeply in her bed. It was the last time he would do so.

It is over. We are no longer heedless children to take these wild risks.

She was the one who must end it. She was the practical one.

Now that the moment had come, she found she could not say the words to him. She slid a new sheet of paper forward, choosing a kind that was cheap and common everywhere. By habit, she wrote in an elegant hand that was not her own, and she did not address him by name. Such reasonable precaution was second nature. Letters can be a source of endless inconvenience.

My friend,

Our time together is finished. We have known from the beginning that this day would arrive when we would set

aside what has been between us. Let us part now, while
there are still no regrets or consequences.

I will send you any news I have of this new matter. You
know how to leave messages for me.

C

C for *chouette.* "Little owl." He sometimes called her that.

She rose. She folded Hawker's clothing and left it on a chair.
She brushed her hair in front of the mirror. She had thought
when women spoke of their heart breaking it was merely a way
of speaking. It was not. Very distinctly, in her chest, she felt the
crack inside her.

She would sleep alone from now on. There was no one else
she wanted.

She folded the several copies of Mr. Millian's letter together
to take with her and laid the original in the center of the table
for Hawker to find.

Her words to Hawker were quite dry. She set the letter on top
of his clothing and left him.

Twenty-seven

JUSTINE STOOD BEFORE THE DESK IN LEBLANC'S
office in the Tuileries and gazed past him, out the window,
down into the courtyard below, and ached tiredness. Her heart
also ached, but that was something she did not think about.

She acknowledged weariness somewhere in the recesses of
her mind and set the knowledge aside since there was nothing she could do about it. She had crisscrossed Paris, delivering
warnings to important, impatient men who did not like being
awakened before dawn. Between those trying interviews, she
had drunk four cups of very strong coffee. Or perhaps five. In
any case, a great deal. Tiny bright lights jittered and blurred at
the corners of her vision.

Leblanc was the last man to whom she must give the Millian
letter, and by far the most unpleasant. She might need his men
and resources, however. One deals with unpleasant men in any
hierarchy. It was the way of the world.

Leblanc's office was on the second floor of the Tuileries Palace with the rest of the Police Secrète. She had quite a good
view of the Louvre.

". . . which you claim is private correspondence," he sneered
at his copy of Millian's letter, "between a diplomat in Paris and

the British Foreign Office in London. Sent in the diplomatic pouch, doubtless."

"That is most likely."

"A letter transported with all elaborate precaution, in inviolate secrecy. Yet you obtained it easily."

"Not easily. It did not drop into my lap like cherry blossoms."

"Then how did it come into your hands?"

Leblanc would keep her standing here an hour, to no purpose whatsoever. He would ask stupid questions he knew she would not answer, merely to show he had the power to do so.

"I asked how you got this letter," he said. "Who gave it to you?"

She must be respectful. He was a senior officer. "I have exceptional sources." *Which I will not reveal to you.* "The letter is authentic."

"I will have his name."

"My sources are also Madame's sources. I do not think she wishes me to share them with you. I am not your agent, Monsieur."

"True. But one never knows what the future will hold, Mademoiselle Justine. You would do well to remember that."

Leblanc always attempted to steal resources, and Madame had been in Italy for months. Perhaps he thought Justine would be careless in Madame's absence, or vulnerable, or easily cowed. She was not.

She did not shrug in an openly disrespectful manner, which would be self-indulgence. She let her eyes drift past him, to the window, and paid no attention while he pointed out that anyone could copy a paper and say it came from some secret source.

She merely nodded and said, "Very true."

In the early morning, a dozen people crossed the pavements of the courtyard below, going from Tuileries to Louvre, or out through the great door that opened onto the Rue de Rivoli. These were not the fashionable, come to see the paintings and statues of the Louvre. These were workers and artists who concerned themselves with the exhibits, or they were men reporting to their work in the Tuileries Palace, to one of the offices of government. A few might be Police Secrète.

Some were servants—Napoleon's servants—sent out to buy peaches or bonbons or take his boots to the bootmaker. He lived in the apartments of the Tuileries, on the floor below this, where royalty had once been housed.

"You waste my time. This is some British stratagem." Leblanc flicked the Millian letter that she had so carefully copied. "If the Secret Police have not heard one whisper of this, it is simply a lie. This is nothing. This is invention."

She was accustomed to working with the master spies of this age. Madame, in an instant, would have brought six clever minds to deciphering this letter. Vauban would have tromped past ranks of Imperial Guard and warned Napoleon, face-to-face, one soldier to another. Soulier would have set informers loose in the Palais Royale, ears open. But Madame was in Italy. Vauban—oh, so greatly mourned—had only last week confounded the odds to die peacefully in bed. Soulier was far away, at his post in England.

Her mentors, who were the great master spies of the Police Secrète, were not in Paris. She was left to make reports to politic, expedient Leblanc, the man of jealousy and mean intrigues. It was inconvenient beyond words.

She said, "The Englishman is dead. Strangely, I find myself convinced."

"Men die." He tossed the letter onto a pile at the side of his desk. "It is the nature of things. The English bedevil us with their little Royalist plots and their secret, overheard conversations. They want to send us running in circles. You are young, Justine. Easily fooled. I am not a Madame Lucille in your Pomme d'Or to coddle you in such matters."

"And if the First Consul is in danger of death?"

"The streets of Paris breed thirty such rumors a week. The Household Guard is alert. They cannot be made more so with constant alarms that come to nothing. I will not bother to mention this to the commander. Or, perhaps . . ." He smiled. It was the smile an eel would make, in some dark pit of the water. "It matters so much to you, Justine?"

"I would not come to you if it did not matter."

He stood. Slowly, he walked toward her. She had the opportunity of backing away, but she did not. If she once retreated from such men, she would never stop. She straightened and faced him. She had faced worse than Leblanc.

"I am susceptible to the arguments of a lovely woman." He came too close. "Persuade me."

She did not mistake his meaning. "Be persuaded by the dead Englishman."

"We have spent many years working at cross purposes, you and I. It was never necessary. I bear you no enmity. You were caught in the old squabble I had with Lucille." He had small, mean eyes, like raisins. They were oddly dark to be set in a long, pale face. "You are an ambitious woman, Justine. Under my guidance, you can rise to any height in the Police Secrète. You have a section of your own and a dozen agents working for you. I can give you more. I can give you the Pomme d'Or and the many agents who report there."

"It is not yours to give. It belongs to Madame."

"All things change, chérie." He came within the length of an easy, casual touch. "I might reconsider this letter of Monsieur Millian. Perhaps it is worth investigating for—"

She caught his wrist, where he came to brush the skin of her neck, and held it, digging her nails in. "I am not one of the women of La Pomme d'Or, Monsieur."

"I did not think you were."

Since she was a child, she had studied the faces of many men, fearing them and hating them. She had catalogued Leblanc's expressions carefully, because he was the enemy of Madame, and thus, her enemy. This was Leblanc, coldly, stiffly furious.

He smiled. "You are more attractive than they are, in so many ways." He turned away. "We will reach a better understanding someday soon. Go. Play with your intrigues of the Englishman and fools and the woman of Tours. Pursue this phantom. Go question this mysterious source of yours. Report to me what progress you make."

Leblanc was a man of cold rages and of long vengeance. She had offended him. If she had been one of his cadre, without Madame's protection, she would have been very afraid.

Twenty-eight

JUSTINE HELD HER CUP AND CLOSED HER EYES, CON-
sidering and reconsidering each phrase of Monsieur Millian's
letter. She whispered, "'*La Dame est prête.*' The woman is
ready."

The day was warm. She sat in the shade of the huge arches of
the Palais Royale. The Café Foy made the most lovely coffee, but
she did not drink it. She only held it and let her thoughts finger
first one phrase and then another from that letter. "What woman
and what is she ready to do?" There were no obvious answers.
Certainly none inside her. "If she is ready, why must they wait
until August?"

"Because the fool hasn't showed up yet."

Hawker.

She jerked in surprise and opened her eyes. A drop, only, of
her coffee spilled and fell upon the table.

Hawker stood beside her, casually inspecting the café and
all within it. He laid his cane down, slantwise. It was elegantly
black with a silver head, in the shape of a skull, which grinned
in her direction, pleased with Hawker's little triumph.

She would not be flustered. She had known Hawker would
track her down and confront her. He had simply been very
quick about it. The letter of Monsieur Millian mentioned the

Palais Royale, where he had overheard the plotters. It was entirely predictable she would come here.

She hated to be predictable. "Go away. We should not be seen together."

He did not leave. "And we never do anything we're not supposed to." As if fastidious, he inspected the chair, then lifted it and placed it just so. He settled himself, arranging his coat, lifting the fabric of his trousers to let it lie easily. A raised index finger signaled the waiter.

Anyone passing saw friends, meeting by chance at the Café Foy.

She said, "I suppose you are angry with me," and did not look at him

"Why the hell should I be angry? I wake up and you've left me a damn letter saying you're tired of me. Fine. Just fine." The civilized veneer of Monsieur Adrian Hawkhurst was sometimes very thin indeed.

She said, "I did not say I was tired of you."

"The hell you didn't."

"I said we will no longer be lovers."

"You didn't say it. You wrote me a buggering letter."

She had seen Hawker truly angry only three times. He became incalculable and menacing when he was angry.

He did not dismay her in the least. "It was a gracefully written letter and took me considerable time to compose. We have been foolish. Now we will cease to be foolish."

"Oh, right. We're going to embrace good sense, you and me. We're going to be prudent. Fuck that."

"There is no need to be crude."

Silence fell because the waiter was hurrying in Hawker's direction to be attentive. This was the same waiter who had been leisurely in attending to her. Now, he chose to bestir himself.

She waited. Hawker ordered coffee and a carafe of water, taking his time. Maddeningly, taking his time. He saw there were pastries. Fresh? They had been made today? The waiter was quite sure? Then he would have one of those. They discussed apple and plum, to settle at last on apple.

The waiter went away. She fumed at Hawker for a time, but silently, and watched him from under her lashes. She drank coffee. Hawker ignored her. At last she said, "I am not tired of you."

"Well, then. That makes it all right."

"We are no longer the young fools to indulge ourselves in this way."

Deep voiced, slowly, he said, "I like indulging you."

Old memories swept in. Nights of generosity shared. The dark of hidden beds. Days side by side in fields and woods, lying, watching the clouds whirl by overhead, talking and touching.

She curled her hands where they rested in her lap and a pang of emotion struck through her. She desired him unreasonably and completely, at this moment, in this inconvenient place. She remembered his body with an intimacy deep as the memory of her own.

She could not help herself. She lifted her eyes to him.

He was dark and vital, every feature finely chiseled, and all of them unreadable.

She had seen him in rags so often, or in the clothes of a laborer or dockworker, it was almost disconcerting to see him dressed respectably. As always, he was perfect in his role. He wore rich gray of several shades. The sober waistcoat carried a thin silver thread. The glint of silver was the small jarring note, almost flirting with vulgarity, which made the disguise human and fallible and utterly believable.

All the world would observe what he wanted them to see—a handsome young fop of the town, lounging at ease, his legs stretched out. Only she saw the iron of his muscle and knew that he carried three, or possibly four, knives. Knew that his pretty walking stick was lead-weighted and heavy as a cudgel.

No one here, except her, saw that he was angry.

The waiter returned to place coffee and apple tart, water and a glass before Hawker, who accepted this service with nonchalance and waved him away, his role today being that of a dandy of means and taste. Arrogance came naturally to Hawker.

He set his fork into the crust of the tart and gave it a taste. Approved. Wiped his lips delicately. Put the napkin on the table. "It's been five years, I guess. Since that first time."

"Almost exactly." She could have told him to the day. She could have told him how many times they had met since then, and where. She suspected he too knew every minute they had stolen to spend together.

He put sugar in his coffee. "Five years. After five years, I fall asleep in your bed and when I wake up, you've ended it. No warning."

"I do not prolong the inevitable."

"You're a practical woman."

"I did what was needed. Quickly. Cleanly. We make a break with our past mistakes. It does not mean there is no fondness between us. It does not mean we cannot meet and talk like rational people. Only one thing has changed." She took a deep breath. "We are no longer lovers."

"And you couldn't say that to my face?"

"There was no reason." She turned her coffee cup so the handle was exactly to the side. So the spoon in the saucer was aligned just so. "There is nothing to discuss."

"We're discussing it now." He said that pleasantly.

"And I find nothing to say." She was not afraid of his anger, which she had encountered before, in full force. He was cold and deadly and he lied routinely, for the Game of Spies, for fun, for profit. She trusted him more than any man she had ever encountered.

In the quiet of the morning, the great expanse of the Palais Royale held only a few dozen loungers and saunterers. The tables of Café Foy were mostly empty under the calm of the stone columns and the huge trees. Men played checkers at one. At another, three soldiers of the garde engaged in a game of cards. An old woman poured coffee into her saucer and set it down for the tiny yappy dog at her feet. Solitary men read newspapers under the clear and blue autumn sky.

"It's always been your right to end it," he said. "Always the woman's prerogative. Ten words would do it. I just thought you'd face me, when the time came."

"Perhaps . . . I have been cowardly."

"Well, yes. Stripping down to the bare and quivering skin of it, you have been." Hawker's bite of sarcasm.

Bold brown sparrows hopped about the ground between the tables, picking up crumbs. She watched them. "There is a long tradition of such letters, you know. They place a necessary distance. They do not release words one will regret later. It is easy to say too much in such cases."

"You got discretion down to a fine art. Why, Owl? Why now?"

She told him. She owed him much more than such a simple explanation. "I have been advanced in the Police Secrète. I have men and women working for me now. I cannot behave foolishly anymore."

"I'll have to congratulate you on your promotion, won't I?"

"It is a small one, as these things go. A cadre of twelve." He thought she had weighed him against advancement in her profession and discarded him as nothing. It was not true. She set him aside because one day she might no longer choose her work over him.

That was why they must end this intimacy between them. Not because it was foolish—though it was. Not because it was dangerous and close to treason. Because they had come to mean too much to each other.

She had hurt him. She had not meant to do that. She had not known she could. "I was wrong to dismiss you, coldly, in a letter. I ask you to forgive me."

"I will eventually."

"You are all that is kind."

"I should let you stew awhile, first."

"That would be salutary. But then, you would not hear my thoughts upon Monsieur Millian's letter, would you?"

"We'll talk about that. In a bit, we'll talk about being lovers. You might," he glanced up, "reconsider."

"Do not delude yourself." She did not trust the many resolves that lurked behind his bland placidity while he toyed with the apple tart. But he was no longer angry. "Meanwhile, there is a trivial little riddle before us that will change the course of the world for the next several centuries. Perhaps it deserves our attention when we are quite through with the matter of who shall sleep with whom?"

"Go ahead." Hawker leaned back and folded his arms before him.

"'*La Dame est prête.*' The woman is ready. She is at the start of this, I think, whoever she is."

"The most efficient of the lot, anyway. So we know one of them is a woman. A Frenchwoman."

"It is not so uncommon for French conspirators to be women. We are a hardy breed in France. There is this also . . . Millian wrote those words with capitals—'*La Dame*'—as if it were a title. That is the way he heard it, I think."

Hawker's hand stilled from the restless play he made, finger upon finger, tapping. "Yes. That makes sense."

"It is an . . . an old-fashioned way to speak. A respectful

way. One might say 'La Dame' of a very old woman. Or an aristo. It adds the flavor of disgruntled Royalists."

"Or he didn't hear 'La Dame' at all. He heard 'La Place Vendôme' or 'the dome of St. Paul's' or some other fool thing."

She opened a gesture around her coffee cup, agreeing. "It may be. Or this may be a code. Amateurs love their codes."

"Oh yes. We have our own amateurs."

"'La Dame' may be a box or a book or a fifty-year-old veteran of the Vendée. 'Tours' may be the steps of Notre Dame. 'Le fou' may be an army unit or gunpowder or a shipment of boots."

"In which case we'll never figure it out." Hawker had become brisk and practical. "Let's stick to possibilities. We got 'The Lady.'" He dipped a finger in his glass and took a drop of water to draw a line on the tabletop. "We got 'Tours.' Something or someone in Tours."

"I would hazard the British Service has sent men to Tours."

"Don't fish for information." He drew another line. "Tours is a sleepy provincial town a hundred miles to the southwest. What's happening in Tours?"

"I have no idea. It is a city that plays a very small part in the life of France. I do not think of Tours from one month to the next."

"Napoleon's not going there?"

"Not at all. I have inquired—not once, but from three sources within the Tuileries Palace. There is no journey to Tours."

"So we think of places in Paris. La Tour du Temple. La Tour Saint-Jacques."

"La Tour is simply 'the tower.' It could be the tower of any church in the city."

"So we stack up another pile of nothing useful." He wet his forefinger again and drew a third line. "'Le fou.' The madman. The fool."

"Which is obvious. Only a mad fanatic would attempt this assassination. It tells us nothing. The supply of fanatics is inexhaustible."

"And we come to the Englishman."

"Of which there is also an endless supply. We have nothing."

Under the canopy of linden trees in the great courtyard, women chattered like exotic monkeys. They pushed their chairs close together and leaned against each other and passed something back and forth to coo over it. Something small that glinted in the sun. She could not see exactly what it was—a jewel, a gilt box, a painted miniature, a bottle of perfume. One could buy anything in the shops of the arcade of the Palais Royale.

They were some years older than she was, entirely lighthearted and pleased with themselves. They made her feel centuries old.

Hawker had barely touched his apple tart. Delicately, she slid his plate to her side of the table and began to eat, using his fork. "I have questioned three senior officers of my service, also several operatives who feel the pulse of Paris in their blood. They know nothing. All morning I have rolled a madman, a lady, an Englishman, and the Palais Royale around in my mind like so many peppermint drops in a mouth. I am no wiser."

"I spent the last three hours talking to Millian's idiot friends at the British embassy. Nobody was with him. Nobody knows where he was when he overheard all that."

"Gaming rooms, restaurants, shops. There is a whorehouse, also, though it calls itself a club. He might even have been here where we sit. The Café Foy is the veteran of many conspiracies." She pointed with the fork to the arches of the colonnade. "See there? Desmoulins stood on that table and sent the mob marching on the Bastille. It was the first great strike of the Revolution. Men are impelled to rashness by the coffee of the Café Foy."

"Might be. But I wouldn't conspire here if a damn Englishman was sitting at the next table."

"I would not also."

"Cross off the cafés. You'd go someplace with men coming and going, crowded together, talking. The gaming rooms."

But he spoke almost at random. The feral animal inside him looked out of his eyes. He reached out. "You have sugar. Here." He touched the side of her mouth. When he took his fingers away, she saw the fine sparkle of sugar grains. He licked his fingers.

She knotted inside and scooped in a sudden breath. She . . . wanted. *This will stop. When I accept that I cannot have him, this will stop.*

He said, "It's been a while since we sat and drank coffee."

The Piazza San Marco of Venice. Carnevale. He had worn the costume of a corsair, his shirt open at the neck, a red sash at his waist, a small gold ring in his ear. The saber was quite genuine.

She was avoiding the corrupt and brutal police of the Austrians that night. England was the ally of the Austrians. But Hawker had taken her to the *pensione* on Via Ottaviano, saying,

"The town's overrun with French spies. You're my spy. Let them find their own."

For all of Carnevale they had strolled the city together, masked, and pretended they were not enemies. She'd kissed the pirate ring in his ear, tasting gold and the hint of blood. He'd pierced himself to wear it. He was always a man of precision in his disguises. The taste of Hawker was . . . She swallowed and remembered. The nights had been a rough insanity and the tenderness that follows madness.

Hawker watched her from the hot core of his eyes. "You're distracting me."

"We distract one another. This must stop. Talk to me about the Palais Royale. If it is our only clue—"

The waiter approached, bringing her a second cup of coffee, taking away the old, glancing into the bowl that held its small lumps of sugar. He came and took himself and his small round tray away, all in a single movement as expert as the transit of a hummingbird to and from a flower.

Hawker said, "I'll come back tonight with some men. We'll walk around, listening in the gaming hells. You do the same with those dozen people you got." He pulled at his lower lip, something he did when he was thinking.

I know his lips. I know the taste and texture of them at every hour of the night. I have kissed his lips a thousand times.

Never again. Never. Never. Never. She made herself pour water from the carafe into her glass. Made herself drink. The fabric of her dress scraped her breasts when she breathed, she had become so sensitive.

Hawker's hand slid across the table till it just touched her, the back of his hand to the back of hers. "I'm not pushing you, Owl. It's your choice. Always been your choice."

"But you will be persuasive." At the core of her body, the memory of him inside her arose, sweet and tenacious.

"I am that." He grinned. "We are about to be invaded by the English."

She could hear them. From the shops of the arcade, commenting loudly in their native language, a pack of four young gentlemen approached. They swaggered in a line, arms linked, loud, expensively rigged out, unkempt, pushing everyone from their path. They came from the gambling rooms on the floors above where they had spent the night drinking and losing money.

She murmured, "I see why Mr. Millian met the end he did. It is surprising the English are not more frequently defenestrated."

"You're too harsh."

Englishmen swooped upon the Café Foy in a jangle of fobs and a great clumping of riding boots, the many capes of their coats flapping as they walked, the lapels of their jackets wide as outspread wings. They would take breakfast, they said to one another and all the world. The waiter tried to lead them to a spot distant from anyone, behind a pillar, but they ignored him and shoved their way between chairs toward where she sat with Hawker. They sprawled into seats at the next table, bare inches away, close enough to share their reek of drink and tobacco.

The waiter brought brandy and glasses for them without being asked and was rude, addressing them as '*tu*,' which they did not have knowledge enough to resent. He pretended to understand no English in the hopes they would go away to find their beefsteak and ham elsewhere.

They were persistent. Beefsteak they would have or know the reason why. Really, what sensible man would eat food served by a waiter he had offended?

The waiter bowed apologetically to her as he left, then to the old woman nearby who had picked up her dog into her arms protectively.

The café was allowed to listen to a recounting of the nighttime exploits of four well-to-do foreign louts. They were frank in their opinion of the women of the Palais Royale and Frenchwomen in general. The old woman and her dog departed. The pretty young ladies under the linden trees arose and went back to shopping their way down the arcade.

Then the Englishmen became interested in her. "Pretty little bird," one said to the other, staring at her rudely. "Damn, but that's a fine pullet. Think she'll come back down when she's finished servicing the black ram?"

"I know where I'd like her to come down."

"Come down for breakfast. She can breakfast on me."

"She can wrap those sweet lips around my sausage anytime."

Men of such high good humor. Did they imagine no one spoke English?

She shrugged ruefully, "It is my fault, 'Awker, that our peace is done. I will leave." It was a tame surrender, to be chased from their coffee by such apes, but agents do not engage in public brawls. "I must arrange for this evening, in any case. Shall we meet at—"

If Leblanc had not been furtive, she would not have noticed him.

Leblanc stood fifty feet away, half hidden by a column, inspecting the merchandise of a seller of opera glasses and scientific instruments. The hunch of his shoulder shouted hidden purpose. The angle of his head spoke of surreptition.

He had not followed her here. She would have noticed. He came because he knew she would, to interest himself in her investigations and to snoop into her sources.

He was no practiced field agent, Leblanc. He was a political and scheming animal. He had not even changed his coat from their meeting this morning.

"Do not turn around," she said. "Face more to the right."

Hawker was so instantly upon guard, the snap of fingers took longer. His arm remained relaxed upon the back of a chair. His dark, ironic expression did not change in the least. But his fingers went to close over his cane.

"Why should I not look left?" he said genially.

"I do not choose to share your face with others. Their curiosity is intrusive."

He slipped a coin on the table, under the edge of the plate. "Someone is interested in us? How delightful. Do we know who it is?"

"A man I know. Do not turn to look."

His snuffbox held a polished mirror inside. He already held it in his hand and examined the world behind him. "The gentleman with an interest in opera glasses. Who is he?"

How annoying he should spot Leblanc at once. "If you do not know him, I will certainly not enlighten you. Stand, bow once, walk away, and do not show your face. I will meet you at the shop that sells fans, at the end of the arcade, at sunset."

"We'll be more creative than that. Watch."

"Do not—"

He took up the cane as he stood. "*Ma chérie*, let us go." He was so gentlemanly. He bowed as he took her hand. His cane . . .

One of the Englishmen had tipped his chair back on two legs so he might sprawl even more inelegantly. Somehow Hawker's cane encountered the chair.

The chair spilled backward. The Englishman fell with a yelp

and a flailing of arms. Hawker sprang back to avoid him and knocked into another Englishmen. Stumbled. Was tossed against a third.

Oh, the consternation. Hawker in his heavily accented English helped one man to his feet, brushed another, unaccountably bumped into the last. Apologizing. Explaining. Dropping his cane. Picking it up. And never showing his face to Leblanc.

Oh, the annoyance and outrage of the Englishmen. The spilled brandy. The curses.

"I make ten thousand apologies." Hawker bobbed from the waist. "It is my fault entirely."

"Watch yourself, damn it."

"I hurry myself. I did not see. I am only concerned to take my lady away from here and I do not notice the so-English polite gentlemen. Come, I will leave coin with the waiter to pay in some small way for this inconvenience I cause you. See. I call for more brandy." And he waved.

"Clumsy oaf."

"I am clumsy. Yes. Unforgivably so. But I think only to avoid the petty thieves. It is the hazard of this place, that it is replete of pickpockets. I forget myself in my fear of them."

"What do ya mean, pickpockets?"

"They are everywhere. Like the ticks of the dog. And this morning, most of all." Hawker reassured himself, pocket by pocket, as he spoke. Pat. Pat. Vest and jacket. "Yes. All is well still. The waiter tells me he recognizes a most notorious pickpocket. A man called the Swift Finger he is so well known." His gesture led the eyes toward the distant Leblanc. "He comes close, that one. Brazen. You, yourself, have passed him not a moment ago. It is a scandal that such fleas prey upon us, is it not?"

And her Hawker slipped fingers into the last man's pocket. No one saw but her. He let her see.

Sometimes, in a play, there will be a single scene that makes it memorable. The actors reach a height of art that surpasses all others. Hawker's bow, as he kissed his hand and bid a ceremonious farewell was that moment. "I wish you an interesting visit to Paris, gentlemen."

He took her arm to lead her away. They had gone perhaps a hundred steps before the first of the Englishmen noticed his watch was missing.

"We just keep walking," Hawker murmured.

"I am not an infant in these matters. I know what to do." So she did not look over her shoulder to see what happened, only listened to the outraged boots inexorably headed in Leblanc's direction.

Twenty-nine

THEY STROLLED, ARM IN ARM, NOT DAWDLING, NOT hurrying, away from the distant commotion that was Leblanc discussing with four Englishmen the theft of . . . "What did you take, 'Awker?"

"A little of this. A little of that. Not everything." He sounded regretful. "I took a ring from the man who talked about your lips."

"He should not have called you a ram, meaning an insult."

"I took that as a compliment, but I took his ring too. Nice heavy piece of gold." His head was up, like a hunting dog scenting the wind. "Let's get out of the open for a while." They passed a shop that sold music boxes. The next displayed violins and violas, in mellow womanly shapes of maple wood.

He pressed something metal into her palm, cold and heavy. "Turn it on your finger, facing in."

Which told her the bare bones of his plan. She put the ring on her left hand, third finger, and faced the signet inward so it was hidden. Only the band showed. That easily, she was a married lady.

The shops of the Palais Royale lined up one after another under the arcade, each one bright and inviting. All the booty of the world was gathered together here, and every example was the best of its kind. Jewels, fans, handkerchiefs, dressing tables, ribbons, ivory carvings, whores. If you could not buy it within the Palais Royale, it was probably not worth buying.

He chose a shop a dozen feet onward and drew her into it. This one sold rugs from the Orient. These were not carpets to cover the floor, but works of art to be displayed on the walls.

A long mahogany counter separated the shop from the walkway of the arcade. The owner, a wizened man who was also the color of mahogany, leaned his elbows on one of the gems of his collection, thrown over the counter. A brass samovar and tiny china cups stood ready at his right for the entertainment of clients. Behind him, two hundred—three hundred—rugs were piled one upon the other in stacks as high as a man.

Hawker was already at the counter, negotiating. ". . . her husband follows." A gold coin appeared between fingers. "He is a dolt. A selfish brute." It would be a coin Hawker had just stolen, of course. A coin from one of the drunken Englishmen. ". . . a man without the taste to appreciate his gentle flower."

Gentle flower? We stray into the realm of fairy tale.

Hawker was speaking now in another language. Arabic? Hebrew? Turkish? He was endlessly curious. It would not amaze her to discover he had involved himself in studying any of these.

The words in his own tongue surprised and delighted the rug merchant. The coin disappeared. They were bowed into the rich cave of a shop, to walk on rugs crossed two and three deep.

"Here. Behind the counter. If you will . . . Yes. It's quite soft. Very soft. These are the finest." A dozen rugs were piled upon one another, laid flat. The brown hand waved. "Sit. No one will see you."

The topmost rug was a checkerboard of squares, each with the design of a flower. Soft as silk. Perhaps it was silk. Rugs could be made of silk. A memory came of her home, the chateau, in the country and long ago, stroking a rug like this, soft as a kitten.

"My cousin keeps the gold shop, there. See. No one will be surprised if I drink tea with him for a few minutes. This time of the morning I am less use in this shop than the cat." The cat, a black fellow with not a hair of white on him, had been motionless on the highest tower of carpets. He sprang down from stack to stack and made a regal exit as the iron lattice rattled its way across the entrance of the shop.

Hawker spoke again in the same language, a phrase that

called forth laughter. Then he ducked down behind the counter, beside her on the pile of rugs. They were together in the dimness of the shop.

"Five or ten minutes should do it, then we'll double back on the trail. We'll leave separately." Hawker let his head rest back against the wood. His knees were folded in close with his arms resting on top. "Our merchant is across the way, and he's watching. Don't try to make off with one of the rugs."

"I had planned to stuff a few in my bodice and disappear into the alleyways. How much did you lighten those Englishmen, *mon vieux*?"

"Couple of watches, two little sacks of coins, and that ring you're wearing."

It was half light inside this shop, like dusk, but she could see him clearly. Everything smelled sleepily pleasant. Cardamom, tobacco, and some thick musk she could not identify. Possibly that was the smell of sheep. "It is a valuable ring. You should dispose of it and the watches. Also any banknotes you have acquired. They are incriminating."

He turned his head, lazily, toward her. "You're teaching me the thieving trade now, are you?"

"I would not presume."

"You'd presume to teach the devil to make fire. What's the name of this man we're hiding from?"

"He is someone I do not like." She allowed herself to smile. Allowed herself to relax, entirely, against this barrier of wood behind her. Truly, when she was with Hawker she lost all sense of prudence. "You set drunken Englishmen upon him. With any luck, they will call the gendarmes. I am altogether delighted with you."

"Are you in trouble, Owl? With your people?" He could have been staring through her like glass, staring into her bones, the way he studied her. "I'm not prying for secrets. I just want to know."

"All is well with me."

"They set somebody to following you—that man who came into the arcade. You're scared of him."

"I am wary of him."

He touched her shoulder lightly, as if he could read what was inside her with the skin of his fingertips. Perhaps he could. "This is fear. I never saw a service eat its own people like the

Police Secrète does." He pushed her hair back behind her ear, so he could look at her. "I make your life difficult, don't I? I put you in danger."

"I have a hundred explanations ready if anyone connects us. I will tell them I seduce secrets out of you. They will believe me."

"It's still not safe. I'm like a boy with honey cakes. I'm hungry—starving really—for you. I don't think." He took his hand away and sat back.

"You are not alone. 'Awker, I starve myself for you as well."

"Right. That makes me feel much better, that does. Both of us starving. Just marvelous."

His jacket fell open around him, pulled by the weight of the knives he carried in the secret pockets inside. He slouched beside her. The gray waistcoat fitted his body as close as skin, showing a man of lean muscle. A tomcat of a man. A sleek, imperturbable hunter. The strength of him, the danger, the coiled spring of unlikely possibilities that was Adrian Hawker— all contained within that elegance.

Honey cakes. He was the very ideal and pattern of forbidden honey cakes, this one.

"You wonder why I did not say good-bye, 'Awker." She pulled her skirts loose and rolled to kneel beside him. Now they were face-to-face, as he had demanded. "This is why. I would have wanted to do this. I would have let myself have one last . . ." Her hands went to one side of his face and to the other. She cradled him and drew herself down to him and kissed his mouth. "Taste."

The effort to touch him lightly—to feel his lips open and not consume him—left her shaking.

He went still, not kissing back. When she opened her eyes, he was looking up at her. "You don't want this."

"Not again. Not anymore. This is saying good-bye."

He eased away. Left her lips. His hands on her shoulders were warm iron covered by velvet, and he held her till there was space between them. "If that's good-bye, it's just as well we didn't start saying it."

"That is what I thought." From her belly, trembling rose in waves. Her skin prickled.

"Don't do that to me again," he said.

"I will not. It is not fair."

"It's likely to get you tupped on a pile of rugs." He ran his hand over the silk beneath them. Over the rug. "It's soft enough. And I could make you like it. Don't think I couldn't."

"I am sorry. I—"

"You're trusting a lot to a man of my background and proclivities. You don't want to find out how we do things in Whitechapel, Chouette." But in the middle of speaking, his voice changed. "It's a chessboard."

"Upon the rug? No. It is only squares. They make such rugs in . . . What?"

He shook her shoulders, where he held her. "I figured it out. I know."

"You have figured what out?"

"*La dame, le fou, la tour.*" He pushed up to his feet. "Chess. They're all chess pieces." He grabbed her hand and pulled her to her feet. "Listen to me. It's chess. *La tour*—it's not Tours, the town. It's 'the tower.' It's the chess piece. The castle. It's chess pieces."

"*Le fou.* What you English call the bishop on the chessboard. *La dame.* What you call the queen. They are chess pieces. And the most famous chess club in the world is the Café de la Régence."

"In the Palais Royal. We could throw a stone from this shop and hit it." He blazed satisfaction. "It makes sense. Chess. Damn, but I'm good."

"You are more than adequate." He was her Hawker, and he was brilliant. "We will meet there tonight. You may walk in the door and play chess, but I must coerce the owner into giving me some plausible role. That is a café for men only."

He was already pacing back and forth across the rugs. Thinking. Plotting. Muttering to himself. Had she not seen this a hundred times? She had never wanted him more.

She said, "I must leave. This will require preparation." And because there was no one else to tell him this, "You have been clever. You are very, very clever."

Thirty

THE CAFÉ DE LA RÉGENCE WAS FULL OF CHESS PLAY-
ers and spies. Hawker had put himself with his back to the wall,
near the door, where he could keep an eye on both.

It was well past midnight. Outside, under the huge lamps in
the arches of the arcade, the nightly promenade of the Palais
Royale had slowed to a trickle. Patrons of the opera strolled
past, headed home. Even this late, a few English tourists wandered about, absorbing Paris sophistication, helping pickpockets earn a living. A trio of Napoleon's garde rattled by in dress
uniform, come from the gambling dens upstairs. The women
who sauntered by in twos and threes were harlots.

In the café, a dozen men were still playing. Another thirty-
odd watched or sat at tables, the way he did, reading the paper
and drinking.

Pax was two tables away, twenty moves into a game. He'd
dressed like a university student—untidy, with a loose, open
collar. His hair was its natural color, loose down his neck, spilling along cheekbones when he leaned to the board. You'd swear
he wasn't thinking about anything but chess.

Owl walked the room, carrying a tray and wiping down
tables, representing the French side of the spying fraternity.

For Hawker, it was the end of a long evening of wandering

from table to table, brushing shoulders, listening. Nobody mentioned killing Bonaparte. They talked about chess. Spying was more of a challenge than stealing, overall, but there were times it'd bore a corpse.

Owl came up behind him. "I have brought more brandy, even though you have not finished what you have." She leaned over him to set a tiny glass on the table. She was entirely plausible as a Parisian serving maid—deft, impudent, graceful.

"Did you have trouble," he looked her over, "slipping in here?"

"None. When an agent of the Police Secrète indicates she wishes to become a serving maid, the owner of a café does not ask questions. They think I am here to listen for sedition. They are all afraid of the Police Secrète, here in Paris, which is wise of them."

"My own service can't throw men in prison, just on our say-so. One of those disadvantages I labor under." He took a sip of brandy. He drank aquavit in the German states, grappa in Italy, brandy in Paris. In London, mostly gin. None of it had much effect on him.

"You will be pleased to know you present the most realistic appearance of a young man of fashion. One is convinced you have plucked the very pomegranate of life and sucked it dry and tossed the husk away."

"That presents a picture."

"*Mais, oui.* To be a serving maid is to observe life at its most raw. I have been entirely disillusioned of all my ideals. Do you see that young man in the corner in the most excellently cut jacket? He has been here all evening. He orders one *vin ordinaire* and is faithful to it as if they were married in church. All this time he has been slipping sugar cubes into his pocket."

"It's a sad and dishonest world."

"When I say this, few people contradict me. I have decided he is a poor artist, starving in a garret in the Latin Quarter."

"Practicing a little larceny on the side . . ."

"You, of all people, should not condemn that."

"He shook his head. "Owl . . . Owl . . . I have dabbled in depraved and iniquitous business, but I have never been an artist. Any luck tonight?"

"For me it has been an evening of no fish whatsoever. And you?"

"Empty nets."

"We will meet tomorrow and plan new strategies. What happens in the great world?"

He'd folded the newspaper, *La Gazette*, and propped it up on the water carafe in front of him, so he could read while he watched the room. "The First Consul attended the opera tonight. A lyric tragedy, it says. Now that sounds like fun."

"The arts are the soul of the nation," Owl said primly. "Of course the First Consul will attend the opera. It is the French way."

"I'd invade Poland, myself, if it was a choice between that and opera."

"It is as well you do not rule France. I spoke to the captain of his Household Guard myself. They will be alert going to and from the opera. But . . ." Owl shook her head, as if arguing with herself. "I do not wish the First Consul to cower in the Tuileries to keep himself safe, but he is hard to protect."

A professional would finish him off within the week. Thank God this lot seemed to be amateurs. He smoothed the newspaper flat on the table. "Here's his schedule for tomorrow, just in case somebody murderous has trouble locating him. First thing, some English collectors are presenting France with an Egyptian relic—one of the ones the French dug up when they were conquering Egypt. This requires Napoleon's presence. That's eight in the morning. He's reviewing troops at ten. Lunch with a couple generals. Meeting the ambassador of Portugal at three. Music again tomorrow night in some private house. Hell of a life, if you ask me."

Across the room, outlined by the big front window, Pax slid a piece across the board. *Le fou*. The bishop. The bishop made short work of a black pawn. Pax's opponent selected the queen's pawn and slid it forward. Right. That was going to be a bloodbath, that was.

Pax held his own in the finest chess club of Europe, even if he did wear damn boring waistcoats.

Owl breathed down over his shoulder. This close, her body was a clamor in the air, tugging at his attention. "Shouldn't you be wiping tables or paying some attention to that nice old fellow—that one—who's been waving at you awhile? Or something?"

"I am tired of serving drinks. It palls quickly. And it is entirely unrealistic that I would pay attention to an old man while there is a handsome young one to flirt with."

Owl, at work, was bright as the edge of a diamond, hot as fire sparks. Tonight heat glowed out of her, from wanting him. He glowed right back, wanting her. They were both trying to ignore that.

She slipped the tray to the table and picked up the glass he hadn't finished. Her fichu was one of those pro forma garments that didn't stop him enjoying a sweet view of her breasts. The way she was leaning over . . .

He said, "You're going to have every man in the room looking this way."

"Not everyone. Some are obsessed with chess, and some are very, very old. But the others—yes. They envy you, *mon ami*."

She was watching the room. Owl didn't do anything by accident. "You're looking for men who have too much on their mind to stare at a woman's tits."

"Conspirators. That. Exactly. Men who do not watch the chess and do not watch me. So far, I have distracted everyone nicely. It is most discouraging."

"Too much to hope it'd be easy." In another hour, he'd go back to British Service headquarters. Maybe Carruthers had uncovered something. He wished he was going home with Owl, though. They could—

He pulled his mind away from the things he wasn't going to do tonight.

The door opened. They had a late visitor to the Café de la Régence. This was a man with chestnut-brown hair, worn in a Brutus. Brown eyes, medium skin, about twenty-five. Estimating by the doorframe . . . five foot ten.

I know him.

The man took off his hat and held it in his hand, looking around. He wore solid tailoring. Not fashionable. His boots, better quality than his coat.

He saw Pax. Just a little catch in his attention. He barely hesitated. Not something a man would notice unless he was already looking for it.

I know him. Why? How do I know him?

The man changed direction so he'd walk by Pax's table.

The eyebrows. The bones of the face.

I remember.

Four years ago. He'd been near Bristol, with Doyle. It was their job, when nothing else was on offer, to track down and expose Cachés. To tell family after family they had a cuckoo in the nest. Saying, "It's not your grandson," "It's not your nephew," "It's not the daughter of your old friend."

He remembered this one. They'd told an old man that the boy he'd been raising as his grandson was a Caché, a nameless French orphan trained to spy for France.

Dacre. That was the name. The boy had been Paul Dacre.

Sometimes the families cried and didn't believe and kept the kids. Sometimes they booted them out. This time, the old man didn't give the Caché time to pack his tooth powder.

He and Doyle found Dacre halfway down the front drive. They gave the same offer to all the Cachés—*We'll find you work and a place to live. You can settle in England honestly. We won't toss you on the streets with nothing.*

Paul Dacre ignored them and walked off.

Seems Paul had come home to France.

He closed in on Pax from behind, pretending to angle to see the board, but looking at Pax's face.

A Caché walked in and headed straight for a Service agent. Not coincidence. And Pax didn't see.

I don't like this. He was already half out of his chair, hand on his knife, when Owl closed a hand down on his wrist.

She had a grip like iron. "He is mine. My friend. You are not to kill him."

"Police Secrète."

"That is no business of yours. Sit down. Nothing will happen here without my command. You will not endanger my operation."

The moment rolled forward, fast. The Caché paused beside Pax. His right hand brushed his left in a nervous gesture. He glanced at the board. "It is the least of my worries whether you believe me or not. Your queen is in danger." He strolled on.

Not a twitch from Pax. Not the blink of an eye.

What did I just see?

Owl fumed. "You knew I was bringing men here. He comes to report. I will not ask how you know him."

"I saw him in England. He's one of your Cachés."

"So. I thought it was that. You are notorious for that work, you know. For sweeping them out of hiding, one after another. They all feared the Black 'Awk. You. The *Faucon Noir.*" She took away his newspaper and folded it under her arm. "At least this one was loyal to France, unlike most of them. I am disgusted with you,

'Awker. You cannot come to France and object to French spies. I do not go to Covent Garden and begin putting knives into your friends. We are not even at war. You must be logical."

He was only half listening. The hand movement. The fingers.

Eight years ago. The height of the Terror. Robespierre was just dead on the guillotine and everyone holding their breath, expecting riots. He'd spent a long, dark night with Owl and Pax, pulling a baker's dozen of Cachés out of the house where they kept them. Out of the Coach House.

Spies in training. Deadly. But they were also just a dozen scared kids, cornered, backed off to the wall of that attic.

They weren't going to budge. In a minute or two, one of those kids would raise an alarm and people were going to get killed—him, being first and foremost among them.

Pax had said, "Is there anybody on the stairs?" There wasn't. He'd turned back in time to see Pax wriggling his fingers and saying, "It is the least of my worries . . ."

The exact phrase. That was when the Cachés started listening.

Paul Dacre made the same curl of the fingers—the *C* of thumb and forefinger. Then the first and second finger lifted and closed to touch the thumb. The same signal. Exactly the same.

Pax met his eyes.

Pax had showed up one day at Meeks Street, son of a Service agent killed in Russia, only survivor of his family. Nobody knew him.

The Service traced hundreds of orphans up and down England, looking for Cachés. They never looked at Pax. Because he was one of them.

On the board, Pax set his finger on the king. He tipped it on its side.

Owl stood silent, holding the tray, watching everything.

He said, "Get your man out of here. Tell the owner it's time to close up shop."

He went over to destroy his friend.

Thirty-one

HAWKER CROSSED THE CAFÉ, KEEPING HIMSELF BE-
tween Pax and the front door. One thing he didn't need was Pax
escaping into Paris before they had a chance to sort this out.

Pax sat like a man kicked in the belly—that first instant
when you're stunned, hot and cold, and you stop still because
the next breath is going to let the pain loose.

He came up to the table, picking the spot behind Pax and to
his left. The weakest point. It was where you stood to defend a
friend or watch an enemy.

The bloke Pax was playing with had been annoyed when he
was losing. Now he was annoyed Pax had given him the game.
He was prepared to argue about it, point by point.

You can't please some people. Waste of time trying. "You.
Leave. They're closing in a minute."

That didn't cut off the comments. Seemed like conceding was
an insult to both players and a lack of respect for the game. Some
Spanish fellow had played for three days straight because he
wouldn't concede. Some Frenchman had played even longer.
Some Russian . . . It could only go downhill from here.

He shifted to a rougher accent, a street argot from the east of
Paris. "You shut your trap and scuttle out of here. You're annoying me."

There is no substitute for frank discourse. The old man stopped huffing about the honorable history of chess and took himself off.

Pax raised both hands to the table and pressed them down, fingers spread, showing he wasn't reaching for his knife. The world had twisted into a shape where Pax had to convince him of that.

There wasn't going to be a fight. He kept an eye on Pax's shoulders, on muscles up and down the neck, on the tendons of his hand, but it was just training and habit. Pax wouldn't go for him. And he wouldn't give any warning if he did. "We have to talk. There's a storeroom behind the counter."

"Quiet spot." Pax said it as if they'd planned this, working together. "That's good."

"After you."

He'd seen Pax backed to a wall, fighting like a maniac. Seen him staggering, with his eyes swelled shut, peering through blood, crawling out of that ditch in Cassano behind the battle lines. Seen him silly drunk. He'd never seen him with his eyes completely empty.

The café was full of men collecting coats and hats, taking newspapers back to the counter to drop in the pile, making note of where the pieces lay on the board, finishing the last of their brandy in a couple swallows. Pax wove through like they were made of straw. The Caché who'd given him away was talking to Justine. Pax passed him without a glance.

The room behind the counter was the usual cubbyhole—storeroom and kitchen, a little hearth, a table, some rough benches. The walls were lined with shelves holding cups, plates, glasses turned upside down, wine bottles lying sideways, and piles of napkins, ironed and stacked neat. A broom kept company with a bucket. The copper water cistern was behind the door.

Pax walked in and stopped, keeping his hands clasped behind his back. He didn't turn around. Maybe he was counting towels. Maybe he was waiting to get executed, abrupt-like. Pax could be a damned dramatic son of a bitch. Should have been on stage.

What do I say? What can I possibly say? "I never understood the business about not stabbing a man in the back. It's safer, for one thing. And if I have to kill somebody, I'd just as soon not watch his face."

"You're a sensitive soul," Pax said.

He came up to stand beside Pax and stare at the inventory of the Café de la Régence. "I'm not sure what comes next. I think I ask questions and you lie. At some point, one of us hurts the other. Matters deteriorate from there."

"Let's skip that part."

"That's my preference. But damned if I know what I'm supposed to do."

"You've caught French agents before."

It was a stab of shock, hearing Pax call himself a Frenchman. Ten minutes ago, they'd been on the same side. Two minutes ago, they hadn't said the words. Now they had. "You admit it?"

"That's a cat that won't stuff back in the bag." Pax pulled his mind back from wherever he'd sent it and faced him, making the turn slowly, with his hands out from his sides to show a lack of weapons. Not that it mattered. Pax didn't need weapons. "I was careless, eight years ago, letting you see the hand signal. I thought I'd kept it hidden."

"That'd be one of your Caché secrets."

"We had a few. I needed to use that one. Those kids were about to tear us to pieces." Pax looked past him, keeping half an eye on the main room of the café, making sure they weren't overheard. "They would have, you know, in another minute."

"Bloodthirsty lot."

"We weren't nice children. That attic they were in . . . It was cold as a Norse hell in February. They gave us one blanket, summer and winter. We were soldiers of France, they said. Soldiers sleep on the ground in any weather."

"I bet soldiers don't like it, either."

"We had to say we liked it. Had to say we wanted to give the day's food to the army. They'd do that to us unexpectedly when we were hungriest. We never knew when."

"That was a mistake on their part."

"It made us good liars, if nothing else."

"I'm trying to work this out. The timing. You would have been—"

"I was one of the first. When they brought me, the strongest kids were bullying the others, taking their food and their blanket. We made rules." His lips twisted. It was almost amusement. "I made rules. It turned out, I was the strongest kid."

"I know all about your rules. 'Don't wear green. Strike low and strike often. Never budge from a good lie.' "

"With them it was more like, 'Elect a leader. Never betray another Caché. Protect each other. Take care of the little kids.'"

In the café, the noise was dying down. The woman who poured drinks and took money at the counter headed their way, got to the storeroom door, ready to stick her head in and say something. She met his eye and had second thoughts. Walked off without whatever she was looking for. Good decision on her part.

Pax went on talking, not making sudden moves, holding his hands still and open. "We named ourselves the Cachés. They started using it later, but it was us, first. They didn't know what we were hiding from, was them." He thought a while. "The ones who came after me kept the rules. In all the Cachés you uncovered, not one of them led you to another."

"Not one."

"When we walked into that attic that night, the kids had a leader, speaking for all of them. They kept the small ones in the back. They knew the hand signal. That was mine. I made that up."

"It gave you away. They have some word . . . that Greek God of bad luck."

"Nemesis."

"That sounds like it. Who were you, before you went to the Coach House and took up being a Caché?"

Pax shook his head.

"Fair enough. It doesn't matter."

"Not anymore."

"You're not English. You've been a spy from the first day you limped into Meeks Street."

"Yes." He jerked his head to the side, abruptly. "No. I was—" He went silent.

Forty feet away, the door of the café banged closed behind some irritated customer. Glass rattled in the front windows. The noise scraped the lines of his nerves. Hell. This was hard. "You're not the son of a British Service agent."

"I'm not James Paxton's son. I took that dead boy's place. I took his name. Let me sit down." He didn't wait for a nod. He collapsed on the bench, putting his hands out in front of him, holding one inside the other. "I didn't expect to get away with it for this long."

"I have to tell Carruthers."

"I wouldn't expect anything else."

"She'll send men after you."

Pax raised stillness to a fine art. Paint on the wall fidgeted, compared to him. "She'll need to know how much I gave the French."

"She'll send them in twos and threes. You won't be easy to take. Not alive. And you have to be alive to interrogate."

It felt eerily familiar, laying the facts out. Predicting, discussing, getting the choices lined up.

"It'll be an interesting little talk." A muscle in Pax's cheek tightened. A sign of cracks in the ice. "I count on Carruthers to finish up neatly. Don't let her turn the work over to you. You deserve better than that."

"I'm not her butcher."

Pax waved for silence. "Both of you can leave it to the French. Justine DuMotier's going to report this. The French execute turncoats."

"You were about twelve, last time you were French."

"It doesn't matter. I have a day, after the French find out. Maybe less."

In the main room, the lamps were getting blown, one by one, leaving the café darker every time. Murmurs, cautious and annoyed, said the owner and his wife were talking quietly between themselves and locking the windows up and down the front.

"They brought me to Russia, fast, by ship." Pax took up a conversation they weren't actually having. "When I was there, they did the rest. I didn't see the fire." He lost momentum, wiped his mouth, and started up again. "They made me go through the ashes and bury what was left. So I'd be convincing." He ran his hand down his arm. "They burned me. For proof."

He'd seen the scar Pax had snaking up his arm. Ugly and deep. "Authentic."

"They were great ones for detail." Pax sounded exhausted. Hoarse. "They told me to get myself to Meeks Street. 'That way,' they said, and pointed west." He closed his hand on his arm, as if it still hurt. "It took me four months to walk across Europe. It'd started snowing by the time I got to England. Maybe the Coach House did make us tough."

"Nobody trains agents like the French."

"Nobody." Pax took a couple of deep breaths. "Let me finish this. I was four months at Meeks Street when my *directeur* showed up. I'd done better than he hoped."

"Your hand right in the candy box. He must have been pleased."

"It's not . . . Damn. It's not a joke." The table held a coffee grinder and a tray with a dozen cups waiting to be washed. Pax picked up dirty cups and began to lay them out in a row. "I gave him papers, Hawk. I followed orders. You have to know that. Three times, I gave him files I filched out of the cupboards in the basement. I picked old work. Dead operations. Agents who'd retired to some sheep farm in the Outer Hebrides."

"You gave him garbage."

"I was green as grass. I didn't know what was important." Pax began to stack dirty cups. "I'll never know how much damage I did."

Now that was vintage Pax, looking on the dark side, even if he had to run round the side and paint it black himself.

"I know what was stored down there. I burned it wholesale when they put me in charge of filing. How'd you kill him?"

Pax shrugged, all austere and disapproving. Did he think the whole damn story wasn't obvious? "A dagger under the sternum, up to the heart. But I didn't do it till the fourth meeting. None of this is going to make any difference to Carruthers."

"No." The seniors in the British Service were a scary lot. Carruthers more than most.

"Nobody showed up to replace him. A couple months went by and I was still waiting for the ax to fall. Robespierre died on the guillotine. The Coach House closed and the French wanted to pretend it never existed. You and Doyle went hunting Cachés up and down the length of England. But you didn't look at me."

"You were one of us."

"By then, I was." He kept stacking cups, one by one. "Somewhere along the line I turned into Thomas Paxton."

"Who is in one hell of a mess."

There wasn't much more to say, so they sat there, not saying it.

Pax set the last cup in place. "It doesn't get easier with waiting. If you're going to kill me, you might as well do it here."

"If I were going to kill you, I'd have done it ten minutes ago instead of listening to that whole maudlin story. "

"I betrayed the Service from the first day I walked in the door."

"You were a kid and it was a long time ago."

"I've lied to everybody for years. I could have been a traitor all along. You'd never know."

"Fine then. You're so bloody traitorous, I'll sharpen up a knife and you can do the deed yourself. That's a private corner over there. Get on with it."

There was enough light to see Pax's lips twitch. "All right, then. How do I live through this?"

"That's a topic of fruitful speculation. My advice is, run like a rabbit. Go to Germany. Maybe Norway. Settle down to a blameless life as a Latin tutor. Collect bugs. You'd enjoy that. I doubt we'll bother to track you down in the frozen north."

"And the French?"

"They don't have to know, if your Caché mate keeps his mouth shut. I'll convince Justine to stay quiet."

That got a short laugh out of him. "Maybe you could at that. Let's say I don't want to teach Latin in the frozen north."

"You can go to Carruthers and throw yourself on the thin and sticky gruel of her mercy. Or you can go to London, to Galba. At least he'll listen to you before he slits your throat." Nothing else to say. "I have money. And a couple watches. I spent the day picking pockets."

"You're a man of parts, Hawk."

"My morality is complicated. Get out of Paris. The Americans tell me New York and Boston are cities of culture and opportunity. They're probably lying through their teeth, but you could go take a look."

"I might do that. I have to think about this."

Too much damn thinking, that was Pax's problem. "I can give you till dawn. Then I have to go to Carruthers."

Thirty-two

HAWKER STOOD AT THE WINDOW OF THE CAFÉ DE
la Régence, waiting for Owl.

The café was silent around him. The owners had grumbled
their way off into the night. It was just him and Owl. She was
off in the storeroom, doing something or other.

It was dark outside. This late, they snuffed the big lamps in the
arches of the arcade. The shops of the Palais Royale closed up
tight. The shopkeepers went home. He could just barely hear the
rumble of voices and music from the gaming rooms upstairs. A
café down at the far end of the colonnade was offering Gypsy
music.

A few fools were still coming and going. Englishmen and
Germans, mostly, determined to lick up the last dregs of foreign
sin. Easy work for pickpockets, that lot. A couple whores hadn't
given up yet. They'd be the ones too old or too shabby to get
into the gaming rooms, out looking for men dimwitted enough
to touch them. Every once in a while, a gendarme walked by,
keeping the peace.

Four hours till dawn.

Carruthers was going to ask him where Pax was headed. He
could say he didn't know. Lots of routes out of Paris when you
knew the city as well as Pax did.

Owl came up behind him, making the right amount of noise. Enough to say she was there, not enough to break his concentration.

She said, "You did not know he was a Caché?"

"No." The French had done a thorough, convincing job. "Your friend told you?"

"Not so exactly. My colleague pretends to know Pax not at all. He has made a poor choice." Owl was reflected a little in the glass of the window, like a serious, disapproving ghost. "He *lies* to me, 'Awker, despite the years we have worked together."

"Does he?"

"He twists like a worm on the hook to avoid betraying a fellow Caché. I am supposed to be blind to the drama enacted under my nose and stupid as well. I have sent my friend away and told him to keep his mouth shut. I will deal with him later. For many reasons, he will keep silent."

"That's good."

She was watching him, first in the surface of the window, then she turned to study him frankly. "You will give Paxton up to your superiors?"

"In the morning."

"You have no choice, I suppose."

"None." When Carruthers set him to tracking down Pax, he didn't know what he'd do.

He was mirrored in the glass, next to Owl. It looked like he was standing out there in the night, staring in.

"Listen to me." Owl unpinned the top of her apron, first one side, and then the other, and untied the band at the waist, businesslike and calm. "Listen, 'Awker."

"I am."

"You are not, but I will let that pass." She discarded the apron impatiently onto a table and pushed in front of him, between him and the window. She put her hand flat on his chest, and he had to look at her. "I will say nothing of this to my superiors."

He wanted to shake his head to clear it. He wasn't thinking well. "Why?"

"It is no honor to France to pursue one of the Cachés, after so many years." She shrugged angrily. "We did not behave well toward them."

If Pax didn't have the French after him, that was better odds. Doyle would say—

Doyle had trained both of them. Him and Pax. He'd have to tell Doyle . . .

"We French speak always of love, but friendship is harder. Incomparably harder. Take your coat off and come help me."

She wanted help with chairs. The tables, each with a chessboard built into the top, stood in an orderly line. Long padded benches went down one side. Chairs on the other.

"Over there." She pointed.

Fine. He moved chairs. They were rush seats and slat, light to handle. Chess players didn't need a lot of creature comforts. He took them two at a time to the front.

"Now the tables." She'd already picked one up.

They fitted tables against the wall. When that was done, she put her hand on his arm and stopped him. "I did not know about Paxton."

"I believe you."

"It was . . ." Her eyes were intense on him, searching his face. "You know it was inevitable that we should plant one or two Cachés in your midst. Le bon Dieu alone knows how many agents you have inserted into the Police Secrète."

"Don't ask me."

"I will not. I will say this also, mon ami." She looked upon the crowded furniture. "I do not know every agent we French keep in England, but I do not think Pax is ours. I think he is loyal to you English."

"Probably."

"Will you have to kill him anyway?"

"Most likely."

She said quietly, "You, yourself?"

"Not with these." He lifted his hands. "I'm just going to give him to the men who will kill him. I'll do it about five hours from now."

Light and fast, she touched his left hand and his right where he held them out. "I see. I see most clearly. It is damnable. Let us finish this."

Finish. Why were they moving tables? Seemed like they were going to shift one of the benches now.

She said, "He has money? Paxton."

"A good bit. All of mine, plus everything I took this morning. And a couple of watches and the ring."

"That will make good bribes. I try always to bribe with

jewelry. It makes men secretive. Take the other end of this. It is heavy, is it not? This is very sturdy furniture in this café."

Owl pointed to where she wanted it relocated. *Fine. Just fine.*

She said, "The hour before dawn is a good time to steal horses. One might be twenty miles away from Paris by noon. Now. You back up. Yes. That is right."

They walked the bench a ways. Set it down next to the other one.

"He will be disguised by now. He is a very good agent if he has your respect, as I think he does. Push this closer." She straightened and wiped the palms of her hands on her skirt. "That is good." The benches, side by side, close together, pleased her. "I will get my cloak. It is in the storage room."

When she came back, she brought the lantern and her cloak. She began removing bits and pieces from her cloak and setting them out on the table. A pouch of coins. A knife. Her little pistol. A box for bullets and powder.

"He is a good agent, your Paxton?"

He cleared his throat. "Very good. The best. Good as I am."

She shook the cloak, testing to see whether anything fell out, and tossed it across the two benches.

"He has money and knowledge of the countryside and five hours' head start. 'Awker, you and I have run from armies of Austrians with far less than that."

The light stood on the table between the two of them. The dark was all around. Quiet. Intimate.

She said, "Tomorrow, you will go to your headquarters and betray an old friendship. Then you will argue for his life. You will bargain and find allies and you will keep him alive. I have faith in you."

She stood before him and picked at the knot in his cravat. He was wearing just a turn around the neck and a square knot in front. Simple. The kind of neckcloth a chess fanatic might wear.

She tugged it loose, pulled the length away, and dropped it.

He saw what he should have seen a while back. "You've made a bed."

"For us."

Thirty-three

THE BLACK EMPTINESS WAS NOT GONE FROM HAWKer's eyes, not entirely, but it had receded. He no longer despaired.

If he were not so focused upon the horrible duty he must do, he would see that Pax's situation was not hopeless. Pax had many friends in the British Service, Hawker not the least of them. Hawker would make the most formidable and wily of allies. There were ways and ways of fighting the masters of the great spy organizations for the life of an agent.

Later, they would discuss strategies. Right now, he needed her.

"It will not be a comfortable bed, *mon vieux*. But it will suffice." A plain gilt brooch, suitable to a maidservant, held her fichu in place. She loosed it and laid it upon the table.

"Why are we doing this?" He was slow upon the buttons of his waistcoat, not taking his eyes off her. "Remind me."

Because you are in such pain it tears at my heart—you who do not allow yourself to be hurt by the world. You, who are so armored by your sarcasm and your wit. Because you are my friend. I could turn aside from a mere lover, but not from you.
"It is one last time."

"It's always been one last time. Every time. We lead dangerous lives."

He was a man of deft and dexterous hands, yet he was awkward with the simple task of removing his waistcoat. The button of his collar also eluded him.

"We will not play games, you and I. Let me." She slipped the button of his collar free.

"They can see in through the window, if anyone comes by."

"We are hidden well enough by the back of this bench. I will blow the lantern out in a moment. Then I will seduce you for a while."

"Unnecessary." He laughed a little. "Why, Owl? Why'd you change your mind?"

This was the Hawker she knew, asking such questions. Awake and alive behind his eyes. Tough, cynical, unsentimental. The lover who was hard stone and hungry fire.

"We are friends."

"I don't need to bounce the mattress with my friends. Neither do you."

She told him a little more. "I am afraid."

Hawker's knives dropped to the table beside her gun, convenient in case there was need of them. He began to unstrap the sheaths. "Afraid of what?"

"I am overwhelmed by a knowledge of mortality tonight. We dance upon the edge of the abyss, and tonight, I cannot stop myself from looking down."

"Damn. You're being philosophical. That's a mistake."

They were both thinking of the agent Paxton, in the dark, alone, running through the streets of Paris. If worse came to worst, all his strength and skill would not save him from death.

She said, "I am a fool to lie with you. It is disaster upon disaster if we are caught. This morning, I was resolved to set you aside and be wise. It seems I am not that wise."

Hawker disentangled himself from the last knife harness. He pulled his shirt over his head. He wore a silver chain around his neck with a medal of Saint Christopher upon it. A gift from Séverine. She had received the twin to it.

His bare chest made cogent arguments up and down her nerves. It always did. But tonight, when she looked upon him, she knew that even Hawker could die. This perfect machinery of his body, this warm muscle and bone that contained him, was not invulnerable.

"I will not be prudent," she whispered. "Death comes to us all. I will not go to meet it with small, cautious steps."

"You're not going to die." Hawker leaned over and blew out the lantern. "You stop thinking that. There is just a myriad of things it doesn't do any good to let into your head. That's the first of them."

"I cannot help it. I have seen your Paxton fall so quickly, so completely." The darkness was not absolute. She could see his outline. See the shape of his features. In some ways, it was easier to talk when she could not see him clearly. "I feel disaster flapping over us like a great bird. If Napoleon dies at the hands of an Englishman, we will be at war in a week. You and I will meet on opposite sides of a battlefield one day. It is not impossible we will be forced to—"

"Hey." He took her hand and lifted it. Turned it. Kissed the palm. "Not tonight. Forget that for tonight."

Such thin skin lay at the cup of the hand. The little touch there, and she was struck with heat between her legs. She glowed there. Ached there.

He kissed her palm again and closed her hand over it and held her hand in both of his. "Take that. Put it away and save it for later."

He was dim and colorless. Speaking to him was like speaking to the night itself.

"I am too fond of you," she said.

"The complaint of women from one side of Europe to another. Come to bed, love." She knew that in the dark he gave an Adrian smile. A Hawker smile. Challenge. Madness. A promise of earthly delights. An elegant depravity.

She left her shoes behind on the floor, untied her garters as she walked and let her stockings drop, pulled her skirt up, and crawled beside him.

"Lie down. I want to . . . Ah. That's good." His lips sucked three, four, five kisses at her throat. "Did I ever tell you your skin cools off when you sleep? You're like silk. Cool when you touch it."

"You may compare me to silk all night long."

He threaded her hair back from her forehead, bit by bit, then kissed there too. He was in no hurry. Hawker was never in a hurry, not even when she buzzed and twitched with wanting him.

She found the texture of his lips. "You are unbearable entice-ment and temptation."

"I try. In my modest way, I try." He played with one strand of her hair, tugging it so slightly she could barely feel the tiny pulse. Waiting for her. He had the cunning of a mathematics text and the patience of a tree growing.

Desire for him clenched inside her. Grabbed her breath. Streaked in lines of heat between her legs. Folded around her like lightning. Overcame her.

She muttered, "We are stupid, stupid, stupid . . ." She rolled and straddled him. He pulled her dress aside so it would not be between them. She kissed his mouth altogether thoroughly.

She heard him say, "I have to have you," in a voice naked as clear glass.

His need made him clumsy, so she pushed his hand aside and undid the buttons of his trousers herself, fumbling her way from button to button. It took her a while to get them all loose. He didn't seem to mind.

Thirty-four

IN THE NIGHT, THE VAST GARDEN AT THE HEART OF the Palais Royale was empty. The shops under the arcades were closed. The last patrons of the opera had eaten their toast and paté at a restaurant and wandered home. On the upper floor, behind closed doors, men gambled and whored, but only a shadow of sound spilled into the night.

The man who still thought of himself as Thomas Paxton stood alone in the middle of the garden, looking up. The moon rode over Paris. Over London too, and Bonn, and the cities of the New World. Lots of world out there. Dozens of places he could hide.

He stretched his arm full length and measured the angle of moon above the horizon against the width of his hand, a rough sextant. Two and a half hours to moonset, which made this about three in morning. Hawker would be staying in the café till morning, giving him a good long head start.

It was August, but the nights had been chilly lately. There was no warmth in moonlight.

He'd have been outside tonight anyway. The meteor showers in the constellation Perseus were at their peak. Only happened once a year.

There. That was one. A streak of white on the sky. He held

his breath to the end of it. It seemed worthwhile to tilt his head back and tell the sky, "The abyss of endless time swallows it all." Marcus Aurelius said that.

In the morning, he'd take Hawk with him when he went to Carruthers.

He didn't have a decision to make. If you were Service and you blotted your copybook, you reported to the Head of Section for judgment. He was Service. He'd made his choice a good long time ago.

Thirty-five

SHE WOKE. LIGHT CAME THROUGH THE WINDOWS OF the café. What woke her, though, was the scritch of broom on pavement and the clatter of pails. The sweepers were out, raking up the fallen leaves, making the Palais Royale fit for another day.

Happiness rested in the small of her stomach, like coals in a hand warmer. *I have been unwise again. With Hawker.*

It felt very good. When she woke up after having been with him, she felt clean. She felt as if he had touched every part of her and burned it clean with fire.

Sometime in the night Hawker had raised himself to sitting and eased her head into his lap. She had slept so deeply she had not noticed. Or if she woke momentarily, it was with the knowledge she was safe and she let herself slip into sleep again.

She opened her eyes and looked up at him. They had not undressed altogether last night, but Hawker was half naked. She had kissed his chest again and again, following the lines of his muscles.

He slept sitting up, his head leaned against the wall, his eyes closed. His right arm was lax at his side. His left arm lay across her and held her.

He had a face like those carved on ancient Greek coins, with straight nose and strong, full lips. His skin was dark with sun, brown even on his chest. In Milan he had passed himself off as a fisherman and worked on the boats, wearing few unnecessary clothes. His beard had grown diligently in the night, as it did. This was not the first time she had awakened beside him.

He could not be of English blood, not with that face. Pole, Gypsy, Lascar, Jew, Greek, Italian, or some joining of nations. He disappeared into a crowd in the Milanese market like a sparrow into a flock of sparrows. His mother had been a whore, he said. His father might be anyone. Hawker might be half French and his father a man from Marseille or Nîmes.

"I'm awake." He did not open his eyes.

"I know that." She followed that lie with a truth, just to keep him guessing. "I was admiring you." She told him the truth fairly often. Not from principle or calculation, just for the simplicity of it.

With that he smiled down at her. "I'm like a porcupine." He stroked the stubble. It was a wholly masculine gesture, that. Men never really stopped being proud of the ability to grow a beard.

She took his forearm and used it to pull herself up to sitting. Then she held his hand in her lap. She could have read his palm, if she'd been a Gypsy.

The thought of Gypsies and fortune-telling had come to her in the night and stayed with her, past waking. She must talk to him about that, later. "What time do you think it is?"

"Before six."

Footsteps shuffled. Voices gradually filled the arcade outside. She could not make out the words, but the tone was comfortable, unexcited, discussing small, ordinary things. Men and boys and some women too were on their way to work in the cafés and shops of the Palais Royale. The creak and clank of a pushcart was fruits and vegetables being delivered to the cafés and restaurants. Outside, at the door of the café, came a faint thump. That would be the earliest newspapers of the day, dropped at the door.

She had slept solidly for two hours, but it left her only a little rested. Her brain was full of the smell and taste of Hawker until she had very little room to think. She wished they could make love again, now, in the daylight.

I have tried and tried to make myself a woman who is not ruled by her emotions. I have failed, somewhat.

"The owners of this café will arrive soon. They must clean or restock or squeeze lemons or some such thing. I will admit I have not the least idea what one does in a café when the doors are closed."

"Water the wine. Cut the bread thin. Chop up cats for the paté."

He'd taken his hand from hers to hold her forearm, so they were linked, arm to arm. She had seen this on old vases taken out from under the earth in Italy. It was the way antique warriors greeted comrades.

She said, "We do not eat paté of cats in Paris, whatever may be the custom of London."

"London. Cat-eating capital of Europe."

It was natural as sunlight to wake up and talk to Hawker this way. She was warm through her whole body because their hands were wrapped upon one another's arms. Neither of them wanted to be the first to let go.

It was always left to the woman to be wise. She opened her hand and drew away from him. She untangled her knees from the complexity of skirts and squirmed herself off the benches. They were separate now.

She said, "I must find water and wash and become civilized."

"Me too." His eyes had become like the points of knives. "I have an unpleasant interview to get through."

He had spent some of the night while she slept, planning. He would not turn Paxton over to his superiors without a fight.

Hawker rose and angled his way across the room, around the end of the counter, and into the storage room behind. With each step, under her eye, he transformed into a man surrounded by an aura of cold. Adrian the spy. The Black Hawk.

"The owners of this café," she raised her voice, "will hope to find me gone, without trace, when they arrive later this morning. No one wishes to see the Police Secrète cluttering their place of business."

He replied from the storeroom, "Try being a thief. Now, that's a profession that makes you unwelcome."

She located her stockings, which had gone their stocking way along the floor last night. Her garters had accompanied them, companionably, and could also be found. She sat to draw them on.

Metallic clatter came and the sound of water pouring from the cistern and trickling into a pan.

"I have had a thought." She said this loudly, so Hawker could hear. "It is clever, but it confuses the issue. You must tell me what you think of it."

A soft tap from the storeroom. "Let me shave first. I can't think when I'm doing this." A pause followed, for the space it would take a man to finish a stroke, shaving. "I put the kettle to heat. Ten minutes and you can wash."

"While you shave yourself in cold water. I am touched."

There are great heroisms in the world. Hawker had saved her life once or twice, performing them. There are also small heroic acts that pass unnoticed. He was full of such attentions.

She had loosened the this and that of her clothing last night, to be comfortable. To be . . . accessible. But what she wore, she could button and tie and lace herself into, unaided. She returned herself to order. She toed into her shoes, and she was dressed and ready. The morning had most thoroughly arrived.

Yesterday's newspapers lay in a rough pile on the counter. She took one back to the table and spread it out where she had left her gun and her kit for reloading. She always carried what she needed to reload. So many problems cannot be solved with a single bullet. She opened the little box with its powder and brushes, set her gun on the newspaper, and began.

Hawker came out a few minutes later, wiping his face with a towel, and sat on the bench next to where she worked. He'd brought a whetstone with him, which he had found somewhere, and picked up one of her knives and began refining the edge. "Have I ever talked to you about your knives?"

"Frequently."

"It's all in the angle. You feather out the edge every so often, because there is nothing more dangerous than a dull knife. Armies have been brought down by dull knives."

"That is unlikely."

"Absolute truth." He did not test her knife with his thumb. That was for those who wished to go about with little cuts across their thumb. He lifted the edge of newspaper and sliced that, separating an illustration of bust improvers from a column of news. "Tell me this clever thought you've had."

"We have words. *La dame. La tour. Le fou* . . ."

He nodded. He was attending to the knife, raising a rhythmic, slow grinding as he perfected the edge of the blade. One would say he was absorbed in that unless one saw his eyes. They were thinking of other things. Whirring with calculation. "Tell me."

"Tarot."

The single word, and his head snapped up. He stared at her, not seeing. *"Nom d'un nom."*

"The card of the queen is called 'the lady.' *La dame.* The card of the tower. *La tour.* The card of *le fou*—the fool. I do not say we are wrong about chess. But that is another possibility."

"Tarot cards. Gypsies. Gypsies come to the Palais Royale."

"Sometimes. Mostly they are chased away again. But sometimes they bribe the gendarmes and are left in peace for a day or two to tell fortunes up and down the cafés. I did not see any yesterday."

He set her knife down on the newspaper. He was perfectly still, going over this in his mind. He shook his head slowly. "They don't mix in politics. Or assassination. Doesn't make sense."

"It does not. And yet I must explore this. I have friends among the Rom, but they come and go. I will have to track them down in the poor *quartiers* to the east of Paris."

"I'll ask around the Palais Royale. See when and where the Gypsies have been."

"It will take days. We do not have days." She rapped her gun impatiently upon the news sheet. Grains of black powder peppered the schedule of the First Consul's activities for the day.

Egyptian artifacts restored to the Louvre . . . *La Dame du Nil.* The Lady of the Nile, brought from England . . . incomparable artwork . . . gift to the people of France . . . celebration of peace.

It was a pity peace did not really come from gifts of pretty statues.

Hawker said, "What I need is Paxton. He's the one who knows the Rom. They take to him like a long-lost cousin, which he's not, with his coloring. If I had him here—"

She said, "You do."

A man stood at the window, looking in. Monsieur Paxton, who should not be here. Who should be miles away by now. "He did not have the sense to leave. Truly, I have no fear for the secrets of France if the British Service is composed of such—"

"The key," Hawker snapped. He found it himself, instantly, on the counter. Opened the door and pulled his friend inside.

They spoke low, being vehement. Arguing. Paxton was determined upon his course. He would not run. He would surrender himself to his superiors in some madness of honor.

Hawker was to accompany him and speak for him. Save him, if he could, and be with him, at the last, if he could not.

It was altogether brave and damnable of both men.

She did not wish to see Hawker's face as the two men spoke together. Anger, she could look upon. This pain—it shouted from both of them—she did not want to see.

She measured powder into the barrel. Wrapped the bullet in a wadding of paper. Tamped it down. The gun and her knives went back to the pockets of her cloak, ready for use.

Beneath her work, scattered with black grains, a drawing looked up at her. *La Dame du Nil*, a statue, stiff and Egyptian. The paper read, "The director of antiquities of the Louvre, Monsieur Julien Latour, prepares to greet *La Dame du Nil* in her historic journey to Paris as she is restored to French hands. Napoleon will receive the English delegation at eight o'clock in a private ceremony . . . expressions of amity and friendship between nations . . ."

Latour. *La tour.*

"*Mon Dieu.*" She grabbed the paper. Back powder spilled across the table. "Look. No. Be silent. None of that matters. Look here." She thrust it under Hawker's eyes. "*La tour.* Latour. *La Dame du Nil.* That is *la dame*. The Englishman. He is the fool. *Le fou.* The madman. This is the assassination. Here. Now. God help us. What time is it?"

Paxton dragged a watch out. Clicked it open. "Seven."

"We are too late." Too late. They would never get there in time.

"Not yet." It took Hawker one instant to take in the whole of the article. Less than an instant to know what to do. "There's no ceremony in the history of the world that's started on time." He passed the paper to his friend. "Get to headquarters. Tell her I need men. I'll go stop it. If it's too late, we make sure that Englishman is dead before he gets questioned."

It would be their foremost concern—that there was no Englishman. That there was no cause for war. But she must save Napoleon. She threw her cloak about her. Set her hand upon the barrel of her gun.

Hawker followed her out the door. He said, over his shoulder, to Pax, "Go. I'll leave a trail inside the Louvre."

Thirty-six

THE LOUVRE WAS HALF ART MUSEUM, HALF CHAOS. In one gallery, scaffolding and ladders, paint buckets and sheets over the statues. In the next, the bourgeois inspected art.

Nobody knew anything about Napoleon's visit or Egyptian antiquities or *La Dame du Nil* or a ceremony. Museum caretakers, guides, guards, passing artists carrying easels—none of them knew a thing. All stupid as mice.

In the courtyard between the buildings of the Louvre a dozen families strolled under the wide, serene sky. She stood with Hawker, both of them out of breath, surrounded by the peaceful and ordinary. Disaster was about to strike France. It would happen here, somewhere within a few hundred yards of her, and she could not find it.

"It hasn't happened yet." Hawker searched door to door, window to window, with cold, impatient eyes.

She'd sent one of the guides running to the post of the Imperial Guard, another to the offices of the Police Secrète in the Tuileries, to Fouché. But they would not be in time. She knew it in her bones.

One minute too late, or a century too late, it was all the same.

Think. She must think. "He is not in the public galleries. Not here, in the main buildings. If Napoleon had come to the open, public rooms, all these people would be trying to get a glimpse of him. They would be full of chatter, pointing, hurrying, watching."

"Big place." Hawker studied one flank of the buildings, dismissed it, moved on to the next.

"The Louvre is immense. A city in itself." If she planned such a ceremony, where would she hold it? Where?

On both sides of the courtyard, carved gray stone and tall window stretched to the Tuileries Palace. The Louvre was filled with the offices of government, workshops, lecture halls, apartments. "This is an endless labyrinth with a thousand obscure corners."

"They're not holding this donnybrook in some dark corner. What's substantial?" He made one of his complex gestures. "What's fancy?"

"He will not be far from the Tuileries. He will review the troops at ten."

"Where?"

"In the courtyard of the Tuileries Palace." She pointed south. "I think . . . I think he will not go to the Louvre, with its long delay of meeting so many people. He will stay in the palace itself. On the ground floor there are a dozen salons and reception rooms, all of them famous. The king of France lived there once."

He ran his hand through his hair. "We have to guess. You take the left side, I'll head down—"

"No. Look. There is a guard. Standing there, doing nothing. That is the only door with a guard. That's it. That door."

She ran. Hawker stayed an instant to mark another arrow in charcoal on the paving stones.

A hundred yards away, where the Pavillon de Marsan connected to the Louvre, the door was open. The guard eyed her suspiciously. "Entrance for the public is at the front. Go back the way you came. Turn, and go through the big door on the left. Walk around."

Hawker came up beside her and slashed a huge, black arrow in charcoal on the stone wall.

"Here now. You can't do that. It's against the law to deface public buildings. There's a fine for—"

Overlooked, she slipped through the door. Sometimes, it was an advantage to be dressed like no one in particular. To be so obviously of no importance.

The Pavillon de Marsan, here in the Tuileries Palace. It would be here. Yes.

Ancient halls covered with gilt and mirrors. A dozen years ago the sister of the king of France had lived in the apartments here. Where else was so secure, private, and close to Napoleon's quarters? She could even name the room. Any such ceremony would be held in the Green Salon. That was worthy of a presentation to Napoleon.

Not far.

Hawker caught up to her in the long corridor. She did not ask him how he had dealt with the guard.

One soldier guarded the door of the Green Salon, stiff and proud, gun on his shoulder, very serious, but so young he scarcely merited his mustache. Did the First Consul of France deserve only one infant to guard him?

It took two breaths before she could speak. "Is he inside? Napoleon? The presentation from Egypt?"

"This is a private meeting. See the secretary at—"

"I am *policière*. I have a message for the chief of your guard. I will enter immediately." And damn it that she looked untidy and unimportant when she must impress this unimaginative dolt. She fumbled for her *lettre d'autorité* with its seals and impressive signatures that would get her through any door in Paris.

"My orders are to—" He swung the gun down in front of her, blocking her from the door. Frowned past her to Hawker who was ready to mark the wallpaper with one of his arrows. "What are you doing! This palace belongs to the people of France. It is a treasure of the nation. Give that to me!"

Hawker, bland as a sheep, innocent as a child, held out the charcoal. When the guard reached for it, Hawker grabbed him by the ears, slammed the man's head down, and cracked it against his knee, The guard fell noiselessly.

Hawker stepped over him and pushed the double door open. She did not need identification papers.

He said, "You get Napoleon out. I'll find the Englishman."

A year ago, when she had walked through this room, the walls were painted with hunting scenes. Gods and cherubs looked down from a high, domed ceiling.

The Green Salon was transformed. White gauze, in thin layers, hung from the ceiling and tented out over four huge wood obelisks at the corners of the room. More white gauze curtained the walls, floor to ceiling, hiding the windows, making everything dim and stuffy. Placards, painted with Egyptian gods, had been set up every few feet between huge, upright mummy cases. Everything smelled strongly of linseed oil.

Napoleon stood with his back to her, but he was unmistakable. He was bareheaded, in a dark blue coat, his arms crossed. He was no taller than the men around him. Shorter, in fact. But the compact energy of him could be felt all the way across the room. He turned to talk to the man next to him. Pale skin and a hooked nose. Slashed, dark eyebrows. In this crowded salon he stood out like an eagle in the midst of chickens.

The man at the front, speaking, was Julien Latour, chief of antiquities at the Louvre. She had heard Latour lecture once. Beside him was a thick beef of a man, middle-aged and florid, with a thick, loose lower lip, the very model of an English hunting squire. That was most likely the Englishman they sought. A glance to the side showed Hawker, sliding forward through the crowd, intent upon him.

Between Latour and the Englishman, on a table covered with more of this wispy gauze, lit by torches, was *La Dame du Nil*, the Lady of the Nile, the carved, painted figure of a woman, a foot tall. It stood on a decorated box, arms outstretched like a bird about to take flight.

La dame. Brought to *la tour*. Latour.

This was the moment. This was the assassination she must stop.

Thirty or forty men, a dozen women, and a few children jammed together into the room, breathing on one another, leaving only a respectful space around Napoleon. Two guards, bored as cows, had their backs against the drapery that lined the walls. Vezier, the garde sergeant, a man she knew, had put himself to the right of Napoleon.

He was alert. He saw her and came to attention.

She started toward him. In a moment someone in this room would try to kill Napoleon. By pistol shot most likely. She must do nothing, nothing to precipitate that.

She elbowed forward through the pack, rammed her shoulder into someone's back, tromped hard on the toes of men who would not move out of her way. Through the slit in the side of her skirt, she found the pouch that held her pistol and put her hand on it.

The room was stifling. The torches in their stands on the presentation table burned with tiny, upright flames. Women fanned themselves with informative pamphlets. The flicker and flitter would be a cover and a distraction for someone pointing a gun. She could not look everywhere at once.

At the front, the Englishman kept his hands possessively on the painted box and the statue. Latour droned, "In Fifteenth Dynasty funerary rites, Isis represents the feminine aspect of rejuvenation . . ."

Latour had been boring when she'd listened to him before.

She reached Vezier. She blessed, blessed a thousand times, the habit and training that taught her to know the best men who did useful work at every level. Not only the captain of the Imperial Guard, but the most responsible sergeants. Vezier was one of the men she'd warned yesterday. He knew everything she knew. She could say to him, "It's here. It's now. Get him out," and waste no time in explanation.

Vezier acted at once, all soldier in this. Decision and deed were close as two sides of a coin. He gathered in the other two guards with a lift of the hand and took the step that brought him to Napoleon's side. Tapped the First Consul's arm to get his attention. Leaned to speak to him.

Napoleon blinked once. The line of his mouth hardened. He said ten words, then looked directly at her. Nodded. He turned to give orders to the men behind him.

She had become a woman whose word would stop this ceremony. Her warning would interrupt the ruler of France. She was proud of that and suddenly terrified, in case she was wrong. If she had made a mistake, she would be disgraced.

She did not think this was a mistake.

Now to get the First Consul away from the room, to safety. In the crowd around her, no one reached into a coat pocket. No woman opened her small bag and removed a pretty pistol. Puzzled looks began, but that was all.

Hawker slid like a shadow along the great swathes of curtains, brushing them to sway as he went by, his left hand down, poised to retrieve a knife from under his coat sleeve. He searched faces as if he were trying to locate some friend, misplaced. He'd recognize murder in a man's eyes. He'd see the first twitch to a weapon. He'd smell intent like a cat smells fish.

He advanced toward the Englishman, coming from behind.

Latour, splendidly oblivious, went on, ". . . to an era of peace and cooperation between our nations, symbolized by this artifact, returned to French hands."

There was a pause. Men began to clap lightly.

The Englishman reached out. She took a step closer. Began to draw her gun. But the Englishman only took up a torch from its holder. Part of the ceremony then.

Then he lowered the torch to the painted box, to the lid beneath the serene figure in white. Flames licked and spread across the patterned box like liquid till it was wrapped in writhing blue fire.

White flames shot upward, four feet high, in a whoosh and a sudden thin column. Sparks flew off in every direction.

Women screamed. The Englishman slipped away behind the curtain of draperies.

She leaped after him, past the fire, around the end of the table, pushing Latour, shocked and openmouthed, aside.

She was in time to see the door close behind the Englishman. Hear it lock.

There were two doors to this room. If this one was locked, the other would be as well.

The door was painted, gilded, ornate, harmless-looking. Solid wood. Locked tight. She grabbed the handle. It didn't turn. Not with all her strength. She slammed herself against it.

"Get out of the way." Hawker pushed her aside and knelt. Pulled his picklocks out, rattling them loose from the black velvet wrapping. Set his forehead to the door and began to work, his hands hard and steady as his picklocks.

They were screaming behind her in the room. Men tried to get past her to claw at the door. She braced herself, hands flat on the door panels, arched over Hawker. Protecting him and what he was doing with her body. She spread her legs wide and put her head down and held in place against fists that pounded at her and tried to batter her aside.

Brilliant light behind her. Stark white. The cloth was on fire everywhere. Heat like she'd been pushed, face-first, into a stove. Three breaths, and she was already choking.

Too hot to see. Her eyeballs hurt.

She was going to die.

Hawker's head pressed under her belly. He was seeing nothing but his work. Not a move out of him but the dance of his hands.

In the room behind her the fire growled like an animal.

She heard the tiny click when the lock turned. Hawker jerked the handle, freed the door, and pushed. The door moved an inch. Stopped. There was a barrier outside the door. Heavy. Immovable.

"It's blocked from outside." Hawker was calm, even as he choked.

He turned. Light rippled grim and red on his face. He said, "Owl. I'm sorry."

Then he set his back to the door. Braced his feet. "You and you. Here. Back to the door. Push.

Four men pushed now, using all their strength. She stepped away and covered her face with her skirt. Bowed her head against the heat.

The door didn't budge. Not much longer for any of them.

Across the room she heard screams and banging. The other door—yes—the other door was locked too, and no one to get it open.

Then Hawker and the desperate, heaving men beside him fell backwards. The door opened outward, abruptly, five inches. Yelling, they pushed again and the door screeched and shuddered an inch more. Then opened enough for the men to edge sideways and through.

She heard the rumble of something being dragged aside. The door flung wide.

The rush of panic and shoving carried her past Hawker and down the hall. Paxton and the first men out of the burning room struggled to shove a heavy bureau out of the way. The guard was limp on the ground next to the wall.

The crowd tumbled out of the room, pushing and choking. Staggering to safety.

She tripped a madman who yammered and tried to run into the blaze. Elbowed him in the belly when he got up and tried again. Saw him held and dragged off by others. She beat at the dress of a woman whose light printed cotton had caught fire. A man—brother or lover or passing stranger—pulled his jacket off and closed it around the girl, smothering the flames.

She yelled at him, over the shouting and the howl of the fire,

"Get her out of here. To the fountain outside. Soak her with water."

Those who had escaped were blocking the path of those still in the room. She pushed one man and another. "Go. Get out of the way." Sent them down the hall. And still Napoleon did not come.

It was bright as fireworks inside. Men and women ran for the door through a corridor of the fire. Through flames that poured like rivers, going upward.

The First Consul was the last man out. His guard pushed two women, a gasping man, and a boy carrying a baby ahead of them. Then Napoleon emerged, even after his guard, covering his face with his arms.

Behind him, in the open doorway, smoke descended like a slow curtain. A hollow roaring built. The fire became solid, flames fingering the doorway. Wind blew from the hall behind her toward the fire.

An inferno of heat. Such heat that she retreated from it. Anyone left inside that room was dead.

Men ran past her, toward the fire. Soldiers carrying buckets of water and sand. Down the hall, outside in the courtyard, men yelled, "Fire," and "Get the pumps," and "This way."

She followed the black, ash-smeared figure of Napoleon. He strode, upright and rigidly controlled, his square, pale countenance set. Men gave way before him. Anyone with clear eyes looked around for orders now. They trailed in his wake or stopped to help the survivors of the Green Salon who coughed and cried out, faces covered with soot.

Smoke snaked over her head, down the corridor, filling the space beneath the ceiling, covering the nymphs and gods.

"Owl." Hawker was in her path. "Your hair's on fire. Hold still." He slapped around her face. Pulled her fichu out from around her neck and pressed it to her head. "You're burned."

Now she felt stinging points of pain. Pieces of falling fire had burned through her clothes. The damage was on her back where she couldn't see. It didn't matter.

"It's nothing." Her throat was raw from breathing in the smoke. She swallowed and tasted ash. "At the other door. There will be a soldier. Go."

"There are men headed that way." Hawker pulled out a handkerchief, spit on it, and swiped across her eyes. "I've got to find the Englishman. For God's sake, get away from the fire. And move these damn idiots along." He was gone, dodging through the crowd, his friend Paxton at his back.

She ran to catch up with Napoleon. He strode through this tumult alone, sending his soldiers to help others. It would be easy, easy, for someone to slip toward him and shoot. That might be their plan all along. In the madness of the fire, to kill him and escape.

Napoleon took his place in the center of the marble entry hall under the great chandelier. Men rushed by in this direction and that, shouting. Then they saw him, and chaos ceased.

Suddenly, officers' voices could be heard. Men formed quickly moving lines, passing buckets. The injured and grimy survivors of the fire were helped outside. The doors cleared.

Napoleon treated this as he would a battlefield. He stayed where he could be seen and consulted. He issued orders to one man and sent him on his way. Spotted another and motioned him forward. Gave more orders. Men came to him in panic and departed with purpose.

She set herself four feet from his back and drew her gun from her pocket, cocked it, and held it at her side, pointed to the floor, hidden by the folds of her skirt. Ready. She studied the eyes of every man who approached him, watched the hands of every man and woman who hesitated in the corridor and stared.

The First Consul had escaped one threat. He must be guarded from the next. That was her job, in this confusion, to guard his back.

Leblanc came from the courtyard outside. He'd washed his face somewhere, but his hair was still full of black ash. He breathed raggedly as he approached the First Consul, whether from exertion or fear, she did not know. "The Englishman got away. We're searching the building for him. I will send—"

"It is not the English." Napoleon commanded armies in the field. Now he raised his voice so it could be heard above the shouting, over the weeping of women who had collapsed on benches in the corridor, over the tromp of soldiers. "This is an unfortunate accident. The fire has been controlled." In a lower voice, he said to Leblanc, "See that nothing else reaches the papers. This is a small fire that accidentally broke out."

"The Englishman lit the—"

"There is no Englishman. This is a plot of the Jacobins. There are a number already under suspicion of treasonous activities. I want them arrested. Find Fouché. I must talk to him."

"Of course, First Consul, I—"

The First Consul would naturally blame the Jacobins. He would take any excuse to harass them. And he did not wish to go to war with England. Not at this minute. Not before he prepared.

Leblanc tried to say more, but Napoleon had already turned away to listen to a sergeant who spoke of pumps. Then he called over to him a man in the clothing of a clerk, saying again that this was an accident only. Not the first fire in these old buildings. This information must appear, just so, in the press.

Vezier came from the direction of the fire, his face smeared, his eyes tearing tracks down to his mustache. He saw the gun she held ready, and at once understood the danger to the First Consul. He gestured three men from the work of carrying buckets to set them in a phalanx around Napoleon. They were ordinary soldiers, but they took up positions, as if by instinct, putting their own bodies between the threat of an assassin and the future of Europe.

Leblanc stalked toward her, determined and furious, and closed his fist around her arm. "We will find the Englishman who did this. Come with me."

Thirty-seven

HE DIDN'T WANT TO LEAVE OWL, BUT HIS JOB WAS to find the Englishman before the French did.

She was alive. Coughing, wheezing, eyes watering, with a nasty burn on her back, but alive. She'd feel the hurt later, when she stood still.

He spent one minute with her, just long enough to hear her breathing clear. No time to say he'd thought she was going to die—thought they both were going to die—and he would have traded his life to get her out.

No time, no place, to kiss her. They'd do that later. He'd find the Englishman and wring his damn neck. Then he'd take Owl to bed.

He signaled Pax, and they took off, following the route the Englishman must have taken, down the corridor and out the door, into the courtyard between the Tuileries and the Louvre.

Ten feet from the door he let himself look back. Owl had attached herself to that bastard Napoleon, playing guard. She was drawn up straight, all steel, ready to shoot anybody who looked at Bonaparte cross-eyed.

The best strike came after the first one failed and the target relaxed. If he was running an operation to kill that cove, he'd do it now.

Clever Owl. Consummate professional. Nothing she didn't see.

Smoke plumed out of a line of windows to his left. The whole side of the building was covered with a blanket of black. Men pumped water into the horse trough, scooped it up, and ran with buckets into the Tuileries.

He motioned Pax to the center of the courtyard and some clear space. "Our Englishman is six foot, built heavy, brown hair going thin on top, red face. Fifty years old. Dark blue coat with brass buttons. Blue vest."

"I got one look at him, running away." Pax kept up. "He won't be out here where everybody can see him."

"He'll stay, though. Stay to see what happens."

"Amateur."

"This all stinks of the amateur."

A hundred people had come out to stare at the fire. Office clerks, maids, cooks, and floor scrubbers from the Tuileries. Gaggles of art lovers running across from the Louvre, pointing and shouting. Soldiers headed in from all quarters, dodging the gawking idiots, trying to get to the fire and do something useful.

The Englishman was here, somewhere.

"A professional would have killed you so you couldn't move that heavy bit of furniture away from the door. He'd have shot Napoleon when he came out of the smoke. And he'd be halfway to Montmartre by now."

"That's what you'd do."

"That's what anyone sensible would do." They were jostled by men wanting a better view of the fire. "Only a bloody amateur traps six dozen people in a fire. When you set out to kill a man, you kill the man. You don't burn half a bloody palace doing it."

"Lots of places for him to hide and watch." Pax looked from door to door, window to window, rooftop to rooftop. "Or set up a gun."

He stripped away the anger and considered the kind of man who put together a plot with so many deaths. "He doesn't have a gun. He planned one big, showy spectacular moment. Mopping up afterward isn't in his calculations."

"He doesn't kill face-to-face."

"Right. It's not the gut hit and the blood he's after. He wants to wind everything up like a clock and set it down and watch it happen. He wants to be . . . like the ceilings in this place. All those gods sneering down from the clouds. Jupiter. That lot."

"The classical gods." Amusement from Pax, but he was thinking about it too.

"He wants to look down on everybody. He's tucked himself up where there's a good view."

Lots of places to hide in the attics of the Louvre. The top floor, up under the roof, had big, wide windows with pointed tops and—what were they called?—plinths running up beside them. Arrogant-looking windows. "What's on the top floor over there?"

Pax would know. He was like Owl, always running over to the Louvre to see some picture or other. He tapped finger to finger as they walked, counting off. "Exhibits on the ground floor. The office of the curator upstairs. Top floor, it's workshops. The studios where they do restoration. There's storage."

"He'll use a storage room. Damn, but I need a map of this place." They were in step, eating the distance across this churned-up gravel. Not moving so fast they stood out in the general mob scene. "He's upstairs, watching the Tuileries."

"Likely."

They crossed one of the charcoal arrows he'd drawn on the ground. "Who did Carruthers send?"

"Hawk, everybody's scattered out. She'll send what she can, but . . ."

"Damn." He thought about it for a while and said, "Damn," again. "We're on our own. There's at least three others with the Englishman. They needed that many to block both doors at once."

"Let's hope we don't run into them all at once." Pax touched one pocket of his coat and then another. "I have two shots."

"The Frenchmen have sense enough to get out of—" In a high window, a patch of light color moved against dark. Somebody stood there. "See that? Someone's taking an interest. What do you want to bet that's the ballock-sucking pustule who sets fire to a room with women and kids?"

"I never bet with you, Hawk."

They ran the last fifty paces. In a minute, Napoleon was going step out into the courtyard and show himself to everybody, letting the world know he was safe. The Englishman was going to realize he'd failed. He'd run.

Through the door, into this piece of the Louvre. Pax drew his gun and cocked it. Acres of white marble on the floor. Marble and bronze people on pedestals, not wearing clothes.

Archways and columns. Three hundred places for some cove to jump out and shoot a hole in you.

At the end of this gallery, the steps going up were more god-damned marble. A hell bitch to run on. Carved marble grapes and cherubs frolicked around the banister, flight after flight, all the way up. Pax followed him up, keeping an eye behind. If anybody had a gun, he and Pax were going to get holes shot in them on these stairs.

On the second floor, they met two men jabbering their way along the hall, all excited.

"Get back in your office. Stay there." It was enough to send them skittering. Ten years of war and riot had taught people to get out of the way fast when somebody barked orders.

Outside, shouts and cheering echoed sharp on the stone. Napoleon must have walked out into the courtyard.

Pax said, "The First Consul of France escapes again. Let joy be unconfined."

"I should have put a knife in him as I passed by. There are some opportunities it is just a sin and a shame to miss."

Pax whispered, "We do not assassinate foreign heads of state." They were at top of the stairs, backed to the wall. He leaned to look down the row of doors. "Without orders."

"I would have saved ten thousand English lives on the battle-fields of Europe."

"It's not that simple."

"Listen." Somebody was up here. Footsteps. The middle door opened, and a man ran past, headlong.

Got 'im. He grabbed the man's coat. Swung him to crash against the wall. *Now we do a little talking.* Twisted an arm behind his back. For all the brute size and muscle, it was easy to force the gasping, thrashing ape to his knees. "Who's in it with you? Talk to me, you bastard."

Pax grabbed the man's hair and pulled his head back so they could see him.

From the man, in English, "I don't understand. I don't speak French."

This wasn't the man in charge. This was somebody's cat-spaw. This was the fool. *Le fou.* He switched languages, "Who are you working for? Give me their names."

"You're English!" Relief filled the man's face. "Thank God. You have to get me out of here. They'll be after us in a minute."

"Who sent you to France?"

"I can't be taken by the *garde*. I have important work to finish."

Killing women and kids. "Who gave the orders?"

"I have to get away. He has to be stopped."

"Who gave you the fire starter?" He ratcheted the man's wrist tighter. It was pointless. The stupid lump was incoherent with fear and frenzy. He didn't feel anything. "You didn't think of this yourself."

"Napoleon must die. No peace till he dies." He was fighting, trying to get up, sputtering, "Have to try again. I'll get him next time."

Pax had his head to the side, listening. "They're coming. A lot of them."

The man was spewing English loud enough to tell the world they were up here. "He killed my boy. Killed my Roger. Roger Cameron, Lieutenant of *The Valorous*. My boy died at the Battle of Aboukir. He killed my boy."

A man willing to murder a hundred innocents because his son died in a naval battle. He'd do this again. The next bomb might go off in the middle of the Comédie-Française.

Shouts from below and the tromp that meant soldiers. They were about to deal with the French authorities.

"Napoleon must die." Spittle and gasps from the Englishman. "Only way to save England. The army's behind me. Important men. Highest levels. They know what he is."

"Give me the names." But this man didn't know anything. He was a tool in somebody's hands. He hadn't been sent here to kill Napoleon. He'd been sent here to be captured and talk.

"I'm doing this is for England. For England."

Casus belli. This blind idiot, this bull-headed, stupid animal would be the cause of war.

Soldiers shouted back and forth in the marble halls downstairs. No getting the Englishman away where they could question him. Only one choice.

"Get back." He wouldn't make Pax part of this. He'd keep the load on his own conscience.

It didn't take strength. It took knowing how to balance the weight. It took being used to the work of killing. It took being the Hawker.

The Englishman rolled over the banister with chilling grace.

The man let out one yelp on the way down. He had a second to be scared. Probably less.

The body sprawled faceup at the bottom. It had a cleanly broken neck, among other things. A fast and clean way out of life. Better than dying in a fire.

Better than what the French would do to him and Pax, if they caught them. "Let's get the hell out of here."

They took off with the soldiers pounding up the stairs after them.

Thirty-eight

THE GALLERIES OF THE LOUVRE WERE ALMOST DE-
serted. Pax didn't see anyone as he strolled past a fine collection
of art looted from Italy. More of Napoleon's contribution to the
history of plunder. The statue of Laocoön wrestling a snake
took most of the end of the hall. A reminder he wasn't the only
one with problems.

He and Hawk had been spotted killing the Englishman. The
soldiers had their description. Time to run.

"Paxton."

Carruthers. She wore crow black, all the respectable widow.
At her side, Althea was in a neat dress and heavy fichu that said
"comfortable, old-fashioned maidservant." God help the man
who thought that's what they were.

"The Englishman is dead," he said, skipping the prelim-
inaries.

"We heard." Carruthers was disapproving. "A regrettable
accident to mar the general rejoicing for the First Consul's escape
from the fire. Did you learn anything before killing him?"

"We didn't have much time."

"That is unfortunate."

"You, my dear boy, are sought as one of the radical Jacobins
who set the fire." Althea smiled. She'd filled a handkerchief

with gray ash from the fire. "You were seen and described. Your hair is most impressively memorable." She moved behind a plinth which carried a Roman copy of a fifth-century bust of Pericles. "Lean down, please. That's right."

He took his hat off and let her dust gray into his hair.

"Not wholly convincing at close quarters." She brushed at his face with the back of her fingers. "It will do from a distance. There. Turn around. I'll tie your hair back."

Carruthers stood, concealing them. "At least his death will placate the French. They'll know we tidied him up. Adrian?"

"Took off the other way. I don't know where he is." Althea had picked up an art pencil from one of the easels standing around. He couldn't speak while she drew lines on his face.

"Enough." Carruthers looked him over. "Let us dodder harmlessly away."

The Head of Section for Paris at his side, a senior agent of the British Service trailing behind, he hobbled down the long gallery. In the jubilation at Napoleon's narrow escape, no one paid attention to an old man, overcome by excitement.

The guards at the door argued over whether a dead Englishman had been shot or tossed out a window and didn't even glance up as he shuffled down the stairs.

Down the Rue de Rivoli, left, two streets over, and one up. They entered the alley behind a *boulangerie*. It was stacked with old barrels, smelling of flour and yeast, hot from the bakery ovens. This led to a storage room that was one of the safe houses of the British Service.

Carruthers said, "I'll send the fiacre for you at dusk. You will grace England with your presence for a while."

He put out a hand. "Wait." And he told her he was a Caché.

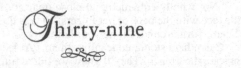

Thirty-nine

JUSTINE FOLLOWED LEBLANC INTO THE CROWD, keeping an eye out for any dark, slim man decorated with ashes. She saw no one of interest, neither Hawker nor his friend with the so-obvious hair. The fire in the Pavillon de Marsan had dusted everyone with bits of black. If Hawker had stupidly remained to hide among the crowd, he would blend in.

"He was seen," Leblanc pointed, "headed that way. We go to the main building."

Two guards followed them, armed. "Yes, monsieur."

It was dim inside, after the bright sun of the courtyard, even with the long windows that reached to the ceiling. They passed no one. All the world was in the courtyard, cheering the arrival of the pumping engine. The galleries of the Louvre led one into another, endless canyons of paintings, studded with statues. It was as good an escape as most, and Hawker would not linger to admire the artwork. He was gone from here. Long gone.

Leblanc muttered to himself, "I saw him at the presentation. Just before the fire. I'll know him when I see him again."

With luck, Leblanc would not see him again.

While Hawker had killed his Englishman, two men from the Department of Antiquities came out to the stairs and looked. Leblanc had questioned them closely. They wore flamboyant cravats and chattered and were as shocked and pleased as if they had done the deed themselves. They were, unfortunately, observant and exact witnesses. They were also artists. Leblanc would soon have pencil sketches of Hawker and Paxton.

Leblanc said, "He set the fire and escaped from the room."

She shook her head. "I do not think so. He was trapped with the rest of us."

"You are wrong. It is the work of a great operative to see these things, Justine. You would do well to take your lessons from me." Leblanc limped mightily from some small injury acquired in the panic of the fire. She hoped it hurt. "The English fight among themselves. One spy has disposed of his accomplice and fled. That is the cause of this murder."

"Or it is Jacobins," she said. "In any case, they are not here."

It was eerie to be in the great vaulted halls, alone. She could have stolen the artwork of centuries at this moment and walked out with it under her cloak. She did not mention this. The guards, following, were unlikely to recognize the theoretical nature of this observation. Leblanc would probably steal something, if it were once suggested to him that he could.

Leblanc said, "You. Search that way. You. Down there." And the guards went to obey. She hoped they would not shoot someone entirely innocent. She also hoped they would not shoot Hawker.

In a gallery at the end of this corridor was a small picture by Vouet that had hung in her bedroom when she was a child and the Mademoiselle de Cabrillac, an aristocrat. The Republic confiscated it when the chateau was sacked. She was not certain whether she would steal it back or not. How strange to almost be given the chance.

Leblanc stalked along, wincing, keeping a half step in front of her so he should look like he was leading. He managed to look both sullen and dangerous, like a spoiled five-year-old playing with munitions. "The First Consul did not listen. I told him it was English spies. I will give him English spies."

He won't thank you for it.

They came to a dead end where a large marble snake strangled several naked men.

"Not here," Leblanc hissed. "Go back. He will escape the other way."

In the distance, an old couple followed by their servant left the hall of sculptures. A museum watchman passed, looking at them curiously.

"I will salvage something from this debacle," Leblanc said. "If only more dead spies."

She saw him then, dark on the white stairs, illuminated pitilessly by the skylight above. He had nowhere to hide in all this grandeur. Slight, black-haired, all ardent grace as he took the steps two at a time. Hawker.

"There. There he is." Leblanc shouted, "Shoot."

Leblanc tore a pistol from his jacket pocket. She stepped in front of him, blocking his aim, and took out her own gun. Raised it. Strange how it seemed so absolutely silent.

"Kill him," Leblanc said.

She held the gun in both hands before her. Shifted, as if by accident, into Leblanc's path. He couldn't get a clear shot.

Her finger found the trigger. She lowered the barrel to her target with the deliberate care of a marksman. She aimed well to the left of him. Her finger tightened. Softly.

Hawker half-turned. In a single snap, their eyes met.

"Out of my way." Leblanc shoved her from behind. And she shot.

Hawker still held her eye. She saw the impact. Blood blossomed on his chest. The bullet hit him high, between heart and shoulder. Blood trickled down over the bright stripes of his waistcoat.

No! No. No. "You spoiled my aim," she heard herself say to Leblanc.

Hawker stayed, standing still, the space of an intake of breath. Shocked with getting hit. Shocked that it was her bullet going into him. Then he turned and ran.

She spun clumsily and managed to knock into Leblanc. Her pistol, empty now, knocked his arm aside.

"Stupid bitch."

She snapped, "He's hit. He can't go far. Get the garde. Search the apartments upstairs. He'll be hiding in one of them."

She ran up the steps.

Hawker had left a trail of blood. He'd turned down this hall. One of the curtains was pulled back unevenly and the window was open.

Even Hawker with his legendary skill could not . . .

But there was blood on the stone outside. Had he managed

to climb down? She searched the ground below, but he was not there. The men and women walking the Rue de Rivoli gave no sign a man had passed, dripping blood. Somehow, he had ambled away, blending into the crowd.

Hawker was alone in Paris, desperate and wounded.

He thought she had tried to kill him.

Forty

1818
Meeks Street, London

JUSTINE WAS DETERMINED TO ARISE AND COME TO
breakfast. She was entirely weary of meeting men in bed when
she was wearing no clothing.

She came downstairs, holding the rail. Séverine went before
her, ready to throw her body down to cushion any fall. Surely
no child wavering onto its feet for the first time was ever so
closely watched.

The banyan robe she wore slithered under her feet when not
persuaded otherwise. Silk brocade lipped about her bare legs,
too heavy to cling. The crimson of it was a shout, a strident
trumpet of a color. One could imagine confronting the emperor
of China in such a garment. It was Hawker's and smelled faintly
of tobacco, sandalwood, and black powder.

At the bottom of the stairs, the carpet was chilly under the
arch of her foot. Three doors were open into the hall and a light
wind blew through. At the back of the house, men's voices rumbled. She would head in that direction. If anyone was talking, it
was probably Hawker.

Séverine said, "Catch your breath. Sit for a minute." She
gave other prudent advice.

"When I sit down, I will not want to stand up again. I am

weak as pudding." Ah, the beauty of great truths. They can be stated so concisely.

It was not so long a journey from the front of the house to the back. She set her right hand upon the wall from time to time and rested because there was no one to impress and she would need all her strength to deal with the men who awaited her at the end of the hall.

Séverine opened the door into a small, perfect dining room with Chinese wallpaper, graceful mahogany furniture, and quite a nice collection of English spies. A mound of untidy gray fur occupied a square of sunlight on the rug. This was the huge dog that visited her room several times a day, sniffed at her, and departed, grave and silent as a physician. The table held breakfast dishes and stacks of notes, folded newspapers, a teapot and cups, and a pair of black knives.

". . . the witness statements. So far, we've talked to—" Doyle swung around in his chair.

Hawker, at the head of the table, looked up.

Silence. She took two . . . three . . . slow breaths and walked through the door to discuss various matters with the British Service.

Hawker was in shirtsleeves. He wore stark white linen of the finest quality, a cream waistcoat, and the impassive containment of a Byzantine icon. He was even thinner than he had been long ago.

He said to Séverine, "You had to bring her, didn't you? I do not understand why nobody ever says 'no' to this woman."

Séverine said, "She can faint as easily downstairs in company as upstairs alone. At worst she will topple over and bloody her nose. At best, one of you can catch her." She went around the table to kiss Doyle on the cheek in a daughterly manner.

"And ain't that a wonderful prospect for a man trying to enjoy his breakfast in peace." Doyle had chosen to be scarred and unshaven today. It would suit his peculiar sense of humor to sit in this exquisite room in the rough, patched clothing of the barely respectable poor.

On the other side of the table, Paxton was a pale, ascetic scholar this morning, wearing shabby black. He had spectacularly proven his loyalty to England many years ago and paid full price for the right to sit among them. It was legend in the circles of spies, how greatly he had redeemed himself from suspicion.

The last man she also knew, though she had never exactly met him. He was the ingenious, insouciant agent known as Fletcher. She knew him only by sight, having avoided a closer introduction.

They had been discussing important matters. All the signs were there—the interrupted gesture, the bodies leaned across the table, the papers and coffee cups pushed aside carelessly. They were wondering, rather obviously, what she had overheard out there in the hall.

Everywhere, she met with suspicion. She, who was an honest shopkeeper. One may retire from spying, but not from one's reputation.

Hawker pushed his chair back from the table and strode over to circle her. "Sit."

"I am hardly in need of advice to—"

"Sit the bloody hell down." He was the sleek animal who flashed from stillness into attack. He did that now. Without pause, without seeming to hurry, all in one long glide of intention, he scooped her up and deposited her in the chair. "Before you fall over."

He used not one feather of force beyond what was needed to take her off balance, to support her as she sank back.

She allowed this because she did, in fact, wish to sit down. The determination that had kept her going packed up its tent and deserted. Little spots swirled before her eyes. She would not faint, but the fringes of this possibility were distracting.

He stood for a long minute looking down at her before he let go. His hold imprinted into her shoulders a sense of the solidity of the banyan's embroidery. Where he held her, the silk remained warm.

The body has memories deeper than thought. Her body remembered him.

He lifted one of the chairs that waited at the wall and brought it to the table so he could sit and glare at her, close and familiar. "Too much to hope you'd spend the day flat in bed." He turned to Séverine. "Too much to expect you'd keep her there."

Séverine made herself comfortable in the chair at the end of the table. "I can't stop her, you know. If you want her in bed, keep her there yourself."

Hawker ignored that. "She's the color of new cheese and she's shaking when she moves." He directed an order to the dark, sullen spy girl in training. "Get her some of that catlap we keep feeding her."

In the long three years apart, she had forgotten the many ways in which he annoyed her. She said, "Coffee. Very strong. I do not wish to drink bouillon in the dawn, and I detest tea. 'Awker, we must talk."

"Right. That's the first thing I said when you fell across my doorstep, bleeding. I said to myself, 'I must talk to this woman.'"

"I did not mean to be stabbed. It is not my fault. In any case, you have discovered most of what I came to tell you. There are two murders."

"With my knife in their gullet. When it's my knives, I like to be the one who puts 'em into people."

"You must contain your disappointment." Black knives lay on the table, close enough that she could have laid hand on them. "Those are the knives?"

He leaned to the side and tapped one, then the other. "Gravois. Patelin. This," he drew from his arm sheath, "is the one that almost finished you."

He spun the knife and caught it, very close to her, all a cold breath of motion that whispered across her skin. He held it out, cutting edge toward her, on the palm of his hand. His eyes were dark, cool, and considering. For the time it took to breathe twice, they were quite, quite still, with the knife between them.

He reversed the knife and set the hilt into her hand. "You didn't know it's poisoned. I wondered about that."

"Poison." She set that morsel of knowledge aside with the rest she had gathered. "I looked upon the corpse of Patelin, but there was no such indication. A little poison is irrelevant when one's heart has been pierced." She became very careful with the knife. "It was poison, then, that almost introduced me to Monsieur Death."

"You were shaking hands with him. It's a nasty poison, as these things go. Slow."

When had she ever seen his knives that they were not immaculate? Doyle, without asking, passed a small magnifying glass to her so she could examine it. The dark smears were her blood. The white film would be poison. She read the history of her stabbing.

His knives had always seemed heavy for their size, as if the savage elegance of design added weight. This was one of the knives she had kept in the box in her shop. Almost certainly, one of those three. She had taken them out and held them sometimes, at night, wondering why she kept them.

She returned it to him, being careful of everyone's skin. "I hope you have not been buttering toast with that."

"I have treated it with circumspection. Nothing more dangerous than sharp objects with poison on them."

She must explain those knives to him. His plate was within easy reach. She selected a strip of bacon he had not yet attended to.

He said, "Should you be eating that?"

"We will find out." The bacon was good. Salty. Her stomach accepted the offering with caution. "I am weary of lying in bed and no one brings me anything to eat."

"She gave her porridge to the dog," Séverine said.

"Who ate it with relish. He is large and strong and will survive an encounter with boiled cereal grains. I may not. It is foolish to survive stabbing and poison and then slowly starve to death on consommé and possets." She found the most comfortable spot in the chair and pulled the banyan across her legs and tucked them under her. Hawker watched with great attention. The other men turned their eyes away. Really, she was covered from head to foot like a beldame. The color of the robe would set fire to loose tinder, but one could not fault it for concealment.

"We need to talk to you, anyway. You're the puzzle piece." Paxton accepted a cup of tea from Séverine with a shade of surprise, as if he had not realized he wanted it. Like everyone else in this room, he looked exhausted. "When we find out why you got stabbed, we'll know who did it."

"That is my hope, certainly. I do not like puzzles that involve my death in the cold rain." She ate in tiny bites, playing with the bacon between her teeth. Three years ago she had turned her back on the games of death and war that spies played. It seemed she was not finished with them.

She stole a second piece of bacon. The gray behemoth of a dog heaved to his feet and thudded toward her. They named him Muffin, instead of Behemoth. They would have their small jokes in this household. He sat—thump—and looked expectant.

It was an ancient policy with her to be on good terms with anything that outweighed her and had so many teeth, so she broke the bacon in two and gave him the smaller piece. He was a dog. He would not realize he had been slighted.

With surprising delicacy the dog picked bacon from her fingers and carried it away to the warm spot in the sun.

Doyle said, "We know the poison. We worked it out from what it did to you."

"I would not wish to die of an unknown poison. It seems impersonal."

Coffee arrived before her, brought by the dark apprentice spy girl, poured and creamed and sugared by Séverine. It was hot, giving off steam in a thin, blue cup. To sit and be alive and discuss poisoning and mayhem with experts while drinking impeccable coffee—it was enough to make one believe in Divine Providence.

"The poison's French." Doyle cut into his ham, getting on with the business of eating.

Or perhaps matters were not so perfect. "You must not assume every exotic deadliness is French. That is a British superstition."

Paxton stacked notes from three piles into one. "The poison's called *la vis*. The ingredients are Hindi and Spanish, but the mixture's French. The Cachés were taught to make it."

"They were taught all kinds of sneakiness, if you're anything to go by." Hawker let light run up and down the blade one last time, then set the knife between the other two. "You can make *la vis* in London. Or Prague or Amsterdam. All the ingredients are here. Assassination's a portable trade."

Three black blades lay in a row, like herrings on straw in a fish market.

Coffee was made in the French style in Meeks Street. One did not merely drink, one indulged.

She considered the knives. "I bribed the coroner's assistant to see Patelin's body, which is why I knew for certain it was he. At Bow Street a more substantial bribe let me see your knives, but I was not able to steal them. They are protective of their murder weapons at Bow Street. Not protective enough, obviously."

"I run tame at Bow Street. They're used to seeing me." Doyle drank ale with his breakfast. One would think he studied how to be the caricature of an Englishman. "Now the knives in evidence boxes have *NB* written in the curlicues, instead of *AH*.

Which is almost the same, and a perfectly natural mistake anybody could make."

Paxton said, "We won't fool Military Intelligence. They'll know we switched them."

Doyle smiled, looking evil. "So they will."

"I wonder if they think I have some particular reason to go killing Frenchmen." Hawker pulled at his lower lip, thinking.

It was good to be back among those who spoke so bluntly, so easily, of death and deceit. She missed this in her exile. "I visited the death scenes of Messieurs Gravois and Patelin. You would never have committed murder in those places. You would never have run from a death, drawing attention to yourself."

"Somebody's painting my name in big letters on these murders." Hawker glanced at her. "Somebody with three of my knives. An enemy."

She ran her thumb down the smooth wood of the chair arm. "Yes. An enemy."

In so short a moment, the atmosphere changed.

She did not know quite how to explain those knives.

Doyle dropped his napkin beside his plate. "Right. I'll leave you two to talk about that. I'm for Soho and hunting down some witness to the first stabbing. That is a neighborhood full of shy game when it comes to flushing out witnesses. Sévie, you got a nice, innocent, confiding look about you today. Come along. Maybe they'll talk to you."

"I am delighted to be your stalking horse." Cup clinked into saucer. Séverine was on her feet. "See that she rests, Hawker. It is no use to nurse her back to health if you are going to badger her to death." Séverine dropped a kiss on her cheek as she passed by. "Do not be cruel to him," she whispered.

Fletcher muttered something about papers from the inquest and slipped out the door. The sullen apprentice spy stacked a pile of dishes in the dumbwaiter and strode after him. By that time, Paxton had already exercised his most excellent talent for vanishing.

"Are you the enemy, turning my knives against me?" Hawker said.

It became very quiet.

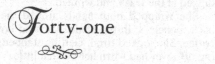

Forty-one

AFTER HE SIGNALED DOYLE AND EVERYBODY CLEARED out, he was left alone with Owl, who wasn't in any shape to go stomping off when he asked awkward questions.

The wooden box from her shop—the one that had played host to his knives for a while—was in the top drawer of the sideboard. He brought it out and laid it on the table. You could call that a conversation piece.

She worked on her coffee in little sips, eking it out as long as she could, avoiding the moment when she'd have to come up with explanations for having three of his knives.

He wasn't in a hurry. He fetched the silver coffeepot and poured into her cup. Added cream the way she liked it. "Two lumps?"

"Thank you."

Enough sugar to set his teeth on edge. That hadn't changed. "We can go to the study, if you like. There's a sofa in there. I can let you lie down." He handed the cup over.

"I have been lying flat for several days. It loses its appeal."

Owl, lying flat, never lost its appeal. He didn't point that out. He was the pattern card of discretion.

The banyan was embroidered with dragons, a gift from an old friend who dealt in cloth. One lascivious lizard curled all comfy on her left breast, tongue out, as if he were tasting her nipple through the cloth. The black dragon on the back, the one with a smile, had his pointy tail hung down so it was caressing the rounded arse underneath.

He didn't let his mind follow that path, however much it tugged at the leash and whined.

She wrapped both hands around the little cup and sank back, boneless, in the chair, her head bowed, considering the coffee. She looked tired. Getting stabbed, poisoned, and fighting off fever had worn her down a little.

She'd primmed the sensual complexity of her hair, scraped it away from her face. Tamed it to an orderly braid to fall down her back. But it wasn't tied up at the bottom. Maybe she hadn't found a ribbon. Even the concerted force of her will wasn't going to keep it from unraveling.

He stood close, breathing down onto all the bare skin at her neck. It wouldn't intimidate her—he couldn't think of anything right off that was likely to intimidate her—and he could catch her if she started to slip sideways.

Always a pleasure to watch Owl. He'd missed that. "You're quiet."

"I am thinking of the several things I must say to you. None of them is easy."

Probably she was weighing her lies. Sorting the big ones from the small ones. Wondering what she could get away with. God, but he loved this woman. "I'm a patient man. Begin at the beginning."

She sighed out slowly. "It is not the beginning, but it is the most recent of our encounters. You rescued me from the Cossacks. I wanted to kill you. You will remember that."

"Vividly."

IT was in the last days before Paris fell. Armies were scattered around the French countryside, fighting off and on. He'd been liaison to the Prussians. Napoleon put up a defense a half day south.

There was gunfire in the distance, but the front line was so mixed up, that could be anybody shooting at anybody else. The Prussians were using him to run messages back and forth and report what was happening, generally. He was so tired he hurt like one big bruise. He smelled like his horse.

Some Cossack officers he knew spotted him and called him over. They needed help interrogating a prisoner. A woman.

He ducked under the tent flap. She was sitting on an old wooden stool, bloodied, with torn clothes. She hadn't been raped. He'd been in time to stop that.

"She fought like a tiger." Pavlo was admiring. "Fortunately, the sergeant she stabbed wasn't popular."

Owl looked up and knew it was over. He watched her face break.

He said, "I know this one. She's harmless."

It had been a dozen years since she'd shot him on the steps in the Louvre. In all those years, all those cities, they hadn't crossed paths often. When they did, it had been interesting.

She'd changed from the woman he'd known. She was exhausted to the edge of endurance, for one thing. Pale, with her eyes set in hollows like two big bruises and her mouth slack. She hadn't given up though. She was calculating, planning, scheming, ready to pay any price and take any chance to get away. Behind her eyes she was . . . she was just more. Everything she'd been when he knew her twelve years before, she was more of now. More strong. More shrewd. More stubborn.

"She's just another courier," he said. "She doesn't know anything."

The papers she had on her were in one of the standard French codes—a message for Napoleon's eyes. The attack on St. Dizier was a feint. The real drive was direct to Paris. He had no idea how she'd found that out.

He said she wasn't worth the trouble of guarding. Said it set a bad example, shooting women. When he took her out of the tent with him, they probably thought he was marching her off for his own use.

He made her walk a mile from the Cossack camp before he stopped his horse. The road ran along the marshes around the lake.

"Your shoes," he said.

Wordlessly, she took the clogs off and handed them over. He threw them as far as he could, in different directions, far out over the marsh.

St. Dizier was fifty miles away. Alone, unarmed, walking barefoot, even Justine wouldn't make it to Napoleon in time. Paris would fall. It was the end.

"I will kill you for this." She stood in the dirt of the road, her arms crossed over her breasts like she was holding her heart inside. "I will wait until you no longer expect it, and then I will kill you. Do not sleep deeply."

SHE sat in his headquarters at Meeks Street in the Chinese dining room, wrapped in his dragons, and drank his coffee.

"That day, outside the Cossack camp. I said a great many things." She consulted her coffee cup. "I was beyond myself."

"I knew that."

"You were the enemy, and you destroyed our last hope."

"It was already too late before I saw you in that tent. Everybody knew that but Napoleon. He was outnumbered. The country was sick of war. All he could do was pick the battleground where he'd lose. If you'd got through to him, he would have taken the final battle to the walls of Paris. Did you want house-to-house fighting across the Latin Quarter? Artillery fire from Montmartre?"

"I see that now. That day, I knew only that I had failed in my duty." The past filled her face. She was a long way away. "I tried to get to Napoleon, and every step of the long way, I planned how I would kill you."

"You were inventive about it, I imagine."

"There has never been a man in the history of the world who was killed as ingeniously as you were, in my mind, that day. I tried so hard, and I failed. When they told me Paris had surrendered, I sat upon the floor of a farmhouse and wept."

Nothing he could say. The war was over. "He had to be stopped."

"I have had a long time to think about this. I do not say you are wrong. But then . . . Paris was full of foreign armies. Prussians strutted about the Champs-Élysées. The cafés were full of Austrians. Cossacks camped on the Champs de Mars. Everywhere I turned, I became sick with rage. I was forsaken and mad with grief. So I blamed you."

"You think I don't understand that?"

"I would have spit upon your understanding, if you had

offered it to me then." She gave a crooked smile. "I was most utterly alone. There was no place for me in the new scheme of things. Even the Police Secrète became suddenly supporters of the monarchy. Those of us who had been loyal to Napoleon found it prudent to leave France."

"To England."

"It is ironic that the safest place for me was here, openly among my old enemies."

"Ironic."

"But I lie." She took a deep breath. "As I lay in bed this morning, I promised myself I would not do that. Habit is very strong. I came to England because you were here." She glanced at the knives that lay in the center of the table, being decorative. "I had decided, very cold-bloodedly, that I would kill you."

"I hope you changed your mind." *Gods, but I hope you changed your mind.*

"I am being honest about complex matters. It is not easy, and you are not helpful in the least." She always got more French when she was annoyed.

He touched her cheek. One brush with his finger. Anybody looking on would have thought it was just friendly. "We never hurt each other. We played fair. Leaving aside that one deplorable incident fifteen years ago, you never shot me."

"I was never put in a position where it was my duty to kill you. Fortune has been kind."

"You should thank the Service." He grinned at her. "After you put a bullet in vital parts of my anatomy, they kept me away from you for years. Sent me to Russia while you were in Paris. Then to France when you were in Italy. To Italy, when you were in Austria. I figured it out later."

Her face flickered like a candle with all those shifting thoughts inside. "Soulier—I became one of Soulier's people, as you know—Soulier said nothing. But you are right. He kept us apart. I have done as much for the women who worked for me when they were enamored of someone unsuitable."

"Nobody more unsuitable than me."

"No one." She negotiated terms with the robe, plucking it up over her thigh where it had slid down, her and the robe having different ideas of what should show and what shouldn't. "I wrote letters to you, do you know? A hundred letters. I explained and explained that the gunshot was an accident. I told you that

I had not meant to hit you. Leblanc struck my arm and the shot went astray."

"Well, that's nice to know."

"I did not mail the letters. I would write them and burn them. If I had once sent the smallest note to you—once—I knew I would wake up the next week and hear you outside my window, asking to come in. And I would open the window. I did not stop being a fool for you, 'Awker. Not for one moment in many long years. They were right to keep us apart."

"Wait a minute. I'm still back thinking about you opening the window and letting me in. What were you wearing?"

"Or I might have opened the window and pulled you inside and strangled you. That is not an impossibility." She didn't finish her coffee. She set it on the table, emphatic-like. "But I am telling you of the time after I left Paris. I went to Socchieve, in Italy, before I went to England. I was still planning to kill you, you understand."

"Italy's a great place for vengeance." He remembered Socchieve. Mountains on all sides like the earth was folded in on you. Snow high up, warm if you walked an hour downhill. Cows. Austria and France had got together to do their fighting in Italy. "That was a long time ago. We never did pay the shot at that inn. Did the Austrians burn the place?"

"It had escaped their notice. It is now run by the son of the old man we met. They kept the luggage, yours and mine, because they had no liking for the Austrians and hoped we would be lucky enough to escape them. Then they continued to keep the bags. It may be they were very honest, but I think they put them in an attic and forgot."

"One of the bags had my knives in it."

"Which you were so proud of and insisted on throwing into the wood of the mantel. The holes are still there. They tell stories about us in that village, none of which are true. Somehow they learned you were the Black Hawk. You would not recognize yourself in those stories."

"I was there less than a week."

"You are credited with a slaughter of Austrians so large I am amazed any still walk the earth. I took out your knives and my tortoiseshell comb and gave the inn everything else to use as they would.

"Three of my knives."

"Those three." She went meditative, considering the knives on the table. "They have been troublesome." Then she said, "It was strange to go through those bags and remember the people we had been. It was like looking at strangers."

They'd made love in a high meadow. Not a flat foot of ground anywhere, just straggly grass and wildflowers. He put his coat down and they crushed flowers underneath them. The smell wrapped his senses till he couldn't think.

Sometime, in between kisses, he said he loved her. She said, "Don't."

Afterward, the sun set and the snow on the mountain peaks turned red and they went off to spy on the Austrian camp. He'd been eighteen. He didn't know what year he was born, so maybe nineteen.

That was a long time ago, as Owl pointed out, and they were different people now. He was talking to a woman who had run major parts of the Police Secrète, not a young girl with her hair down over her breast and yellow wildflower pollen brushed on her skin.

"On the way to England, I had time to think. I found myself leaving old parts of my life behind me, discarded in the mountains, or floating on the sea. It was as if I were unpacking heavy trunks and tossing out things I no longer needed. I had ceased to be a spy for France. The France I had known was gone forever." She pulled her braid forward, over her shoulder, and took to rummaging in the little curves and valleys of it.

Her hair was darker than it had been in that mountain village. He remembered holding a handful of her hair to his face, feeling it with the skin of his nose and his lips, smelling it, when they made love.

"When I came to England, I no longer hated you. I brought no dark purposes with me from the past."

He believed her. He'd interrogated his share of men and women. They didn't lie with their eyes looking inward. They didn't lay out their souls and dissect them on the table in front of him, the way Owl was doing.

She rubbed her arm where the bandage was. The lines at the corners of her mouth said it hurt and she was ignoring that. "I remade myself yet again. I opened my shop, Voyages, and became a dealer in maps and optical instruments and dried fruit. I am the best at what I do. Perhaps the best in the world."

"I've seen your shop. Impressive."

She leaned forward, into a long ray of sun. The fine hair that sprang up at her temples, small and unruly, caught the light just right, and everything glinted in fifty or a hundred sparks. "Men come to me—even famous men—when they are determined to risk their lives in dangerous places. I sell them what they must have to survive. I send them out prepared, as I once sent my agents out to do their work."

"Military Intelligence comes to you." More irony. Military Intelligence, outfitted by a former French spy.

"But the British Service do not. Not ever. They know about the little weakness you had for me once, 'Awker, and they keep their distance." For an instant that amused her and she smiled. But she clouded over the next minute. "This is important. This is what I have to tell you. You know that I mount weapons upon the left wall of my shop. You will have seen them. Some are for sale. Some only for display because they are interesting. Men like to look at weapons. Three years ago, that first day I opened the door or my shop, while Thompson and Chetri were polishing the windows one last time, I put your knives on the wall."

"Ah." Now this he hadn't known.

"I told myself they were a sort of trophy. Or a challenge. Or a memory of the past. I do not know. I think I expected you to walk in one morning and claim them back and we would talk . . . But you did not come. After a few weeks, I took them down and put them away."

"I was in France. Owl, I was in France for months."

"I learned that later." The banyan had a thick, red brocaded belt. She untied the knot and pulled the belt closer about her and tied it again. "I knew when you came to England. You walked by the shop sometimes. But you never came in." She added another knot. "It was because of the words I said outside of Paris. I have told more lies than any woman you will meet in your life. Not one of my lies has been as bitter to me as the truth that I told that day."

"Owl—"

"I should have returned your knives to you at that time. I did not know quite how. There is nothing more embarrassing than importunity from a lover of long ago."

"I should have opened the damn door and walked in. I almost did, a few times." *He'd been stupid. And a coward.*

"There was no reason for you to do so. What we felt for one another was gone. You had become Head of the British Intelligence Service. You were Sir Adrian, no longer the 'Awker I had once known. You had made yourself rich. I was the discredited spy of a fallen empire."

She was going paler as she talked, probably getting ready to pitch forward in a faint. He wasn't going to let this go on much longer.

"You think any of that mattered?"

"You did not come to me."

"I made a mistake," he said.

"We have both made more mistakes in our life than it is possible to count." She smiled wryly, and she was Justine DuMotier, French spymaster, the woman who'd routed some of his best operations. "That is past. We will concentrate upon the present. I read of a stabbing, a Frenchman. It was some time ago, now. I did not take particular notice, since I am no longer in the business of watching and analyzing such matters. Then the next stabbing came. Another Frenchman, and there was mention of a black knife." Her eyes were very clear, very fierce, when they met his. "I have not forgotten my old skills. I did not need to see those knives at Bow Street. I knew at once."

"So you came to me."

"Not immediately. I went first to look upon Patelin's corpse, laid out in the back room of a tavern, and to see the place where he was killed. Then I visited Bow Street and bribed my way into the evidence room to see the knives. Perhaps that was where your enemies picked up my trail and began following. Or perhaps they were watching Voyages. Mr. Thompson has said for months he feels eyes upon us. Somewhere, between Voyages and Meeks Street, they acted."

"Used that third knife on you."

"One man, very young, but already with experience. I had a glimpse of the side of his face. The knives that were stolen from me were used to attack you."

He put his hand on her shoulder, being careful, because that was the arm that hurt her. "Used against you, actually."

"It is the same thing."

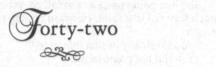

Forty-two

THE HEAD OF THE BRITISH INTELLIGENCE SERVICE
sounded like a powerful man. Anybody'd think he'd be able to
tell Justine DuMotier to go upstairs and sleep for the afternoon.
Not so.

She sat beside him in the coach and lifted the edge of the
curtain to peer out the window. "I hate carriages," she said. A
line of bright light painted itself across her face and down her
body. A thin triangle of street showed, going by. "They are
traps. One might as well pin a target on the chest and be done
with it. A carriage is the worst place to be if someone wants to
kill you."

He made a two-finger width, opening his own curtain.
"Maybe they're tired of trying to kill you. Maybe they'll kill
Pax for a change. Or me."

"That is unduly optimistic." She went back to being suspicious of the pedestrians.

Pax sat forward, across from them, one pistol on the seat beside
him and another in his lap. He was still loading the second, polishing the frizzen and pan with a clean handkerchief, taking off the
last film of damp before he poured in the powder.

Owl was right. A coach was a moving target, easy to follow,
easy to hit. Every street was an ambush about to happen. The

wood and leather on the sides of a coach weren't any use. They might as well have been riding around in a paper sack.

Because he had never learned not to argue with this woman, he pointed out, "You were safe at Meeks Street."

"I am safe at home."

"If you would give me a damn week to find out who's behind this, we might avoid getting anybody killed. And you could let your bloody arm heal."

"My apartment is secure. Mr. Thompson and Mr. Chetri will sleep in the shop. Séverine will spend the nights with me, and she is protective as a mother tiger. She is also a very good shot. The crown jewels are more carelessly protected. 'Awker, we do not know anyone is after me at all. I was not attacked until I came to see you."

"Oh, you're part of it, all right." He knew better than to keep arguing. He never won an argument with Owl. "Your knives from your shop. Your stab wound. Your blood all over the streets of London."

"You exaggerate, as always."

"I'll station a man in the alley at the back. And I'm staying with you."

She didn't answer. She did that trick where she raised one eyebrow and looked superior.

He was wondering whether staying with her in the apartment meant he'd get to go to bed with her. It was too soon, probably. Almost certainly. He was playing the old friend card now. Sneaking up on her, like. He'd put his arm across the back of the coach seat and waited till the coach jolted hard to let it settle down on her shoulders.

An old friend could put an arm around another old friend.

Besides, if she had Sévie with her in the apartment, she wouldn't be getting into bed with him. Looked like he'd be sleeping on a patch of floor in front of her door. Like Muffin.

That was a humiliating comparison. On the other hand, Muffin had spent most of lunchtime with his head in her lap, which was not a bad place to be.

Another long delay on the street while some ham-handed squire from the country got his wheels unlocked from another carriage. Then they turned the corner, onto Exeter. Pax, hands steady as rock, tapped a nicely graded quantity of powder into the pan.

Nobody followed them on foot down Exeter Street. Didn't seem to be any carriages or wagons making the same turn.

When the coach slowed down, coming up outside the shop, nobody took any notice. As far as he could see, there was nothing moving in the buildings across the way. He had a clear, bright view. The rain had washed all the soot out of the air. It was sunny now, and not too hot. Couldn't be a nicer day for doing this damned stupidity.

Pax said, "I'll be back." Before the coach stopped, Pax opened the door, swung down, dodged an oncoming horse, and crossed the street. He lounged his way up the row of houses and shops, blending in, his hand in his pocket keeping company with the gun. He turned the corner and disappeared.

Owl frowned at the shop front of Voyages. Maybe even the shimmering clean glass wasn't clean enough for her. She was probably hurting. There was just no way a man could protect and coddle a woman like Owl. Pointless to try.

He pushed past her, opened the coach door, and kicked the step down.

One old idiot in a dove gray jacket and maroon vest toddled past the shop, rubbing his nose like he was exploring someplace interesting and foreign. That was not an assassin. Left of Voyages the shop that sold travel books and botanical prints was empty. Beyond that, the milliner's and the watchmaker were open for business, but also quiet. On the right hand, the confectioner's had two women inside. They didn't look immediately dangerous.

He stepped down to the pavement. Took in every twitch of movement along the street. Stillwater, a good man, was driving the hackney and also keeping an eye out.

Inside Voyages, Thompson had seen them. He started down the length of the counter, headed out to meet them. Two customers were absorbed in something exotic and expeditionary laid out on a table. One woman left the confectioner's, turning to walk in the opposite direction.

Owl held the sides of the doorframe to take the first step down, because she needed the support and shouldn't have been running around in coaches at this stage in the recovery period from getting stabbed, for God's sake. Stubborn as a mule. Anybody else would . . . But if she was anybody else, he wouldn't give a hang about her.

He picked her up and put her on her feet. Flipped the step up and slapped the door closed. The hackney rolled away. "Let's go. Off the street. Into the shop." This open space grated on his nerves. He wished he could be on all sides of her.

"We are in equal danger, you and I. But it is a sensible suggesti—"

He heard the shot. Heard the thud of lead hitting wood.

He ducked. Owl was down, face to the pavement, scrambling toward the shop. He crowded so he was half on top of her and pushed her ahead of him to the door.

No one in sight. That was rifle fire. No cover anywhere. Some idiot came out of the bookshop to peer around.

"Get the hell back inside."

Owl pushed the door to her shop open and threw herself in. He followed.

The three men in the shop were all on the floor. He lifted himself up off Owl enough to roll her over and have a look at her. "You're not hit anywhere."

"Of course I am not hit. If I were hit I would be bleeding."

Oh, that's useful to know, that is. Across the street all the windows were open. The sniper was in one of them. No movement. No sign. Look for it . . . Look for it . . . There. Ten yards to the left, two floors up. A puff of smoke was just now drifting out the window into the street.

Owl was looking over his shoulder. Saw the same thing. "Go. Go out the back way and around. Do not waste this."

"Oh, hell. You did this on purpose." Bait. She'd set herself up as bait. Damn the woman. Damn him for a fool, not seeing it.

"Go. Now is the time to catch him. Go and be careful with yourself."

"Right." He kissed her hard on the lips and unglued himself from the most beautiful woman in London and went to find out who was trying to kill her.

THE house where the sniper had been had one of those doors you could just kick down if you hit it right. The hall was filled with squawking tenants who wanted to get in his way. The room on the top floor was left with the door swinging. It was empty except for a pair of chairs, a table under the window, a Baker rifle left lying on it, and the smell of black powder.

Outside, the street was full of gawkers and talkers. Some of them were inspecting a bullet hole in the wood framing of the bookshop's window. Pax was doubled over, propped on the wall next to Voyages. Not hurt. Just out of breath. No prisoner with him. Pax said, "Was anyone hit?"

He shook his head.

"Good." A couple deep breaths. "I lost the sniper." Pax wiped his mouth. "I saw her face."

"A woman?"

"Thin. Very pretty. Light hair." Pax's eyes cut in and out through the crowd around them. Always the chance there was another killer on the job. "I chased her to Gorton Street and lost her. She faded into the crowd. Lots of practice. Lots of skill. Professional."

"Which way?"

"Headed toward Piccadilly. Hawk, I know who she is."

This might be the end of it. This might be the answer. He didn't take his eyes off the hands and arms and faces around them. "Who?"

"You know her too. Think back. Paris. End of the Terror. The Coach House. We took Cachés out of there."

"Ten of them. Four girls. Last I heard they were married and raising kids. They didn't take the mail coach down to London to shoot at us."

Pax shook his head. "Not the ones we rescued. We left one girl behind. Remember? Scrawny girl with straw-colored hair."

Some moments from that night were starkly clear. Not that girl's face, though. She'd been a shadow, off in a corner, away from the lantern. "It was dark. You were the one arguing with her."

"I had a good look. Justine probably saw her through field glasses back when she was reconnoitering the Coach House. When we get back to Meeks Street, I'll draw you a picture."

Forty-three

IT TOOK ONLY A MOMENT TO BE SHOT AT. IT TOOK hours to deal with Bow Street.

The watchman from the end of Exeter Street must come to bustle about like a chicken. Then those most closely concerned—she and Hawker and an officious old man who had been passing on the pavement—must go to Bow Street. A report must be taken. Lengthily and in detail. She must ceremoniously meet Sir Nathaniel Conant, the magistrate, who was apparently a great friend of Hawker. Then a Runner and a subsidiary youth, whose job it was to nod at intervals, must return with her to her to her shop to inspect the bullet lodged in the wall and dig it out and discover that nothing whatsoever could be determined except that it had not hit her.

Hawker was of no assistance whatsoever. He said very little, only hovered over her and kept himself between her and every window and made her sit down in chairs.

The watchman, the Bow Street Runner, his assistant, and the local constable must then blunder their way around her shop, sniffing at bottles and looking in drawers and remarking upon the maps which were, she agreed, of very rum places indeed.

They pointed out several times that she had also been stabbed in Braddy Square, with which she agreed. It was strange so many people wanted to kill her. Yes, it was. When that had been discussed sufficiently, the officials and Hawker departed en masse to the tavern to gossip.

That was when Paxton came to stand over her and be alert. Then Séverine arrived and took her upstairs to pack a bag. Séverine did not advise against staying at the shop. She said, "You will need this at Meeks Street," and "You will not need that at Meeks Street," and kept packing. Séverine was a veritable bully about this.

The hackney stopped at the door of her shop. Séverine carried the bag out. Paxton stood, his arms crossed, looking so patient one wanted to kick him.

Hawker, it turned out, had gone to take dinner with the Bow Street magistrate, Conant, and could not be argued with because he was not there.

So she returned to Meeks Street. There was no reason against it, since she had accomplished her purpose in going to Voyages and flushing her attacker.

She let herself be fussed into bed by Séverine while it was still daylight. She slept, profoundly, for hours, past all need for sleeping. That was why she lay awake in bed in the still dark of the night when the clocks struck two, and heard Hawker return to the house.

This was a solid old house that enclosed sounds and secrets within it. She heard the front door open and close, but she did not precisely hear Hawker's footsteps. She heard the dog Muffin, guarding her door, stir and whine and knew that someone had passed. Of Hawker, there was only a sense of him approaching and passing down the long hall, past her room, to his own.

She did not want him to pass her bedroom door without hesitation. She did not want to lie in the darkness and think about him. There had been quite enough of that in her life.

After she had entertained such thoughts for a long time, she rose and wrapped silk about herself and ventured into the hall. She stepped over Muffin, who seemed interested but unalarmed.

The door to Hawker's bedroom was not locked. He sat on the hearthrug, cross-legged, naked except for caleçons, facing the low fire, dark against that red light.

"This is a surprise," he said.

She did not think he was truly surprised. Hawker would always know what she was going to do before she did it. They had worked together and against each other for too many years. They knew even the small crevices of each other's minds.

She said, "You have stayed several nights in my bedchamber. It seemed polite to return the favor."

His face flickered with red light and his eyes glittered. "I wonder if you know what you're doing, coming here like this."

"I always know what I'm doing." She closed the door behind her.

The click, click, click sound that had followed her down the hall ceased. There was a thump as Muffin threw himself down outside the door.

"I bribe your dog, the Muffin, with tidbits, and he lets me invade your room. He is not a good watchdog."

"Almost perfectly useless. Can I ask why you're here?"

"I was restless."

He said, "So you came to be restless with me. I'm glad."

Logs burned blue and orange on the grate. The study downstairs and three of the bedrooms used logs. The other hearths were modern and heated with coal, as was usual in London. The fire of logs made her feel as if she were at home in France. In her own apartment above the shop, her fire was made with logs.

With Hawker, she did not trouble to be proper. She sat the way a man does, cross-legged, and pulled the robe around her knees.

She wore his crimson robe de banyan. Nothing else at all. To clasp his robe upon her was to feel surrounded by masculine arms. The color warmed her like the sun. Red silk for grand gestures, for luxurious desires and recklessness.

They would talk for a while, however. She said, "Paxton has drawn the face of the Caché sniper. Did you see it?"

"When I came in. He hung a copy in the hall. I don't recognize the face."

"Your Ladislaus made five or six copies. I was no help at all. I must have seen her through the glasses in the courtyard of the Coach House, but I have no memory of her. It was long ago."

"She's probably the one who stabbed you. You might know her if you were face-to-face."

"That is what Paxton said. He is planning to search the expensive brothels tomorrow with a pack of men and several copies of his portrait. He tells me I am not well enough to accompany him, as if he were denying me a treat."

"No brothels for you, then." Hawker smiled at her easily. He set his hand to her knee. It was an easy, brief encounter with her knee, as if they were still used to sitting like this, chatting back and forth. "You and me, we'll deck ourselves out and winnow through the ton. We can hunt for a murderess among the guests at the Pickerings' ball. That should add some interest to an otherwise dull affair."

"I do not go to such entertainments. I will ask Séverine to lend me a dress."

Another soft touch to her. This time he slid fingers along the lapel of the robe. "I wish you could wear this color."

The swelling of his cock was not hidden by the caleçons, but he took no notice of it. His physical reaction to her had always seemed to amuse him more than anything else.

She was intensely aware of his smallest movement. Of his hand, as it dropped back to rest on his thigh. Of his breathing.

The red glow of the fire slid over him, appreciating the excellences of his body, lingering on hard lines of muscle. She had never met a man who made nakedness seem so natural. Always, he lived easily within his flesh, like some mythical half human, a selkie or satyr, unacquainted with modesty. He could have been a savage on one of the far islands of the world who had never been clothed.

She knew, of her own knowledge, that he made love without the least shame. Perhaps the men who lived in simplicity at the edges of the world did, also. "Do you think the Caché will be at this great party? It seems a forlorn hope."

"If she's in the beau monde, she should be." He studied his own hand, as if he could add and subtract probabilities there. As if it held answers. "We missed a good many. They're still out there, Cachés infiltrated into the best families."

"For that girl, though, there was no rich family waiting. The Tuteurs would not have been gentle in their treatment."

"I know. After Pax looks in on the richer side of demimonde tomorrow. I'll take the cheaper brothels. I have old friends I can ask." He leaned to nudge the fire, pushing at a log with the tips of his fingers. Sparks flew up. "She's not young. We both know what life is like when a whore isn't young anymore."

She said, "I left her to face that."

"We both did. Mostly me."

"It was my operation."

"I was the expert. You listened to me." He shoved a log till he had it placed just right. "Years of experience later, I still say it. We couldn't have got her out."

"Some people one cannot save." She had her own years of learning this. "It was her choice. She will blame us, though. It is the way of things."

"I imagine she hates us reasonably well."

"But even if she hates us, why destroy you, now, after so long? Why use me in this circuitous way? There is a calculation in this, Hawker, and long planning. She would . . ." The night was not chilly and the fire was hot upon her face. But she was suddenly cold. Since the stabbing she had been cold all the time. "She would direct her greatest hate to Gravois and Patelin. Yet those killings were almost merciful—one brief thrust and it is over. The deadly malice is aimed at you, *mon ami*. You are the one hated."

"That's what I'm thinking." Having perfected the fire, he settled back, his hands at rest on his knees. "I recognize hate when I see it."

He would not be dismayed by the hatred of enemies. He could be hurt only by his friends. What she had done . . . "I do not hate you. I have not hated you for a long time."

His narrow, ruthless face turned to her. He smiled. It was like the sun coming from behind a black and ominous thundercloud. "Do you think I don't know that?"

On his chest, high on the shoulder, a farthing-sized mark in the shape of a star. That was where she'd shot him, long ago, on the marble stairway of the Louvre. She touched it. "I did this."

"An accident." He laughed, deep in his eyes. "I have that from an authoritative source."

"You think it is funny, that I shot at you."

"Not while it was happening, no. Looking back, it does have its humorous side."

No one else in the entire world would be amused by being shot. Only Hawker. "We should not quibble about one small bullet."

She rose onto her knees and leaned over to kiss him, there, on the scar. It was soft as silk and warm to the touch. Warmer than the rest of his skin. Scars left a shallow place in the body's defensive wall. One could feel life beat close to the surface where there had been so much pain. One could feel the very Hawker of him. The stupid disregard for his own safety among the hazards of the world. Gallantry and sarcasm. The reality of Hawker.

He stroked her hair, just as if matters between them were that simple. He must have seen *yes*. He must have seen it in her face.

"I want to take time with this." With great authority, calmly, he pulled her against him till he held her, resting. By chance, her cheek lay against the very wound she had made in him.

He held her, both arms wrapped around her. They watched the fire, and gradually she relaxed against him.

Forty-four

HE HAD REARRANGED HIMSELF TO ENCLOSE HER, supporting her against his knee so she did not have to lean upon her wound. He stroked down her side as one would caress a lazy cat that had come to curl in the lap. There was a combination of deep appreciation and slight wariness. She found both of those arousing.

He had taken upon himself the smell of smoke when he laid the fire and played with it. He also smelled of brandy. She said, "You had good brandy for dinner."

"Nathaniel likes the best. It's wasted on me. I think I prefer gin."

Nathaniel Conant, the chief magistrate of Bow Street, would not serve gin with his dinners. "You do not know if you prefer gin? That is strange."

"When I'm Hawker, I like gin. Sir Adrian Hawkhurst drinks brandy."

"And you are both of them. Both Hawker and Sir Adrian. You must find it confusing."

"Moderately."

It was pleasant to be stroked through the red silk. It would be pleasant also to encounter his skin. She pulled the robe away from her legs and let it slither down beside her thighs. She raised her knee and invited him to touch.

"When I'm Sir Adrian and I do this . . ." He cupped his hand on her knee. She was open to him, thigh and belly and the light brown curls between her legs. "I'm appreciating art."

"You are a connoisseur, in fact."

"It's a pretty knee. Strong. Interesting. A couple of scars. And here, I'm sliding down an arch the color of sunrise and finding a friendly, silky little animal. A rabbit, they call it in English. Coney."

"In French, as you know, it is *chatte*. The little cat."

"Stroking the little cat. Did you know . . . in the middle there you're the color of one of those shells you find on the coast of Italy."

He trailed a fingertip across her there, playing with the hair, smoothing it apart. Her breath caught in her chest. Her senses jerked madly, pulling at her body to do something. Anything. She was breathing quickly when he returned on his slow way back up to her knee. He applied great concentration to the task.

He said, "When I'm Sir Adrian, I love to look at you. When I'm Hawker, I just want to lay you back and get inside you and make us both happy." The path of his hand upon her was iron and honey. "God, but it feels good to touch you. I'm never easy having dinner with Nathaniel, fine fellow though he is. I got tried at Bow Street, once. For theft."

Hawker lived an interesting life. "You did not hang, obviously."

"There was what you might call a miscarriage of justice. I was guilty as charged, but my old master—he was the King Thief of London—bribed me some witnesses. That was my first brush with the magistrates at Bow Street. The beginning of a long, interesting association, as it turned out." He said, "Sit up. We got a hard piece of floor under us." He was gone for an instant.

Her back felt cold where he had left her. Then there were pillows and blankets behind her. He slipped the last of the crimson silk from her shoulders, being gentle along the bandage of her arm. At some point he had divested himself of the last of his clothes.

"We could get into bed," she said. "Many people do. Every

night." But she did not want to leave the circle of light cast by the fire. It was a small world of their own. The rest of the room was dark.

"I like the color of you in the firelight," he said. "Let's lie down so I can get to you better." He leaned over and kissed her knee.

"That is good," she whispered. "I like that."

"I like it too." He kissed the inside of her knee several times. Lingeringly.

Little strikes of lighting played over every soft place between her legs. They were skin to skin. More than naked. Stripped to the soul. Her longing for his body was fire and need and a distraction beyond bearing. She said, "I have wanted you. For three years I have gone about London, and every day I have thought of you."

His hand was possessive on her thigh. "I'd walk down Exeter Street, casual-like, and look in the windows of your shop. I could have stepped inside any day and said, 'Remember me? We used to be lovers.' Sometimes I thought you knew I was there."

"Sometimes I did." He laid himself defenseless against her with such truths. And she . . . What could she do but speak the truth back to him? She was vulnerable to him, undefended as an open oyster. "I saw you once, six months ago. You were on Jermyn Street."

She had stopped in the road and watched him. Perhaps some part of him had sensed her attention. He had raised his head suddenly, as if he sniffed the air. She'd slipped away. A moment longer, and he would have turned around to see her.

She whispered, "We have lost so much time."

"And now?"

She rolled to face him, to kneel beside him. His hand stayed upon her the whole time, sliding over her skin to end up resting on her back. She was glad to be connected to him. Glad her thigh rested next to his.

"And now . . . this." She kissed his lips. Men need simple answers—even Hawker, who was the most wise of his species.

His lips were filled with complicated response, heavy with meaning. She was enmeshed in the taste and smell of him. Along his jaw and his neck he tasted like soap when she licked him.

The persuasion of his hands was infinite. Hands that loosened every muscle of her back as they ran up and down her spine. He leaned to kiss her breasts, to murmur at their beauty and kiss them again. She was urged toward him, lifted as if she had no weight. She was upon him, upon his lap, and she wrapped her legs around him so they were even closer.

He kissed one breast. Then the other. "Here's my old friends. Pretty girls. How have you two been?" He teased her nipple between his fingers. "And look at this. You're glad to see me too."

He was altogether foolish. But, oh, her body delighted in his games. She plunged into his nonsense and let him take her where he would.

"Your turn." He went from breast to breast. "Now yours. Just no choice between you."

He nibbled where her breasts were drawn up and sensitive. Played his tongue fast across her there. Her heart expanded into joy. She filled her senses with him, drowned in him, dug her fingers into his shoulder, and lost herself in the smell of his hair.

He entered her. Hard and overwhelming and so good.

"I have missed this," he said.

She felt herself tipped backward, down to the blankets. He never left her. Never parted from her. She held him to her tightly, with arms, with thighs.

"Please." She had no words. "Please. Now."

He began to drive each stroke strongly inside her. She pulled herself to him, meeting him. Matching him.

Arched and straining, gasping for breath, plucked like a bow, she became the exultation. She convulsed around him. She felt him join her, losing control. He groaned deeply, hard and low, in triumph.

She heard that and let herself fall into red pleasure and was consumed by it.

SHE watched him through lazy and half-closed eyes, not wanting to move. He was so perfectly beautiful. He was skilled beyond measure. She felt wonderful.

He touched across the bandage on her arm, seeing that all was safe. Then he sat, his half of the blanket across his lap, gazing down at her with an unreadable expression in his eyes.

She reached to hold his hand. Even with all the intimacy between them, the straightforward holding of hand in hand was one more.

He said, "Will you marry me?"

"No." She sat up.

"Ah. That's your considered reply, that is?" One might spend a week with a magnifying glass and not read one iota of expression upon that face. She tried to take her hand away, and he did not let go.

"I mean, 'No, what are you saying?'"

"Then you shouldn't make it sound so much like, 'No, we can't get married.'"

"That is also true." She paused. "Probably." When he was silent, she said, "I have not thought this through."

"Think it through."

She would have jumped up and put more space between the breath and heat and immediacy of his body. She would have liked to become somewhat more clothed. Almost no rational thinking occurs when one is naked.

He held her hand and looked at her, quietly serious. "There is no one else for me. Never has been. The war's been over a long time."

"It is not a matter of our nations at war."

"Just pointing out that that small impediment no longer exists. We're not enemies anymore—England and France. I heard the speeches. Nobody on either side will care if we marry." He turned her hand over to look at the palm. Stroked across it as if he brushed dust away. "Is it me being a gutter rat? Me coming from nothing at all?"

"You know that does not matter to me."

"It should. You deserve better." His lips quirked. "But since you haven't picked anybody better, why not me? I have money. I came by it honestly, picking good investments. Property mostly. There's a house in the West End I've never bothered to live in much. It has a Grecian foyer and an Adam fireplace in the dining room." Startlingly, suddenly, he grinned. "I have a damn butler. You can help me intimidate him."

"I do not give one penny for your butler and your thousands of pounds and the blood you carry in your veins. I have fought all my life to make a world where such things do not matter."

"But the answer is still no," he said.

"How can I say yes? We have been apart for years and years. We do not know each other."

"You know every alley in my mind, every broken bottle and rat scuttling in there. You put me in my place when I get above myself. Austria, Prussia, Italy, all up and down France—you always figured out where I was going to mount the next operation. Half the time, you blocked me. Just uncanny that way." He hadn't let go of her hand. "I know you pretty well too."

"I have some familiarity with the workings of your mind. That does not mean we should get married."

He kissed her knuckles. One, two, three, and four. She was twitching inside by the time he finished. "No, we should get married so we can go to bed together and do all these interesting things with each other and still stay respectable."

"You, who are a paragon of respectability, always." Never, not once, had she expected to marry. She had not considered the possibility.

Perhaps it was being naked, which befuddled her mind. Perhaps it was being wholly happy, with every inch of her body exultant. Perhaps it was merely that this was Hawker, and he could always make his mad notions seem possible. "I do not say, 'No,' precisely. I feel very strange about the whole idea."

He stood and used the hand he was still holding to pull her to her feet. "Let's go to bed—my bed—and talk about this in the morning. I want to lie beside you and soak up the warmth coming off of you."

His bed was very nice, so much so that they made love again almost as soon as they had wriggled down into the sheets.

When she sank into sleep at the end of it, she felt Hawker pull the covers over her. He did that after they made love, however far the blankets and sheets had strayed. It was an act of most gentlemanly kindness, the sort of habit a man might follow with a cherished wife.

She could not imagine herself, married.

Forty-five

PAX SAT AT THE DESK IN THE LIBRARY, DRAWING the face of the Caché woman with pen and charcoal. This was his tenth copy, and they were going faster now. He'd got the face close to right. The nose and the shape of the eyes hadn't changed from when she was a child.

The study on the ground floor of Meeks Street held a couch and armchairs. The walls were stocked with some of the books in the house, the ones that weren't upstairs. The day's newspapers, as always, had been opened and folded at random and left on the tables everywhere or stuffed sideways in the shelves.

Felicity had come at dark to close the curtains. She hadn't cleaned away the dirty teacups or lighted the lamps. Back when he was doorkeeper and errand boy, he'd been more conscientious.

He'd lit the stand of candles from the mantelpiece and taken it over to the desk to give him light to work.

Doyle was in a big chair by the fire with his feet up on the andirons. He had a pile of file folders on the table at his elbow and was leafing through them, taking out reports and news clippings, leaving a strip of red paper with his name and the date behind as a marker.

A little stack was growing on the floor beside Doyle. News

of men who disappeared. Men who died with a single knife stroke to the heart. Unexpected deaths in the night where men forgot how to breathe. Rumors about Cachés. Anything in the files that might touch on this business.

He'd be going through the files himself, if he weren't busy drawing. "Are we going to pick up the ones who gave evidence to Bow Street, saying the killer looked like Hawk?"

"Three false names." Doyle didn't look up. "Which is not what you'd call useful, and an army captain who didn't crack like an egg when I questioned him. He's being watched."

"They'll turn out to be Cachés."

"Likely."

"Blackmailed into it. I may know them from Paris." He blew charcoal dust off the portrait, studied it, and set it aside on the edge of the desk. "From when I was training to spy on the English."

"Now you spy for the English. France's loss. Our gain."

"I like to think so. I'm glad Galba decided not to garrote me." He flexed his fingers and pulled a sheet to him. "This is going slow." He picked up the finest of the pencils, and drew the oval of the face.

It wasn't just copying. Each time, he had to catch what made the face unique. "I'll do two or three for Bow Street. Hawk can drop them by tomorrow."

Hawk had come back to Meeks Street an hour before. The only sign of him was Felicity muttering her way down the hall to open the door and then muttering her way back to bed. He hadn't poked his head into the study. There was no sound of his footsteps on the stairs. No click of a bedroom door closing. Hawk didn't make noise moving around a house at night.

Doyle said, "I'd guess everything went smoothly with Conant."

"Seems so." Lines horizontal. Lines vertical. The geography of the face that set the longitude and latitude of eyes, nose, mouth. "They're an odd pair to be friends."

"They sit around and talk about murder. Conant helps the Service when he can and Hawk doesn't kill people in London. Bow Street appreciates the courtesy. This one's interesting." Doyle picked a clipping from a file. "Two years ago an MP from the wilds of Buckinghamshire got himself stabbed in Mayfair walking home from a dinner party."

"I remember. Vessey. William, I think. Never solved."

"Good memory. Six months before that . . ." Doyle indicated the papers on the floor beside him, "a Thomas Daventry was taken out of the Thames with stab wounds in him. Not an MP, but active in politics. A Radical with money."

"If somebody's planning to wipe out the Whigs, they're taking their time about it." He sketched the shape of the lips.

"And this is a bloke from the Foreign Office. George Reynolds, politics unknown. Death by a surfeit of steel through his belly." Doyle closed one file and reached for another.

Upstairs, in the hall, there was a scratching of dog toenails. Muffin tapped claws down the hall, transferring his guarding duties from Justine DuMotier's door to Hawk's.

Justine had gone into Hawk's room.

Doyle tilted his head back to look at the ceiling. "They're keeping Muffin awake."

"Nobody's getting any sleep tonight."

A solid, comfortable thump from the upstairs hall. Muffin settled down, meaning Justine was staying for bit.

"Be nice if this simplified matters," Doyle said.

"And about time."

"But they don't do anything simple, do they?"

"Not so far." The Caché's mouth wasn't wide, but the lips were full. She had a flat bridge on the nose. He'd finish that up with white chalk, last thing. "You're Hawk's executor, if he dies, aren't you?"

Doyle didn't look surprised. Hard to make Doyle look surprised. "Have been for years."

"Who gets the money?"

Doyle pulled a new file into his lap, opened it, and started through. "There are easier ways to kill somebody if you just want his money."

"Humor me."

"Ask Hawk."

"No." He worked on the eyebrows. Then went over it with pen and India ink.

Doyle said, "Setting aside that it's illegal for me to talk about this and Hawk wouldn't like it, it's not useful."

"We have to cross it off the list. He's a rich man."

After another minute of thought. Doyle said, "He's left houses and businesses to old friends who are already running them or living in them. A gold watch to George. Justine DuMotier gets a silver chain with a medal on it. He's set up fifty or sixty annuities. Retired agents, mostly."

"I don't see Hawk leaving property to somebody who'd kill him for it."

A grunt from Doyle.

"What about the rest? That's a good many tens of thousands of pounds. Who gets that?"

"Well, that goes to me, you see. Which is a technicality, meaning it goes to Maggie."

"For the orphanages."

"What Hawk calls, 'those damn brats too clumsy to make a living at theft.'" Doyle had worked his way through the files for April. He set that down and opened up May. "I could steal the lot, if he obliged me by dying."

"And you'd step in as Head of the British Service."

"I would indeed," Doyle said. "You keep coming up with reasons for me to kill him."

"Except you don't need the money and you don't want to run the Service. You've spent a long career avoiding it."

"There's that," Doyle agreed amiably.

Forty-six

THE SMELL OF A FANCY BALL IN LONDON WAS SWEET wine, sweat, and perfume. In winter, add damp wool to that. It didn't smell too different from a whorehouse, really.

"I hate seeing her without a gun," Hawker said.

"Here I thought you didn't like guns." Doyle strolled at his side, looking stupid and benign and well-groomed. The quintessence of English aristocrat.

"I don't. But Justine does." He followed the lilac silk weaving through the forest of black coats and pastel debutante gowns. That was Owl, with Séverine beside her, working her way around the reception room. "I let her talk me into sending her in with one wing out of commission and no gun. I must be out of my mind."

"You and the generality of mankind."

The Pickerings' ballroom, reception room, all the antechambers, and every damn room in the place was noisy, crowded, and covered with gilt and mirrors. Overheated, over-scented, over-decorated. Pax and Owl searched, dancer by dancer, wallflower by wallflower, looking into every face, trying to spot one sparrow out of the flock.

"She has a knife in her sleeve," Doyle said. "She's got another under her dress. She's been in worse places, with less—so has Sévie, for that matter—and we got five men wandering around, armed to the teeth. I've seen pitched battles with less weaponry."

That was an exaggeration. "It only takes one bullet."

"Which our Caché is not going to contribute unless she's stuffed a gun down her titties." Doyle shook his head. "You're staring at Justine again. I taught you better than that."

"I'm keeping track of an operation."

"You're staring. This is why I never put a husband and wife in the field together."

"We're not married."

"I don't put lovers together, either." Doyle nodded to a man Hawker didn't know. When they were out of earshot, Doyle murmured, "Richard Shaw, Justice of the Peace, up from the country. Rabid Tory. Probably trying for an introduction to Liverpool."

Liverpool, the Prime Minister, was standing in an alcove on the far side of the room. Eight or ten men had gathered in close, basking in the glow of power, chatting. A respectful distance cleared around them.

"Castlereagh, Granville, and Melbourne." Doyle named them.

"Liverpool is knee deep in Whig politicians."

"Diplomatic business, since it's Castlereagh. Probably the Prussian tariffs." Doyle said, "Cummings is busy."

Lord Cummings had wedged himself into a place on Liverpool's right hand. He was taller than the other men around Liverpool, gray-haired and distinguished, but he seemed flimsy next to the others.

"Small fish for that pond." Lordship or no, Cummings wasn't the equal of the other men in Liverpool's circle. "He's talking nineteen to the dozen. I wonder what he's up to."

"At a guess, he's mending bridges. Military Intelligence is unpopular in England. Liverpool's being criticized in the newspapers, and he doesn't like it. He's not cozy with Cummings lately."

"Who shall blame Liverpool? Let us go trolling for a Caché."

The ton parted to let them through—diplomats, MPs, bankers and bishops, staid country gentry, the aristocracy of Europe. They moved aside for the boy from the rookeries of St. Giles.

There'd been a time when his greatest ambition was to be a

gentleman. Gentlemen—he was sure of this—ate all the sausages and eel pie they wanted. They kept coal fires burning on every grate. They wore silk nightshirts to bed and they pissed in gold chamber pots.

He'd set out to make himself a nob. He'd succeeded. Trouble was, it had stopped being an act years ago. Somebody named Sir Adrian had crawled into his skin and set up housekeeping. The boy from St. Giles wasn't quite comfortable in there anymore.

"Hawkhurst. I thought you were out of town."

"Jeremy." Greet a friend. Shake hands. Promise to talk when they met for cards next week at Mortimer's house. Walk on.

For all he was a friend, Jeremy knew Sir Adrian. He didn't know Hawker. In St. Giles, men knew Hawker but not Sir Adrian. Sometimes, it felt like neither half of him was the real one.

"You're watching her again," Doyle said.

"I like watching her." He kept his eye on Owl as she slipped along, inconspicuous, looking at faces. A flock of women milled around her, fluttering, gesturing. Any one of them could be carrying a knife.

For a decade, she'd kept herself alive on battlefields and in back alleys. She was watching her back. He had to believe she could survive one night at the Pickerings.

Besides, Pax was following her, ten paces behind.

He turned away, casual-like, so he didn't have to notice Mrs. Gaite-Hartwick waving cheerily in his direction. The Gaite-Hartwicks weren't the only family making it clear they'd overlook any amount of Hawkhurst mysterious origin as long as he owned a snug little manor near Oxford, part of a shipping company, and considerable London property.

Doyle said, "If I were her husband, I'd drink. Let's get out of the main thoroughfare."

"Suits me. Looks like Owl's about finished."

"Let's go down and take inventory of the latecomers in the lobby. Terrington party next. Anybody who wasn't here is going to be there. It'll be larger than this."

"Always a silver lining."

"There's more of a foreign contingent at the Terringtons'. Our Caché may have gone back to being French." Doyle narrowed his eyes. "Cummings is whispering in Liverpool's ear, and they're both looking this way."

"Have we done anything to irritate Liverpool in the last little space of time?"

"Not that I know of."

"Let us hope Cummings is annoying him with the antics of the Yorkshire Luddites. Ah . . . Reams comes this way, being impolite to all the nice old ladies in his path. How very direct the military is."

Colonel Reams arrived in all the glory of his scarlet coat, dress sword at his side, a big, red-coated slab of aging muscle. He wouldn't think of himself as a messenger boy, but that was his role. "Liverpool wants to talk to you."

Reams might as well have capered in triumph. Cummings had something clever planned, and Reams knew what it was. The Prime Minister was involved.

Interesting.

Nothing like walking into a trap to set the blood pumping. Plots and machinations littered the ground like caltrops. The game was in play.

He signaled Pax to move in closer to Owl. "Keep an eye on things," he told Doyle.

"I'll keep an eye on you instead." Doyle slipped a thumb into his fob pocket and turned to be at his side.

Reams blocked the way. "I was told to bring Hawkhurst, not you."

Doyle didn't twitch a muscle. He just transformed from a large, indolent gentleman enjoying himself at a party into Lord William Doyle Markham, Viscount Markham, heir to the Earl of Dunmott, cousin, in one degree or other, to everybody important in the room, and married into one of the great aristocratic houses of Europe.

And him . . . he let himself be Sir Adrian Hawkhurst, who was God knew what, from God knew where, but rich, powerful, and at home in this ballroom.

Possibly Reams recalled the reputation for deadliness hovering over the men he confronted.

It was time to behave like an aristocrat. Time to be damn-your-eyes arrogant. He said, "Get the hell out of my way." He and Doyle walked past Reams like a jackass in uniform didn't even exist.

They didn't hurry. Reams got left in their wake anyhow.

Liverpool beckoned when they got close, inviting them in. "Hawkhurst. Markham. Sorry to interrupt your evening."

"Sir." The Head of the British Intelligence Service met fairly often with the Prime Minister. So far, they'd dealt well. Liverpool liked to get reports face-to-face. Liked to ask questions. He understood there was just a startling flock of secrets that never got set down on paper.

Nods exchanged all around the circle. He knew these men, some better than others. On every face, he saw the kind of avid curiosity given to carriage wrecks.

The Prime Minister was an amiable man in private, pig-stubborn politically, and nobody's fool. He was not pleased at the moment, which was likely to be bad news for somebody. His big twitchy eyebrows drew together. "Tell me about these two dead Frenchmen."

Cummings made placating gestures. "I'm not accusing Hawkhurst. I am entirely convinced of his integrity. I merely raise the question of whether he should temporarily step down from his position until—"

Liverpool interrupted, "I want to hear what he has to say. Well, Hawkhurst?"

Cummings planted his cane on the marble floor, set both hands to the head of it, and gloated in a genteel manner.

Well, well, well. This was the duel. This was facing an enemy, weapons drawn. Him against Cummings. High stakes. He couldn't grin and rub his hands. Instead, he drew himself up, stiff and offended. "What do you mean, 'step down?' "

Cummings gave an elegant tilt to the cane. "In light of certain allegations that have been brought against you, it would be wisest if the government replaced you with someone outside your—" Cummings didn't get to finish.

"Tell me about the dead men," Liverpool said.

The Head of the British Service played political games as well the Great Game of spying. This was the cross-and-jostle work of British politics. He let himself look exasperated, with a dash of mysterious spicing it up. "There have been two deaths, both French émigrés. They're being investigated by Bow Street. The first murder—"

"The stabbings are the work of the same man," Cummings said quickly. "He—"

Liverpool snapped, "Let him talk."

Good. Liverpool wasn't on Cummings's side. Not necessarily on his side, either, but not on Cummings's.

"Stabbed. Yes. We know a good bit about the circumstances." He paused. The circle of men leaned forward, listening. Nothing like murder to entertain the nobility. "There's more to it than brutal murder."

"What do you mean?" That was Castlereagh. You could be foreign secretary and still hungry for the details of violent death.

Time to lift the corner of the curtain and reveal some shadow. Damn, he should have been a street performer. "The same method was used in both cases. One stroke to the heart." He jerked his fist upward, suddenly. "It takes timing and skill and—I hate to say it—practice. We're dealing with an expert."

Castlereagh muttered, "Cowardly. Cowardly work."

"In London, you say?" That was an MP from Suffolk. "What's the world coming to when there's bloody murder in London?"

Men die worse than that in London every day, in Whitechapel and St. Giles. "Bow Street called us in because of the connection with France. We've learned that both the dead men were former French Secret Police. They left France during the Revolution, changed their names, and set up in London as shopkeepers."

Reams, who'd been hanging around the outskirts, shouldered forward. "Should have been hanged the day they arrived." One man raised an eyebrow. Liverpool looked annoyed. Reams plowed on, oblivious. "Too many damn French in England anyway. The war's over, but they're still stirring up trouble."

Ass. Didn't he know these men had ties and ties again to France? Blood, marriage, friendship. He paused to let the idiocy of Reams sink in, then went on. "We think the murderer is French, too, from the method. The knives used—"

"They're your bloody knives." Reams didn't have the sense to keep his mouth closed. "Your name's on them, for God's sake. The initials *A* and *H*. Do you think you can stand here and pretend not to know?"

Noblemen are born knowing how to freeze impertinence. He'd had to learn. "I beg your pardon."

"Your knives. I've seen them, you murdering little—"

"Enough." He rapped it out. He lifted ice from inside his belly and put it in his voice. "I've had enough of this. Silence!"

Reams didn't dare—didn't quite dare—to answer back.

"There's a superficial resemblance to knives used in overseas operations a decade ago. If you had military experience in the field," he looked deliberately up and down the uniform, "or if you'd taken two minutes to examine the knives, the differences would be obvious."

"I'll be damned if—"

He cut it off. "That's enough, Colonel. If one of my men went off half-cocked like that, I'd break him to sergeant. Be glad you don't answer to me."

He turned his back on Reams. "The knives are the crux of the matter." He gathered the group with his eyes. They were all listening. "The blades are marked L'Atelier de Paris. That makes them very possibly French Military issue. French steel." He glanced scathingly at Reams. "Not British."

Reams wasn't in a position to contradict, not knowing French steel from Italian sausage.

"A quarrel between Frenchmen?" Liverpool offered.

"Not as simple as that, unfortunately. The knives are engraved on the hilt, yes. But not *AH*. The letters are *N* and *B*—"

Castlereagh understood instantly. "The devil you say."

"*NB* for *Napoleon Bonaparte*. The knives were left at the scene as a warning. These are undoubtedly political murders. We're looking at French revolutionary groups operating in London. There are still fanatics out there."

There were murmurs of agreement. Significant glances back and forth. Napoleon might be an old man, embittered and sick, exiled to a remote outpost in the North Atlantic, but his name was still imperial. Every one of these powerful lords had been afraid of Napoleon's *Grande Armée*.

Cummings knew he'd been outmaneuvered. What he'd seen in the evidence boxes at Bow Street was gone now. The face under the graying hair was pale as a fish belly. His mouth stretched in a tight smile, holding back rage.

Let's finish this before he gets his balance back.

Time to frown and look serious. "I've sent word to our branch in Paris. We hope . . ." He was judicious for a second or two. "We hope this is some old revenge against two particular men, but we have to take into account the possibility of a larger plot." His gesture spoke of a hundred secrets not told. "We're investigating."

One man nodded to the next. Before dawn, half the ton would know there was a plot to free Napoleon from St. Helena. Prime Minister to ten-year-old schoolboy, everyone loved plots.

Reams said, "Damn it! I know what I saw."

Cummings knew when to retreat. "That's enough, Colonel." Whatever wormwood was, Cummings had bitten off a wad of it. "You were mistaken, obviously."

Liverpool said, "It would be best to avoid such mistakes in the future." From him, in this company, that was enough.

Castlereagh wanted to know if there was blood on the knives still. Fortunately, he was able to say, "There is. Yes." Nothing like attention to detail.

It could have gone the other way. He could have been the one humiliated. He could even have been removed from the British Service. That quick. That easy. Whoever wanted to ruin Adrian Hawkhurst had found a fine instrument in Lord Cummings.

"Give me a few minutes with Sir Adrian." Liverpool glanced around.

Men separated off in groups. Doyle chatted with Melbourne, who was with him at Cambridge. Reams stalked off muttering about "that upstart foreign bastard," Hawkhurst, who was "half a Hindu, probably," till Cummings put a lid on him.

Liverpool's grandmother was Indian. Melbourne was, famously, Egremont's bastard. Somebody should have shared this with the colonel.

When they were alone, Liverpool said, "I dislike settling quarrels between my intelligence departments." That was both support and a warning. Liverpool was the consummate politician and, above all, a practical man. They understood each other reasonably well. "I don't want to know what you did with those knives. Will the government be embarrassed in the newspapers?"

"It will not."

"Cummings says there's a Frenchwoman living at your headquarters. The implication is she's a spy and involved in those murders."

"A spy?" He allowed himself a wry smile. "Hardly. Markham's foster daughter, Séverine, is staying with us while he's in London. Also her sister, Mademoiselle Justine DeCabrillac. She goes by the name DuMotier in England."

"DeCabrillac . . . ?"

"Daughters of the last Comte DeCabrillac."

"Ah. Killed in the Revolution, wasn't he? Terrible business for the daughters. I know the current comte. They'd be DuMotiers on the mother's side. Some kind of cousin to Lafayette."

That was the nobs for you. Always knowing who was related which way. "As to being spies . . . I'll ask you to keep this sub rosa, but those two gathered intelligence in France during the war." Which was true enough. No need to say who Justine had been working for.

"Admirable." Liverpool ran eyes over the reception room, knowing everyone, noticing who was talking to who. "Someone asked me, the other day, if you were one of the Kent Hawkhursts. Nobody knew. You're quite the mysterious figure."

"I have never attempted to be. Merely . . . private."

"Quite so. In your position, it's natural." Liverpool pursed his lips. "Markham took in a three or four French orphans, didn't he, back during the Terror? Séverine DeCabrillac and one of the Villards—the old duc's heir. There were some others. You're a protégé of Markham, yourself, I understand." He added delicately, "Another of those French orphans?"

"I've known Lord Markham a good long while. The DeCabrillac daughters are here tonight. Over there by the—"

"One of the difficulties with the French war was the pack of hungry émigrés that washed up in England. French second cousins we'd never heard of, mostly. A few turned out to be worth their salt. Some of them made fine army officers. I suppose Markham steered you in the direction of his own service."

"You might say that." Doyle had been persuasive about joining the British Service back when he was a kid. There'd been some mention that the other choice was hanging.

Liverpool nodded. "You know there are rumors about your background? Someone mentioned the translation of Hapsburg into English is Hawkhurst."

I didn't know that when I made the name up. "A coincidence. Speaking of émigrés who settled in England, both the DeCabrillacs are interesting women. Very independent. The older one keeps a shop in Exeter Street."

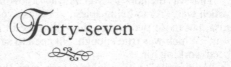

Forty-seven

ON THE OTHER SIDE OF THE FOYER, CUMMINGS COL-
lected his overcoat. A footman helped him into it, handed him
hat and cane, and went to attend three men who'd walked in the
front door and were shedding belongings.

Hawker didn't glance in that direction. He'd humiliated the
man in public. Dealing with him was now dangerous as hand-
feeding a rabid dog. Next week or next month he'd need to work
with Military Intelligence again.

Or maybe not. Cummings and his happy lads had been
brought back to England to enforce order upon an unruly popu-
lace. The papers were already calling it "England's secret
police." Letters to the editor talked about dissolving Military
Intelligence for good.

Cummings definitely had the wind up. Whoever wrote the
letter that sent Cummings off to Bow Street understood his
lordship right down to the ground.

His Lordship twitched his cuffs smooth under the coat
sleeves with brisk little motions. Upright, distinguished, dis-
dainful, he was all an important gentleman should be. You'd
never guess he'd lost the skirmish in front of Liverpool. Reams
was significantly absent.

Cummings was headed this way. Looked like he wanted to

exchange a few words. But then, Cummings was an old campaigner. Maybe he took the setback philosophically.

"I must congratulate you." Cummings said it the same way he'd say, "I must flay the flesh off your still-twitching bones."

"Thank you."

"You switched the knives at Bow Street."

"That would be clever of me."

Cummings developed a tight, white line around his mouth. He gripped his cane like they'd had an argument and it wanted to leave. "We both know what happened."

"Truth is so elastic. Within an hour, the polite world will talk of nothing but the Bonapartist plot." He allowed himself to become very French, and shrug. It maddened Cummings when he acted French. "Who can contradict what the world knows so thoroughly?"

"Don't challenge me, Hawkhurst. You don't want me for an enemy." He turned and swept away, his cane swinging angrily, his heels clicking the marble floor toward Castlereagh who stopped and exchange a few words.

"There is a long tradition," a voice said from behind his shoulder, "that senior intelligence agents should hate one another."

Owl draped her lace shawl at her back, arm to arm. She looked like one of the great ladies of the ton. Dignified and aristocratic. Prettier than any of the others, though.

He said, "I've heard that."

"It is a matter of testing their competence. If they cannot emerge victorious among their colleagues, how can they outfox their enemies? I believe a similar method is used in training gamecocks."

"We had an encounter just a few minutes ago and I am now the chief gamecock on this particular hill. Are you tired? Doyle can take you home if you're getting tired."

"I am weary, of course. It is embarrassing to walk about, rudely staring at women, comparing their faces with my memory of a young girl. I have only one glimpse of an assassin in the rain and a tiny figure seen through glasses many years ago. I do not know if I would recognize her again. And she will have changed. It is sad, sometimes, to see what life makes of pretty young girls."

"I liked you as a pretty young girl." He let men and women brush past on either side of him and only looked at her. "I like the woman you became better than the girl you were. I like the story you've written on your face."

"I will not say you speak flattery. I will only point out that you say most exactly what I want to hear."

"Truth, then. You want to hear truth." He couldn't touch Owl, except with his eyes, so he let his imagination slide across her, planning where he'd kiss her later on tonight. He liked kissing beauty and he'd done a certain amount of that over the years. With Owl, he'd start with beauty and go on to kissing ruthlessness and ideals in the lines at the corners of her eyes. Passion and practicality sitting around her mouth. Not a comfortable woman, his Owl. Not ordinary.

She wrapped her hand on that bandage she was wearing under the sleeve of that silk dress. "The next party is bigger than this and noisier. More people."

"I am not fragile."

"I have never been an admirer of fragile. I think we have to do this tonight, before she hears we're looking for her."

"I think so too." Owl was faced the right way. She spotted Fletcher and gave a little tilt of her head toward him.

Fletcher came, ducking through a line of young girls, so carefully groomed they were almost indistinguishable one from the other. He brought a bright-eyed maid with him.

"This is Mary, maid to Lady McLean." Fletcher handed her the Caché drawing he'd been showing around the kitchen and stables. "Tell them."

"I have seen this woman." She unrolled it to look at one last time. To hold out and show. Her English was careful, with Scots underneath. "Twice. Once outside a shop on Oxford Street. Once in Portman Square, watching a street player."

The West End. Still a big place to search. "Do you remember anything else? Was she with somebody? How she was dressed?"

"On her own, both times. Not a maid in sight. It was by that I noticed her, because a woman dressed as she was should have her maid about her." She tapped the paper with the back of her hand. "She was wearing Madame Elise."

Owl slipped in, "The dressmaker."

"It was a walking dress in Pomona poplin, the first time. Satin trim and a perline cape, long, with scallops." She made shapes in the air. "The second time, she was in Portman Square.

That was a carriage dress in spotted silk. And a very pretty color it was. Amber. Lined with sarcenet."

Owl leaned close to his ear. "This may be the one. I have thought it would be a woman who recognized her."

"We'll try the dressmaker. You and Doyle come with me. I'll send the rest off to the next party."

"The dressmaker will live near her shop. With luck, there may even be someone working this late. Give me three minutes more and I will come." Owl touched the maid's arm and drew her a little aside, into a quiet space beside the stairs. "Tell me more about the dresses. Satin and braid on the Pomona one? What color was the braid?"

When he they left Cummings was walking out too. He watched their carriage drive away, looking grim.

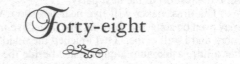

Forty-eight

IT HAD TAKEN MORE THAN THREE HOURS TO TRACK down the dressmaker, Elise, who was in a bed not her own. A nicely calculated mixture of bribery and threat was required to cajole this address from her. It was almost dawn when they came to Percy Street.

Jane Cardiff, a woman of the demimonde, lived above a neat milliner's shop. It was, Justine thought, exactly the sort of place she had chosen for herself when she retired from spying. Here was a quiet street and neighbors busy enough with their own affairs that they would not meddle with hers.

The bow window of the shop held five hats, tilted attractively on their posts like flower heads on stalks. The windows of that apartment upstairs were silent and dark, as they should be at this hour. To the right of the shop was the door that led upward. She allowed Hawker to do the business of opening it.

Monsieur Doyle had already circled to the back, looking into the state of the alley and the garden of the shop, prepared to deal with anyone who fled in that direction. She watched the street, the other shops and houses, and all the windows.

Jane Cardiff had shown a tendency to shoot people from windows. This should not be encouraged by inattention.

The breath of the waking city surrounded her, a grumble

compounded of sleepy tradesmen opening shutters, sparrows chittering, the drivers of delivery wagons being emphatic to one another, and milk carts rumbling over cobblestones. This was the best hour for breaking into houses. Suspicion was at a low ebb this time of the day. There is something respectable about dawn.

When Hawker leaned close to the lock to work his skill upon it, his white shirt was hidden. His black coat and her own dark gray cloak were almost invisible against the door. They would not be apparent unless someone looked carefully.

Hawker set his first pick in the keyhole. Wriggled it. Frowned and tried the knob. The door opened. "It's not locked."

"We break into the only house in London that is not locked. How fortuitous."

"I wouldn't want to calculate the odds."

"It is almost certainly a trap. We will be lured to the top of the stairs and shot and lie there in a slowly widening pool of blood while Mademoiselle Jane Cardiff steps over our corpses and escapes. Or possibly, even as we stand here, she is in a window, aiming a rifle at us."

"Now you've got me nervous." He put his picklocks away inside his jacket and pushed the door back. A long, straight stair led upward. "Why don't you stay a ways behind me."

"Certainly. We will allow Mademoiselle Cardiff to attempt your life instead of mine. That will be a nice change."

He was already padding soft-footed upward. She left the door to the street ajar, drew her pistol, and followed, guarding behind them.

He did not fill the dusty stairwell with unnecessary chatter. The next sound she heard was the door at the top of the stair swinging open. Another door had been left invitingly unlocked.

Hawker led the way into the apartment, radiating a cautious readiness, setting his feet with the grace of a cat on a high wall. Hearing, smelling, sensing everything. She was content to send him and his great cunning ahead while she held the gun and followed. She would, at the least sign of hazard, shoot someone. Hawker could explain to the authorities later. Much of life is wasted worrying about the authorities.

The foyer was a scene of malicious disorder. The little tables were thrown down. A vase of indigo-blue Sèvres-ware was broken. The roses had been crushed underfoot.

All the delicate, elegant rooms were torn apart. The sofa was ripped open and the feathers spilled out in white piles. Every book was ripped from the bookcase and thrown to the floor. She stepped over a marquetry cabinet, its glass in pieces, the china boxes from the shelves crushed to white chips. The poker that had smashed them was across the room beneath the black mark it made where it was hurled against the wall.

"Someone is in a rage." One does not meet rage with rage. One does not become afraid. But this destruction was very ugly. "This is not a proper search. This is a tantrum."

"Fast and sloppy." Hawker stalked around, poking into what was broken and what was not, disgusted. "Even setting aside the damage, this is a poor job of searching the place."

Wide glass doors let in the dawn and showed a balcony where the pots of ferns and flowers had been overturned. She eased her pistol to half cock and stepped out. The garden below was shadowed. It possibly contained Doyle.

"I don't know why people always check the flowerpots." Hawker joined her. "I have never yet found anything in a flowerpot."

"I do not see Doyle. I gather one doesn't."

"He'll drop by when he's through breaking into the shop downstairs. It shouldn't take long."

Hawker pushed a spindly table out of the way in the hall. An open door revealed the kitchen, ransacked. It would be a desperate or stupid man who searched for secrets in a kitchen, where maids would poke about in every cranny and crevice. Smashed china and spilled flour covered the floor, full of boot prints.

He said, "This was done after the salon. There's no flour in there. I make it the foyer first, then the salon. Here, in the kitchen. Then down the hall toward the bedroom."

She knelt, holding her pistol at her side, not getting flour on her dress, and touched the pattern of a boot heel. "It was one man in this room."

"If we got one man, it took him an hour. Two men go a little faster. Not twice as fast. They get in each other's way." Hawker would always make a good estimate of the time needed for theft.

She agreed with a nod. "This destruction was done recently. The roses in the foyer have only begun to wilt."

"An hour or two."

"We have just missed him. Almost certainly he was alerted by your search of the brothels today."

"Or he saw us in the Pickerings' ballroom. He came looking for something smaller than this." Hawker touched the broken pieces of the salt box with his boot. "Less than eight inches long."

"Something important that belongs to Jane Cardiff." She did not say, "Where is she?" but they were both thinking that. "This is an evil man. I can taste it in what he has done."

Crescents of flour marked the long carpet toward the door at the end of the hall. Jane Cardiff's bedroom.

A hand lantern stood on the writing desk, still lit. The embroidered bedspread, the red velvet pillows, and the mattress were thrown to the floor and slit open. The drawers upended. Dresses, cloaks, and bonnets were tumbled in heaps.

"And we have more random breakage." Hawker curled his lip. "He didn't find what he was looking for."

She saw what Hawker saw. This was the last room searched—the lamp had been left behind here. There was no corner left undisturbed. No sign a search ended and the searcher picked up his prize and departed.

She said, "Perhaps Jane Cardiff grabbed it up and ran. Perhaps he was too late."

She uncocked her gun and laid it beside the lantern where it would be handy if she needed it. Every cubbyhole in the desk had been emptied. The secret drawer—such desks always contain one—was pulled out. On the blotter, six fabric-covered boxes, such as jewelers use, were open and empty. Séverine would be able to tell her which jewelers these were. She did not know, herself. She had no reason to buy jewels. "This is robbery. But it is an afterthought."

"I never trust a man who is not attracted to valuable objects." Papers had been shoved from the desk onto the floor. Hawker picked them up and shuffled through, making sense of them. "They're crumpled up one by one."

"Ah. Bon. And these books were opened one by one before they were tossed down. See how they fell? That is true in the salon, also. All the books were searched." The bookends had been bawdy figures, the shepherdess with her dress raised high, the shepherd with his breeches lowered. They were smashed against the fireplace. More malice. "He is looking for a paper or a book, almost certainly."

"Stupid to keep secret papers lying about in your bedroom."

"A wise agent does not produce incriminating papers at all."

"Not everybody's as careful as you and me. Sad fact." He began to circle the room, deft and deliberate. Not touching anything. Looking and thinking. "Let's say Jane Cardiff has secrets to hide, being a woman who lives a full and interesting life. Where does a woman hide secrets, Owl?"

"Women do not think alike, *mon vieux*. Do not expect me to understand her merely because I am a woman."

"But you're a sneaky woman. Have I ever told you how much I admire that? We can eliminate the easy places—all the drawers and bookcases."

"Certainly, that is a foolish place to hide something." She set aside her distaste for the man who searched this apartment. It was not the vandal she must understand. It was Jane Cardiff.

"I'll send men to pick the place apart. It'll take a few hours." But she did not want to wait for that. Neither did Hawker.

"She is no sweet squire's daughter to trust a secret drawer in her desk." She had picked up the poor, sad obscenity of the broken shepherdess. The lingering of malevolence disturbed her more than she had realized. "The man who did this was one of her lovers. He comes to her apartment and searches it as such a man would."

She had Hawker's attention. "Tell me."

"He gives his time to the places he knows. His world. The salon, where she entertained him. This bedroom, where she practiced her art upon him. These are important to him, so he thinks they are important to her."

"What he searches, he destroys."

"Her clothes, this pretty dressing table, the sofa in the salon. This vulgar object." She set the little shepherdess upon the desk. "He crushes all the trappings of a harlot. And he takes his jewelry back."

Hawker pulled at his bottom lip, thumb and forefinger. "Searches the familiar territory. His territory. What he feels like he owns."

"You see that. But Jane Cardiff has lived a different life in this apartment. This bed is the stage upon which the courtesan plays her role. Whatever power she found there, she did not enjoy. This room . . . I will tell you. I have been in rooms like this."

"You don't have to say it."

"But I will. I have acted horrible games upon exactly such a bed. Long ago. I understand this room."

"Owl, you're not Jane Cardiff."

"It is the same."

"Well, bugger that for a lie."

He stomped off to look out the window. She had made him angry, in that sudden way she sometimes did.

She said, "I was also a whore."

"Don't say that."

He was angry for her sake. Even after all these years, always angry. Perhaps she had healed, because she knew her anger still lived inside Hawker. "I understand her this well. She doesn't sleep in that ugly, red bed. Look here."

She opened the door of the small room beyond and brought the lamp. There was barely space for both of them. The disorder was less. Here was only a narrow bed with wool blankets and the simplest of rough linen sheets—something a young maid might have been given. The table held an oil lamp and an oak box, flat-topped, a foot square. It had been pried open. A rush-bottomed chair stood under the window. The white curtains were closed, leaving the room dim in the earliest light.

She said, "This is her place."

"You think she slept here?"

"When she was alone, yes. This is her private place. There are nuns who own more, but everything here is hers. If she has secrets, we'll find them here."

They would not find clandestine drawers under the bed frame or secret panels in the table. Such hiding places were for fools and amateurs.

"Floorboards." Hawker did not sound enthusiastic. It was a tedious job, on hands and knees, pulling at floorboards. He was examining the pieces of the ruined box. And frowning.

"Lift the light, will you?"

"You have found something?"

"I think . . ." Hawker ran his thumb along the back of the box where the wood was pried away and turned the wood to a slant against the light. "We have something . . ." He picked it out between thumb and forefinger.

A tiny triangle of metal glinted on his palm.

"That is the point of a knife," she said.

"Second-rate steel. Dagger point. Half an inch of it broken off. Somebody was impatient in his prying. I keep telling people a knife is a delicate instrument, not a pry bar. No one ever listens." He pulled out a handkerchief and wrapped the bit of metal. "A gentleman always carries a handkerchief," he murmured. "There's a knife in London missing its tip. Needle in a haystack comes to mind."

"It is likely someone will try to stab you with it soon."

"I will hold that happy thought in mind."

"He did not find what he sought in that box." In this spare, childish room, there was nowhere else. "I think it is above this table. Whatever it is, when she wants it she climbs the table and steps upon that box and reaches up."

She moved the chair from the window. When she stepped up on the table, it was obvious what section of the molding had been touched again and again. She pressed, and the spring released. The panel slid away easily.

She took a small black leather book out. Hawker's hands around her waist lifted her down and set her upon her feet on the floor.

THEY did not stay in that stark room. The light was better on the terrace, but that was not why they went to stand there.

"In code . . ." She turned the pages.

Hawker read over her shoulder. "French. And old. I think that's the first of your codes I ever learned. I can probably read it better than you."

"Almost certainly. You are good with codes. It was expunged many years ago. If she had been working with the Police Secrète, she would have changed to a more recent one." She flipped through the pages. "Everything is undated, but see how the ink has gone pale at the beginning of the book. This is years of writing."

"Let's see the last pages." He opened the book near the end. A minute passed. "She's not just using the old symbols. She's added new stuff. And it's in English." He frowned. "It says, 'I have failed in my . . .' There's something I can't read here. 'In my mission once again. The rifle was inaccurate. Le Maître will not be pleased.' Owl, we're going to find it all. It's in here."

"Her mission. Her Master. She was working for someone."

"She says, 'I have been seen. I must wait until their suspicions are—' "

She heard a whistle below, from the garden. A snatch of song.

She would have ignored it. A boy in the lane on an errand.

Hawker leaned over the railing of the balcony and watched the man who had entered the garden. Watched hand signs. Made one of his own and then another.

"Outside," he said. He headed for the front door of the apartment, hurrying.

She did not make complications when important matters went forward. But she also did not follow blindly. "What is happening? Give me ten words."

"There's a body on the street out back. A woman. I think we know what became of Jane Cardiff."

They went downstairs and circled the house to go look at the body.

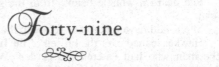

Forty-nine

JUSTINE PULLED THE SHADES OF THE WINDOWS OF the coach. She did not think anyone was observing Jane Cardiff's house, but there was no reason to advertise their presence here, where a murder had so recently happened.

She was not stunned by the death she had confronted. She had seen many men die, and women too. But it had seemed Jane Cardiff's blank eyes stared at her accusingly before Doyle had reached his big hand to close them.

She sat beside Hawker in the coach. The dead woman and Doyle, who must deal with the grim formalities of death, receded behind them. She said what she had been thinking for a time. "She was what I might have become."

"You're not Jane Cardiff," Hawker said. "You're not anything like her."

"If things had gone differently—"

"Never."

"We cannot know."

"I know," Hawker said. "You'd have woke up one fine morning and stabbed the bastard. Nothing more certain."

"I hope so."

"We'll deal with him now, you and me." He shifted on the seat so he held her against the motion of the coach as they turned the corner, not letting it jostle her arm. Always, at every instant, he was careful of her. "I know how I'm going to do it. Just a matter of settling some of the details."

"Always, it is the small details that trip one up."

"I've never wanted to kill anyone as much as I want to kill the man who sent a knife after you."

Adrian Hawkhurst sprawled beside her on the seat of the coach and constructed the scheme that would end in a man's death. She imagined she could see the plan stretching through his mind, weaving itself in strong simplicity, like the threads of a snare.

They were still dressed for the evening party at the Pickerings. He, in black coat and starched neckcloth. She, in lilac silk.

Last night, she had watched Sir Adrian Hawkhurst weave his way among the charming, flirtatious women of the ton. They had followed him with their eyes, admiring and speculative. Not one had seen beneath the deceptive surface of him.

"You're thinking," he said. "Tell me."

"I am thinking of what we have become over the years, you and I. Where we ended up."

"The head of an obscure government department. A shopkeeper. Ordinary folk." He spread his fingers over the silk of her sleeve, appreciating it. She saw the smile in his eyes before it showed up on his lips. "Let me hold you, shopkeeper."

"I would like that."

His arm came around her waist. He did not merely hold her. He lifted her to sit sideways upon him, leaning against his chest. It would have been entirely innocent, except that he began immediately to stroke her breast, taking pleasure in it, making a deep sound in his throat. "This silk thing doesn't just look like a flower. It feels like one. Like stroking a petal, with you inside it."

It was a comfort beyond description to be held with such care and knowledge. To be caressed by a man who delighted in the textures of her body. To relax into the strength and the old familiarity. Shoulder, ribs, along her thigh, he drew her in to him again and again, closer.

The coach ground and rumbled forward at a walking pace, swaying, and the street was filled with the sound of carts and wagons. She lay her cheek on his jacket and closed her eyes and enjoyed this moment. In all of her life, there had been so few times she could rest from wariness.

"You are not a restful person, Adrian Hawkhurst. I have

never understood why I feel at peace with you, sometimes, at moments like these."

"One of life's mysteries." He ran his fingers over her nipple and lanced a shock through her body, downward, deep inside, like a star falling from the sky. Her nipples crinkled up, feeling his hand through silk, through the linen shift she wore beneath the silk.

"That's nice," he said, speaking of the shudder she made. He was a man entirely too perceptive.

He kissed her forehead. Little shivers began at the edges of her, everywhere. Her skin, wanting. Her nerves, anticipating.

She said, "This is good. I like you touching me."

"I could do it for the next decade or two. Have you given any thought to marrying me? It's probably slipped your mind, what with so much going on, but I did ask."

"It has not, as you put it, slipped my mind. I have decided to leave things as they are."

"Good reasons for that, I suppose." He did not seem dismayed. He kissed across her forehead and down her face to her ear. She heard his breath there. Warmth. Whispers. *Chouette. Mignonne.* His breath and murmured love words filled her. *Mon adorée. Ti amo.*

The coach that moved through the streets of London was their universe, a little world where they were alone. There was no reason to refrain from this indulgence. No need to hold back. No cautions to lay upon the surface of her mind. She could give herself wholly to the moment and to him. He held her in his lap, and she felt every impact of the horse's hooves, every irregularity that jolted the wheels, through him. Through his body.

She put her hand upon his shoulder and turned to him to take his mouth. She kissed him deeply and inventively.

She said, "We are idiots to tease ourselves this way. We should stop."

"You're right about that, luv." He slid his hand between her legs to begin sparks and persuasion there. The road vibrated beneath them steadily, and her desire for him was almost unbearable.

When she moved in his lap, he closed his eyes and groaned.

"We will be at Meeks Street soon," she said.

His hand upon her, stroking, went still. When he took his touch away, the pulses of pleasure inside her did not stop. They breathed into each other's faces, deep, almost in unison. Ten breaths. Twenty.

He said, "You feel this, don't you?"

"Desire? It is fire and madness in me. I want you very much."

He shook his head impatiently. "I don't mean that."

Abruptly, he brought his hands up into her hair. His long, clever, lock-picking fingers held her face as if she were infinitely precious. He kissed, once, just upon the threshold of her mouth. "We got a rare amount of wanting between us. That's fine. That's good. I want you more than I've ever wanted anything in this world."

She would have looked away if she had not been held so closely. When a man so hard and secret opens his heart, there is no way to reply except with honesty. "I have never wanted anyone else."

"But it's never been just wanting, has it? Not even the first time." He shook his head impatiently. "It's the rest of it. You and me, we belong together. We always have." The carriage jolted over the road, turning a corner. His hold didn't waver. "Marry me."

Years lie between us. Years when I made dark and difficult choices. "I am not the woman I was at twenty."

"I'm not that man. But there's never been anybody else for either of us. It's not going to change if we wait a dozen more years."

"You don't know me."

"I know you like skin knows an itch. All that time in Italy and Austria, everywhere, working against each other, we could always figure out what the other one was going to do. We might as well have been sitting like this the whole time, we were so close." The nape of her neck, the bare skin of her shoulders, her back beneath the silk . . . he ran his hand over her. "There is not an inch of you, inside or outside, that I don't know."

"There is no reason—"

Fingers crossed her lips, stealing the words. His breath was warm on her face. He whispered, "Dammit. I love you."

"I am not an easy woman," she said.

"I'm a bloody difficult man."

She had no words for what she needed to say. She had thought they were not in her. Then, somehow, they were.

"She said, "It has always been you."

His fingers sank into her shoulders. "Marry me."

She said, "Yes."

It was not enough for him. Dark and intent, he demanded, "Why? Why are we getting married, Owl?"

She said what he needed to hear. She said, "I love you."

Fifty

HAWKER DIDN'T LOOK UP WHEN FELICITY CAME IN.

He stood in the middle of the study at Meeks Street, holding the knife, waiting for the play to start. This was the knife that had been sent after Owl. The poison was still on it, filmed across the working edge of the blade. Owl's blood was dried on it too.

Felicity said, "He didn't come alone. He brought that lickspittle dog with him. Reams." She scowled at the teacups sitting on every bare surface in the study. "I suppose you expect me to clean up in here."

"That would be nice."

"It's not like people couldn't walk over here and put away their own dishes." She clattered cups together and thumped through to the dining room to tumble them into the dumbwaiter. "Not as if they have something more important to do, like standing around in the middle of the room staring at the wallpaper."

He said, "Did you know, there are waiters across London who could remove every cup in the room so silent and swift you'd never see them."

"How very adroit of them."

"I didn't think that would work. You are the most annoying

chit. Where did you leave Cummings and his dog? In my office?"

"Front parlor."

"A wise and moderate choice." The big desk was clear except for a two-inch pile of papers and a black leather book. He set the knife beside the book, blade facing him, the engraved initials upward. "I need Justine. Find her."

"I suppose I can."

"She is not in the Outer Hebrides. Try the library. Get Doyle and Pax too. And Fletcher. He's downstairs in the workroom. And find Sévie. Tell them it's time."

Felicity shrugged, deposited a few more cups into the dumb-waiter, and left, slamming the door behind her.

The desk in the study carried expensive and formidable locks. He'd picked them a dozen times, back in the old days. Now he was the man with the key. Times change.

He took an envelope out of the top drawer and tapped the broken knife tip out onto his palm. A tiny triangle of shiny silver metal. A lesson not to use fine knives for prying into wood boxes. He put the tip on the envelope, centered on the desk. Almost ready.

These papers should go somewhere artistic and obvious. Stage-setting. A show of power. So. Half on the table beside the sofa—yes—stacked up as if somebody'd just finished reading them. A few left on the desk chair. Another pile on the window-sill. He was satisfied when he'd finished. This was a picture of men called away in the middle of a consultation. Felicity had missed a few coffee cups, adding to the fine, heedless air of haste.

And the black book. He was deciding whether to leave it on the desk or put it up on the mantelpiece when Owl walked in.

"You are looking pensive," she said. "I dislike it when you are introspective. Matters always become enigmatic. Is it time?"

"Cummings is here. I'm wondering where to put this." He let the pages fall open. If it had been Jane Cardiff's journal, it would have been symbols across the page. Since it was one of Sévie's old copybooks, it was line after line of ordinary script. "I want him to see it but not lay hands on it."

"The far side of the desk." Owl took the book from him and arranged it herself. "Good. It lies there, slanted just so, obviously important. I have never seen a book hold such an aspect of importance."

"I could add bookmarks hanging out everywhere."

"We will not ice the cake. We will be simple. You will try to keep the very direct Colonel Reams from tossing it into the fire. Séverine will be annoyed if it is damaged." She frowned at the knife that had almost killed her. "Will you reconsider this plan? I am not easy in my mind with the chance you will take. That knife is dangerous."

"I'm more dangerous." There was a comfortable patch of wall over to the side. He backed her up there so she'd have something to lean on. "We have a minute. Use it to kiss me."

"Doyle may walk in at any instant. Paxton may—"

"Let's not make a list of everybody who's going to walk in on us."

A brief kiss. Lips touching once, friendly-like. A *petit dejeuner* of a kiss. A roll and coffee in the morning of a kiss. Not the main course, but he gave it his entire expertise.

Owl said, "That was nice."

"That's why husbands and wives kiss a lot. Because it's nice. It'll take some practice, but we'll eventually get it right."

"I am not yet used to the idea of becoming a wife. I have no idea what kind of kisses to expect in that state."

"We'll find out. We're going to fall into the ravening maw of respectability, you and I." He kissed her. It tasted significant, as if everything they did, every word they said, meant more now. It wasn't just pleasure between them, though God knew there was a mort of that. It wasn't friendship.

This was his lady. This would be his wife.

He pulled her to him, using the amount of persuasion he thought he could get away with, feeling her answer back with the next kiss, warm and willing.

They did that for a while.

"We have no time for this." She shoved him away. "I am in no mood to fool with you. I am hungry for vengeance. You, I will indulge myself with later."

Wonderful Owl. "I'm feeling peckish for some vengeance myself."

Doyle came in, looking grim and angry from a morning spent handing a corpse over to the coroner. Pax was with him,

Fletcher a few steps behind. The rustle coming downstairs was Sévie.

Nobody needed to say much. Doyle took in the stage setting. Eyes lingered on the knife. "We have Cummings?"

"Waiting in the front parlor."

A brusque nod from Doyle. Sévie, dignified as a judge, sat in the big chair, the one next to the fire, and folded her hands in her lap. She'd done most of the work on Jane Cardiff's book, since she could decode as fast as write. Pax, Fletcher, and Doyle took the corners of the room and stood like guards. They wouldn't interfere with what was going to happen.

The door opened. Cummings came in, trailed by a belligerent-looking Reams. "What the devil do you mean by this, Hawkhurst? That was a damned peremptory note you sent."

"This won't take long."

His lordship glanced around and assessed his audience. His voice became a shade more conciliatory. "I have better things to do than run across town at your beck and call."

Cummings was shaved pink, his hair clipped and polished, his clothes without a speck of dust on them. He was tightly decorous. A little overdressed for the informality of Meeks Street. He'd dropped his hat and coat somewhere, but he carried his cane.

Good. As good as could be.

Reams came up behind Cummings and whispered into his ear. ". . . knives . . . Bow Street . . ." There was more, but Cummings ignored him. Because Cummings had spotted the black book sitting enticingly on the desk.

He put himself between Cummings and the desk and turned to Owl. "Lord Cummings and Colonel Reams came to ask after your health when you were stabbed. How long ago was it, mademoiselle? Five days?"

"It has been longer than that. A week, I think. I lose track of time, we have been so very busy." She came toward him, strolling across the landscape of the study, running her hand from chair to chair, taking every eye with her. "It has been day after day, talking to people, discovering secrets. I have barely had time to draw my breath."

She paused by the sofa and touched two fingers to the papers he'd piled there. "Then there is this. It is tedious work, the making of copies from old French codes into the vernacular." She tilted her head and considered the words written on the top sheet. "And now we have finished. Many people will be fascinated by that little book. It is instructive reading."

Cummings whipped his attention from the papers she touched to the book on the desk and back again.

Reams, edging along at Cummings's side, hadn't stopped muttering. ". . . sneaking bastards. They got into Bow Street somehow. We can prove it. That knife on the desk has to be—"

"Not now, Colonel." Cummings brushed his shoulder. "Hawkhurst, I'm not here to play games. What's this about?"

"Treason. Greed. Murder. Trifles like that. A woman's body was found in Percy Street, at dawn. But you already know that."

Cummings knew. His face was closed, barred, and shuttered, but the smugness showed.

Owl said, "It was a particularly cowardly murder. She was killed by someone she knew. Someone looked into her eyes while he killed her."

The cane swung in Cummings's hand, being arrogant. "All very affecting, of course, but not the province of the British Service. Unless you stumbled on the body, Hawkhurst. Really, Bow Street is going to wonder why women keep getting stabbed when you're around."

He gave Cummings time to realize what he'd let slip. "Did I say she was stabbed?"

Sévie and the three men standing at the wall didn't change expression. They were silent and impassive witnesses. Even Reams was a witness.

Cummings clenched his teeth. "A guess. Maybe she died of the pox or fell under a carriage. It's nothing to me how some whore died."

"I didn't say she was a whore, either." Time to lean against the desk and get comfortable, like a man settled down for a long talk. "Her apartment was ransacked. I don't believe I've ever seen such a clumsy job."

"I can't share your familiarity with the ransacking of a whore's living quarters."

Reams had got into the pile of papers at the end of the sofa. He shoveled through them like a pig, rooting. "What's this?" He squinted at the top page. "'R.T. will do what he is told. He is snared. Le Maître is very pleased with me.' What's that supposed to mean?"

Sévie answered him. "That is the transcript of a book kept by a woman of the demimonde." She sounded like she was discussing something ordinary. Vegetables, maybe. "For many years she blackmailed the men she slept with. She did not ask for money. She demanded political favors. Votes. Influence. Le Maître—the Master—was her patron. He gave the orders."

He watched Cummings's face. The house of cards was falling, and Cummings would fall with it. "A few dozen men were blackmailed. We know some of the names. We'll figure out the rest in the next couple days. It's all in the book."

"It was not merely blackmail," Sévie said. "She killed men when Le Maître gave the order. We know those names as well."

Reams wasn't paying attention to that. He shuffled through sheet after sheet, reading them and crumpling them in his fist, throwing the pages away. "'He lay down naked. I began rubbing the ointment on his—' By God, man. It says, 'on his genitals!' This is obscenity. What kind of a book do you have here? This is some of that French muck."

Owl, cool as marble, turned slowly to consider Reams. "It is a journal. Did you not know hired women often write of their lives? It is a passion with some of them. Every small detail of what they do, they set down in writing." She smiled and looked very French indeed. "It is one of several reasons a wise man does not share his secrets with harlots."

Reams tore a page in half. Listen to this. "'. . . with the smaller cane there will be fewer marks. I do not wish to be bruised for the visit of G.R. I must entice him to yet another betrayal of his Foreign Office, and he has developed a conscience of late. I will use—' This is vile. This is filth." Reams swept the pile of paper across the table onto the floor.

Sévie said, "It is filth that will splash upon many people. G.R. is George Reynolds. Later, she explains how she killed him."

He wanted Cummings's attention on him. Wanted the man close. "We'll find everything in here." When he took the black book from the desk, he handled it as if it were genuine. "The man who killed her didn't find this."

Cummings took a step closer. "Say what you have to say and be done with it."

"I'll do better than that. Look for yourself." He tossed the book at Cummings. The pages flapped and rippled like bird's wings. Cummings dropped his cane and grabbed for the book.

He snapped the cane from the air as it left Cummings's hand. The head unscrewed in a single twist. The fancy hilt, hexagonal with embossed gold points, separated from the shaft.

Everybody at Meeks Street knew that cane. Cummings had swaggered around with it for years. But this was the first time they'd seen the dagger inside. It was thin, six inches long, and missing the tip.

On his desk, the tiny point of metal he'd picked out of a wooden chest in Jane Cardiff's bedroom glinted. He laid the dagger beside it. They matched. Matched exactly.

Proof absolute. Whatever he did from here on out, he had the proof. This was the man who killed Jane Cardiff. The man who'd tried to kill Owl.

Cummings fumbled with the book and leafed from page to page, gobbling indignation. "This isn't her book." Cummings's voice was a terrible hoarse whisper. He slammed the book closed. "This is some schoolgirl's drivel."

"We have the real journal." He tapped the metal triangle back into its envelope and set it and Cummings's dagger into the desk drawer. He turned the key. "We've all seen it. We all know. I'll give the real book to Liverpool."

Rigid with rage, livid as death, Cummings threw Sévie's composition book across the room. "I will destroy you."

When he turned to face Cummings, the black knife, the poisoned one, lay between them on the desk. "All those years ago the Service sent word to look for the Cachés. You did. You found some. But you didn't turn them in. You kept them for your own dirty use. You bought Jane Cardiff from Gravois and Patelin. She was twelve. Even in the cesspit of Whitechapel, they spit on men who buy children."

"I see a silly copybook anyone could have written and no one can read. You have no evidence. Gravois and Patelin won't testify to anything."

The dead are notably silent. "You bought her. You hurt her. Little by little, you made her an obedient tool." He understood evil. What Cummings had done to a child was pure evil.

"She was a French spy and a whore. No one's going to care what I did to her." Cummings's eyes slid to Owl. "She's not the only French whore in England. Does Liverpool know you're sleeping with that one?"

Sévie looked angry and Owl, grimly amused. Doyle, with

his back to the bookshelves and his arms crossed over his chest could have been thinking about other matters altogether.

"Liverpool knows the war is long over. Her cousin's a Minister of France. Nobody's looking closely at what the French got up to under the last regime."

Cummings's cane, empty of the dagger, was still heavy. Clumsy, to his way of thinking. Stiff malacca, brown as a walnut. His gut told him Cummings had used this cane to beat and break a half-grown girl. "You didn't know about that journal, did you? She must have told you about it when she was dying." He saw the flicker in Cummings's eyes. He'd guessed right. "You didn't have time to find it."

Owl seated herself on the arm of the sofa. She laced her hands together, wrapped about her knee. "Did you think of the irony? You destroyed Jane Cardiff. Now she destroys you."

"She can't touch me. None of you can." Cummings's lip lifted in a sneer, and it was Adrian Hawkhurst he looked at. "I've held my position longer than you've been alive. I know every powerful man in London. I know secrets about everyone. If I call the journal a fake, I'll be believed."

Cummings had centuries of breeding behind him, generations of ordering men around, getting away with murder. He had it in his bones.

"If you try to use those ravings against me, Hawkhurst, I'll see you in prison for murder." Coldly, Cummings gazed from face to face, at every man and woman in the room. "I'll ruin the rest of you. I'll make it my life's work."

Nobody even blinked.

"I'll grant you this. I didn't see it, at first." He began to pace, crossing in front of Cummings. "I like puzzles, but this one just about drove me mad. Why would anyone go to this much trouble just to disgrace me? Easier to point a rifle and shoot. Killing's the easiest thing in the world. You agree with that, don't you, Cummings?"

Cummings let his eyes agree. He was probably thinking how much Adrian Hawkhurst needed killing.

Death lurked in this room. But Cummings wasn't the one dealing it.

I am. "When I found out you were behind it—Do you know how we found out?"

"He does not." Owl was bright-eyed and mocking. "So I will

tell him. Do not stab anyone with a fancy dagger, my lord. Especially not when the hilt leaves its mark pressed into the corpse." She touched her chest. "Here. Monsieur Doyle and Monsieur Hawkhurst had no difficulty in recognizing the pattern of your cane."

Reams looked up from the papers he was still reading. "There's a damned lot of accusation going—"

"Quiet," Cummings said. "I'm handling this."

Then they both ignored Reams.

"Once I knew who was behind this, I knew why. Military Intelligence is a dead horse, and we all know it. You wanted the Service. Killing me wouldn't give it to you. You needed a scandal in the Service so embarrassing Liverpool would bring in an outsider to clean house. You were sure he'd bring you in."

Owl rearranged the skirt of her dress, being the great lady, untouchable and disapproving. "It is all ambition, which is very ugly. The Whigs call for the Military Intelligence to be dissolved, as they do not like secret police set to spy upon Englishmen. Over the years, for advancement, you have ordered the death of innocent men. You have blackmailed and ruined dozens more. When we take vengeance for Jane Cardiff, we collect it for them also."

Unrepentant, condescending, Cummings shook his head.

We'll finish this. He glanced at Doyle. At Sévie, all grim determination. At Pax's careful detachment. At Owl, who knew what came next and approved.

Doyle's deep, flat, matter-of-fact voice carried utter conviction. "When we take the book and the transcription to Liverpool, everything comes out. You're ruined. But every innocent man named in that journal falls with you. You disgrace Military Intelligence. Good men worked for you in the war. They don't deserve this."

"How dramatic." Cummings took a casual stand by the desk.

"You have a mother still living. You have two sons and grandchildren. You have a wife. When this comes out, you shame every one of them." Doyle waited.

They all did.

Looked like they expected the Head of Service to say the rest of it. "This is when a gentleman goes home and has an accident cleaning his gun." Deliberately, he walked to the desk and laid his hands down flat on it. He leaned across, close to Lord Cummings. "You have until tomorrow noon."

Cummings laughed. Actually laughed. "You're bluffing, Hawkhurst. You're all bluff. I know you. I've watched you for years. You won't destroy that many people to get to me. You won't show that book to anyone." His gaze dropped to the desk.

He'll do it now.

From the corner of his eye, he saw Cummings scoop up the black knife. Grip the hilt. Stab down. Stab toward the hand so temptingly flat on the desktop.

He jerked out of way. Rapped up hard and broke Cummings's hold on the knife. Caught it away from him.

He slashed Cummings across the palm, up the forearm. A long, shallow cut that opened up red.

Judge. Jury. He let the knife drop. He didn't need it anymore. Executioner.

"You bastard." Cummings's eyes bulged out of his head, staring at his hand and the blood dripping across it.

"You have to be more careful, sir." Reams was beside Cummings, pressing a handkerchief on a wound that bled sluggishly. "It's not deep. We'll have it stopped in a minute."

"Get me out of here." Cummings pulled away. He stared at his hand, trembling, wiping at the seeping blood. "I have to get out of here."

"Let me stop the bleeding." Reams looked around at all the men and women who watched and did nothing. "Goddammit, one of you help me."

"Use mine." Hawker shook his handkerchief out and handed it over to Reams.

Cummings backed away, nursing his hand, bleeding. "They saw. Everybody saw what you did."

"They saw that you were clumsy where you pointed a knife. That's always a mistake."

"You'll hang for this. I swear it. You'll hang if it's the last thing I do." Cummings shrugged Reams off. "Let go of me, idiot. That's not going to help. I'm poisoned. Poisoned. He's killed me." He was pale as death when he staggered toward the door. But it would be a while before he died.

Fifty-one

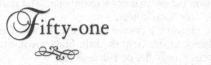

HAWKER FOUND HER IN THE APARTMENT ABOVE her shop. Thompson pointed him up the stairs and said Mademoiselle had been expecting him and the door at the top was open.

Owl had thirty blue-glass bottles sitting out on a table that she was filling with something. She sat in a red brocade chair, leaning over, tapping powder from a paper down the mouth of a bottle. He stood awhile and watched. About every fifth one she'd straighten up, lean to the fire for the kettle, and fill the bottles with hot water.

He said, "Shouldn't somebody else do this? An apothecary?"

"That would be nice, but I prefer to make my own mixtures." After a minute, Owl said, "He is dead, then?"

"Last night, about two. I waited outside the house till I was sure."

"And his accusations toward you?"

"I bribed the footman to give me the letter. Anything he said, they took as the ravings of a dying man."

A mortar with a handful of green powder in it sat on the table. She pulled it to her and put it in her lap and began to grind. "I am not sorry. Perhaps there is a woman somewhere who is more forgiving than I am. I feel only relief that this is over."

He sat down in the chair across from hers and sniffed the powder she was working with. "There was a time I could have killed three bastards like Cummings before tea and enjoyed doing it. I didn't enjoy this. I'm getting soft."

"Not noticeably. I would not put that vial too close to your nose."

He set it down. "Poison?"

"We have dealt too much in poison lately. That will only make you sneeze. It is a fine antiseptic, though. That is what I am making here." She kept grinding. "I hope his wife was not there."

"She took off years ago." He wondered whether to tell her, and then decided he would. "He was at it awhile, dying. Couple of hours. His sons didn't come."

"It is the death he intended for me." She didn't quite shrug. "He was an evil man. You intended this from the first hour, when I was struck by that poison. That is why you did not clear the knife."

"Yes."

She was doing some deep thinking, apparently, so he left her to it and began to sift powder into bottles. There were five papers already measured, so he tapped them into the next bottles in the row. He didn't scatter much around. Either he was doing it right or she was being mannerly.

"He would have escaped justice?"

"We couldn't show anyone that book. I'd have talked to Liverpool and Cummings would be out of Military Intelligence. Doyle would see that he had to resign from his clubs."

"He was right, then, in saying that nothing much would happen to him. That we could not touch him."

"Well, he's dead, you see. So he wasn't entirely correct."

He helped himself to the kettle and topped the bottles up with hot water while neither of them talked for a while.

"I think the world needs people like us to destroy evil men," she said. "It requires people who are not entirely good to do this."

"Sounds like me."

"That is what I was thinking."

The grinding was going to take a while. He ran out of green powder to put in bottles, so he stood up to wander around her parlor. She had some of her knife collection up here. The kris was pretty to look at but wouldn't throw worth a damn.

It was peaceful, being here, watching her work. A couple strands of brown hair started off at her forehead, let loose, and fell down almost straight till they made little hooks at the end. She kept brushing them off her nose and they kept coming back. Even her hair was stubborn.

It was just impossible to say how much he loved this woman. It felt like he'd been waiting his whole life to walk in a door and there would be Owl, doing something interesting.

She had a fine fire burning in the hearth, so he went over and sat down on the hearthrug and leaned against her, setting his head against her thigh, looking into the flames.

After a minute, her hand came down on his head, into his hair. She said, "I will come to live with you in your great mansion and be a lady again. I will be a DeCabrillac, and face down the world if they make accusations. I will shake out your haughty mansion like an old rag and make it comfortable to live in."

"Funny. I was thinking I'd come to live with you here, over the shop. It's an easy walk to Meeks Street."

"The Head of the British Service must live somewhere grander than this little *appartement*. But we could come here sometimes." She took a deep breath. "I would like to marry you, 'Awker. I have loved you for many, many years."

"Well. That's fine then." He turned his face to the cloth on her lap. Beneath the dress she wore, she was energy and strength. She seduced the hell out of him.

They met halfway. Him, coming up to kiss her. Her, leaning down to take his lips.

He drew her down from her seat. She flowed over him like water, refreshing him and filling every empty part of him. Her face was enchanting, infinite in its secrets.

Clothing wasn't a problem. They had coupled hastily in the most ridiculous situations. Here there was silence and safety, privacy and a warm fire, the hearthrug under one back and then under the other as they touched and resettled. It was right. It was simple. He'd come home.

Keep reading for a special excerpt
from Joanna Bourne's

The Spymaster's Lady

Available now from Berkley Sensation!

SHE WAS WILLING TO DIE, OF COURSE, BUT SHE HAD not planned to do it so soon, or in such a prolonged and uncomfortable fashion, or at the hands of her own countrymen.

She slumped against the wall, which was of cut stone and immensely solid, as prison walls often are. "I do not have the plans. I never had them."

"I am not a patient man. Where are the plans?"

"I do not have—"

The openhanded slap whipped out of the darkness. For one instant she slipped over the edge of consciousness. Then she was back again, in the dark and in pain, with Leblanc.

"Just so." He touched her cheek where he had hit her and turned her toward him. He did it gently. He had much practice in hurting women. "We continue. This time you will be more helpful."

"Please. I am trying."

"You will tell me where you have hidden the plans, Annique."

"They are a mad dream, these Albion plans. A chimera. I never saw them." Even as she said it, the Albion plans were clear in her mind. She had held the many pages in her hands, the dog-eared edges, maps covered with smudges and fingerprints, the lists in small, neat writing. *I will not think of this. If I remember, it will show on my face.*

"Vauban gave you the plans in Bruges. What did he tell you to do with them?"

He told me to take them to England. "Why would he give me plans? I am not a valise to go carrying papers about the countryside."

His fist closed on her throat. Pain exploded. Pain that stopped her breath. She dug her fingers into the wall and held on. With such a useful stone wall to hold on to, she would not fall down.

Leblanc released her. "Let us begin again, at Bruges. You were there. You admit that."

"I was there. Yes. I reported to Vauban. I was a pair of eyes watching the British. Nothing more. I have told you and told you." The fingers on her chin tightened. A new pain.

"Vauban left Bruges empty-handed. He went back to Paris without the plans. He must have given them to you. Vauban trusted you."

He trusted me with treason. She wouldn't think that. Wouldn't remember.

Her voice had gone hoarse a long time ago. "The papers never came to us. Never." She tried to swallow, but her throat was too dry. "You hold my life in your hands, sir. If I had the Albion plans, I would lay them at your feet to buy it back."

Leblanc swore softly, cursing her. Cursing Vauban, who was far away and safe. "The old man didn't hide them. He was too carefully watched. What happened to them?"

"Look to your own associates. Or maybe the British took them. I never saw them. I swear it."

Leblanc nudged her chin upward. "You swear? Little Cub, I have watched you lie and lie with that angel face since you were a child. Do not attempt to lie to me."

"I would not dare. I have served you well. Do you think I'm such a fool I've stopped being afraid of you?" She let tears brim into her eyes. It was a most useful skill and one she had practiced assiduously.

"Almost, one might believe you."

He plays with me. She squeezed her lids and let tears slide in cold tracks down her cheeks.

"Almost." He slowly scratched a line upon her cheek with

his thumbnail, following a tear. "But, alas, not quite. You will be more honest before morning, I think."

"I am honest to you now."

"Perhaps. We will discuss this at length when my guests have departed. Did you know? Fouché comes to my little soiree tonight. A great honor. He comes to me from meetings with Bonaparte. He comes directly to me, to speak of what the First Consul has said. I am becoming the great man in Paris these days."

What would I say if I were innocent? "Take me to Fouché. He will believe me."

"You will see Fouché when I am satisfied your pretty little mouth is speaking the truth. Until then . . ." He reached to the nape of her neck to loosen her dress, pulling the first tie free. "You will make yourself agreeable, eh? I have heard you can be most amusing."

"I will . . . try to please you." *I will survive this. I can survive whatever he does to me.*

"You will try very, very hard before I am finished with you."

"Please." He wanted to see fear. She would grovel at once, as was politic. "Please. I will do what you want, but not here. Not in a dirty cell with men watching. I hear them breathing. Do not make me do this in front of them."

"It is only the English dogs. I kennel some spies here till I dispose of them." His fingers hooked the rough material of her dress at the bodice and pulled it down, uncovering her. "Perhaps I like them to watch."

She breathed in the air he had used, hot and moist, smelling of wintergreen. His hand crawled inside the bodice of her dress to take hold of her breast. His fingers were smooth and dry, like dead sticks, and he hurt her again and again.

She would not be sick upon Leblanc in his evening clothes. This was no time for her stomach to decide to be sincere.

She pressed against the wall at her back and tried to become nothing. She was darkness. Emptiness. She did not exist at all. It did not work, of course, but it was a goal to fix the mind upon.

At last, he stopped. "I will enjoy using you."

She did not try to speak. There was no earthly use in doing so.

He hurt her one final time, pinching her mouth between thumb and forefinger, breaking the skin of her dry lips and leaving a taste of blood.

"You have not amused me yet." He released her abruptly. She heard the scrape and click as he lifted his lantern from the table. "But you will."

The door clanged shut behind him. His footsteps faded in the corridor, going toward the stairs and upward.

"PIG." She whispered it to the closed door, though that was an insult to pigs, who were, in general, amiable.

She could hear the other prisoners, the English spies, making small sounds on the other side of the cell, but it was dark, and they could no longer see her. She scrubbed her mouth with the back of her hand and swallowed the sick bile in her throat. It was amazingly filthy being touched by Leblanc. It was like being crawled upon by slugs. She did not think she would become even slightly accustomed to it in the days she had left.

She pulled her dress into decency and let herself fold onto the dirt floor, feeling miserable. This was the end then. The choice that had tormented her for so long—what should be done with the Albion plans that had been entrusted to her—was made. All her logic and reasoning, all her searchings of the heart, had come to nothing. Leblanc had won. She would withstand his persuasions for only a day or two. Then he would wrest the Albion plans from her memory and commit God knew what greedy betrayals with them.

Her old mentor Vauban would be disappointed in her when he heard. He waited in his small stone house in Normandy for her to send word. He had left the decision to her, what should be done with the plans, but he had not intended that she give them to Leblanc. She had failed him. She had failed everyone.

She took a deep breath and let it out slowly. It was strange to know her remaining breaths were numbered in some tens of thousands. Forty thousand? Fifty? Perhaps when she was in unbearable pain later on tonight, she would start counting.

She pulled her shoes off, one and then the other. She had been in prisons twice before in her life, both times completely harrowing. At least she had been above ground then, and she had been able to see. Maman had been with her, that first time. Now Maman was dead in a stupid accident that should not have killed a dog. *Maman, Maman, how I miss you.* There was no one in this world to help her.

In the darkness, one feels very alone. She had never become used to this.

The English spy spoke, deep and slow, out of the dark. "I would stand and greet you politely." Chain clinked. "But I'm forced to be rude."

It was a measure of how lonely she was that the voice of an enemy English came like a warm handclasp. "There is much of that in my life lately. Rudeness."

"It seems you have annoyed Leblanc." He spoke the rich French of the South, without the least trace of a foreign accent.

"You also, it would seem."

"He doesn't plan to let any of us leave here alive."

"That is most likely." She rolled off her stockings, tucked them into her sleeve so she would not lose them, and slipped the shoes back on. One cannot go barefoot. Even in the anteroom to hell, one must be practical.

"Shall we prove him wrong, you and I?"

He did not sound resigned to death, which was admirable in its way, though not very realistic. It was an altogether English way of seeing things.

In the face of such bravery, she could not sit upon the floor and wail. French honor demanded a Frenchwoman meet death as courageously as any English. French honor always seemed to be demanding things of her. Bravery, of a sort, was a coin she was used to counterfeiting. Besides, the plan she was weaving might work. She might overcome Leblanc and escape the chateau and deal with these Albion plans that were the cause of so much trouble to her. And assuredly pigs might grow wings and fly around steeples all over town.

The English was waiting for an answer. She pulled herself to her feet. "I would be delighted to disappoint Leblanc in any way. Do you know where we are? I was not able to tell when I was brought here, but I hope very much this is the chateau in Garches."

"A strange thing to hope, but yes, this is Garches, the house of the Secret Police."

"Good, then. I know this place."

"That will prove useful. After we deal with these chains," he clinked metallically, "and that locked door. We can help each other."

He made many assumptions. "There is always the possibility."

"We can be allies." The spy chose his words carefully, hoping to charm her so she would be a tool for him. He slipped velvet upon his voice. Underneath, though, she heard an uncompromising sternness and great anger. There was nothing she did not know about such hard, calculating men.

Leblanc took much upon himself to capture British agents in this way. It was an old custom of both French and British secret services that they were not bloodthirsty with one another's agents. This was one of many rules Leblanc broke nowadays.

She worked her way along the wall, picking at the rocks, stealing the gravel that had come loose in the cracks and putting it into her stocking to make her little cosh. It was a weapon easy to use when one could not see. One of her great favorites.

There was a whisper of movement. A younger voice, very weak, spoke. "Somebody's here."

Her English spy answered, "Just a girl Leblanc brought in. Nothing to worry about."

". . . more questions?"

"Not yet. It's late at night. We have hours before they come for us. Hours."

"Good. I'll be ready . . . when the chance comes."

"It'll be soon now, Adrian. We'll get free. Wait."

The mindless optimism of the English. Who could comprehend it? Had not her own mother told her they were all mad?

It was a tidy small prison Leblanc kept. So few loose stones. It took a while before the cosh was heavy enough. She tied the end of the stocking and tucked it into the pocket hidden beneath her skirt. Then she continued to explore the walls, finding nothing at all interesting. There is not so much to discover about rooms that are used as prisons. This one had been a wine cellar before the Revolution. It still smelled of old wood and good wine as well as less wholesome things. Halfway around the cell she came to where the Englishmen were chained, so she stopped to let her hands have a look at them as well.

The one who lay upon the ground was young, younger than she was. Seventeen? Eighteen? He had the body of an acrobat, one of those slight, tightly constructed people. He had been wounded. She could smell the gunpowder on his clothes and the wound going bad. She would wager money there was metal still inside him. When she ran her fingers across his face, his lips were dry and cracked, and he was burning hot. High fever.

They had chained him to the wall with an excellent chain, but a large, old-fashioned padlock. That would have to be picked if they were to escape. She searched his boots and the seams of his clothing, just in case Leblanc's men had missed some small, useful object. There was nothing at all, naturally, but one must always check.

"Nice . . ." he murmured when she ran her hands over him. "Later, sweetheart. Too tired . . ." Not so young a boy then. He spoke in English. There might be an innocent reason for an English to be in France, in these days when their countries were not exactly at war, but somehow she was sure Leblanc spoke truly. This was a spy. "So tired." Then he said clearly, "Tell Lazarus I won't do that anymore. Never. Tell him."

"We shall speak of it," she said softly, "later," which was a promise hard to fulfill, since she did not expect to have so very many laters. Though perhaps a few more than this boy.

He struggled to sit up. "Queen's Knight Three. I have to go. They're waiting for me to deliver the Red Knight." He was speaking what he should not, almost certainly, and he would injure himself, thrashing about. She pushed him gently back down.

Strong arms intervened. "Quiet. That's all done." The other man held the boy, muffling his words.

He need not have worried. She was no longer interested in such secrets. In truth, she would as soon not learn them.

"Tell the others."

"I will. Everyone got away safe. Rest now."

The boy had knocked over the water jug, struggling. Her hands found it, rolled on its side, empty. It was perfectly dry inside. The thought of water stabbed sour pinpricks in her mouth. She was so thirsty.

Nothing is worse than thirst. Not hunger. Not even pain. Maybe it was as well there was no water to tempt her. Perhaps she would have become an animal and stolen from these men, who suffered more than she did. It was better not to know how low she could have fallen. "When was the last time they gave you water?"

"Two days ago."

"You have not much longer to wait, then. Leblanc will keep me alive for a while, in the hopes I may be useful to him. And to play with." *In the end, he will kill me. Even when I give him*

the Albion plans—every word, every map, every list—he will
still kill me. I know what he did in Bruges. He cannot let me live.

"His habits are known."

He was large, the English spy of the deep voice and iron sternness. She sensed a huge presence even before she touched him. Her
hands brought her more details. The big man had folded his coat
under the boy, accepting another measure of discomfort to keep
his friend off the cold floor. It was a very British courage, that
small act. She felt his fierce, protective concentration surrounding
the boy, as if force of will alone were enough to hold life in him. It
would be a brave man indeed who dared to die when this man had
forbidden it.

She reached tentatively and discovered soft linen and long,
sinewy courses of muscle down his chest and then, where his
shirt lay open at the neck, a disconcerting resilience of masculine skin. She would have pulled away, but his hand came to
cover hers, pressing it down over his heart. She felt the beat
under her palm, startling and alive. Such power and strength.

He said, "I know what Leblanc does to women. I'm sorry
you've fallen into his hands. Believe that."

"Me, I am also extremely sorry." This one was determined
to be nice to her, was he not? She took her hand back. She
would free him, if she could, and then they would see exactly
how delightful he was. "These locks," she jiggled his manacle,
"are very clumsy. One twiddle, and I could get them off. You do
not have a small length of wire about you, do you?"

She could hear the smile in his voice. "What do you think?"

"I do not expect it to be so simple. Life is not, in my experience."

"Mine also. Did Leblanc hurt you?"

"Not so much."

He touched her throat where she was sore and bruised. "No
woman should fall into Leblanc's hands. We'll get out of here.
There's some way out. We'll find it." He gripped her shoulder,
heavy and reassuring.

She should get up and search the cell. But somehow she
found herself just sitting next to him, resting. Her breath trickled out of her. Some of the fear that had companioned her for
weeks drained away too. How long had it been since anyone
had offered her comfort? How strange to find it here, in this
fearful place, at the hands of an enemy.

After what seemed a long time, she roused herself. "There is another problem. Your friend cannot walk from here, even if I get him free of the chain."

"He'll make it. Better men than Leblanc have tried to kill him." Not everyone would have heard the anguish beneath the surface of that voice, but she did. They both knew this Adrian was dying. In a dozen hours, in at most another day, his wound and thirst and the damp chill of the stones would finish him off.

The boy spoke up in a thin thread of polished Gascon French. "It is . . . one small bullet hole. A nothing." He was very weak, very gallant. "It's the . . . infernal boredom . . . I can't stand."

"If we only had a deck of cards," the big man said.

"I'll bring some . . . next time."

They would have made good Frenchmen, these two. It was a pity Leblanc would soon take her from this cell. One could find worse companions for the long journey into the dark. At least the two of them would be together when they died. She would be wholly alone.

But it was better not to speculate upon how Leblanc would break her to his will and kill her, which could only lead to melancholy. It was time to slide from beneath the touch of this English spy and be busy again. She could not sit forever, hoping courage would seep out of his skin and into her.

She stood, and immediately felt cold. It was as if she had left a warm and accustomed shelter when she left the man's side. That was most silly. This was no shelter, and he did not like her much despite the soft voice he used. What lay between them was an untrusting vigilance one might have carved slices of.

Perhaps he knew who she was. Or perhaps he was one of those earnest men who go about spying in total seriousness. He would die for his country in a straightforward English fashion in this musty place and hate her because she was French. To see the world so simply was undoubtedly an English trait.

So be it. As it happened, she was not an amicable friend of big English spies. A French trait, doubtless.

She shrugged, which he would not see, and began working her way around the rest of the cell, inspecting the floor and every inch of the wall as high as she could reach. "In your time here, has Henri Bréval visited the cell?"

"He came twice with Leblanc, once alone, asking questions."

"He has the key? He himself? That is good then."

"You think so?"

"I have some hopes of Henri." There was not a rusted nail, not a shard of glass. There was nothing useful anywhere. She must place her hope in Henri's stupidity, which was nearly limitless. "If Fouché is indeed upstairs drinking wine and playing cards, Leblanc will not leave his side. One does not neglect the head of the Secret Police to disport oneself with a woman. But Henri, who takes note of him? He may seize the moment. He wishes to use me, you understand, and he has had no chance yet."

"I see." They were most noncommittal words.

Was it possible he believed she would welcome Henri? What dreadful taste he thought she had. "Leblanc does not let many people know about this room. It is very secret what he does here."

"So Henri may come sneaking down alone. You plan to take him." He said it calmly, as if it were not remarkable that she should attack a man like Henri Bréval. She was almost certain he knew what she was.

"I can't help you," the chain that bound him rattled, "unless you get him close."

"Henri is not so stupid. Not quite. But I have a small plan."

"Then all I can do is wish you well."

He seemed a man with an excellent grasp of essentials. He would be useful to her if she could get his chains off. That she would accomplish once those pigs became like the proverb and grew wings and went flying.

Exploring the cell further, she stubbed her toe upon a table, empty of even a spoon. There were also chairs, which presented more opportunity. She was working at the pegs that held a chair together when she heard footsteps.

"We have a visitor," the big English said.

"I hear." One man descended the steps into the cellar. Henri. It must be Henri. She set the chair upright, out of her way, and drew her cosh into her hand and turned toward the sound of footsteps. A shudder ran along her spine, but it was only the cold of the room. It was not fear. She could not afford to be afraid. "It is one man. Alone."

"Leblanc or Henri, do you think?"

"It is Henri. He walks more heavily. Now you will shut up

quietly and not distract me." She prayed it was Henri. Not Leblanc. She had no chance against Leblanc.

The Englishman was perfectly still, but he charged the air with a hungry, controlled rage. It was as if she had a wolf chained to that wall behind her. His presence tugged and tugged at her attention when it was desperately important to keep her mind on Henri.

Henri. She licked her lips and grimly concentrated on Henri, an unpleasant subject, but one of great immediacy. There were twenty steps on the small curved staircase that led from kitchen to cellar. She counted the last of them, footstep by footstep. Then he was in the corridor that led to the cell.

Henri had always thought her reputation inflated. When he had brought her the long way to Paris to turn her over to Leblanc, she had played the spineless fool for him, begging humbly for food and water, stumbling, making him feel powerful. She was so diminished in her darkness he thought her completely harmless. He had become contemptuous.

Let him come just a little close, and he would discover how harmless she was. Most surely he would.

She knew the honey to trap him. She would portray for him the Silly Young Harlot. It was an old favorite role of hers. She had acted it a hundred times.

She licked her lips and let them pout, open and loose. What else? She pulled strands of hair down around her face. Her dress was already torn at the neckline. She found the spot and ripped the tear wider. Good. He would see only that bare skin. She could hold a dozen coshes and he would never notice.

Quickly. Quickly. He was coming closer. She took another deep breath and let the role close around her like a familiar garment. She became the Harlot. Yielding, easy to daunt, out of her depth in this game of intrigue and lies. Henri liked victims. She would set the most perfect victim before him and hope he took the bait.

Hid beneath layer upon layer of soft and foolish Harlot, she waited. Her fist, holding the cosh, never wavered. She would not allow herself to be afraid. It was another role she had crafted; the Brave Spy. She had played this one so long it fit like her skin.

Probably, at the center of her being, under all the pretense, the real Annique was a quivering mouse. She would not go prying in there and find out.

THE grilled window in the door glowed ghostly pale, then brightened as a lantern came closer. Grey could see again. The details of his cell emerged. Rough blocks of stone, a table, two chairs. And the girl.

She faced the door, stiff and silent and totally intent upon the man out in the corridor. Not a move out of her. Not the twitch of a fingernail. Her eyes, set in deep smudges of exhaustion, were half-closed and unfocused. She didn't once glance in his direction.

He watched her draw a deep breath, never taking her attention from that small barred window in the door. Her lips shaped words silently, praying or talking to herself. Maybe cursing. Again, she combed her fingers through her hair in staccato, purposeful, elegant flicks that left wild elflocks hanging across her face.

She was totally feminine in every movement, indefinably French. With her coloring—black hair, pale skin, eyes of that dark indigo blue—she had to be pure Celt. She'd be from the west of France. Brittany, maybe. Annique was a Breton name. She carried the magic of the Celt in her, used it to weave that fascination the great courtesans created. Even as he watched, she licked her lips again and wriggled deliberately, sensually. A man couldn't look away.

She'd torn her own dress. The curve of her breast showed white against the dark fabric—a whore, bringing out her wares. She was a whore, a liar, and a killer . . . and his life depended on her. "Good luck," he whispered.

She didn't turn. She gave one quick, dismissive shake of her head. "Be still. You are not part of this."

That was the final twist of the knife. He was helpless. He measured out his twenty inches of chain, picturing just how far a fast kick could reach. But Henri wasn't going to wander that close. She'd have to subdue Henri Bréval on her own, without even a toothpick to fight with.

There were red marks on her skin where Leblanc had been tormenting her and the tracks of tears on her cheeks. She couldn't have looked more harmless. That was another lie, of course.

He knew this woman. He'd recognized her the moment Leblanc pushed her stumbling into this cell. Feature by feature, that face was etched in his memory. He'd seen her the day he found his men, ambushed, twisted and bloody, dead in a cornfield near Bruges. If he'd had any doubt, the mention of the Albion plans would have convinced him. The Albion plans had been used to lure them to Bruges.

He'd been tracking this spy across Europe for the last six months. What bloody irony to meet her here.

He'd have his revenge. Leblanc was an artist in human degradation. Pretty Annique wouldn't die easily or cleanly or with any of that beauty intact. His men would be avenged.

If he got out of here . . . No, *when* he got out of here, Annique would come with him. He'd take her to England. He'd find out every damn thing she knew about what happened at Bruges. He'd get the Albion plans from her. Then he'd take his own vengeance.

She'd be supremely useful to British intelligence. Besides, he wouldn't leave a rabid hyena to Leblanc.

The peephole went bright as Henri held the lantern up. His heavy, florid face pressed to the grill. "Leblanc is furious with you."

"Please." The girl wilted visibly, leaning on the table for support, a sweet, succulent curve of entrapped femininity. "Oh, please." The drab blue of her dress and the crude cut of the garment marked her as a servant and accessible. Somehow her disheveled hair, falling forward over her face, had become sensuality itself. "This is all a mistake. A mistake. I swear . . ."

Henri laced fingers through the bars. "You'll talk to him in the end, Annique. You'll beg to talk. You know what he'll do to you."

There was a sniffle. "Leblanc . . . He does not believe me. He will hurt me terribly. Tell him I know nothing more. Please, Henri. Tell him." Her voice had changed completely. She sounded younger, subtly less refined, and very frightened. It was a masterful performance.

"He'll hurt you no matter what I tell him." Henri gloated.

The girl's face sank into her upturned palm. Her hair spilled in dark rivers through her fingers. "I cannot bear it. He will use me . . . like a grunting animal. I am not meant to be used by peasants."

Clever. Clever. He saw what she was doing. Henri's voice marked him as Parisian, a man of the city streets. Leblanc, for all his surface polish, was the son of a pig farmer. And Henri worked for Leblanc.

Henri's spite snaked out into the cell. "You were always Vauban's pet—Vauban and his elite cadre. Vauban and his important missions. You were too good for the rest of us. But tonight the so-special Annique that nobody could touch becomes a blind puppet for Leblanc to play with. If you'd been kind to me before, maybe I'd help you now."

"Leblanc has become Fouché's favorite. With the head of the Secret Police behind him, he can do anything. You cannot help me. You would not dare defy him." She rubbed her eyes with the back of her hand. "I will do whatever he wishes. I have no choice."

"I'll have you when he's through with you."

She went on speaking. She might not have heard Henri. "He will make me oil my body and do the Gypsy dances I learned when I was a child. I will dance in the firelight for him with nothing but a thin bit of silken cloth upon me. Red silk. He . . . he prefers red. He has told me."

Grey wrapped the chain around his hand, gripping tight, seized by the image of a slim body writhing naked, silhouetted in the golden glow of fire. He wasn't the only one. Henri gripped the crossed bars of the grill and pressed his face close, salivating.

Annique, eyes downcast, swayed as if she were already undulating in the sensual dance she described. "I will draw the crimson silk from my body and caress him with it. The silk will be warm and damp with the heat of the dance. With my heat." Her left hand stroked down her body, intimately.

Grey ached from a dozen beatings, thirst was a torment every second, and he knew exactly what she was doing. He still went hard as a rock. He was helpless to stop it. God, but she was good.

Huskily, dreamily, she continued. "He will lie upon his bed and call me to him. At first, only to touch. Then to put my mouth upon him, wherever he directs. I have been trained to be skillful with my mouth. I will have no choice, you see, but to do as he demands of me."

Henri clanked and fumbled with the lock. In a great hurry,

was Henri. If the Frenchman was half as aroused by Annique's little act as Grey was, it was a wonder he could get the door open at all.

The door banged back against the stone wall. "You must not come in here, Henri," she said softly, not moving, "or touch me in any way without the permission of Leblanc."

"Damn Leblanc." Henri slapped the lantern down and cornered her against the table. His fist twisted into her skirt and pulled it up. He grabbed the white shift beneath.

"You should not . . . You must not . . ." She struggled, pushing futilely at his hands with no more strength than a tiny, captured bird.

"No." He threw himself at Henri. And jerked short on his iron leash. The circle of pain at his wrist brought him back to reality. He couldn't get to her. He couldn't fight Henri for her. There wasn't a bloody thing he could do but watch.

"Do not . . ." Her flailing arm hit the lantern. It tilted and skidded off the table and clattered to the floor and extinguished. Darkness was instant and absolute.

"Stupid bitch," Henri snarled. "You . . ."

There was a small squashed thud. Henri yelped in pain. More thuds—one, two, three. The table scraped sideways. Something large and soft fell.

No movement. He heard Annique breathing hard, the smallness of it and the contralto gasps uniquely hers.

Planned. She'd planned it all. He crouched, tense as stretched cord, and acknowledged how well he'd been fooled. She'd planned this from start to finish. She'd manipulated both of them with that damned act of hers.

There was a long silence, broken by intriguing rustling sounds and Annique grunting from time to time. Her footsteps, when she walked toward him, were sure and unhesitating. She came in a straight line across the cell as if it were not dark as a tomb.

"What did you do to Henri?" The issue, he thought, had never really been in doubt.

"I hit him upon the head with a sock full of rocks." She seemed to think it over while she sat down beside him. "At least I am almost sure I hit his head once. I hit him many places. Anyway, he is quiet."

"Dead?"

"He is breathing. But one can never tell with head wounds. I may have yet another complicated explanation to make to God when I show up at his doorstep, which, considering all things, may be at any moment. I hope I have not killed him, quite, though he undoubtedly deserves it. I will leave that to someone else to do, another day. There are many people who would enjoy killing him. Several dozen I can call to mind at once."

She baffled him. There was ruthlessness there, but it was a kind of blithe toughness, clean as a fresh wind. He didn't catch a whiff of the evil that killed men in cold blood, from ambush. He had to keep reminding himself what she was. "You did more than knock him over the head. What was the rest of it, afterwards?"

"You desire the whole report?" She sounded amused. "But you are a spymaster, I think, Englishman. No one else asks such questions so calmly, as if by right. Very well, I shall report to you the whole report—that I have tied Henri up and helped myself to his money. There was an interesting packet of papers in a pocket he may have thought was secret. You may have them if you like. Me, I am no longer in the business of collecting secret papers."

Her hands patted over him lightly. "I have also found a so-handy stickpin, and if you will lift your pretty iron cuff here. Yes. Just so. Now hold still. I am not a fishwife that I can filet this silly lock while you wriggle about. You will make me regret that I am being noble and saving your life if you do not behave sensibly."

"I am at your disposal." He offered his chained wrist. At the same time he reached out and touched her hair, ready to grab her if she tried to leave without freeing him.

She put herself right in his power—a man twice her size, twice her strength, and an enemy. She had to know what her writhing and whispering did to a man. Revenge and anger and lust churned in his body like molten iron. The wonder was it didn't burn through his skin and set this soft hair on fire.

"Ah. We proceed," she said in the darkness. "This lock is not so complicated as it pretends to be. We are discussing matters."

She edged closer and shifted the manacle to a different angle, brushing against his thigh. With every accidental contact, his groin tightened and throbbed. All he could think of was her soft voice saying, "I will oil my body and dance in the firelight." He was no Henri. He wasn't going to touch her. But how did he get a picture like that out of his head?

"And . . . it is done." The lock fell open.

She made it seem easy. It wasn't. He rubbed his wrist. "I thank you."

He stood and stretched to his full height, welcoming the pain of muscles uncramping. Free. Savage exultation flooded him. He was free. He bunched and unbunched his fists, glorying in the surge of power that swept him. He felt like he could take these stones apart with his bare hands. It was dark as the pit of hell and they were twenty feet under a stronghold of the French Secret Police. But the door hung open. He'd get them out of here—Adrian and this remarkable, treacherous woman—or die trying. If they didn't escape, it would be better for all of them to die in the attempt.

While that woman worked on Adrian's manacle, he groped his way across the cell to Henri, who was, as she had said, breathing. The Frenchman was tied, hand and foot, with his stockings and gagged with his own cravat. A thorough woman. Checking the bonds was an academic exercise. There was indeed a secret pocket in the jacket. He helped himself to the papers, then tugged Henri's pants down to his ankles, leaving him half naked.

"What do you busy yourself with?" She'd heard him shifting Henri about. "I find myself inquisitive this evening."

"I'm giving Henri something to discuss with Leblanc when they next meet." It might buy them ten minutes while Henri explained his plans for the girl. "I may eventually regret leaving him alive."

"If we are very lucky, you will have an eventually in which to do so." There was a final, small, decisive click. "That is your Adrian's lock open. He cannot walk from here, you know."

"I'll carry him. Do you have a plan for getting out of the chateau with an unconscious man and no weapons and half the Secret Police of France upstairs?"

"But certainly. We will not discuss it here, though. Bring your friend and come, please, if you are fond of living."

He put an arm under Adrian's good shoulder and hauled him upright. The boy couldn't stand without help, but he could walk when held up. He was conversing with unseen people in a variety of languages.

"Don't die on me now, Hawker," he said. "Don't you dare die on me."

From the author of *The Spymaster's Lady*

JOANNA BOURNE

THE
Forbidden Rose

The only person she can trust with her life . . .
is a man who trusts no one.

Marguerite de Fleurignac, once a glittering aristocrat in
a world of privilege, is on the run, disguised as Maggie
Duncan, British governess. Penniless and alone, cornered
by fanatics of the revolution, she falls into the hands of
a compelling stranger. There's no chance this menacing
rogue with the rough voice and the sinister scar is an innocent bookseller. Why does he risk his life to save her?
Are his secrets as desperate as her own?

Praise for Bourne's Spymaster novels

"Distinct, fresh, and engaging."
—Madeline Hunter, *New York Times* bestselling author
of *Dangerous in Diamonds*

"What a terrific story!"
—Diana Gabaldon, *New York Times* bestselling author
of *An Echo in the Bone*

penguin.com

JOANNA BOURNE

presents her stunning and award-winning debut novel

THE
Spymaster's Lady

She's never met a man she couldn't deceive . . .
until now.

She's braved battlefields. She's stolen dispatches from under the noses of heads of state. She's played the worldly courtesan, the naive virgin, the refined British lady, even a Gypsy boy. But Annique Villiers, the elusive spy known as the Fox Cub, has finally met the one man she can't outwit.

"A FLAT-OUT SPECTACULAR BOOK."
—*All About Romance*

"Love, love, LOVED it!"
—Julia Quinn

Now available in trade paperback